EX LIBRIS

VINTAGE CLASSICS

THE WHITE GUARD

Mikhail Afanasievich Bulgakov was born in Kiev on 15 May 1891. He graduated as a doctor from Kiev University in 1916, but gave up the practice of medicine in 1920 to devote himself to literature. In 1925 he completed the satirical novel *The Heart of a Dog* which remained unpublished in the Soviet Union until 1987. This was one of the many defeats he was to suffer at the hands of the censors. By 1930 Bulgakov had become so frustrated by the political atmosphere and the suppression of his works that he wrote to Stalin begging to be allowed to emigrate if he was not to be given the opportunity to make his living as a writer in the USSR. Stalin telephoned him personally and offered to arrange a job for him at the Moscow Arts Theatre instead. In 1938, a year before contracting a fatal illness, he completed his prose masterpiece, *The Master and Margarita*. He died in 1940. In 1966–7, thanks to the persistence of his widow, the novel made a first, incomplete appearance in *Moskva*, and in 1973 appeared in full.

ALSO BY MIKHAIL BULGAKOV

MIKHAIL BULGAKOV

The White Guard

TRANSLATED FROM THE RUSSIAN BY
Michael Glenny

VINTAGE BOOKS
London

Published by Vintage 2006

8 10 9

English translation © McGraw-Hill Co. 1971
English translation of 'Alexei's Dream' (p.72-77) © Michael Glenny 1990

First published in Great Britain by Collins and The Harvill Press in 1967

Vintage
Random House, 20 Vauxhall Bridge Road,
London SW1V 2SA

www.vintage-classics.info

Addresses for companies within The Random House Group Limited
can be found at: www.randomhouse.co.uk/offices.htm

The Random House Group Limited Reg. No. 954009

A CIP catalogue record for this book
is available from the British Library

ISBN 9780099490661

The Random House Group Limited supports The Forest Stewardship
Council (FSC®), the leading international forest certification organisation.
Our books carrying the FSC label are printed on FSC® certified paper.
FSC is the only forest certification scheme endorsed by the leading
environmental organisations, including Greenpeace. Our
paper procurement policy can be found at
www.randomhouse.co.uk/environment

Printed and bound in Great Britain by Clays Ltd, St Ives PLC

To Lyubov Yevgenievna Belozerskaya

A light snow was falling, which suddenly changed to thick, heavy flakes. The wind began to howl; it was a snowstorm. Within a moment the dark sky had merged with the ocean of snow. Everything disappeared.

'Looks bad, sir,' shouted the coachman. 'A blizzard!'

Pushkin *The Captain's Daughter*

... and the dead were judged out of those things which were written in the books according to their works ....

Revelation, XX, 12.

One

GREAT and terrible was the year of Our Lord 1918, of the Revolution the second. Its summer abundant with warmth and sun, its winter with snow, highest in its heaven stood two stars: the shepherds' star, eventide Venus; and Mars – quivering, red.

But in days of blood as in days of peace the years fly like an arrow and the thick frost of a hoary white December, season of Christmas trees, Santa Claus, joy and glittering snow, overtook the young Turbins unawares. For the reigning head of the family, their adored mother, was no longer with them.

A year after her daughter Elena Turbin had married Captain Sergei Talberg, and in the week in which her eldest son Alexei Turbin returned from years of grim and disastrous campaigning to the Ukraine, to the City of Kiev and home, the white coffin with the body of their mother was carried away down the slope of St Alexei's Hill towards the Embankment, to the little church of the St Nicholas the Good.

Their mother's funeral had been in May, the cherry and acacia blossom brushing against the narrow lancet windows of the church. His cope glittering and flashing in the golden sunlight, their parish priest Father Alexander had stumbled from grief and embarrassment while the deacon, his face and neck mauve, vested in beaten gold down to the tips of his squeaky boots, gloomily intoned the words of the funeral service for the mother who was leaving her children.

Alexei, Elena, Talberg, Anyuta the maid who had grown up in the Turbins' house, and young Nikolka, stunned by the death, a lock of hair falling over his right eyebrow, stood at the foot of the ancient brown ikon of St Nicholas. Set deep on either side of his long bird-like nose, Nikolka's blue eyes had a wounded, defeated look. Occasionally he raised them towards the ikon screen, to the vaulted apse above the altar where that glum and enigmatic old man, God, towered above them and winked. Why had he inflicted such a wrong on them? Wasn't it unjust? Why did their mother have to be taken away, just when they had all been reunited, just when life seemed to be growing more tolerable?

As he flew away through the crack that had opened up in the sky, God vouchsafed no answer, leaving Nikolka in doubt whether the things that happened in life were always necessary and always for the best.

The service over, they walked out on to the ringing flagstones of the porch and escorted their mother across the vast City to the cemetery, to where their father had long lain under a black marble cross. And there they buried their mother . . .

*

For many years before her death, in the house at No. 13 St Alexei's Hill, little Elena, Alexei the eldest and baby Nikolka had grown up in the warmth of the tiled stove that burned in the dining-room. How often they had followed the story of Peter the Great in Holland, 'The Shipwright of Saardam', portrayed on its glowing hot Dutch tiles; how often the clock had played its gavotte; and always towards the end of December there had been a smell of pine-needles and candles burning on evergreen branches. In answer to the gavotte played by the bronze clock in their mother's bedroom – now Elena's – the black clock on the wall had struck its steeple chimes. Their father had bought both clocks long ago, in the days when women had worn funny leg-of-mutton sleeves. Those sleeves had gone, time had slipped by like a flash, their father the professor had died, and they had all grown, but the clock remained the same and went on chiming. They had all grown used to the idea that if by some miracle that clock ever fell off the wall, it would be as sad as if a beloved voice had died and nothing could ever be hung there in its place. But clocks are fortunately quite immortal, as immortal as the Shipwright of Saardam, and however bad the times might be, the tiled Dutch stove, like a rock of wisdom, was always there to radiate life and warmth.

The stove; the furniture covered in old red velvet; the beds with their shiny brass knobs; the worn carpets and tapestries, some plain red, some patterned, one with a picture of Tsar Alexei Mikhailovich, another showing Louis XIV reclining beside a silken lake in paradise; the Turkish carpets with their gorgeous oriental curlicues which had danced in front of little Nikolka's eyes when he was once delirious from scarlet fever; the bronze lamp and its shade; the finest bookshelves in the world full of books that smelled mysteriously of old chocolate with their Natasha Rostovs and their Captain's Daughters, gilded cups, silver, portraits, drapes: all seven of those crammed, dusty rooms in which the young Turbins had been raised; all this, at a time of great hardship, was bequeathed to the children by their mother who as she lay gasping, her strength failing, had clutched the hand of the weeping Elena and said:

'Go on living . . . and be kind to one another . . .'

*

But how, how were they to go on living? Alexei Turbin, the eldest and a doctor, was twenty-eight, Elena twenty-four. Her husband Captain Talberg was thirty-one, and Nikolka seventeen and a half. Their life had been darkened at its very dawning. Cold winds had long been blowing without cease from the north and the longer they persisted the worse they grew. The eldest Turbin had returned to his native city after the first blast had shaken the hills above the Dnieper. Now, they thought, it will stop and we can start living the kind of life they wrote about in those chocolate-smelling books. But the opposite happened and life only grew more and more terrible. The snow-storm from the north howled and howled, and now they themselves could sense a dull, subterranean rumbling, the groaning of an anguished land in travail. As 1918 drew to an end the threat of danger drew rapidly nearer.

*

The time was coming when the walls would fall away, the terrified falcon fly away from the Tsar's white sleeve, the light in the bronze lamp would go out and the Captain's Daughter would be burned in the stove. And though the mother said to her children 'Go on living', their lot would be to suffer and die.

One day at twilight, soon after their mother's funeral, Alexei Turbin called on Father Alexander and said:

'It has been a terrible blow for us, Father Alexander. Grief like ours is even harder to bear when times are so bad . . . The worst is, you see, that I'd only just come home from the war and we were looking forward to straightening things out and leading a reasonable life, but now . . .'

He stopped and as he sat at the table in the half light he stared thoughtfully into the distance. Branches of the churchyard trees overshadowed the priest's little house. It was as if just out there, beyond the walls of his cramped, book-lined study was the edge of a tangled, mysterious, springtime forest. From outside came the muffled evening hum of the City and the smell of lilac.

'What can we do?' muttered the priest awkwardly. (He always felt embarrassed when he had to talk to people.) 'It is the will of God.'

'Perhaps all this will come to an end one day? Will things be any better, then, I wonder?' asked Turbin of no one in particular.

The priest shifted in his armchair.

'Yes, say what you like, times are bad, very bad', he mumbled. 'But one mustn't lose heart . . .'

Then drawing it out of the black sleeve of his cassock he suddenly laid his white hand on a pile of books, and opened the topmost one at the place marked by a bright embroidered ribbon.

'We must never lose heart', he said in his embarrassed yet somehow profoundly convincing voice. 'Faintness of heart is a great sin . . . Although I must say that I see great trials to come. Yes, indeed, great trials', he said with growing certainty. 'I have been spending much of the time with my books lately, you know. All concerned with my subject of course, mostly books on theology . . .'

He raised the book so that the last rays of the sun fell on the open page and read aloud:

'And the third angel poured out his vial upon the rivers and fountains of waters; and they became blood.'

Two

WHITE with hoar-frost, December sped towards its end. The glitter of Christmas could already be felt in the snowbound streets. The year 1918 would soon be over.

Number 13 was a curious building. On the street the Turbins' apartment was on the second floor, but so steep was the hill behind the house that their back door opened directly on to the sloping yard, where the house was brushed and overhung by the branches of the trees growing in the little garden that clung to the hillside. The back-gardens filled up with snow, and the hill turned white until it became one gigantic sugar-loaf. The house acquired a covering like a White general's winter fur cap; on the lower floor (on the street side it was the first floor, whilst at the back, under the Turbins' verandah, it was the basement) the disagreeable Vasily Lisovich – an engineer, a coward and a bourgeois – lit his flickering little yellow lamps, whilst upstairs the Turbins' windows shone brightly and cheerfully.

One evening Alexei and Nikolka went out into the yard for some firewood.

'Hm, damn little firewood left. Look, they've been pinching it again.'

A cone of bluish light burst out from Nikolka's pocket flash-light, and they could see clearly where the planking of the wood-shed had been wrenched away and clumsily pushed back into place from the outside.

'I'd shoot the swine if I caught them, by God I would. Why don't we keep watch out here tonight? I know it's that shoemaker's family from Number 11. And they've got much more firewood than we have, damn them!'

'Oh, to hell with them . . . Come on, let's go.'

The rusty lock creaked, a pile of logs tumbled down towards the two brothers and they lugged them away. By nine that evening the tiles of Saardam were too hot to touch.

The gleaming surface of that remarkable stove bore a number of historic inscriptions and drawings, painted on at various times during the past year by Nikolka and full of the deepest significance:

> If people tell you the Allies are coming to help us out of this mess, don't believe them. The Allies are swine.
>
> He's a pro-Bolshevik!

A drawing of a head of Momus, written underneath it:

> Trooper Leonid Yurievich.
>
> News is bad and rumours humming –
> People say the Reds are coming!

A painting of a face with long drooping moustaches, a fur hat with a blue tassel. Underneath:

> Down with Petlyura!

Written by Elena and the Turbins' beloved childhood friends – Myshlaevsky, Karas and Shervinsky – in paint, ink and cherry-juice were the following gems:

> Elena loves us all,
> the thin, the fat and the tall.
>
> Lena dear, have booked tickets for Aida
> Box No. 8, right.
>
> On the twelfth day of May 1918 I fell in love.
>
> You are fat and ugly.
>
> After a remark like that I shall shoot myself.

(followed by an extremely realistic drawing of an automatic)

14

Long live Russia!
Long live the Monarchy!

June. Barcarolle.

All Russia will recall the day
of glorious Borodino.

Then printed in capitals, in Nikolka's hand:

> I hereby forbid the scribbling of nonsense on this stove. Any comrade found guilty of doing so will be shot and deprived of civil rights.
> signed: Abraham Goldblatt,
> Ladies, Gentlemen's and Women's Tailor.
> Commissar, Podol District Committee.
> 30th January 1918.

The patterned tiles were luxuriously hot, the black clock going tonk-tank, tonk-tank, as it had done for thirty years. The elder Turbin, clean-shaven and fair-haired, grown older and more sombre since October 25th 1917, wearing an army officer's tunic with huge bellows pockets, blue breeches and soft new slippers, in his favourite attitude – in an upright armchair. At his feet on a stool Nikolka with his forelock, his legs stretched out almost as far as the sideboard – the dining-room was not big – and shod in his buckled boots. Gently and softly Nikolka strummed at his beloved guitar, vaguely . . . everything was still so confused. The City was full of unease, of vague foreboding . . .

On his shoulders Nikolka wore sergeant's shoulder-straps to which were sewn the white stripes of an officer cadet, and on his left sleeve a sharp-pointed tricolor chevron. (Infantry, No. 1 Detachment, 3rd Squad. Formed four days ago in view of impending events.)

Yet despite these events, all was well inside the Turbins' home: it was warm and comfortable and the cream-colored blinds were drawn – so warm that the two brothers felt pleasantly languorous.

The elder dropped his book and stretched.

'Come on, play "The Survey Squad".'
Thrum-ta-ta-tum, thrum-ta-ta-tum . . .

'Who look the smartest?
Who move the fastest?
The Cadets of the Engineers!'

Alexei began to hum the tune. His eyes were grim, but there was a sparkle in them and his blood quickened. But not too loud, gentlemen, not too loud . . .

'No need to run, girls,
Life can be fun, girls –'

The guitar strummed away in time to the marching feet of an engineer company – left, right, left, right! In his mind's eye Nikolka saw a school building, peeling classical columns, guns. Cadets crawling from window to window, firing. Machine-guns at the windows. A handful of soldiers was besieging the school, literally a handful. But it was no use. General Bogoroditzky had turned yellow and surrendered, surrendered with all his cadets. The shame of it . . .

'No need to run, girls,
Life can be fun, girls –
The Survey Squad is here!'

Nikolka's eyes clouded again. Heat-haze over the red-brown Ukrainian fields. Companies of cadets, white with powdery dust, marching along the dusty tracks. All over now. The shame . . . Hell.

Elena pushed aside the drapes over the door, and her auburn head appeared in the dark gap. She glanced affectionately at her brothers but anxiously at the clock. With good reason; where on earth was Talberg? Their sister was worried. To hide it, she started to sing the tune with her brothers, but suddenly stopped and raised her finger.

'Wait. Did you hear that?'

On all seven strings the company came to a halt. All three listened. There was no mistaking the sound: gunfire. Low,

16

muffled and distant. There it was again: boo-oo-om . . . Nikolka put down his guitar and jumped up, followed, groaning, by Alexei.

In the lobby and drawing-room it was quite dark. Nikolka stumbled over a chair. Outside it was exactly like a stage-setting for *The Night Before Christmas* – snow and twinkling, shimmering lights. Nikolka peered through the window. Heat-haze and school house vanished as he strained his ears. Where was that sound? He shrugged his tabbed shoulders.

'God knows. I get the impression it's coming from the Svyato-shino direction. Funny, though. It can't be as near as that.'

Alexei was standing in the dark, but Elena was nearer to the window and her eyes were shadowed with fear. Why had Talberg still not come home? What did it mean? The elder brother sensed her anxiety and because of it he said nothing, although he very much wanted to speak his thoughts. There was not the slightest doubt that it was coming from Svyatoshino. The firing was no more than eight miles outside the City. What was going on?

Nikolka gripped the window-catch and pressed his other hand against the pane as if to break it open, and flattened his nose against the glass.

'I'd like to go out there and find out what's going on . . .'

'Maybe; but it's no place for you right now . . .' said Elena anxiously. Her husband should have been home at the latest – the *very* latest – at three o'clock that afternoon, and now it was ten.

They went silently back into the dining-room. The guitar lay glumly silent. Nikolka went out to the kitchen and carried in the samovar, which hissed angrily and spat. The table was laid with cups that were pastel-colored inside and decorated outside with gilded caryatids. In their mother's day this had been the family's best tea-service for special occasions, but her children now used it for everyday. Despite the gunfire, the alarms and anxiety, the tablecloth was white and starched. This was thanks to Elena, who instinctively saw to such things, and to Anyuta who had grown up in the Turbin household. The hem of the tablecloth gleamed, and although it was December, in the tall, pillar-shaped matt glass vase stood a bunch of blue hortensias and two languorous roses to affirm the beauty and permanency of life – despite the fact that out there, on the roads leading into the City, lay the cunning enemy, poised to crush the beautiful snowbound City and grind the shattered remnants of peace and quiet into fragments beneath the heel of his boot. The flowers were a present from Elena's faithful admirer, Lieutenant Leonid Shervinsky of the Guards, a friend of the salesgirl at La Marquise, the famous confectioners, and a friend of the salesgirl at the florist's shop, Les Fleurs de Nice. In the shadow of the hortensias was a blue-patterned plate with a few slices of sausage, butter under a glass bell, lumps of sugar in the sugar-bowl and a long loaf of white bread. Everything one could want for a delicious supper if only the situation . . .

The teapot was covered by a bright woolen tea-cosy in the shape of a rooster, while the gleaming side of the samovar reflected the three distorted faces of the Turbins, making Nikolka's cheeks look as round and puffed as the face of Momus scribbled on the stove.

Elena looked miserable and her red curls hung lankly down.

Talberg and his trainload of the Hetman's money had gone astray somewhere, and the evening was ruined. Who knows what might have happened to him? The two brothers listlessly ate some slices of bread and sausage. A cold cup of tea and *The Gentleman from San Francisco* lay on the table in front of Elena. Misty and unseeing, her eyes stared at the words:

'. . . darkness, sea, storm.'

Elena was not reading.

Finally Nikolka could restrain himself no longer:

'Why is the gunfire so close, I'd like to know? I mean, they can't have . . .'

He broke off, his reflection in the samovar distorting as he moved. Pause. The hands of the clock crawled past the figure ten and moved on – tonk-tank – to a quarter past ten.

'They're firing because the Germans are swine', his elder brother barked unexpectedly.

Elena looked up at the clock and asked:

'Surely, surely they won't just leave us to our fate?' Her voice was miserable.

As if at by unspoken command the two brothers turned their heads and began telling lies.

'There's no news', said Nikolka and bit off a mouthful.

'What I said was purely, h'm . . . conjectural. Rumors.'

'No, it's not rumors', Elena countered firmly. 'That wasn't a rumor – it was true; I saw Shcheglova today and she said that two German regiments had withdrawn from Borodyanka.'

'Rubbish.'

'Now just think,' Alexei began. 'Is it conceivable that the Germans should let that scoundrel Petlyura come anywhere near the city? Is it? Personally I can't imagine how they could ever come to terms with him for one moment. Petlyura and the Germans – it's utterly absurd. They themselves regard him as nothing but a bandit. It's ridiculous.'

'I don't believe you. I know what these Germans are like by now. I've seen several of them wearing red arm-bands. The other day I saw a drunken German sergeant with a peasant woman – and she was drunk too.'

'What of it? There may be isolated cases of demoralisation even in the German army.'

'So you don't think Petlyura will break through?'

'H'm . . . No, I don't think it's possible.'

'*Absolument pas.* Pour me another cup of tea, please. Don't worry. Maintain, as the saying goes, complete calm.'

'But where's Sergei, for God's sake? I'm certain that train has been attacked and . . .'

'Pure imagination. Look – that line is completely out of any possible danger.'

'But something *might* happen, mightn't it?'

'Oh, God! You know what railroad journeys are like nowadays. I expect they were held up for about three hours at every single station.'

'That's what a revolution does to the trains. Two hours' delay for every hour on the move.'

With a deep sigh Elena looked at the clock, was silent for a while, then spoke again:

'God, if only the Germans hadn't acted so despicably everything would be all right. Two of their regiments would have been enough to squash that Petlyura of yours like a fly. No, I can see perfectly well that the Germans are playing some filthy double game. And where are our gallant Allies all this time? Ugh, the swine. Promises, promises . . .'

The samovar, silent until then, suddenly whistled and a few glowing coals, forced down by a heap of gray ash, fell on to the tray. Involuntarily the two brothers glanced towards the stove. There was the answer. Didn't it say: 'The Allies are swine'?

The minute hand stopped on the quarter-hour, the clock cleared its throat sedately and struck once. Instantly the clock's chime was answered by the gentle, tinkling ring of the front-door bell.

'Thank God; it's Sergei', said Alexei joyfully.

'Yes, it must be', Nikolka agreed and ran to open the door.

Flushed, Elena stood up.

*

But it was not Talberg. Three doors slammed, then Nikolka's astonished voice could be heard coming from the staircase. Another voice answered. The voices coming upstairs were gradually drowned by the noise of hobnailed boots and a rifle-butt. As the cold air flooded in through the front door Alexei and Elena were faced by a tall, broad-shouldered figure in a heel-length greatcoat and cloth shoulder-straps marked in grease pencil with a first lieutenant's three stars. The hood of the coat was covered with hoar-frost and a heavy rifle fixed with a rusty bayonet filled the whole lobby.

'Hello there', piped the figure in a hoarse tenor, pulling at the hood with fingers stiff with cold.

'Viktor!'

Nikolka helped the figure to untie the drawstring and the hood fell away to reveal the band of an officer's service cap with a faded badge; on the huge shoulders was the head of Lieutenant Viktor

Myshlaevsky. His head was extremely handsome, with the curiously disturbing good looks of centuries of truly ancient inbred lineage. His attractive features were two bright eyes, each of a different colour, an aquiline nose, proud lips, an unblemished forehead and 'no distinguishing marks'. But one corner of his mouth drooped sadly and his chin was cleft slantwise as though a sculptor, having begun by modelling an aristocratic face, had conceived the wild idea of slicing off a layer of the clay and leaving an otherwise manly face with a small and crooked feminine chin.

'Where have you come from?'

'Where've you been?'

'Careful,' replied Myshlaevsky weakly, 'don't knock it. There's a bottle of vodka in there.'

Nikolka carefully hung up the heavy greatcoat, from whose pocket there protruded the neck of a bottle wrapped in a piece of torn newspaper. Next he hung up a Mauser automatic in a wooden holster, so heavy that it made the hatstand of stag's antlers rock slightly. Only then did Myshlaevsky turn round to Elena. He kissed her hand and said:

'I've come from the Red Tavern district. Can I spend the night here, please, Lena? I'll never make it home tonight.'

'My God, of course you can.'

Suddenly Myshlaevsky groaned, tried to blow on his fingers, but his lips would not obey him. His face grew moist as the frost on his eyebrows and smooth, clipped moustache began to melt. The elder Turbin unbuttoned Myshlaevsky's service tunic, pulled out his dirty shirt and ran his finger down the seam.

'Well, of course . . . Thought so. You're crawling with lice.'

'Then you must have a bath.' Frightened, Elena had moment-arily forgotten about Talberg. 'Nikolka, there's some firewood in the kitchen. Go and light the boiler. Oh, why did I have to give Anyuta the evening off? Alexei, take his tunic off, quickly.'

By the tiled stove in the dining-room Myshlaevsky let out a groan and collapsed into a chair. Elena bustled around, keys clinking. Kneeling down, Alexei and Nikolka pulled off Mysh-laevsky's smart, narrow boots strapped around the calf.

'Easy now . . . oh, take it easy . . .'

They unwound his dirty, stained puttees. Under them was a pair of mauve silk socks. Nikolka at once put the tunic out on to the cold verandah, where the temperature would kill the lice. In his filthy cotton shirt, criss-crossed by a pair of black suspenders and blue breeches strapped under his instep Myshlaevsky now looked thin, dark, sick and miserable. He slapped his frozen palms together and rubbed them against the side of the stove.

'News . . . rumors . . . People . . . Reds . . .'

'. . . May . . . fell in love . . .'

'What bastards they are!' shouted Alexei Turbin. 'Couldn't they at least have given you some felt boots and a sheepskin jerkin?'

'Felt boo-oots', Myshlaevsky mimicked him, weeping. 'Felt boo . . .'

Unbearable pain gripped his hands and feet in the warmth. Hearing Elena's footsteps go into the kitchen, Myshlaevsky screamed, in tears, screamed furiously:

'It was a shambles!'

Croaking and writhing in pain he collapsed and pointing at his socks, groaned:

'Take them off, take them off . . .'

There was a sickening smell of methylated spirits as frozen extremities thawed out; from a single small wineglass of vodka Lieutenant Myshlaevsky became intoxicated in a moment, his eyes clouding.

'Oh Lord, don't say they'll have to be amputated . . .' he said bitterly, rocking back and forth in his chair.

'Nonsense, of course not. You'll be all right . . . Yes. The big toe's frostbitten. There . . . The pain will go.'

Nikolka squatted down and began to pull on some clean black socks while Myshlaevsky's stiff, wooden hands inched into the sleeves of a towelling bathrobe. Crimson patches began to appear on his cheeks and Lieutenant Myshlaevsky, grimacing in clean underwear and bathrobe, loosened up and came back to life. A stream of foul abuse rattled around the room like hail on a window-sill. Squinting with rage, he poured a stream of obscenities on the headquarters staff in their first-class railroad cars, on a certain Colonel Shchetkin, the cold, Petlyura, the Germans and the snowstorm and ended by heaping the most vulgar abuse on the Hetman of All the Ukraine himself.

Alexei and Nikolka watched the lieutenant's teeth chatter as he thawed out, making occasional sympathetic noises.

'The Hetman? Mother-fucker!' Myshlaevsky snarled. 'Where were the Horse Guards, eh? Back in the palace! And *we* were sent out in what we stood up in . . . Days on end in the snow and frost . . . Christ! I thought we were all done for . . . Nothing but a row of officers strung out at intervals of two hundred yards – is that what you call a defensive line? It was only by the grace of God that we weren't slaughtered like chickens!'

'Just a minute', Turbin interrupted, his head reeling under the flow of abuse. 'Who was with you at the Tavern?'

'Huh!' Myshlaevsky gestured angrily. 'You've no idea what it was like! How many of us d'you think there were at the Tavern? For-ty men. Then that scoundrel Colonel Shchetkin drove up and said (here Myshlaevsky twisted his expression in an attempt to imitate the features of the detested Colonel Shchetkin and he began talking in a thin, grating lisp): "Gentlemen, you are the City's last hope. It is your duty to live up to the trust placed in you by the Mother of Russian Cities and if the enemy appears – attack, God is with us! I shall send a detachment to relieve you after six hours. But I beg you to conserve your ammunition . . ." (Myshlaevsky spoke in his ordinary voice again) – and then he and his aide vanished in their car. Dark – it was like being up the devil's arsehole! And the frost – needles all over your face.'

'But why were you there, for God's sake? Surely Petlyura can't be at Red Tavern?'

'Christ knows. By morning we were nearly out of our minds. By midnight we were still there, waiting for the relief. Not a sign of them. No relief. For obvious reasons we couldn't light fires, the nearest village was a mile and a half away, the Tavern half a mile. At night you start seeing things – the fields seem to be moving. You think it's the enemy crawling up on you . . . Well, I thought, what shall we do if they really do come? Would I throw down my rifle, I wondered – would I shoot or not? It was a temptation. We stood there, howling like wolves. When you shouted someone along the line would answer. Finally I burrowed in the snow with my rifle-butt and dug myself a hole, sat down and tried not to fall asleep: once you fall asleep in that temperature you're done for. Towards morning I couldn't hold out any longer – I was beginning to doze off. D'you know what saved me? Machine-gun fire. I heard it start up at dawn, about a mile or two away. And, believe it or not, I found I just didn't want to stand up. Then a field-gun started booming away. I got up, feeling as if each leg weighed a ton and I thought: "This is it, Petlyura's turned up." We closed in and shortened the line so that we were near enough to shout to each other, and we decided that if anything happened we would form up into a tight group, shoot our way out and withdraw back into town. If they overran us – too bad, they overran us. At least we'd be together. Then, imagine – the firing stopped. Later in the morning we took it in turns to go to the Tavern three at a time to warm up. When d'you think the relief finally turned up? At two o'clock this afternoon. Two hundred officer cadets from the 1st Detachment. And believe it or not they were all properly dressed in fur hats a..d felt boots and they had a machine-gun squad. Colonel Nai-Turs was in command of them.'

'Ah! He's one of ours!' cried Nikolka.

'Wait a minute, isn't he in the Belgrade Hussars?' asked Alexei.

'Yes, that's right, he's a hussar . . . well, you can imagine, they were appalled when they saw us: "We thought you were at least two companies with a machine-gun – how the hell did you stand it?" Apparently that machine-gun fire at dawn was an attack on Serebryanka by a horde of about a thousand men. It was lucky they didn't know that *our* sector was defended by that thin line, otherwise that mob might have broken into the City. It was lucky, too that our people at Serebryanka had a telephone line to Post-Volynsk. They signalled that they were under attack, so some battery was able to give the enemy a dose of shrapnel. Well, you

24

can imagine that soon cooled their enthusiasm, they broke off the attack and vanished into thin air.'

'But who were they? Surely they weren't Petlyura's men? It's impossible.'

'God knows who they were. I think they were some local peasants – Dostoyevsky's "holy Russia" in revolt. Ugh – mother-fuckers . . .'

'God almighty!'

'Well,' Myshlaevsky croaked, sucking at a cigarette, 'thank God we were relieved in the end. We counted up and there were thirty-eight of us left. We were lucky – only two of us had died of frostbite. Done for. And two more were carried away. They'll have to have their legs amputated . . .'

'What – two were frozen to death?'

'What d'you expect? One cadet and one officer. But the best part was what happened at Popelukho, that's the village near the Tavern. Lieutenant Krasin and I went there to try and find a sledge to carry away the men who'd been frostbitten. The village was completely dead – not a soul to be seen. We hunted around, then finally out crawled some old man in a sheepskin coat, walking with a crutch. He was overjoyed when he saw us, believe it or not. I felt at once that something was wrong. What's up, I wondered? Then that miserable old bastard started shouting: "Hullo there, lads . . ." So I put on an act and spoke to him in Ukrainian. "Give us a sledge, dad", I said. And he said: "Can't. Them officers have pinched all the sledges and taken them off to Post." I winked at Krasin and asked the old man: "God damn the officers. Where've all your lads disappeared to?" And what d'you think he said? "They've all run off to join Petlyura." How d'you like that, eh? He was so blind, he couldn't see that we had officers' shoulder-straps under our hoods and he took us for a couple of Petlyura's men. Well, I couldn't keep it up any longer . . . the cold . . . I lost my temper . . . I grabbed hold of the old man so hard he almost jumped out of his skin and I shouted – in Russian this time: "Run off to Petlyura, have they? I'm going to shoot you – then you'll learn how to run off to Petlyura! I'm going to make you run

25

off to Kingdom Come, you old wretch!" Well, then of course this worthy old son of the soil (here Myshlaevsky let out a torrent of abuse like a shower of stones) saw what was up. He jumped up and screamed: "Oh, sir, oh sir, forgive an old man, I was joking, I can't see so well any more, I'll give you as many horses as you want, right away sir, only don't shoot me!" So we got our horses and sledge.'

'Well, it was evening by the time we got to Post-Volynsk. The chaos there was indescribable. I counted four batteries just standing around still limbered up – no ammunition, apparently. Innumerable staff officers everywhere, but of course not one of them had the slightest idea of what was going on. The worst of it was, we couldn't find anywhere to unload our two dead men. In the end we found a first-aid wagon. If you can believe it they threw our corpses away by force, wouldn't take them. Told us to drive into the City and dispose of them there! That made us really mad. Krasin wanted to shoot one of the staff officers, who said: "You're behaving like Petlyura" and vanished. Finally at nightfall I found Shchetkin's headquarters car – first class, of course, electric light . . . And what d'you think happened? Some filthy little man, a sort of orderly, wouldn't let us in. Huh! "He's asleep," he said, "the colonel's given orders he's not to be disturbed." Well, I pinned him to the wall with my rifle-butt and all our men behind me started yelling. This brought them tumbling out of the railroad car. Out crawled Shchetkin and started trying to sweeten us. "Oh, my God", he said, "how terrible for you. Yes, of course, right away. Orderly – soup and brandy for these gentlemen. Three days' special furlough for all of you. Sheer heroism. It's terrible about your casualties, but they died in a noble cause. I was so worried about you . . ." And you could smell the brandy on his breath a mile away . . . Aaah!' Suddenly Myshlaevsky yawned and began to nod drowsily. As though asleep he muttered:

'They gave our detachment a car to themselves and a stove . . . But I wasn't so lucky. He obviously wanted to get me out of the way after that scene. "I'm ordering you into town, lieutenant.

Report to General Kartuzov's headquarters." Huh! Rode into town on a locomotive . . . freezing . . . Tamara's Castle . . . vodka . . .'

The cigarette dropped out of Myshlaevsky's mouth, he leaned back in the chair and immediately started snoring.

'God, what a story . . .' said Nikolka, in a bemused voice.

'Where's Elena?' enquired the elder brother anxiously. 'Take him to get washed. He'll need a towel.'

Elena was weeping in the bathroom, where beside the zinc bath dry birch logs were crackling in the boiler. The wheezy little kitchen clock struck eleven. She was convinced Talberg was dead. The train carrying money had obviously been attacked, the escort killed, and blood and brains were scattered all over the snow. Elena sat in the half-darkness, the firelight gleaming through her rumpled halo of hair, tears pouring down her cheeks. He's dead, dead . . .

Then came the gentle, tremulous sound of the door bell, filling the whole apartment. Elena raced through the kitchen, through the dark library and into the brighter light of the dining-room. The black clock struck the hour and ticked slowly on again.

But after their first outburst of joy the mood of Nikolka and his elder brother very quickly subsided. Their joy was in any case more for Elena's sake. The wedge-shaped badges of rank of the Hetman's War Ministry had a depressing effect on the Turbin brothers. Indeed dating from long before those badges, practically since the day Elena had married Talberg, it was as if some kind of crack had opened up in the bowl of the Turbins' life and imperceptibly the good water had drained away through it. The vessel was dry. The chief reason for this, it seems, lay in the double-layered eyes of Staff Captain Sergei Ivanovich Talberg . . .

Be that as it may, the message in the uppermost layer of those eyes was now clearly detectable. It was one of simple human delight in warmth, light and safety. But deeper down was plain fear, which Talberg had brought with him on entering the house. As always, the deepest layer of all was, of course, hidden, although naturally nothing showed on Talberg's face. Broad, tightly-

27

buckled belt; his two white graduation badges – the university and military academy – shining bravely on his tunic. Beneath the black clock on the wall his sunburned face turned from side to side like an automaton. Although Talberg was extremely cold, he smiled benevolently round at them all. But there was fear even in his benevolence. Nikolka, his long nose twitching, was the first to sense this. In a slow drawl Talberg gave an amusing description of how he had been in command of a train carrying money to the provinces, how it had been attacked by God knows who somewhere about thirty miles outside the City. Elena screwed up her eyes in horror and clutched at Talberg's badges, the brothers made suitable exclamations and Myshlaevsky snored on, dead to the world, showing three gold-capped teeth.

'Who were they? Petlyura's?'

'Well if they were,' said Talberg, smiling condescendingly yet nervously, 'it's unlikely that I would be . . . er . . . talking to you now. I don't know who they were. They may just have been a stray bunch of Nationalists. They climbed all over the train, waving their rifles and shouting "Whose train is this?" So I answered "Nationalist". Well, they hung around for a while longer, then I heard somebody order them off the train and they all vanished. I suppose they were looking for officers. They probably thought the escort wasn't Ukrainian at all but manned by loyalist Russian officers.' Talberg nodded meaningfully towards the chevron on Nikolka's sleeve, glanced at his watch and added unexpectedly: 'Elena, I must have a word with you in our room . . .'

Elena hastily followed him out into the bedroom in the Talbergs' half of the apartment, where above the bed a falcon sat perched on the Tsar's white sleeve, where a green-shaded lamp glowed softly on Elena's writing desk and on the mahogany bedside table a pair of bronze shepherds supported the clock which played a gavotte every three hours.

With an incredible effort Nikolka succeeded in wakening Myshlaevsky, who staggered down the passage, twice crashing into doorways, and fell asleep again in the bath. Nikolka kept watch on him to make sure that he did not drown. Alexei Turbin, without conscious reason, paced up and down the dark living-room, pressed his face to the windowpane and listened: once again, from far away and muffled as though in cotton wool came the occasional distant harmless rumble of gunfire.

Elena, auburn-haired, had aged and grown uglier in a moment. Eyes reddened, her arms dangling at her sides she listened miserably to what Talberg had to say. As stiff as though he were on parade he towered over her and said implacably:

'There is no alternative, Elena.'

Reconciled to the inevitable, Elena said:

'Oh, I understand. You're right, of course. In five or six days, d'you think? Perhaps the situation may have changed for the better by then?'

Here Talberg found himself in difficulty. Even his patient, everlasting smile disappeared from his face. His face, too, had aged; every line in it showed that his mind was made up. Elena's hope that they could leave together in five or six days was pathetically false and ill-founded . . .

Talberg said: 'I must go at once. The train leaves at one o'clock tonight . . .'

Half an hour later everything in the room with the falcon had been turned upside down. A trunk stood on the floor, its padded inner lid wide open. Elena, looking drawn and serious, wrinkles at the corners of her mouth, was silently packing the trunk with shirts, underclothes and towels. Kneeling down, Talberg was fumbling with his keys at the bottom drawer of the chest-of-drawers. Soon the room had that desolate look that comes from the chaos of packing up to go away and, worse, from removing the shade from the lamp. Never, never take the shade off a lamp. A lampshade is something sacred. Scuttle away like a rat from danger and into the unknown. Read or doze beside your lampshade; let the storm howl outside and wait until they come for you.

Talberg was running away. He straightened up, trampling on the pieces of torn paper littered around the heavy, closed trunk. He was fully dressed in his long greatcoat, neat black fur cap with ear-muffs and gray-blue Hetmanite badge, his sword belted to his side.

On the long-distance departure track of the City's No. 1 Passenger Station the train was already standing, though still without a locomotive, like a caterpillar without a head. It was made up of nine cars, all shining with blindingly white electric light, due to leave at 1 a.m. carrying General von Bussow and his headquarters staff to Germany. They were taking Talberg with them; he had influence in the right quarters . . . The Hetman's ministry was a stupid, squalid little comic opera affair (Talberg liked to express himself in cutting, if unoriginal terms) – like the Hetman himself, for that matter. All the more squalid because . . .

'Look, my dear (whisper) the Germans are leaving the Hetman in the lurch and it's extremely likely that Petlyura will march in . . . and you know what that means . . .'

Elena knew what that meant. Elena knew very well. In March 1917 Talberg had been the first – the first, you realise – to report to the military academy wearing a broad red armband. That was in the very first days of the revolution, when all the officers in the City turned to stone at the news from Petersburg and crept away down dark passages to avoid hearing about it. As a member of the Revolutionary Military Committee it had been none other than Talberg who had arrested the famous General Petrov. Towards the end of that momentous year many strange and wonderful things happened in the City and certain people began appearing – people who had no boots but who wore broad, baggy Ukrainian trousers called *sharovary* which showed beneath their army great-coats. These people announced that they would not leave the City for the front on any account because the fighting was none of their affair and they intended to stay in the City. This irritated Talberg, who declared curtly that this was not what was required, that it was a squalid comic opera. And to a certain extent he turned out to be right: the results were operatic, though so much blood was shed that they were hardly comic. The men in baggy trousers were twice driven out of the City by some irregular regiments of troops who emerged from the forests and the plains from the direction of

Moscow. Talberg said that the men in *sharovary* were mere adventurers and that the real roots of legitimate power were in Moscow, even though these roots were Bolshevik roots.

But one day in March the Germans arrived in the City in their gray ranks, with red-brown tin bowls on their heads to protect them from shrapnel balls; and their hussars wore such fine busbies and rode on such magnificent horses that Talberg at once realised where the roots of power grew now. After a few heavy salvoes from the German artillery around the City the men from Moscow vanished somewhere beyond the blue line of the forests to eat carrion, and the men in *sharovary* slunk back in the wake of the Germans. This was a great surprise. Talberg smiled in embarrassment, but he was not afraid because as long as the Germans were there the *sharovary* behaved themselves, did not dare to kill anyone and even walked the streets with a certain wariness, like guests who were none too sure of themselves. Talberg said they had no roots, and for about two months he had no work to do. One day when he walked into Talberg's room, Nikolka Turbin could not help smiling: Talberg was seated and writing out grammatical exercises on a large sheet of paper, whilst in front of him lay a thin text-book printed on cheap gray paper:

Ignatii Perpillo

UKRANIAN GRAMMAR

At Easter in April 1918 the electric arc-lights hummed cheerfully in the circus auditorium and it was black with people right up to the domed roof. A tall, crisp, military figure, Talberg stood in the arena counting the votes at a show of hands. This was the end of the *sharovary*, there was to be a Ukrainian state but a 'hetmanite' Ukraine – they were electing the 'Hetman of All the Ukraine'.

'We're safely insulated from that bloody comic opera in Moscow', said Talberg, his strange Hetmanite uniform clashing with the dear familiar old wallpaper in the Turbins' apartment. The clock's tonk-tank was choked with scorn and the water drained away from the bowl. Nikolka and Alexei found that they had nothing in common with Talberg. Talking to him would in any case have been extremely difficult because Talberg lost his temper whenever the conversation turned to politics and especially on those occasions when Nikolka was tactless enough to begin with the remark: 'What was it that you were saying in March, Sergei . . .?' Then Talberg would instantly bare his strong, widely-spaced teeth, yellow sparks would flash in his eyes and he would start to lose his temper. Conversation thus went out of fashion.

Comic opera . . . Elena knew what those words meant on her husband's puffy, Baltic-German lips. But now the comic opera was becoming a real threat, and this time not to the *sharovary*, not to the Bolsheviks in Moscow, not just to other people, but to Sergei Talberg himself. Every man has his star and it was with good reason that court astrologers of the Middle Ages cast their horoscopes to predict the future. They were wise to do so. Sergei Talberg, for instance, had been born under a most unfortunate, most unsuitable star. Life would have been fine for Talberg if everything had proceeded along one definite straight line, but events in the City at that time did not move in a straight line; they followed fantastic zig-zags and Sergei Talberg tried in vain to guess what was coming next. He failed. Still far from the City, maybe a hundred miles away, a railroad car stood on the tracks, brilliantly lit. In that car, like a pea in a pod, a clean-shaven man sat talking, dictating to his clerks and his aides. Woe to Talberg if that man were to reach the City – and he might! Everybody had read a certain issue of the *Gazette*, everybody knew the name of Captain Talberg as a man who had voted for the Hetman. In that newspaper there was an article written by Sergei Talberg, and the article declared:

'Petlyura is an adventurer, who threatens the country with destruction from his comic-opera régime . . .'

'You must understand, Elena, that I can't take the risk of having to go into hiding and facing the uncertainties of the immediate future here. Don't you agree?'

Elena said nothing in reply, being a woman of pride.

'I think,' Talberg went on, 'that I shall have no difficulty in getting through to the Don by way of Roumania and the Crimea.

Von Bussow has promised me his co-operation. They appreciate me. However, the German occupation has deteriorated into a comic opera. The Germans are leaving. (Whisper) By my calculations Petlyura will collapse soon, too. The real power is in the South – Denikin. You realise, of course, that I can't afford not to be there when the army of the forces of law and order is being formed. Not to be there would ruin my career – especially as Denikin used to be my divisional commander. I'm convinced that in three months' time – well, by May at the latest – we shall be back in the City. Don't be afraid. No one is going to touch you and in a real emergency you still have your passport in your maiden name. I shall ask Alexei to make sure that no possible harm comes to you.'

Elena looked up with a jerk.

'Just a moment,' she said, 'shouldn't we tell Alexei and Nikolka at once that the Germans are betraying us?'

Talberg blushed deeply.

'Of course, of course, I will certainly . . . On second thoughts, you had better tell them yourself. Although it makes very little real difference to the situation.'

For an instant Elena had a strange feeling, but she had no time to reflect on it. Talberg was kissing her and there was a moment when his two-layered eyes showed only a single emotion – tenderness. Elena could not prevent herself from bursting into tears, although she cried silently. She was, after all, her mother's daughter and a strong woman. Then came Talberg's leave-taking with her brothers in the living-room. A pinkish light shone from the bronze lampstand, flooding the corner of the room. The piano bared its familiar white teeth and the score of *Faust* lay open at the passage where the flamboyant lines of notes weave across the stave in thick black clusters and the gaily-costumed, bearded Valentine sings:

> 'I beg you, beg you for my sister's sake,
> Have mercy on her – mercy!
> Guard her well, I pray you.'

At that moment even Talberg, who had never been a prey to sentimental feelings, recalled the dense black chords and the tattered pages of the age-old family copy of *Faust*. Never again would Talberg hear the cavatina 'Oh God Almighty', never again hear Elena accompanying Shervinsky as he sang. But long after the Turbins and Talbergs have departed this life the keys will ring out again and Valentine will step up to the footlights, the aroma of perfume will waft from the boxes and at home beautiful women under the lamplight will play the music, because *Faust*, like the Shipwright of Saardam, is quite immortal.

Talberg stood beside the piano as he said his piece. The brothers listened in polite silence, trying not to raise their eyebrows – the younger from pride, the elder from lack of courage. Talberg's voice shook.

'You will look after Elena, won't you?' The upper layer of Talberg's eyes looked at them anxiously, pleadingly. He stuttered, glanced awkwardly at his pocket watch and said nervously: 'It's time to go.'

Elena embraced her husband, hastily made a fumbling sign of the cross over him and kissed him. Talberg brushed his brothers-in-law on the cheek with his clipped, bristly moustache. With a nervous glance through his wallet he checked the thick bundle of documents in it, re-counted the thinner wad of Ukrainian money and German marks; then smiling tensely he turned and went. The light went on in the lobby, there came the sound of his trunk bumping downstairs. Leaning over the banisters, the last thing that Elena saw was the sharp peak of his hood.

At one o'clock in the morning an armored train like a gray toad pulled out from Track 5, through the dark graveyards of rows of idle, empty freight cars, snorting and picking up speed as it spat hot sparks from its ash-pit and hooted like a wild beast. Covering six miles in seven minutes it reached Post-Volynsk with a roar and a rattle and a flash of its lights, arousing a vague sense of hope and pride in the cadets and officers huddled in railroad cars or on guard duty. Without slowing down the armored train was switched off the main line and headed boldly away towards the German frontier. After it, ten minutes later, a passenger train with a colossal locomotive and dozens of brilliantly-lit windows passed through Post-Volynsk. Massive as obelisks and swathed to the eyes, German sentries flashed by on the platforms at the end of the cars, their black bayonets glinting. Hunched up from the cold and lit by rapid shafts of light from the windows, the switchmen watched as the long pullman cars rattled over the junction. Then everything vanished and the cadets were seized with envy, resentment and alarm.

'Ah, the swine . . .' a voice groaned from the switches as the blistering gust of a snowstorm lashed the railroad cars housing the cadets. That night Post was snowed up.

In the third car back from the locomotive, in a compartment upholstered in checkered calico, smiling politely and ingratiatingly, Talberg sat opposite a German lieutenant and spoke German.

'Oh, ja', drawled the fat lieutenant from time to time and chewed his cigar.

When the lieutenant had fallen asleep, when all the compartment doors were shut and all that could be heard in the warm, brilliantly lit car was the monotonous click of the wheels, Talberg went out into the corridor, opened one of the pale-colored blinds with their transparent letters 'S. – W.R.R.' and stared long into the darkness. Occasional sparks, snow flickered past, and in front the locomotive raced on and with a howl that was so sinister, so threatening that even Talberg was unpleasantly affected by it.

Three

IN the downstairs apartment at No. 13, which belonged to Vasily Lisovich, engineer and householder, absolute silence reigned at that hour of the night, a silence only occasionally disturbed by a mouse in the dining-room. Busily and insistently the mouse gnawed and gnawed away at an old rind of cheese, cursing the meanness of the engineer's wife, Wanda Mikhailovna. The object of this abuse, the bony and jealous Wanda, was sound asleep in the dark bedroom of their damp, chilly apartment. Lisovich himself was still awake and ensconced in his study, a draped, book-lined, over-furnished and consequently extremely cosy little room. The standard lamp, in the shape of an Egyptian queen and shaded in green flowered material, lit the room with a gentle mysterious glow; there was something mysterious, too, about the engineer himself in his deep leather armchair. The mystery and ambiguity of those uncertain times was expressed above all in the fact that the man in the armchair was not Vasily Lisovich at all, but Vasilisa . . . He, of course, called himself Lisovich, many of the people he met called him Vasily, but only to his face. Behind his back no one ever called him anything but Vasilisa. This had come about because since January 1918, when the strangest things began happening in the City, the owner of No. 13 altered his distinctive signature, and from a vague fear of committing himself to some document that might be held against him in the future, instead of a bold 'V. Lisovich' he began signing his name on questionnaires, forms, certificates, orders and ration cards as 'Vas. Lis.'

On January 18th 1918, with a sugar ration card signed by Vasily Lisovich, instead of sugar Nikolka had received a terrible blow on his back from a stone on the Kreshchatik and had spat blood for two days. (A shell had burst right over the heads of some brave people standing in line for sugar.) When he reached home, clutching the wall and turning green, Nikolka had managed to smile so as not to alarm Elena. Then he had spat out a bowlful of blood and when Elena shrieked: 'God – what's happened to you?' he replied: 'It's Vasilisa's sugar, damn him!' After that he turned white and collapsed. Nikolka was out of bed again two days later, but Vasily Lisovich had ceased to exist. At first only the people living at No. 13, then soon the whole City began calling him Vasilisa, until the only person who introduced him as Lisovich was the bearer of that girl's name himself.

After making sure that the street was quiet at last, with not even the occasional creak of sleigh-runners to be heard, and listening attentively to the whistling sound coming from his wife in the

36

bedroom, Vasilisa went out into the lobby. There he carefully checked the locks, bolt, chain and door-handle and returned to his study, where he produced four shiny safety-pins from a drawer of his massive desk. He tiptoed away somewhere into the darkness and returned with a rug and a towel. Again he stopped and listened, even putting his finger to his lips. He pulled off his jacket, rolled up his sleeves and took down from a shelf a pot of glue, a length of wallpaper neatly rolled into a tube, and a pair of scissors. Then he sidled up to the window and, shielded by his hand, looked out into the street. With the aid of the safety-pins he hung the towel over the top half of the left-hand window and the rug over the right-hand window, arranging them with care lest there should be any cracks. Taking a chair he climbed up on it and fumbled for something above the topmost shelf of books, ran the point of a little knife vertically down the wallpaper, then side-ways at a right angle; next he inserted the blade under the cut to reveal a small, neat hiding-place the size of two bricks, made by himself during the previous night. He removed the cover – a thin rectangle of zinc – climbed down, glanced fearfully at the windows and patted the towel. From the depths of a lower drawer, which opened with a tinkling double turn of the key, there came to light a package carefully wrapped in newspaper, sealed and tied criss-cross with string. This Vasilisa immured in his secret cache and replaced the cover. For a long while he stood on the red cloth of the chair-cover and cut out pieces of wallpaper until they exactly fitted the pattern. Smeared with glue, they covered the gap perfectly: half a spray of flowers matching its other half, square matching square. When the engineer climbed down from his chair, he was positive that there was not a sign of his secret hiding-place in the wall. Vasilisa rubbed his hands with exultation, crumpled up the scraps of wallpaper and burned them in the little stove, then pounded up the ashes and hid the glue.

Out in the black and deserted street a gray, ragged, wolf-like creature slid noiselessly down from the branches of an acacia, where he had been sitting for half an hour, suffering badly from the cold but avidly watching Lisovich at work through a tell-tale gap above the upper edge of the towel. It had been the oddness of a green towel being draped over the window which had attracted the snooper's attention. Dodging behind snowdrifts, the figure disappeared up the street, whence it loped through a maze of side-streets until the storm, the dark and the snow swallowed it up and obliterated all its traces.

Night. Vasilisa in his armchair. In the green shadows he looks exactly like the Taras Bulba. Long, bushy, drooping moustaches: he's no Vasilisa – he's a man, dammit! After another gentle tinkle of keys in his desk drawer, there lay on the red cloth several wads of oblong bills like green stage-money, with a legend in Ukrainian:

State Bank Certificate
50 Roubles
Circulates at Parity with Credit Notes

Pictured on one side of the bill was a Ukrainian peasant with drooping moustaches and armed with a spade, and a peasant woman with a sickle. On the reverse in an oval frame were the reddish-brown faces of the same two peasants magnified in size, the man complete with typical long moustaches. Above it all was the warning inscription:

The Penalty for Forgery is Imprisonment

and beneath it the firm signature:

Director of the State Bank:
Lebid-Yurchik.

Mounted on his horse, a bronze Alexander II, his face framed in a ragged lather of metal sideburns, glanced angrily at Lebid-Yurchik's work of art and smirked at the Egyptian queen disguised as a lampstand. From the wall one of Vasilisa's ancestors, a civil servant painted in oils with the Order of St Stanislav around his neck, stared down in horror at the banknotes. The spines of Goncharov and Dostoyevsky glowed gently in the green light, whilst nearby the green and black volumes of Brockhaus and Ephron's encyclopedia stood drawn up in mighty ranks like Horse Guards on parade. A world of comfort and security.

The five-per-cent state bonds were safely hidden in the secret cache under the wallpaper, along with fifteen Tsarist 1000-rouble bills, nine 500-rouble bills, twenty-five silver spoons, a gold watch and chain, three cigar-cases (presents 'To our Esteemed Colleague', although Vasilisa did not smoke), fifty gold 10-rouble pieces, a pair of salt-cellars, a six-person canteen of silver cutlery and a silver tea-strainer. The second cache was a large one, outside in the woodshed – two paces straight forward from the doorway, one pace to the left, then one pace on from the chalk-mark on one of the planks of the wall. Everything was packed in tin boxes that had once held Einem's Biscuits, wrapped in oilcloth with tarred seams, then buried five feet deep.

The third cache was in the loft, a hollow in the plaster under a beam six feet north-east of the chimney-stack. In this were a pair of sugar-tongs, one hundred and eighty-three gold 10-rouble pieces and state bonds to a nominal value of twenty-five thousand roubles.

Lebid-Yurchik was for current expenses.

Vasilisa glanced around, as he always did when counting money, licked his finger and started to flick through the wad of stage money. Suddenly he went pale.

'Forgeries', he growled angrily, shaking his head. 'Disgraceful!'

Vasilisa's blue eyes glowered morosely. In the third bundle of ten bills there was one forgery, in the fourth – two, in the sixth – two, in the ninth three bills in succession were unmistakeably of the kind for which Lebid-Yurchik threatened to imprison him. A hundred and thirteen bills in all and, if you please, eight of them with obvious signs of being forged. The peasant had a sort of gloomy look instead of being cheerful, they lacked the proper quotation marks and colon, and the paper was better than Lebid's. Vasilisa held one up to the light and an obvious forgery of Lebid's signature shone through from the other side.

'One of these will do for the cab fare tomorrow', said Vasilisa aloud to himself. 'And I've got to go down to the market, anyway. They don't look too hard at them there.'

He carefully put the forged notes aside, to be given to the cab-driver and used in the market, then locked the wad in the drawer with a tinkle of keys. He shuddered. Footsteps were heard along the ceiling overhead, laughter and muffled voices broke the deathly silence. Vasilisa said to Alexander II:

'You see – no peace . . .'

There was silence again upstairs. Vasilisa yawned, stroked his wispy moustache, took down the rug and the towel from the windows and switched on the light in the sitting-room, where a large phonograph horn shone dully. Ten minutes later the apartment was in complete darkness. Vasilisa was asleep beside his wife in their damp bedroom that smelled of mice, mildew and a peevish sleeping couple. In his dream Lebid-Yurchik came riding up on a horse and a gang of thieves with skeleton keys discovered his secret hiding-place. The jack of hearts climbed up on a chair, spat at Vasilisa's moustache and fired at him point-blank. In a cold sweat Vasilisa leaped up with a shriek and the first thing that he heard was the mouse family hard at work in the dining-room on a packet of rusks; then laughter and the gentle sound of a guitar came through the ceiling and the carpets . . . Suddenly from the floor above a voice of unusual strength and passion struck up, and the guitar swung into a march.

'There's only one thing to be done – turn them out of the apartment', said Vasilisa as he muffled himself up in the sheets. 'This is outrageous. There's no peace day or night.'

> 'The guards' cadets
> Are marching along –
> Swinging along,
> Singing a song.'

'Still, in case anything happened . . . Times are bad enough. If you kick them out you never know who you'll get instead – they are at least officers and if anything happened, they would defend us . . . Shoo!' Vasilisa shouted at the furiously active mouse.

The sound of a guitar . . .

*

Four lights burning in the dining-room chandelier. Pennants of blue smoke. The french windows on to the verandah completely shut out by cream-colored blinds. Fresh bunches of hot-house flowers against the whiteness of the tablecloth, three bottles of vodka and several narrow bottles of German white wine. Long-stemmed glasses, apples in glittering cut-crystal vases, slices of lemon, crumbs everywhere, tea . . .

On the armchair a crumpled sheet of the humorous magazine *Peep-show*. Heads muzzy, the mood swinging at one moment towards the heights of unreasoning joy, at the next towards the trough of despondency. Singing, pointless jokes which seemed irresistibly funny, guitar chords, Myshlaevsky laughing drunkenly. Elena had not had time to collect herself since Talberg's departure . . . white wine does not remove the pain altogether, only blunts it. Elena sat in an armchair at the head of the table. Opposite her at the other end was Myshlaevsky, shaggy and pale in a bathrobe, his face blotchy with vodka and insane fatigue. His eyes were red-ringed from cold, the horror he had been through, vodka and fury. Down one of the long sides of the table sat Alexei and Nikolka, on the other Leonid Shervinsky, one-time First Lieutenant in His Majesty's Own Regiment of Lancers and now an aide on the staff of Prince Belorukov, and alongside him Second Lieutenant Fyodor Stepanov, an artilleryman, still known by his high school nickname of 'Karas' – the carp. Short, stocky and really looking very like a carp, Karas had bumped into Shervinsky at the Turbins' front door about twenty minutes after Talberg had left. Both had brought some bottles with them. In Shervinsky's package were four bottles of white wine, while Karas had two bottles of vodka. Beside that Shervinsky was loaded with an enormous bouquet, swathed in three layers of paper – roses for Elena, of course. Karas gave him his news on the doorstep: he was back in artillery uniform. He had lost patience with studying at the university, which was pointless now anyway; everybody had to go and fight, and if Petlyura ever got into the City time spent at the university would be worse than useless. It was everyone's duty to volunteer and the mortar regiment needed trained gunnery officers. The commanding officer was Colonel Malyshev, the regiment was a fine one – all his friends from the university were in it. Karas was in despair because Myshlaevsky had gone off to join that crazy infantry detachment. All that death-or-glory stuff was idiotic, and now where the hell was he? Maybe even killed at his post somewhere outside the City . . .

But Myshlaevsky was here – upstairs! At her mirror, with its frame of silver foliage, in the half-light of the bedroom the lovely Elena hastily powdered her face and emerged to accept her roses. Hurrah! They were all here. Karas' golden crossed cannon on his crumpled shoulder-straps and carefully pressed blue breeches. A shameless spark of joy flashed in Shervinsky's little eyes at the news of Talberg's departure. The little hussar immediately felt himself in excellent voice and the pink-lit sitting-room was filled with a positive hurricane of gorgeous sound as Shervinsky sang an epithalamion to the god Hymen – how he sang! Shervinsky's voice was surely unique. Of course he was still an officer at present, there was this stupid war, the Bolsheviks, and Petlyura, and one had one's duty to do, but afterwards when everything was back to normal he would leave the army, in spite of all his influential connections in Petersburg – and they all knew what sort of connections *those* were (knowing laughter) – and . . . he would go on the stage. He would sing at La Scala and at the Bolshoi in Moscow – as soon as they started hanging Bolsheviks from the lamp-posts in the square outside the theatre. Once at Zhmerinka, Countess Lendrikov had fallen in love with him because when he had sung the Epithalamion, instead of C he had hit E and held it for five bars. As he said 'five', Shervinsky lowered his head slightly and looked around in an embarrassed way, as though someone else had told the story instead of him.

'Mm'yes. Five bars. Well, let's have supper.'

And now the room was hung with wispy pennants of smoke . . .

'Where are these Senegalese troops? Come on, Shervinsky, you're at headquarters: tell us why they aren't here. Lena, my dear, drink some more wine, do. Everything will be all right. He was right to go. He'll make his way to the Don and come back here with Denikin's army.'

42

'They're coming,' said Shervinsky in his twinkling voice, 'reinforcements are coming. I have some important news for you: today on the Kreshchatik I myself saw the Serbian billeting-officers and the day after tomorrow, in a couple of days' time at the latest, two Serbian regiments will arrive in the City.'

'Listen, are you sure?'

Shervinsky went red in the face.

'Well, really. If I say I saw them myself, I consider that question somewhat out of place.'

'That's all very well, but what good are two regiments?'

'Kindly allow me to finish what I was saying. The prince himself was telling me today that troop-ships are already unloading in the port of Odessa: Greek troops and two divisions of Senegalese have arrived. We only have to hold out on our own for a week – and then we can spit on the Germans.'

'Treacherous bastards.'

'Well, if all that's true it won't be long before we catch Petlyura and hang him! String him up!'

'I'd like to shoot him with my own hands.'

'And strangle him too. Your health, gentlemen.'

Another drink. By now minds were getting fogged. Having drunk three glasses Nikolka ran to his room for a handkerchief, and as he passed through the lobby (people act naturally when there's no one watching them) he collapsed against the hat-stand. There hung Shervinsky's curved sabre with its shiny gold hilt. Present from a Persian prince. Damascus blade. Except that no prince had given it to him and the blade was not from Damascus, but it was still a very fine and expensive one. A grim Mauser in a strap-hung holster, beside it the blued-steel muzzle of Karas' Steyr automatic. As Nikolka stumbled against the cold wood of the holster and fingered the murderous barrel of the Mauser he almost burst into tears with excitement. He suddenly felt an urge to go out and fight, now, this minute, out on the snow-covered fields outside the City. He felt embarrassed and ashamed that here at home there was vodka to drink and warmth, while out there his fellow cadets were freezing in the dark, the snow and the blizzard.

They must be crazy at headquarters – the detachments were not ready, the students not trained, no sign of the Senegalese yet and they were probably as black as a pair of boots . . . Christ, that meant they'd freeze to death – after all, they were used to a hot climate, weren't they?

'As for your Hetman,' Alexei Turbin was shouting, 'I'd string him up the first of all! He's done nothing but insult us for the past six months. Who was it who forbade us to form a loyalist Russian army in the Ukraine? The Hetman. And now that things have gone from bad to worse, they've started to form a Russian army after all. The enemy's practically in sight and now – *now!* – we have to rake up troops, form detachments, headquarters, – and in conditions of total disorder! Christ, what lunacy!'

'You're spreading panic', Karas said coolly.

Turbin lost his temper.

'Me? Spreading panic? You are simply shutting your eyes to the facts. I'm no panic-monger. I just want to get something off my chest. Panic? Don't worry. I've already decided to go and enrol in that Mortar Regiment of yours tomorrow, and if your Malyshev won't have me as a doctor I shall enlist in the ranks. I'm fed up with the whole damn business! It's not panic . . .' A piece of cucumber stuck in his throat, he began to cough furiously and to choke, and Nikolka started thumping him on the back.

'Well done!' Karas chimed in, beating the table. 'In the ranks hell – we'll fix you to be the regimental doctor.'

'Tomorrow we'll all go along together,' mumbled the drunken Myshlaevsky, 'all of us together. The whole of our class from the Alexander I High School. Hurrah!'

'He's a swine,' Turbin went on with hatred in his voice, 'why, he can't even speak Ukrainian properly himself! Hell – the day before yesterday I asked that bastard Kuritsky a question. Since last November, it seems, he's forgotten how to speak Russian. Changed his name, too, to make it sound Ukrainian . . . Well, so I asked him – what's the Ukrainian for "cat"? "Kit" he said. All right, I said, so what's the Ukrainian for "kit"? That finished him.

44

He just frowned and said nothing. Now he doesn't say good-morning any longer.' Nikolka roared with laughter ...

'Mobilisation – huh', Turbin continued bitterly. 'A pity you couldn't have seen what was going on in the police stations yesterday. All the black marketeers knew about the mobilisation three days before the decree was published. How d'you like that? And every one of them had a hernia or a patch on his lung, and any one of them who couldn't fake lung trouble simply vanished as if he'd fallen through a hole in the ground. And that, my friends, is a very bad sign. If the word's going round all the cafés even before mobilisation is officially announced and every shirker has a chance to dodge it, then things are really bad. Ah, the fool – if only he had allowed us to form units manned by Russian officers back in April, we could have taken Moscow by now. Don't you see? Here in the City alone he could have had a volunteer army of fifty thousand men – and what an army! An élite, none but the very best, because all the officer-cadets, all the students and high school boys and all the officers – and there are thousands of them in the City – would have gladly joined up. Not only would we have chased Petlyura out of the Ukraine, but we would have reached Moscow by now and swatted Trotsky like a fly. *Now* would have been the time to attack Moscow – it seems they're reduced to eating cats. And Hetman Skoropodsky, the son of a bitch, could have saved Russia.'

Turbin's face was blotchy and the words flew out of his mouth in a thin spray of saliva. His eyes burned.

'Hey, you shouldn't be a doctor – you should be the Minister of Defense, and that's a fact', said Karas. He was smiling ironically, but Turbin's speech had pleased him and excited him.

'Alexei is indispensable at meetings, he's a real orator', said Nikolka.

'Nikolka, I've told you twice already that you're not funny', his brother replied. 'Drink some wine instead of trying to be witty.'

'But you must realise,' said Karas, 'that the Germans would never have allowed the formation of a loyalist army – they're too afraid of it.'

'Wrong!' exclaimed Alexei sharply. 'All that was needed was someone with a good head on his shoulders and we could have always come to terms with the Hetman. Then we should have made it clear to the Germans that we were no threat to them. *That* war is over, and we have lost it. Now we have something much worse on our hands, much worse than the war, worse than the Germans, worse than anything on earth – and that is Trotsky. We should have said to the Germans – you need wheat and sugar, don't you? Right – take all you want and feed your troops. Occupy the Ukraine if you like, only help us. Let us form our army – it will be to your advantage, we'll help you to keep order in the Ukraine and prevent these God-forsaken peasants of ours from catching the Moscow disease. If there were a Russian-manned army in the City now we would be insulated from Moscow by a wall of steel. And as for Petlyura . . . k-khh . . .' Turbin drew his finger expressively across his throat and was seized by a furious coughing fit.

'Stop!' Shervinsky stood up. 'Wait. I must speak in defense of the Hetman. I admit some mistakes were made, but the Hetman's plan was fundamentally correct. He knows how to be diplomatic. First of all a Ukrainian state . . . then the Hetman would have done exactly as you say – a Russian-manned army and no nonsense. And to prove that I'm right . . .' – Shervinsky gestured solemnly toward the window – ' the Imperial tricolor flag is already flying over Vladimirskaya Street.'

'Too late!'

'Well, yes, you may be right. It is rather late, but the Hetman is convinced that the mistake can be rectified.'

'I sincerely hope to God that it can', and Alexei Turbin crossed himself in the direction of the ikon of the Virgin in the corner of the room.

'Now the plan was as follows,' Shervinsky announced solemnly. 'Once the war was over the Germans would have recovered, and turned to help us against the Bolsheviks. Then when Moscow was captured, the Hetman would have laid the allegiance of the Ukraine at the feet of His Majesty the Emperor Nicholas II.'

At this remark a deathly silence fell on the room. Nikolka turned white with agony.

'But the Emperor is dead', he whispered.

'What d'you mean – Nicholas II?' asked Alexei Turbin in a stunned voice, and Myshlaevsky, swaying, squinted drunkenly into Shervinsky's glass. Obviously Shervinsky had had one too many to keep his courage up.

Leaning her head on one hand, Elena stared in horror at him.

But Shervinsky was not particularly drunk. He raised his hand and said in a powerful voice:

'Not so fast. Listen. But I beg you, gentlemen, to remain silent until I've finished what I have to say. I suppose you all know what happened when the Hetman's suite was presented to Kaiser Wilhelm?'

'We haven't the slightest idea', said Karas with interest.

'Well, I know.'

'Huh! He knows everything', sneered Myshlaevsky.

'Gentlemen! Let him speak.'

'After the Kaiser had graciously spoken to the Hetman and his suite he said: "I shall now leave you, gentlemen; discussion of the future will be conducted with . . ." The drapes parted and into the hall came Tsar Nicholas II. "Go back to the Ukraine, gentlemen," he said, "and raise your regiments. When the moment comes I shall place myself in person at the head of the army and lead it on to the heart of Russia – to Moscow." With these words he broke down and wept.'

Shervinsky beamed round at the whole company, tossed down a glass of wine in one gulp and grimaced. Ten eyes stared at him and silence reigned until he had sat down and eaten a slice of ham.

'See here . . . that's all a myth', said Alexei Turbin, frowning painfully. 'I've heard that story before.'

'They were all murdered,' said Myshlaevsky, 'the Tsar, the Tsarina and the heir.'

Shervinsky glanced sideways towards the stove, took a deep breath and declared:

'You're making a mistake if you believe that. The news of His Imperial Majesty's death . . .'

'Is slightly exaggerated', said Myshlaevsky in a drunken attempt at wit.

Elena shivered indignantly and boomed out of the haze at him.

'You should be ashamed at yourself, Viktor – you, an officer.'

Myshlaevsky sank back into the mist.

'. . . was purposely invented by the Bolsheviks', Shervinsky went on. 'The Emperor succeeded in escaping with the aid of his faithful tutor . . . er, sorry, of the Tsarevich's tutor, Monsieur Gilliard and several officers, who conveyed him to er, to Asia. From there they reached Singapore and thence by sea to Europe. Now the Emperor is the guest of Kaiser Wilhelm.'

'But wasn't the Kaiser thrown out too?' Karas enquired.

'They are both in Denmark, with Her Majesty the Empress-Dowager Maria Fyodorovna, who is a Danish princess by birth. If you don't believe me, I may tell you that I was personally told this news by the Hetman himself.'

Nikolka groaned inwardly, his soul racked with doubt and confusion. He wanted to believe it.

'Then if it's true,' he suddenly burst out, jumping to his feet and wiping the sweat from his brow, 'I propose a toast: to the health of His Imperial Majesty!' His glass flashed, the cut-crystal arrows on its side piercing the German white wine. Spurs clinked against chair-legs. Swaying, Myshlaevsky stood up and clutched the table. Elena stood up. Her crescent braid of golden hair had unwound itself and her hair hung down beside her temples.

'I don't care – even if he is dead', she cried, hoarse with misery. 'What does it matter now? I'll drink to him.'

'He can never, never be forgiven for his abdication at Dno Station. Never. But we have learned by bitter experience now, and we know that only the monarchy can save Russia. Therefore if the Tsar is dead – long live the Tsar!' shouted Alexei and raised his glass.

'Hurrah! Hur-rah! Hur-ra-ah!' The threefold cry roared across the dining-room.

Downstairs Vasilisa leaped up in a cold sweat. Suddenly weakened, he gave a piercing shriek and woke up his wife Wanda.

'My God, oh my God . . ' Wanda mumbled, clutching his nightshirt.

'What the hell's going on? At three o'clock in the morning!' the weeping Vasilisa shrieked at the black ceiling. 'This time I really am going to lodge a complaint!'

Wanda groaned. Suddenly they both went rigid. Quite clearly, seeping down through the ceiling, came a thick, greasy wave of sound, dominated by a powerful baritone resonant as a bell:

'. . . God Save His Majesty,
Tsar of all Russia . . .'

Vasilisa's heart stopped and even his feet broke out into a cold sweat. Feeling as if his tongue had turned to felt, he burbled:

'No . . . it can't be . . . they're insane . . . They'll get us into such trouble that we'll never come out of it alive. The old anthem is illegal now! Christ, what are they doing? They can be heard out on the street, for God's sake!'

Wanda had already slumped back like a stone and had fallen asleep again, but Vasilisa could not bring himself to lie down until the last chord had faded away upstairs amid a confused babble of shouts.

'Russia acknowledges only one Orthodox faith and one Tsar!' shouted Myshlaevsky, swaying.

'Right!'

'Week ago . . . at the theater . . . went to see *Paul the First*', Myshlaevsky mumbled thickly, 'and when the actor said those words I couldn't keep quiet and I shouted out "Right!" – and d'you know what? Everyone clapped. All except some swine in the upper circle who yelled "Idiot!" '

'Damned Yids', growled Karas, now almost equally drunk.

A thickening haze enveloped them all . . . Tonk-tank . . . tonk-tank . . . they had passed the point when there was any longer any sense in drinking more vodka, even wine; the only remaining stage was stupor or nausea. In the narrow little lavatory, where the lamp jerked and danced from the ceiling as though bewitched, every-thing went blurred and spun round and round. Pale and miserable, Myshlaevsky retched violently. Alexei Turbin, drunk himself, looking terrible with a twitching nerve on his cheek, his hair plastered damply over his forehead, supported Myshlaevsky.

'Ah-aakh . . .'

Finally Myshlaevsky leaned back from the bowl with a groan, tried painfully to focus his eyes and clung to Alexei's arms like a limp sack.

'Ni-kolka!' Someone's voice boomed out through the fog and black spots, and it took Alexei several seconds to realise that the voice was his own. 'Nikolka!' he repeated. A white lavatory wall swung open and turned green. 'God, how sickening, how dis-gusting. I swear I'll never mix vodka and wine again. Nikol . . .'

'Ah-ah', Myshlaevsky groaned hoarsely and sat down on the floor.

A black crack widened and through it appeared Nikolka's head and chevron.

'Nikol . . . help me to get him up. There, pick him up like this, under his arm.'

'Poor fellow', muttered Nikolka shaking his head sympathetically and straining himself to pick up his friend. The half-lifeless body slithered around, twitching legs slid in every direction and the lolling head hung like a puppet's on a string. Tonk-tank went the clock, as it fell off the wall and jumped back into place again. Bunches of flowers danced a jig in the vase. Elena's face was flushed with red patches and a lock of hair dangled over her right eyebrow.

'That's right. Now put him to bed.'

'At least wrap him in a bathrobe. He's indecent like that with me around. You damned fools – you can't hold your drink. Viktor! Viktor! What's the matter with you? Vik . . .'

'Shut up, Elena. You're no help. Listen, Nikolka, in my study . . . there's a medicine bottle . . . it says "Liquor ammonii", you can tell because the corner of the label's torn off . . . anyway, you can't mistake the smell of sal ammoniac.'

'Yes, right away . . .'

'You, a doctor – you ought to be ashamed of yourself, Alexei . . .'

'All right, I know . . .'

'What? Has his pulse stopped?'

'No, he's just passed out.'

'Basin!'

'Ah-aah . . .'

'Christ!'

Violent reek of ammonia. Karas and Elena held Myshlaevsky's mouth open. Nikolka supported him while Alexei twice poured white cloudy liquid into his mouth.

'Aah . . . ugh . . . urkhh . . .'

'The snow . . .'

'God almighty. Can't be helped, though. Only way to do it . . .'

On his forehead lay a wet cloth dripping water, below it the swivelling, bloodshot whites of his eyes under half-closed lids, bluish shadows around the sharpened nose. For an anxious quarter of an hour, bumping each other with their elbows, they strove with the vanquished officer until he opened his eyes and croaked:

'Aah . . . let me go . . .'

'Right. That's better. He can stay and sleep here.'

Lights went on in all the rooms and beds were quickly made up.

'Leonid, you'd better sleep in here, next to Nikolka's room.'

'Very well.'

Copper-red in the face but cheerful, Shervinsky clicked his spurs and, bowing, showed the parting in his hair. Elena's white hands fluttered over the pillows as she arranged them on the divan.

'Please don't bother . . . I can make up the bed myself.'

'Nonsense. Stop tugging at that pillow – I don't need your help.'

'Please let me kiss your hand . . .'

'What for?'

'Gratitude for all your trouble.'

'I can manage without hand-kissing for the moment . . . Nikolka, you're sleeping in your own bed. Well, how is he?'

'He's all right, sleeping it off.'

Two camp beds were made up in the room leading to Nikolka's, behind two back-to-back bookcases. In Professor Turbin's family the room was known as the library.

*

As the lights went out in the library, in Nikolka's room and in the dining-room, a dark red streak of light crawled out of Elena's bedroom and into the dining-room through a narrow crack in the door. The light pained her, so she had draped her bedside lamp with a dark red theater-cloak. Once Elena used to drive to an evening at the theater in that cloak, once when her arms, her furs and her lips had smelled of perfume, her face had been delicately powdered – and when under the hood of her cloak Elena had looked like Liza in *The Queen of Spades*. But in the past year the cloak had turned threadbare with uncanny rapidity, the folds grown creased and stained and the ribbons shabby. Still looking like Liza in *The Queen of Spades*, auburn-haired Elena now sat on the turned-down edge of her bed in a négligé, her hands folded in her lap. Her bare feet were buried deep in the fur of a well-worn old bearskin rug. Her brief intoxication had gone completely, and now deep sadness enveloped her like a black cloak. From the next room, muffled by the bookshelf that had been placed across the closed door, came the faint whistle of Nikolka's breathing and Shervinsky's bold, confident snore. Dead silence from Myshlaevsky and Karas in the library. Alone, with the light shining on her nightgown and on the two black, blank windows, Elena talked to herself without constraint, sometimes half-aloud, sometimes whispering with lips that scarcely moved.

'He's gone . . .'

Muttering, she screwed up her dry eyes reflectively. She could not understand her own thoughts. He had gone, and at a time like this. But then he was an extremely level-headed man and he had done the right thing by leaving . . . It was surely for the best.

'But at a time like this . . .'

Elena whispered, and sighed deeply.

'What sort of man is he?' In her way she had loved him and even grown attached to him. Now in the solitude of this room, beside

52

these black windows, so funereal, she suddenly felt an overwhelming sense of depression. Yet neither at this moment, nor for the whole eighteen months that she had lived with this man had there been in her heart of hearts that essential feeling without which no marriage can survive – not even such a brilliant match as theirs, between the beautiful, red-haired, golden Elena and a career officer of the general staff, a marriage with theater-cloaks, with perfume and spurs, unencumbered by children. Married to a sensible, careful Baltic German of the general staff. And yet – what was he really like? What was that vital ingredient, whose lack had created the emptiness in the depth of Elena's soul?

'I know, I know what it is', said Elena to herself aloud. 'There's no respect. Do you realise, Sergei? I have never felt any respect for you', she announced meaningfully to her cloak, raising an admonitory finger. She was immediately appalled at her loneliness, and longed for him to be there at that moment. He had gone. And her brothers had kissed him goodbye. Did they really have to do that? But for God's sake, what am I saying? What else should they have done? Held back? Of course not. Well, maybe it was better that he shouldn't be here at such a difficult time and he was better gone, but they couldn't have refused to wish him Godspeed. Of course not. Let him go. The fact was that although they had gone through the motions of embracing him, in the depth of their hearts they hated him. God, yes – they did. All this time you've been lying to yourself and yet when you stop to think for a moment, it's obvious – they hate him. Nikolka still has some remnants of kindness and generosity toward him, but Alexei . . . And yet that's not quite true either. Alexei is kind at heart too, yet he somehow hates him more. Oh my God, what am I saying? Sergei, what am I saying about you? Suddenly we're cut off . . . He's gone and here am I . . .

'My husband,' she said with a sigh, and began to unbutton her négligé, 'my husband . . .'

Red and glowing, her cloak listened intently, then asked:

'But what sort of a man is your husband?'

*

'He's a swine, and nothing more!' said Alexei Turbin to himself, alone in his room across the lobby from Elena. He had divined what she was thinking and it infuriated him. 'He's a swine – and I'm a weakling. Kicking him out might have been going too far, but I should at least have turned my back on him. To hell with him. And it's not because he left Elena at a time like this that he's a swine, that has really very little to do with it – no, it's because of something quite different. But what, exactly? It's only too clear, of course. He's a wax dummy without the slightest conception of decency! Whatever he says, he talks like a senseless fathead – and he's a graduate of the military academy, who are supposed to be the élite of Russia . . .'

Silence in the apartment. The streak of light from Elena's room was extinguished. She fell asleep and her thoughts faded away, but for a long time Alexei Turbin sat unhappily at the little writing desk in his little room. The vodka and the hock had violently disagreed with him. He sat looking with red-rimmed eyes at a page of the first book he happened to pick up and tried to read, his mind always flicking senselessly back to the same line:

'Honor is to a Russian but a useless burden . . .'

It was almost morning when he undressed and fell asleep. He dreamed of a nasty little man in baggy check pants who said with a sneer:

'Better not sit on a hedgehog if you're naked! Holy Russia is a wooden country, poor and . . . dangerous, and to a Russian honor is nothing but a useless burden.'

'Get out!' shouted Turbin in his dream. 'You filthy little rat – I'll get you!' In his dream Alexei sleepily fumbled in his desk drawer for an automatic, found it, tried to shoot the horrible little man, chased after him and the dream dissolved.

For a couple of hours he fell into a deep, black, dreamless sleep and when a pale delicate light began to dawn outside the windows of his room that opened on to the verandah, Alexei began to dream about the City.

54

Four

BEAUTIFUL in the frost and mist-covered hills above the Dnieper, the life of the City hummed and steamed like a many-layered honeycomb. All day long smoke spiralled in ribbons up to the sky from innumerable chimney-pots. A haze floated over the streets, the packed snow creaked underfoot, houses towered to five, six and even seven storeys. By day their windows were black, while at night they shone in rows against the deep, dark blue sky. As far as the eye could see, like strings of precious stones, hung the rows of electric globes suspended high from the elegant curlicues of tall lamp-posts. By day the streetcars rolled by with a steady, comfortable rumble, with their yellow straw-stuffed seats of handsome foreign design. Shouting as they went cabmen drove from hill to hill and fur collars of sable and silver fox gave beauty and mystery to women's faces.

The gardens lay silent and peaceful, weighed down with white virgin snow. And there were more gardens in the City than any other city in the world. They sprawled everywhere, with their avenues of chestnuts, their terraces of maples and limes.

The beautiful hills rising above the Dnieper were made even lovelier by gardens that rose terrace-wise, spreading, at times flaming into colour like a million sunspots, at others basking in the perpetual gentle twilight of the Imperial Gardens, the terrifying drop over the escarpment quite unprotected by the ancient, rotting black beams of the parapet. The sheer hillsides, lashed by snowstorms, fell away to the distant terraces below which in turn spread further and wider, merging into the tree-lined embankments that curved along the bank of the great river. Away and away wound the dark river like a ribbon of forged steel, into the haze, further than the eye could see even from the City's highest eminence, on to the Dnieper Rapids, to the Zaporozhian Sech, to the Chersonese, to the far distant sea.

In winter, more than in any other city in the world, quiet fell over the streets and alleyways of the two halves of the City – the Upper City on the hilltops and the Lower City spread along the curve of the frozen Dnieper – and the City's mechanical roar retreated inside the stone buildings, grew muffled and sank to a low hum. All the City's energy, stored up during a summer of sunshine and thunderstorms, was expended in light. From four o'clock in the afternoon light would start to burn in the windows of the houses, in the round electric globes, in the gas street-lamps, in the illuminated house-numbers and in the vast windows of electric power-stations, turning people's thoughts towards the terrifying prospect of man's electric-powered future, those great windows through which could be glimpsed the machines whose desperate, ceaselessly revolving wheels shook the earth to its very core. All night long the City shone, glittered and danced with light until morning, when the lights went out and the City cloaked itself once more in smoke and mist.

But the brightest light of all was the white cross held by the gigantic statue of St Vladimir atop Vladimir Hill. It could be seen from far, far away and often in summer, in thick black mist, amid the osier-beds and tortuous meanders of the age-old river, the boatmen would see it and by its light would steer their way to the City and its wharves. In winter the cross would glow through the dense black clouds, a frozen unmoving landmark towering above the gently sloping expanse of the eastern bank, whence two vast bridges were flung across the river. One, the ponderous Chain Bridge that led to the right-bank suburbs, the other high, slim and urgent as an arrow that carried the trains from where, far away, crouched another city, threatening and mysterious: Moscow.

*

In that winter of 1918 the City lived a strange unnatural life which is unlikely ever to be repeated in the twentieth century. Behind the stone walls every apartment was overfilled. Their normal inhabitants constantly squeezed themselves into less and less space, willy-nilly making way for new refugees crowding into the City, all of whom arrived across the arrow-like bridge from the direction of that enigmatic other city.

Among the refugees came gray-haired bankers and their wives, skilful businessmen who had left behind their faithful deputies in Moscow with instructions to them not to lose contact with the new world which was coming into existence in the Muscovite kingdom; landlords who had secretly left their property in the hands of trusted managers; industrialists, merchants, lawyers, politicians. There came journalists from Moscow and Petersburg, corrupt, grasping and cowardly. Prostitutes. Respectable ladies from aristocratic families and their delicate daughters, pale depraved women from Petersburg with carmine-painted lips; secretaries of civil service departmental chiefs; inert young homosexuals. Princes and junk-dealers, poets and pawnbrokers, gendarmes and actresses from the Imperial theatres. Squeezing its way through the crack, this mass of people converged on the City.

All spring, beginning with the election of the Hetman, refugees had poured into the City. In apartments people slept on divans and chairs. They dined in vast numbers at rich men's tables. Countless little restaurants were opened which stayed open for business until far into the night, cafés which sold both coffee and women, new and intimate little theatres where the most famous actors bent themselves into contortions to raise a laugh among the refugees from two capitals. That famous theatre, the Lilac Negro, was opened and a gorgeous night club for poets, actors and artists called Dust and Ashes kept its cymbals ringing on Nikolaevsky Street until broad daylight. New magazines sprang up overnight and the best pens in Russia began writing articles in them abusing the Bolsheviks. All day long cab-drivers drove their passengers from restaurant to restaurant, at night the band would strike up in the cabaret and through the tobacco smoke glowed the unearthly beauty of exhausted, white-faced, drugged prostitutes.

The City swelled, expanded, overflowed like leavened dough rising out of its baking-tin. The gambling clubs rattled on until dawn, where some gamblers were from Petersburg and others from the City itself, others still were stiff, proud German majors and lieutenants whom the Russians feared and respected, card-sharpers from Moscow clubs and Russo-Ukrainian landlords whose lives and property hung by a thread. At Maxim's café a plump, fascinating Roumanian made his violin whistle like a nightingale; his gorgeous eyes sad and languorous with bluish whites, and his hair like velvet. The lights, shaded with gypsy shawls, cast two sorts of light – white electric light downwards, orange light upwards and sideways. The ceiling was draped star-like with swathes of dusty blue silk, huge diamonds glittered and rich auburn Siberian furs shone from dim, intimate corners. And it smelled of roasted coffee, sweat, vodka and French perfume.

All through the summer of 1918 the cab-drivers did a roaring trade and the shop windows were crammed with flowers, great slabs of rich filleted sturgeon hung like golden planks and the two-headed eagle glowed on the labels of sealed bottles of Abrau, that delicious Russian champagne. All that summer the pressure of newcomers mounted – men with gristly-white faces and grayish, clipped toothbrush moustaches, operatic tenors with gleaming polished boots and insolent eyes, ex-members of the State Duma in pince-nez, whores with resounding names. Billiard players took girls to shops to buy them lipstick, nail-polish, and ladies' panties in gauzy chiffon, cut out in the most curious places.

They sent off letters through the only escape-hole across tur-bulent, insecure Poland (not one of them, incidentally, had the slightest idea what was going on there or even what sort of place this new country – Poland – was) to Germany, that great nation of honest Teutons – begging for visas, transferring money, sensing that before long they would have to flee Russian territory al-together to where they would be finally and utterly safe from the terrible civil war and the thunder of Bolshevik regiments. They dreamed of France, of Paris, in anguish at the thought that it was extremely difficult, if not nearly impossible to get there. And there were other thoughts, vague and more frightening, which would suddenly come to mind in sleepless nights on divans in other people's apartments.

'And what if . . . what if that steel cordon were to snap . . . And the gray hordes poured in. The horror . . .'

These thoughts would come at those times when from far, far away came the dull thump of gunfire: for some reason firing went on outside the City throughout the whole of that glittering, hot summer, when those gray, metallic Germans kept the peace all around, whilst in the City itself they could hear the perpetual muffled crack of rifle-fire on the outskirts. Who was shooting at whom, nobody knew. It happened at night. And by day people were reassured by the occasional sight of a regiment of German hussars trotting down the main street, the Kreshchatik, or down Vladimir Street. And what regiments they were! Fur busbies crowning proud faces, scaly brass chinstraps clasping stone-hard jaws, the tips of red 'Kaiser Wilhelm' moustaches pointing upward like twin arrows. Squadrons of horses advancing in tight ranks of four, powerful seventeen-hand chestnuts, all six hundred troopers encased in blue-gray tunics like the cast-iron uniforms on the statues of their ponderous Germanic heroes that adorned the city of Berlin.

People who saw them were cheered and reassured, and jeered at the distant Bolsheviks, who were furiously grinding their teeth on the other side of the barbed wire along the border.

They hated the Bolsheviks, but not with the kind of aggressive hatred which spurs on the hater to fight and kill, but with a cowardly hatred which whispers around dark corners. They hated by night, choking with anxiety, by day in restaurants reading newspapers full of descriptions of Bolsheviks shooting officers and bankers in the back of the neck with Mausers, and how the Moscow shopkeepers were selling horsemeat infected with glanders. All of them – merchants, bankers, industrialists, lawyers, actors, landlords, prostitutes, ex-members of the State Council, engineers, doctors and writers, felt one thing in common – hatred.

*

And there were officers, officers who had fled from the north and

59

from the west – the former front line – and they all headed for the City. There were very many of them and their numbers increased all the time. They risked their lives to come because being officers, mostly penniless and bearing the ineradicable stamp of their profession, they of all refugees had the greatest difficulty in acquiring forged papers to enable them to get across the frontier. Yet they did manage to cross the line and appeared in the City with hunted looks, lousy and unshaven, without badges of rank, and adopted any expedient which enabled them to stay alive and eat. Among them were old inhabitants of the City who had returned home with the same idea in their minds as Alexei Turbin – to rest, recuperate and start again by building a new life, not a soldier's life but an ordinary human existence; there were also hundreds of others for whom staying in Petersburg or Moscow was out of the question. Some of them – the Cuirassiers, Chevalier Guards, Horse Guards and Guards Lancers – swam easily in the murky scum of the City's life in that troubled time. The Hetman's bodyguard wore fantastic uniforms and at the Hetman's tables there was room for up to two hundred people with slicked-down hair and mouthfuls of decayed yellow teeth with gold fillings. Anyone who was not found a place in the Hetman's bodyguard was found an even softer billet by women in expensive fur coats in opulent, panelled apartments in Lipki, the most exclusive part of town, or settled into restaurants or hotel rooms.

Others, such as staff-captains of shattered and disbanded regiments of the line, or hussars who had been in the thick of the fighting like Colonel Nai-Turs, hundreds of ensigns and second lieutenants, former students like Karas, their careers ruined by the war and the revolution, and first lieutenants, who had also enlisted from university but who could never go back and study, like Viktor Myshlaevsky. In their stained gray coats, with still un-healed wounds, with a torn dark strip on each shoulder where their badges of rank had been, they arrived in the City and they slept on chairs, in their own homes or in other people's, using their great-coats as blankets. They drank vodka, roamed about, tried to find something to do and boiled with anger. It was these men who hated the Bolsheviks with the kind of direct and burning hatred which could drive them to fight.

And there were officer cadets. When the revolution broke out there were four officer-cadet schools in the City – an engineers' school, an artillery school and two infantry schools. They were closed and broken up to a rattle of gunfire from mutinous soldiery and boys just out of high school and first-year students were thrown out on to the street crippled and wounded. They were not children and not adults, neither soldiers nor civilians, but boys like the seventeen-year-old Nikolka Turbin . . .

*

'Of course I'm delighted to think that the Ukraine is under the benevolent sway of the Hetman. But I have never yet been able to discover, and in all probability never will until my dying day, just exactly who is this invisible despot with a title that sounds more appropriate to the seventeenth century than the twentieth.'

'Yes – exactly who is he, Alexei?'

'An ex-officer of the Chevalier Guards, a general, rich land-owner, his name is Pavel Petrovich Skoropadsky . . .'

By some curious irony of fate and history his election, held in April 1918, took place in a circus – a fact which will doubtless provide future historians with abundant material for humor. The people, however, in particular the settled inhabitants of the City who had already experienced the first shocks of civil war, not only failed to see the humor of the situation but were unable to discern any sense in it at all. The election had taken place with bewildering speed. Before most people knew it had happened it was all over – and God bless the Hetman. What did it matter anyway, just so long as there was meat and bread in the market and no shooting in the streets, and so long – above all – as the Bolsheviks were kept out and the common people were kept from looting. Well, more or less all of this was put into effect under the Hetman – indeed to a considerable degree. At least the Moscow and Petersburg refugees and the majority of people in the City itself, even though they laughed at the Hetman's curious state and like Captain

Talberg called it a ludicrous operetta, sincerely blessed the Hetman, and said to themselves 'God grant that it lasts for ever'.

But whether it could last for ever, no one could say – not even the Hetman himself.

For the fact was that although life in the City went on with apparent normality – it had a police force, a civil service, even an army and newspapers with various names – not a single person in it knew what was going on around and about the City, in the real Ukraine, a country of tens of millions of people, bigger than France. They not only knew nothing about the distant parts of the country, but they were even, ridiculous though it seems, in utter ignorance of what was happening in the villages scattered about twenty or thirty miles away from the City itself. They neither knew nor cared about the real Ukraine and they hated it with all their heart and soul. And whenever there came vague rumors of events from that mysterious place called 'the country', rumors that the Germans were robbing the peasants, punishing them mercilessly and mowing them down by machine-gun fire, not only was not a single indignant voice raised in defense of the Ukrainian peasants but, under silken lampshades in drawing-rooms, they would bare their teeth in a wolfish grin and mutter:

'Serve them right! And a bit more of that sort of treatment wouldn't do 'em any harm either. I'd give it 'em even harder. That'll teach them to have a revolution – didn't want their own masters, so now they can have a taste of another!'

'You're so mistaken . . .'

'What on earth d'you mean, Alexei? They're nothing more than a bunch of animals. The Germans'll show 'em . . .'

The Germans were everywhere. At least, they were all over the Ukraine; but away to the north and east beyond the furthest line of the blue-brown forest were the Bolsheviks. Only these two forces counted.

Five

THEN suddenly, out of the blue, a third force appeared on the vast chessboard. A poor chess-player, having fenced himself off from his opponent with a line of pawns (an appropriate image, as Germans in their steel helmets look very like pawns) will surround his toy king with his stronger pieces – his officers. But suddenly the opponent's queen finds a sly way in from the side, advances to the back line and starts to knock out pawns and knights from the rear and checks the terrified king. In the queen's wake comes a fast-moving bishop, the knights zig-zag into action and in no time the wretched player is doomed, his wooden king checkmated.

All of this happened very quickly, but not suddenly, and not before the appearance of certain omens.

One day in May, when the City awoke looking like a pearl set in turquoise and the sun rose up to shed its light on the Hetman's kingdom; when the citizens were already going about their little affairs like ants; and sleepy shop-assistants had begun opening the shutters, a terrible and ominous sound boomed out over the City. No one had ever heard a noise of quite that pitch before – it was unlike either gunfire or thunder – but so powerful that many windows flew open of their own accord and every pane rattled. Then the sound was repeated, boomed its way around the Upper City, rolled down in waves towards Podol, the Lower City, crossed the beautiful deep-blue Dnieper and vanished in the direction of distant Moscow. It was followed instantly by shocked and blood-stained people running howling and screaming down from Pechyorsk, the Upper City. And the sound was heard a third time, this time so violently that windows began shattering in the houses of Pechyorsk and the ground shook underfoot. Many people saw women running in nothing but their underclothes and shrieking in terrible voices. The source of the sound was soon discovered. It had come from Bare Mountain outside the City right above the Dnieper, where vast quantities of ammunition and gunpowder were stored. There had been an explosion on Bare Mountain.

For five days afterwards they lived in terror, expecting poison gas to pour down from Bare Mountain. But the explosions ceased, no gas came, the bloodstained people disappeared and the City regained its peaceful aspect in all of its districts, with the exception of a small part of Pechyorsk where several houses had collapsed. Needless to say the German command set up an intensive investigation, and needless to say the City learned nothing of the cause of the explosions. Various rumors circulated.

'It was done by French spies.'

'No, the explosion was produced by Bolshevik spies.'

In the end people simply forgot about the explosions.

The second omen occurred in summer, when the City was swathed in rich, dusty green foliage, thunder cracked and rumbled and the German lieutenants consumed oceans of soda-water. The second omen was truly appalling.

One day on Nikolaevsky Street, in broad daylight, just beside the cab-stand, no less a person than the commander-in-chief of the German forces in the Ukraine, that proud and inviolable military pro-consul of Kaiser Wilhelm, Field Marshal Eichhorn was shot dead! His assassin was, of course, a workman and, of course, a socialist. Twenty-four hours after the death of the Field Marshal the Germans had hanged not only the assassin but even the cab driver who had driven him to the scene of the incident. This did nothing, it is true, towards resurrecting the late distinguished Field Marshal, but it did cause a number of intelligent people to have some startling thoughts about the event.

That evening, for instance, gasping by an open window and unbuttoning his tussore shirt, Vasilisa had sat over a cup of lemon tea and said to Alexei Turbin in a mysterious whisper:

'When I think about all these things that have been happening I can't help coming to the conclusion that our lives are extremely insecure. It seems to me that the ground (Vasilisa waved his stubby little fingers in the air) is shifting under the Germans' feet.

64

Just think . . . Eichhorn . . . and where it happened. See what I mean.' (Vasilisa's eyes looked frightened.)

Alexei listened, gave a grim twitch of his cheek and went.

Yet another omen appeared the very next morning and burst upon Vasilisa himself. Early, very early, when the sun was sending one of its cheerful beams down into the dreary basement doorway that led from the backyard into Vasilisa's apartment, he looked out and saw the omen standing in the sunlight. She was incomparable in the glow of her thirty years, the glittering necklace on her queenly neck, her shapely bare legs, her generous, resilient bosom. Her teeth flashed, and her eyelashes cast a faint, lilac-colored shadow on her cheeks.

'Fifty kopecks today', said the omen in a lilac-colored voice, pointing to her pail of milk.

'What?' exclaimed Vasilisa plaintively. 'For pity's sake, Yavdokha – forty the day before yesterday, forty-five yesterday and now today it's fifty. You can't go on like this.'

'It's not my fault. Milk's dear everywhere', replied the lilac voice. 'They tell me in the market it's fetching a rouble in some places.'

Again her teeth flashed. For a moment Vasilisa forgot about the price of milk, forgot about everything and a deliciously wicked shiver ran through his stomach – the same cold shiver that Vasilisa felt whenever this gorgeous sunlit vision appeared before him in the morning. (Vasilisa always got up earlier than his wife.) He forgot everything and for some reason he imagined a clearing in the forest, the scent of pinewoods. Ah, well . . .

'See here, Yavdokha', said Vasilisa, licking his lips and looking quickly round in case his wife was coming. 'You've blossomed since this revolution. Look out, or the Germans will teach you a lesson or two.' 'Dare I kiss her or daren't I?' Vasilisa wondered agonisingly, unable to make up his mind.

A broad alabaster ribbon of milk spurted foaming into the jug.

'If they try and teach us a lesson we'll soon teach them it doesn't pay', the omen suddenly replied, flashing, glittering, rattling her pail; swung her yoke and herself, even brighter than the sunlight, started to climb up the steps from the basement into the sunlit yard. 'Ah, what legs', groaned Vasilisa to himself.

At that moment came his wife's voice and Vasilisa, turning round, bumped into her.

'Who were you talking to?' she asked, giving a quick, suspicious glance upward.

'Yavdokha', Vasilisa answered casually. 'Can you believe it – milk's up to fifty kopecks today.'

'What?' exclaimed Wanda. 'That's outrageous! What cheek! Those farmers are impossible . . . Yavdokha! Yavdokha!' she shouted, leaning out of the window. 'Yavdokha!'

But the vision had gone and did not come back.

Vasilisa glanced at his wife's angular figure, her yellow hair, bony elbows and desiccated legs and suddenly felt so nauseated by everything to do with his life that he almost spat on the hem of Wanda's skirt. Sighing, he restrained himself, and wandered back into the semi-darkness of the apartment, unable to say exactly what was depressing him. Was it because he had suddenly realised how ugly Wanda looked, with her two yellow collar bones protruding like the shafts of a cart? Or was it something vaguely disturbing that the delicious vision had said?

'What was it she said? "We'll teach 'em it doesn't pay"?' Vasilisa muttered to himself. 'Hell – these market women! How d'you like that? Once they stop being afraid of the Germans . . . it's the beginning of the end. ". . . teach 'em it doesn't pay" indeed! But what teeth – bliss . . .'

Suddenly he seemed to see Yavdokha standing in front of him stark naked, like a witch on a hilltop.

'What cheek . . . "we'll teach 'em" . . . But those breasts of hers . . . my God . . .'

The thought was so disturbing that Vasilisa felt sick and dizzy and had to go and wash his face in cold water.

Imperceptibly as ever, the fall was creeping on. After a ripe, golden August came a bright, dust-laden September and in September there came not another omen but a happening that at first sight was completely insignificant.

It was one bright September evening that a piece of paper, signed by the appropriate official of the Hetman's government, arrived at the City's prison. It was an order to release the prisoner being held in cell No. 666. That was all.

That was *all*?! Without any doubt that piece of paper was the cause of the untold strife and disaster, all the fighting, bloodshed, fire and persecution, the despair and the horror that were to come . . .

The name of the prisoner was quite ordinary and unremarkable: Semyon Vasilievich Petlyura. Both he and the City's newspapers of the period from December 1918 to February 1919 used the rather frenchified form of his first name – Simon. Simon's past was wrapped in deepest obscurity. Some said he had been a clerk.

'No, he was an accountant.'

'No, a student.'

On the corner of the Kreshchatik and Nikolaevsky Street there used to be a large and magnificent tobacco store. Its oblong shop-sign was beautifully adorned with a picture of a coffee-colored Turk in a fez, smoking a hookah and shod in soft yellow slippers with turned-up toes. There were people who swore on their oath that not long ago they had seen Simon in that same store, standing elegantly dressed behind the counter and selling the cigarettes and tobacco made in Solomon Cohen's factory. But then there were others who said:

'Nothing of the sort. He was secretary of the Union of Municipalities.'

'No, not the Union of Municipalities, the Zemstvo Union,' countered yet a third opinion; 'a typical Zemstvo official.'

A fourth group (refugees) would close their eyes as an aid to memory and mutter:

'Now just a minute . . . let me think . . .' Then they would describe how, apparently, ten years ago – no, sorry, eleven years ago – they had seen him one evening in Moscow walking along Málaya Brónnaya Street carrying under his arm a guitar wrapped in a black cloth. And they would add that he had been going to a party given by some friends from his home town, hence the guitar. He had been going, it seems, to a delightful party where there were lots of gay, pretty girl students from his native Ukraine, bottles of delicious Ukrainian plum-brandy, songs, a Ukrainian band . . . Then these people would grow confused as they described his appearance and would muddle their dates and places . . .

'He was clean-shaven, you say?'

'No, I think . . . yes, that's right . . . he had a little beard.'

'Was he at Moscow University?'

'Well no, but he was a student somewhere . . .'

'Nothing of the sort. Ivan Ivanovich knew him. He was a schoolteacher in Tarashcha.'

Hell, maybe it wasn't him walking down Málaya Brónnaya, it had been so dark and misty and frosty on the street that day . . . Who knows? . . . A guitar . . . a Turk in the sunlight . . . a hookah . . . chords on a guitar, it was all so vague and obscure. God, the confusion, the uncertainty of those days . . . the marching feet of the boys of the Guards' Cadet School marching past, lurking figures shadowy as bloodstains, vague apparitions on the run, girls with wild, flying hair, gunfire, and frost and the light of St Vladimir's cross at midnight.

> Marching and singing
> Cadets of the Guards
> Trumpets and drums
> Cymbals ringing . . .

Cymbals ringing, bullets whistling like deadly steel nightingales, soldiers beating people to death with ramrods, black-cloaked Ukrainian cavalry-men are coming on their fiery horses.

The apocalyptic dream charges with a clatter up to Alexei Turbin's bedside, as he sleeps, pale, a sweaty lock of black hair plastered damply to his forehead, the pink-shaded lamp still burning. The whole house was asleep, – Karas' snores coming from the library, Shervinsky's sibilant breathing from Nikolka's room . . . Darkness, muzzy heads . . . A copy of Dostoevsky lay open and unread on the floor by Alexei's bed, the desperate characters of *The Possessed* prophesying doom while Elena slept peacefully.

68

'Now listen: there's no such person. This fellow Simon Petlyura never existed. There was no Turk, there was no guitar under a wrought-iron lamp-post on the Málaya Brónnaya, he was never in the Zemstvo Union . . . it's all nonsense.' Simply a myth that grew up in the Ukraine among the confusion and fog of that terrible year 1918.

. . . But there was something else too – rabid hatred. There were four hundred thousand Germans and all around them four times forty times four hundred thousand peasants whose hearts blazed with unquenchable malice. For this they had good cause. The blows on the face from the swagger-canes of young German subalterns, the hail of random shrapnel fire aimed at recalcitrant villages, backs scarred by the ramrods wielded by Hetmanite cossacks, the IOU's on scraps of paper signed by majors and lieutenants of the German army and which read:

'Pay this Russian sow twenty-five marks for her pig.' And the derisive laughter at the people who brought these chits to the German headquarters in the City. And the requisitioned horses, the confiscated grain, the fat-faced landlords who came back to reclaim their estates under the Hetman's government; the spasm of hatred at the very sound of the words 'Russian officers'.

That is how it was.

Then there were the rumors of land reform which the Lord Hetman was supposed to carry out . . . and alas, it was only in November 1918, when the roar of gunfire was first heard around the City, that the more intelligent people, including Vasilisa, finally realised that the peasants hated that same Lord Hetman as though he were a mad dog; and that in the peasants' minds the Hetman's so-called 'reform' was a swindle on behalf of the land-lords and that what was needed once and for all was the true reform for which the peasants themselves had longed for centuries:

All land to the peasants.
Three hundred acres per man.
No more landlords.
A proper title-deed to those three hundred acres, on official

69

paper with the stamp of authority, granting them perpetual
ownership that would pass by inheritance from grandfather
to father to son and so on.

No sharks from the City to come and demand grain. The
grain's ours. No one else can have it, and what we don't eat
ourselves we'll bury in the ground.

The City to supply us with kerosene oil.

No Hetman – or anyone else – could or would carry out reforms
like those. There were some wistful rumors that the only people
who could kick out both the Hetman and the Germans were the
Bolsheviks, but the Bolsheviks themselves were not much better:
nothing but a bunch of Yids and commissars. The wretched
Ukrainian peasants were in despair; there was no salvation from
any quarter.

But there were tens of thousands of men who had come back
from the war, having been taught how to shoot by those same
Russian officers they loathed so much. There were hundreds of
thousands of rifles buried under-ground, hidden in hayricks and
barns and not handed in, despite the summary justice dealt out
by the German field courts-martial, despite flailing ramrods and
shrapnel-fire; buried in that same soil were millions of cartridges,
a three-inch gun hidden in every fifth village, machine-guns in
every other village, shells stored in every little town, secret ware-
houses full of army greatcoats and fur caps.

And in those same little towns there were countless teachers,
medical orderlies, smallholders, Ukrainian seminarists, whom fate
had commissioned as ensigns in the Russian army, healthy sons of
the soil with Ukrainian surnames who had become staff-captains –
all of them talking Ukrainian, all longing for the Ukraine of their
dreams free of Russian landlords and free of Muscovite officers;
and thousands of Ukrainian ex-prisoners of war returned from
Austrian Galicia.

All these plus tens of thousands of peasants could only mean
trouble . . .

And then – this prisoner . . . the man with the guitar, the man

70

from Cohen's tobacco store, Simon, the one time Zemstvo official? All nonsense, of course. There was no such man. Rubbish, mere legend, a pure mirage. But when the wise Vasilisa, clasping his head in horror, had exclaimed on that fateful November day 'Quem deus vult perdere, prius dementat!' and cursed the Hetman for releasing Petlyura from the filthy City prison, it was already too late.

'Nonsense, impossible,' they said. 'It can't be Petlyura – it's another man. No, it's someone else.'

But the time for omens was past and omens gave way to events. The second crucial event was nothing so trivial as the release of some mythical figure from prison. It was an event so great that all mankind will remember it for centuries to come. Far away in western Europe the Gallic rooster in his baggy red pantaloons had at last seized the steel-gray Germans in a deathly grip. It was a terrible sight: these fighting-cocks in Phrygian caps, crowing with triumph, swarmed upon the armor-plated Teutons and clawed away their armor and lumps of flesh beneath it. The Germans fought desperately, thrust their broad-bladed bayonets into the feathered breasts of their adversaries and clenched their teeth; but they could not hold out, and the Germans – the Germans! – begged for mercy.

The next event was closely connected with this and was directly caused by it. Stunned and amazed, the whole world learned that the man whose curled moustache-ends pointing upwards like two six-inch nails and were as famous as his name, and who was undoubtedly made of solid metal without a trace of wood, had been deposed. Cast down, he ceased to be Emperor. Everyone in the City felt a shiver of horror: they watched with their own eyes as the color drained from every German officer, as the expensive material of their blue-gray uniforms was metamorphosed into drab sackcloth. All this happened in the City within the space of a few hours: every German face paled, the glint vanished from the officers' monocles and nothing but blank poverty stared out from behind those broad glass discs.

It was then that the reality of the situation began to penetrate the brains of the more intelligent of the men who, with their solid rawhide suitcases and their rich women-folk, had leaped over the barbed wire surrounding the Bolshevik camp and taken refuge in the City. They realised that fate had linked them with the losing side and their hearts were filled with terror.

'The Germans are beaten', said the swine.

'We are beaten', said the intelligent swine.

And the people of the City realised this too. Only someone who has been defeated knows the real meaning of that word. It is like a party in a house where the electric light has failed; it is like a room in which green mould, alive and malignant, is crawling over the wallpaper; it is like the wasted bodies of rachitic children, it is like rancid cooking oil, like the sound of women's voices shouting obscene abuse in the dark. It is, in short, like death.

Of course the Germans will leave the Ukraine. As a result some people will have to run away, others to stay and face the City's next wave of new, unpredictable and uninvited guests. And some, no doubt, will have to die. The ones who run away will not die; who, then will die? . . .

'Dying is not remotely like playing dead in a game of soldiers,' said Colonel Nai-Turs, burring his 'R's, as he suddenly appeared from nowhere to the sleeping Alexei Turbin.

He was wearing a peculiar uniform: on his head was a shining helmet, his body was encased in chain-mail and he was leaning on a long sword such as has not been seen in any army since the days of the crusades. A celestial radiance followed Nai like a cloud.

'Are you in heaven, colonel?' asked Turbin, feeling a pleasurable shiver of a kind that no man feels in the waking state.

'I am,' replied Nai-Turs in a voice as pure and crystalline as a forest brook.

'How strange, how strange,' said Turbin. 'I thought paradise was, well . . . a figment of man's imagination. And what a strange uniform you're wearing. Would you mind telling me, colonel – are you still an officer in heaven?'

'The colonel's in the Crusaders' Brigade now, Doctor Turbin,' replied Sergeant-Major Zhilin – a soldier, as Alexei well knew, who had been mown down by enemy fire in the fighting around Vilno in 1916.

The sergeant-major towered above Alexei Turbin like a hero of legend and light radiated from his chain-mail. His craggy features – which Doctor Turbin remembered perfectly, having himself dressed Zhilin's mortal wounds – were now unrecognisable, and the sergeant-major's eyes exactly resembled those of Nai-Turs – pure, unfathomable, aglow from within.

More than anything else on earth, Alexei Turbin's stricken soul loved women's eyes. Ah, but what a treasure the Lord God fashioned when he made women's eyes! Yet they were as nothing compared with the sergeant-major's eyes.

'But how is it,' Doctor Turbin asked with curiosity, feeling an unutterable delight, 'how is it that you're wearing boots and spurs in heaven? And have you also got your horses, your lances, your supply waggons and everything?'

'You can believe me, doctor,' boomed Sergeant-Major Zhilin in his cello-like bass voice, looking straight into Alexei's eyes with a sky-blue gaze that warmed the heart. 'The whole squadron, horses and all, arrived at full strength. We even had our accordion-player. Of course, we felt a bit awkward . . . It's all as clean as a whistle there, you may like to know, with marble floors like in church.'

'Really?' said Turbin in amazement.

'There was an old civilian gentleman there, dignified but very polite, who must have been St Peter. Of course, I reported in regulation fashion: "No. 2 Squadron, Belgrade Hussars, reporting to heaven, sir. What are your orders, sir?" Well, reporting's one thing, but I was thinking to myself' – the sergeant-major coughed modestly into his fist – 'I was thinking St Peter would probably tell us to clear off out of it . . . Because, well, where could we go, what with the horses and all, and . . . (the sergeant-major scratched the back of his head in embarrassment) between you and me, doctor, a few women had joined us on the way. I told this to St Peter, but I tipped the wink to my troop, meaning – get rid of the women for the time being, till we see what's what. Let them go and sit over there behind that cloud till things have sorted themselves out. But although St Peter's a man who knows his own mind, you see, he's not one to chuck his weight about. One flash of his eyes and I could see he'd spotted the women riding on the waggons. 'Course, with their bright headscarves you could see 'em a mile off. This is it, I thought to myself. The whole squadron's going to get it in the neck now . . .

"Aha," says he, "so you've got some women with you, have you?" And he shook his head.

"Yes, sir," say I, "but don't worry – we'll make 'em clear off, Mr saint, sir."

"No, you won't," says he, "we'll have none of your violence here!"

How about that, eh? What could I do? He was a decent old fellow. After all, you know, doctor, a squadron on active service can't get by without a few women.'

And the sergeant-major gave a crafty wink.

'That's true enough.' Lowering his gaze, Alexei Turbin had to agree. A pair of black, black eyes above a birthmark on a soft right cheek flickered dimly in the mists of sleep. He coughed to hide his embarrassment. The sergeant-major went on:

'Well, sir, right away he says: "I'll go and see about this". So off he went, came back and said: "All right, we'll fix them up too." And we were so chuffed about this, I can't tell you. Only then there was a slight hitch. You'll have to wait a bit, says St Peter. But we didn't have to wait more than a minute. I looked round and who should it be' – the sergeant-major pointed to the proud and silent Nai-Turs, who was just vanishing from the dream into the dark of the unknown – 'but our squadron leader himself on his charger. And a little later after him came an infantry cadet, dismounted –' here the sergeant-major glanced sideways at Turbin and looked down for a moment as if wanting to hide something from the doctor – nothing sad, but on the contrary a splendid and joyful secret. Then he thought better of it and went on:

'Well, St Peter shields his eyes with his hand and says: "Right," he says, "That's the lot!" And there and then he opens the gates and – "In you go," he says, "by the right in columns of threes."'

Dunya, Dunya, Dunya mine!

Dunya, sweet as a berry . . .

Suddenly a choir of steel-hard voices, accompanied by an Italian accordion, swelled up as in a dream, singing the marching song.

'Keep in step!' shouted the several voices of the troop leaders . . .

Oh Dunya, Dunya, Dunya mine!

Love me, Dunya, please . . . !

. . . and the choir died away in the distance.

'So you all went in? Women and all?' Turbin gasped in amazement.

The sergeant-major laughed with the excitement of it and spread his arms in a gesture of delight.

'Good Lord above, Doctor Turbin. The space there – it stretches as far as the eye can see. And clean . . . At first glance I'd say there was room there for five army corps plus reserve squadrons . . . What am I saying, five – it was more like ten! And near us there were such mansions, heavens above – why the rooms were so high you couldn't even see the ceilings! So I say: "May I ask," say I, "Who those places are for?" 'Cos they looked sort of funny, red stars, red clouds the colour of those soft leather boots our womenfolk wear . . . "That", says St Peter, "is for the Bolsheviks who'll be coming from Perekop."'

'Perekop? Why from Perekop?' asked Turbin, in vain racking his weak, earthbound brain.

'Ah, you see, sir, they know about everything beforehand. When the Bolsheviks stormed the Isthmus of Perekop in 1920, they had terrible casualties. So they'd got a place ready for them.'

'The Bolsheviks?' Turbin was deeply disturbed. 'You must have made a mistake, Zhilin. That can't be right. They wouldn't let *them* in there.'

'Yes, that's just what I thought myself, doctor. I was a bit upset, so I asked the Lord God . . .'

'God? Oh, really, Zhilin!'

'No cause to doubt me, doctor – I'm telling you the truth. I couldn't lie about that. I've talked to Him myself more than once.'

'What is he like?'

Zhilin's eyes flashed and pride gave his features an even finer cast.

'I couldn't tell you, even if you was to kill me. A shining face – although no-one can tell what it's like . . . Sometimes you look at Him and you turn cold. You get the feeling He looks like you, which frightens you stiff, and you wonder – can it be? But nothing happens to you, and you go away. His face is sort of different all the time. But when He speaks, you feel such joy, such joy . . . And then He goes, and it's like a blue light going away . . . H'mm . . . well, no, it's not exactly blue' – the sergeant-major thought for a moment – 'I really can't say. It goes right through you from a thousand miles away . . . Anyway, sir, I go up to Him and I say: "How's this, Lord? Your priests all say the Bolsheviks will go to hell. So," I say, "what's all this? They don't believe in You, yet You've built these splendid quarters for them."

"Oh, don't they believe in Me?" He asks.

"Honest to God," say I – and I gave myself a real fright, I can tell you: fancy saying *that* to God! But then I look at Him and He's smiling. What a fool I am, thinks I, telling Him all this when He knows it already, better than me. But I was curious to know just what He'd say. And He says:

"So what," says He, "If they don't believe in Me? That's their business. It doesn't bother Me, and it shouldn't bother you, either," He says. "Because it's neither profit nor loss to Me whether you believe or not. One man may believe and another may not, but you all behave the same as each other – at any moment you may be at each others' throats. And as for quarters, Zhilin, you've got to realize that up here with Me you're all equal – all who fell on the field of battle. You must understand that, Zhilin – not every-body does. Anyway, Zhilin," He says, "don't bother yourself with questions like this. Off you go and carry on with your life."

Gave it to me straight, didn't He, doctor? Eh? "But the priests," say I. He just waved His hand. "Zhilin," says He, "you'd do better

76

not to remind Me about those priests. I'm at my wits' end to know what to do about them. I mean, there are no bigger fools on earth than your priests. I'll tell you a secret, Zhilin – they're not priests, they're nothing but a disgrace."

"That's right," say I. "You should get rid of them bag and baggage! Why should You keep feeding those parasites?!"

"I feel sorry for them, Zhilin, that's the trouble" says he.'

The radiance around Zhilin began to turn blue, and an inexpressible joy filled the heart of the sleeping man. Stretching out his arms to the glowing sergeant-major, he groaned in his sleep:

'Zhilin, Zhilin, isn't there a chance I could be posted to your brigade as the medical officer?'

Zhilin beckoned, nodding his head in kindly affirmation. Then he began to move away and left Alexei Turbin, who woke up. In front of him, instead of Zhilin, there was the window, paling slightly in the first light of dawn. The doctor wiped his hand over his face and felt it wet with tears. For a long time he lay sighing in the morning twilight, but then he fell asleep again and this time he slept soundly, without dreaming . . .

As the fall turned to winter death soon came to the Ukraine with the first dry, driven snow. The rattle of machine-gun fire began to be heard in the woods. Death itself remained unseen, but its unmistakable herald was a wave of crude, elemental peasant fury which ran amok through the cold and the snow, a fury in torn bast shoes, straws in its matted hair; a fury which howled. It held in its hands a huge club, without which no great change in Russia, it seems, can ever take place. Here and there 'the red rooster crowed' as farms and hayricks burned, in other places the purple sunset would reveal a Jewish innkeeper strung up by his sexual organs. There were strange sights, too, in Poland's fair capital of Warsaw: high on his plinth Henryk Sienkiewicz smiled with grim satisfaction. Then it was as if all the devils in hell were let loose. Priests shook the green cupolas of their little churches with bell-ringing, whilst next door in the schoolhouses, their windows shattered by rifle bullets, the people sang revolutionary songs.

It was a time and a place of suffocating uncertainty. So – to hell with it! It was all a myth. Petlyura was a myth. He didn't exist. It was a myth as remarkable as an older myth of the non-existent Napoleon Bonaparte, but a great deal less colorful. But something had to be done. That outburst of elemental peasant wrath had somehow to be channelled into a certain direction, because no magic wand could conjure it away.

It was very simple. There would be trouble; but the men to deal with it would be found. And there appeared a certain Colonel Toropetz. It turned out that he had sprung from no less than the Austrian army . . .

'You can't mean it?'

'I assure you he has.'

Then there emerged a writer called Vinnichenko, famous for two things – his novels and the fact that as far back as the beginning of 1918 fate had thrown him up to the surface of the troubled sea that was the Ukraine, and that without a second's delay the satirical journals of St Petersburg had branded him a traitor.

'And serves him right . . .'

'Well, I'm not so sure. And then there's that mysterious man who was released from prison.'

Even in September no one in the City could imagine what these three men might be up to, whose only apparent talent was the ability to turn up at the right moment in such an insignificant place as Belaya Tserkov. By October people were speculating furiously about them, when those brilliantly-lit trains full of German officers pulled out of the City into the gaping void that was the new-born state of Poland, and headed for Germany. Telegrams flew. Away went the diamonds, the shifty eyes, the slicked-down hair and the money. They fled southwards, south-wards to the seaport city of Odessa. By November, alas, everyone knew with fair certainty what was afoot. The word 'Petlyura' echoed from every wall, from the gray paper of telegraph forms. In the mornings it dripped from the pages of newspapers into the coffee, immediately turning that nectar of the tropics into dis-gusting brown swill. It flew from tongue to tongue, and was tapped out by telegraphists' fingers on morse keys. Extraordinary things began happening in the City thanks to that name, which the Germans mispronounced as 'Peturra'.

Individual German soldiers, who had acquired the bad habit of lurching drunkenly around in the suburbs, began disappearing in the night. They would vanish one night and the next day they would be found murdered. So German patrols in their tin hats were sent around the City at night, marching with lanterns to put an end to the outrages. But no amount of lanterns could dissolve the murky thoughts brewing in people's heads.

Wilhelm. Three Germans murdered yesterday. Oh God, the Germans are leaving – have you heard? The workers have arrested Trotsky in Moscow!! Some sons of bitches held up a train near Borodyanka and stripped it clean. Petlyura has sent an embassy to Paris. Wilhelm again. Black Senegalese in Odessa. A mysterious, unknown name – Consul Enno. Odessa. General Denikin. Wilhelm again. The Germans are leaving, the French are coming.

'The Bolsheviks are coming, brother!'

'Don't say such things!'

The Germans have a special device with a revolving pointer – they put it on the ground and the pointer swings round to show where there are arms buried in the ground. That's a joke. Petlyura has sent a mission to the Bolsheviks. That's an even better joke. Petlyura. Petlyura. Petlyura. Peturra. . . .

*

There was not a single person who really knew what this man Peturra wanted to do in the Ukraine though everyone knew for sure that he was mysterious and faceless (even though the newspapers had frequently printed any number of pictures of Catholic prelates, every one different, captioned 'Simon Petlyura') and that he wanted to seize the Ukraine. To do that he would advance and capture the City.

Six

MADAME ANJOU'S shop, Le chic parisien, was in the very center of the City, on Theater Street, behind the Opera House, on the first floor of a large multi-storied building. Three steps led up from the street through a glass door into the shop, while on either side of the glass door were two large plate-glass windows draped with dusty tulle drapes. No one knew what had become of Madame Anjou or why the premises of her shop had been put to such uncommercial use. In the left-hand window was a colored drawing of a lady's hat with 'Chic parisien' in golden letters; but behind the glass of the right-hand window was a huge poster in yellow cardboard showing the crossed-cannon badge of the artillery. Above it were the words:

'You may not be a hero – but you must volunteer.'

Beneath the crossed cannon it read:

'Volunteers for the Mortar Regiment may enlist here.'

Parked at the entrance to the shop was a filthy and dilapidated motor-cycle and sidecar. The door with its spring-closure was constantly opening and slamming and every time it opened a charming little bell rang – trrring-trrring – recalling the dear, dead days of Madame Anjou.

After their drunken evening together Alexei Turbin, Myshlaevsky and Karas got up next morning almost simultaneously. All, to their amazement, had thoroughly clear heads, although the hour was a little late – around noon in fact. Nikolka and Shervinsky, it seemed, had already gone out. Very early that morning Nikolka had wrapped up a mysterious little red bundle and creaking on tiptoe out of the house had set off for his infantry detachment, whilst Shervinsky had returned to duty at General Headquarters.

Stripped to the waist in Anyuta's room behind the kitchen, where the geyser and the bath stood behind a drape, Myshlaevsky poured a stream of ice-cold water over his neck, back and head, and shouted, howling with the delicious shock; 'Ugh! Hah! Splendid!' and showered everything with water for a yard around him. Then he rubbed himself dry with a Turkish towel, dressed, anointed his head with brilliantine, combed his hair and said to Alexei:

'Er, Alyosha . . . be a friend and lend me your spurs, would you? I won't be going home and I don't like to turn up without spurs.'

'You'll find them in the study, in the right-hand desk drawer.'

Myshlaevsky went into the study, fumbled around, and marched out clinking. Dark-eyed Anyuta, who had returned that morning from staying with her aunt, was flicking a feather duster over the chairs in the sitting room. Clearing his throat Myshlaevsky glanced at the door, made a wide detour and said softly:

'Hullo, Anyuta . . .'

'I'll tell Elena Vasilievna', Anyuta at once whispered automatically. She closed her eyes like a condemned victim awaiting the executioner's axe.

'Silly girl . . .'

Alexei Turbin appeared unexpectedly in the doorway. His expression turned sour.

'Examining our feather duster, Viktor? So I see. Nice one, isn't it? Hadn't you better be on your way? Anyuta, remember in case he tells you he'll marry you, don't believe it – he never will.'

'Hell, I was only saying hullo . . .' Myshlaevsky reddened at the undeserved slight, stuck out his chest and strode clinking out of the drawing-room. At the sight of the elegant, auburn-haired Elena in the dining-room he looked uncomfortable.

'Good morning, Lena my sweet. Err . . . h'mmm' (Instead of a metallic tenor Myshlaevsky's voice came out of his throat as a low, hoarse baritone), 'Lena, my dear,' he burst out with feeling, 'don't be cross with me. I'm so fond of you and I want you to be fond of me. Please forget my disgusting behaviour yesterday. You don't think I'm really such a beast, do you?'

So saying he clasped Elena in an embrace and kissed her on both cheeks. In the drawing-room the feather duster fell to the ground with a gentle thud. The oddest things always happened to Anyuta whenever Lieutenant Myshlaevsky appeared in the Turbins' apartment. All sorts of household utensils would start slipping from her grasp: if she happened to be in the kitchen knives would cascade to the floor or plates would tumble down from the dresser. Anyuta would look distracted and run out into the lobby for no reason, where she would fiddle around with the overshoes, wiping them with a rag until Myshlaevsky, all cleft chin and broad shoulders, swaggered out again in his blue breeches and short, very low-slung spurs. Then Anyuta would close her eyes and sidle out of her cramped hiding-place in the boot-closet. Now in the drawing-room, having dropped her feather duster, she was standing and gazing abstractedly into the distance past the chintz curtains and out at the gray, cloudy sky.

'Oh, Viktor, Viktor,' said Elena, shaking her carefully-brushed diadem of hair, 'you look healthy enough – what made you so feeble yesterday? Sit down and have a cup of tea, it may make you feel better.'

'And you look gorgeous today, Lena, by God you do. That cloak suits you wonderfully, I swear it does', said Myshlaevsky ingratiatingly, his glance darting nervously back and forth to the polished sideboard. 'Look at her cloak, Karas. Isn't it a perfect shade of green?'

'Elena Vasilievna is very beautiful', Karas replied earnestly and with absolute sincerity.

'It's the electric light that makes it look this color', Elena explained. 'Come on, Viktor, out with it – you want something, don't you?'

'Well, the fact is, Lena dearest, I could so easily get an attack of migraine after last night's business and I can't go out and fight if I've got migraine . . .'

'All right, it's in the sideboard.'

'Thanks. Just one small glass . . . better than all the aspirin in the world.'

With a martyred grimace Myshlaevsky tossed back two glasses of vodka one after the other, in between bites of the soggy remains of last night's dill pickles. After that he announced that he felt like a new-born babe and said he would like a glass of lemon tea.

'Don't let yourself worry, Lena,' Alexei Turbin was saying hoarsely, 'I won't be long. I shall just go and sign on as a volunteer and then I shall come straight back home. Don't worry, there won't be any fighting. We shall just sit tight here in the City and beat off "president" Petlyura, the swine.'

'May you not be ordered away somewhere?'

Karas gestured reassuringly.

'Don't worry, Elena Vasilievna. Firstly I might as well tell you that the regiment can't possibly be ready in less than a fortnight; we still have no horses and no ammunition. Even when we are ready there's not the slightest doubt that we shall stay in the City. The army we're forming will undoubtedly be used to garrison the City. Later on, of course, in case of an advance on Moscow . . .'

'That's pure guess-work, though, and I'll believe it when I see it . . .'

'Before that happens we shall have to link up with Denikin . . .'

'You don't have to try so hard to comfort me', said Elena. 'I'm not afraid. On the contrary, I approve of what you're doing.'

Elena sounded genuinely bold and confident; from her expression she was already absorbed with the mundane problems of daily life: sufficient unto the day is the evil thereof.

'Anyuta,' she shouted, 'Anyuta dear, Lieutenant Myshlaevsky's dirty clothes are out there on the verandah. Give them a good hard brush and then wash them right away.'

The person who had the most calming effect on Elena was the short, stocky Karas, who sat there very calmly in his khaki tunic, smoking and frowning.

They said goodbye in the lobby.

'God bless you all', said Elena grimly as she made the sign of the cross over Alexei, then over Karas and Myshlaevsky. Myshlaevsky hugged her, and Karas, his greatcoat tightly belted in at the waist, blushed and gently kissed both her hands.

*

'Permission to report, colonel', said Karas, his spurs clinking gently as he saluted.

The colonel was seated at a little desk in a low, green, very feminine armchair on a kind of raised platform in the front of the shop. Pieces of blue cardboard hat boxes labelled 'Madame Anjou, Ladies' millinery' rose behind him, shutting out some of the light from the dusty window hung with lacy tulle. The colonel was holding a pen. He was not really a colonel but a lieutenant colonel, with three stars on broad gold shoulder-straps divided lengthwise by two coloured strips and surmounted by golden crossed cannon. The colonel was slightly older than Alexei Turbin himself – about thirty, or thirty-two at the most. His face, well fed and clean shaven, was adorned by a black moustache clipped American-style. His extremely lively and intelligent eyes looked up, obviously tired but attentive.

Around the colonel was primeval chaos. Two paces away from him a fire was crackling in a little black stove while occasional blobs of soot dripped from its long, angular black flue, extending over a partition and away into the depths of the shop. The floor, both on the raised platform and in the rest of the shop, was littered with scraps of paper and green and red snippets of material. Higher still, on a raised balcony above the colonel's head a typewriter pecked and clattered like a nervous bird and when Alexei Turbin raised his head he saw that it was twittering away behind a balustrade almost at the height of the shop's ceiling. Behind the railings he could just see someone's legs and bottom encased in blue breeches, but whose head was cut off by the line of the ceiling. A second typewriter was clicking away in the left-hand half of the shop, in a mysterious pit, in which could be seen the bright shoulder-straps and blond head of a volunteer clerk, but no arms and no legs.

Innumerable people with gold artillery badges milled around the colonel. To one side stood a large deal box full of wire and field-telephones, beside it cardboard cases of hand-grenades looking like cans of jam with wooden handles; nearby were heaps of coiled machine-gun belts. On the colonel's left was a treadle sewing-machine, while the snout of a machine-gun protruded beside his right leg. In the half-darkness at the back of the shop, behind a curtain on a gleaming rail came the sound of a strained voice, obviously speaking on the telephone: 'Yes, yes, speaking . . . Yes, speaking . . . Yes, this is me speaking!' Brrring-drring went the bell . . . 'Pee-eep' squeaked a bird-like field-telephone somewhere in the pit, followed by the boom of a young bass voice:

'Mortar regiment . . . yes, sir . . . yes . . .'

'Yes?' said the colonel to Karas.

'Allow me to introduce, sir, Lieutenant Viktor Myshlaevsky and Doctor Turbin. Lieutenant Myshlaevsky is at present in an infantry detachment serving in the ranks and would like to be transferred to your regiment as he is an artillery officer. Doctor Turbin requests enrolment as the regimental medical officer.'

Having said his piece Karas dropped his hand from the peak of his cap and Myshlaevsky saluted in turn. 'Hell, I should have come in uniform', thought Turbin with irritation, feeling awkward without a cap and dressed up like some dummy in his black civilian overcoat and Persian lamb collar. The colonel briefly looked the doctor up and down, then glanced at Myshlaevsky's face and army greatcoat.

'I see', he said. 'Good. Where have you served, lieutenant?'

'In the Nth Heavy Artillery Regiment, sir', replied Myshlaevsky, referring to his service in the war against Germany.

'Heavy artillery? Excellent. God knows why they put gunnery officers into the infantry. Obviously a mistake.'

'No, sir', replied Myshlaevsky, clearing his throat to control his wayward voice. 'I volunteered because there was an urgent need for troops to man the line at Post-Volynsk. But now that the infantry detachment is up to strength . . .'

'Yes, I quite understand, and I thoroughly approve . . . good', said the colonel, giving Myshlaevsky a look of thorough approval. 'Glad to know you . . . So now – ah yes, you, doctor. You want to join us too. Hmm . . .'

Turbin nodded in silence, to avoid saying 'Yes, sir' and saluting in his civilian clothes.

'H'mmm . . .' the colonel glanced out of the window. 'It's a good idea, of course, especially since in a few days' time we may be . . . Ye-es . . .' He suddenly stopped short, narrowed his eyes a fraction and said, lowering his voice: 'Only . . . how shall I put it? There is just one problem, doctor . . . Social theories and . . . h'mm . . . Are you a socialist? Like most educated men, I expect you are?' The colonel's glance swivelled uncomfortably, while his face, lips and cajoling voice expressed the liveliest desire that Doctor Turbin should prove to be a socialist rather than anything else. 'Our regiment, you see, is called a "Students' Regiment",' the colonel gave a winning smile without looking up. 'Rather sentimental, I know, but I'm a university man myself.'

Alexei Turbin felt extremely disappointed and surprised. 'The devil . . . why didn't Karas tell me?' At that moment he was aware of Karas at his right shoulder and without looking at him he could sense that his friend was straining to convey him some unspoken message, but he had no idea what it was.

'Unfortunately,' Turbin suddenly blurted out, his cheek twitching, 'I am not a socialist but . . . a monarchist. In fact I can't even bear the very word "socialist". And of all socialists I most detest Alexander Kerensky.'

The colonel's little eyes flicked up for a moment, sparkling. He gestured as if politely to stop Turbin's mouth and said:

'That's a pity. H'mm . . . a great pity . . . The achievements of the revolution, and so on . . . I have orders from above to avoid recruiting monarchist elements in view of the mood of the people . . . we shall be required, you see, to exercise restraint. Besides, the Hetman, with whom we are closely and directly linked, as you know is . . . regrettable, regrettable . . .'

As he said this the colonel's voice not only expressed no regret at all but on the contrary sounded delighted and the look in his eyes totally contradicted what he was saying.

'Aha, so that's how the land lies', Turbin thought to himself. 'Stupid of me . . . and this colonel's no fool. Probably a careerist to judge from his expression, but what the hell.'

'I don't quite know what to do in your case . . . at the present

86

moment' – the colonel laid heavy stress on the word 'present' – 'as I say, at the present moment, our immediate task is the defence of the City and the Hetman against Petlyura's bands and, possibly, against the Bolsheviks too. After that we shall just have to see . . . May I ask, doctor, where you have served to date?'

'In 1915, when I graduated from university I served as an extern in a venereological clinic, then as a Junior Medical Officer in the Belgrade Hussars. After that I was a staff medical officer in a rail-borne mobile field hospital. At present I am demobilised and working in private practice.'

'Cadet!' exclaimed the colonel, 'ask the executive officer to come here, please.'

A head disappeared into the pit, followed by the appearance of a dark, keen-looking young officer. He wore a round lambskin fur hat with gold rank-stripes crosswise on its magenta top, a long gray coat like Myshlaevsky's tightly belted at the waist, and a revolver. His crumpled gold shoulder-straps indicated that he was a staff-captain.

'Captain Studzinsky,' the colonel said to him, 'please be kind enough to send a message to headquarters requesting the immediate transfer to my unit of Lieutenant . . . er . . .'

'Myshlaevsky,' said Myshlaevsky, saluting.

'. . . Lieutenant Myshlaevsky from the second infantry detachment, as he is a trained artillery officer. And another request to the effect that Doctor . . . er?'

'Turbin.'

'. . . Doctor Turbin is urgently required to serve in my unit as regimental medical officer. Request their immediate appointment.'

'Very good, colonel', replied the officer, with a noticeable accent, and saluted. 'A Pole', thought Turbin.

'There is no need for you, lieutenant, to return to your infantry outfit' (to Myshlaevsky). 'The lieutenant will take command of Number 4 Battery' (to the staff-captain).

'Very good, sir.'

'Very good, sir.'

'And you, doctor, are on duty as of now. I suggest you go home and report in an hour's time at the parade ground in front of the Alexander I High School.'

'Yes, sir.'

'Issue the doctor with his uniform at once, please.'

'Yes, sir.'

'Mortar Regiment headquarters?' shouted a deep bass voice from the pit.

'Can you hear me? No, I said: no . . . No, I said . . .' came a voice from behind the screen.

Rrring . . . peep, came the bird-like trill from the pit.

'Can you hear me?'

*

'*Voice of Liberty, Voice of Liberty!* Daily paper – *Voice of Liberty!*' shouted the newsboys, muffled up past their ears in peasant women's headscarves. 'Defeat of Petlyura! Black troops land in Odessa! *Voice of Liberty!*'

Turbin was home within the hour. His silver shoulder-straps came out of the dark of the desk drawer in his little study, which led off the sitting-room. White drapes over the glass door on to the balcony, desk with books and ink-well, shelves of medicine bottles and instruments, a couch laid with a clean sheet. It was sparse and cramped, but comfortable.

'Lena my dear, if I'm late for some reason this evening and someone comes, tell them that I'm not seeing anyone today. I've no regular patients at the moment . . . Hurry, child.'

Hastily Elena opened the collar of his service tunic and sewed on the shoulder-straps . . . Then she sewed a second pair, field-service type, green with black stripes, on to his army greatcoat.

A few minutes later Alexei Turbin ran out of the front door and glanced at his white enamel plate:

Doctor A. V. Turbin
Specialist in venereal diseases
606 – 914
Consulting hours: 4 pm to 6 pm.

88

He stuck a piece of paper over it, altering the consulting hours to: '5 pm to 7 pm', and strode off up St Alexei's Hill.

'Voice of Liberty!'

Turbin stopped, bought a paper from a newsboy and unfolded it as he went:

THE VOICE OF LIBERTY.

A non-party, democratic newspaper.

Published daily.

December 13th 1918.

The problems of foreign trade and, in particular of trade with Germany, oblige us . . .

'Come on, hurry up! My hands are freezing.'

Our correspondent reports that in Odessa negotiations are in progress for the disembarkation of two divisions of black colonial troops – Consul Enno does not admit that Petlyura . . .

'Dammit boy, give me my copy!'

Deserters who reached our headquarters at Post-Volynsk described the increasing breakdown in the ranks of Petlyura's bands. Three days ago a cavalry regiment in the Korosten region opened fire on an infantry regiment of nationalist riflemen. A strong urge for peace is now noticeable in Petlyura's bands. Petlyura's ridiculous enterprise is heading for collapse. According to the same deserter Colonel Bolbotun, who has rebelled against Petlyura, has set off in an unknown direction together with his regiment and four guns. Bolbotun is inclined to support the Hetmanite cause.

The peasants hate Petlyura for his requisitioning policy. The mobilisation, which he has decreed in the villages, is having no success. Masses of peasants are evading it by hiding in the woods.

'Let's suppose . . . damn this cold . . . Sorry.'

'Hey, quit pushing. Why don't you read your paper at home . . .'
'Sorry.'

We have always stressed that Petlyura's bid for power . . .

'Petlyura – the scoundrel. They're all rogues . . .'

Every honest man and true
Volunteers – what about you?

'What's the matter with you today, Ivan Ivanovich?'

'My wife's caught a dose of Petlyura. This morning she did a Bolbotun and left me . . .'

Turbin grimaced at this joke, furiously crumpled up his newspaper and threw it down on the sidewalk. Then he pricked up his ears.

Boo-oom, rumbled the guns, answered by a muffled roar from beyond the City that seemed to come from the bowels of the earth.

'What the hell?'

Alexei Turbin turned sharply on his heel, picked up his scrap of newspaper, smoothed it out and carefully re-read the report on the first page:

In the Irpen region there have been clashes between our patrols and groups of Petlyura's bandits . . .

All quiet in the Serebryansk sector.

No change in the Red Tavern district.

Near Boyarka a regiment of Hetmanite cossacks dispersed a fifteen-hundred strong band. Two men were taken prisoner.

Boo-oo-oom roared the gray winter sky far away to the south west. Suddenly Turbin opened his mouth and turned pale. Mechanically he stuffed the newspaper into his pocket. A crowd of people was slowly moving out of the boulevard and along Vladimirskaya Street. The roadway was full of people in black overcoats . . . Peasant women started filling the sidewalks. A horseman of the Hetman's State Guard rode ahead like an outrider. His large horse laid back its ears, glared wildly, walking sideways. The rider's expression was perplexed. Occasionally he would give a shout and crack his whip for order, but no one listened to his outbursts. In the front ranks of the crowd could be seen the golden copes of bearded priests and a religious banner flapped above their heads. Little boys ran up from all sides.

'*Voice of Liberty!*' shouted a newsboy and dashed towards the crowd.

A group of cooks in white, flat-topped chef's caps ran out of the nether regions of the Metropole Restaurant. The crowd scattered over the snow like ink over paper.

Several long yellow boxes were bobbing along above the crowd. As the first one drew level with Alexei Turbin he was able to make out the rough charcoal inscription on its side:

Ensign Yutsevich.

On the next one he read:

Ensign Ivanov.

And on the third:

Ensign Orlov.

Suddenly a squeal arose from the crowd. A gray-haired woman, her hat pushed on to the back of her head, stumbled and dropping parcels to the ground, rushed forward from the sidewalk into the crowd.

'What's happening? Vanya!' she yelled. Turning pale, a man dodged away to one side. A peasant woman screamed, then another.

'Jesus Christ Almighty!' muttered a voice behind Turbin. Somebody nudged him in the back and breathed down his neck.

'Lord . . . the things that happen these days. Have they started killing people? What is all this?'

'I know no more than you do.'

'What? What? What? What's happened? Who are they burying?'

'Vanya!' screamed the voice in the crowd.

'Some officers who were murdered at Popelyukha', growled a voice urgently, panting with the desire to be first to tell the news. 'They advanced to Popelyukha, camped out there and in the night they were surrounded by peasants and men from Petlyura's army who murdered every last one of them. Every last one . . . They gouged out their eyes, carved their badges of rank into the skin of their shoulders with knives. Completely disfigured them.'

'Was that what happened? God . . .'

Ensign Korovin.

Ensign Herdt –

more yellow coffins bobbed past.

'Just think . . . what have we come to . . .'

'Internecine war.'

'What d'you mean . . .'

'Apparently they had all fallen asleep when . . .'

'Serve 'em right . . .' cried a sudden, black little voice in the crowd behind Alexei Turbin and he saw red. There was a mêlée of faces and hats. Turbin stretched out his arms like two claws, thrust them between the necks of two bystanders and grabbed the black overcoat sleeve that belonged to the voice. The man turned round and fell down in a state of terror.

'What did you say?' hissed Turbin, and immediately relaxed his grip.

'Sorry sir', replied the voice, shaking with fright. 'I didn't say anything. I didn't open my mouth. What's the matter?' The voice trembled.

The man's duck-like nose paled, and Turbin realised at once that he had made a mistake and had grabbed the wrong man. A face of utter loyalty peered out from behind the duck-bill nose. It was struck dumb and its little round eyes flicked from side to side with fright.

Turbin let go the sleeve and in cold fury he began looking around amongst the hats, backs of heads and collars that seethed about him. He kept his left hand ready to grab anything within reach, whilst keeping his right hand on the butt of the revolver in his pocket. The dismal chanting of the priests floated past, beside him sobbed a peasant woman in a headscarf. There was no one to seize now, the voice seemed to have been swallowed up by the earth. The last coffin marked 'Ensign Morskoy' moved past, followed by some people on a sledge.

'*Voice of Liberty!*' came a piercing contralto shriek right beside

Alexei Turbin's ear. Senseless with rage he pulled the crumpled newspaper out of his pocket and twice rammed it into the boy's face, grinding his teeth and saying as he did so:

'There's your damned *Voice of Liberty*! You can damn well have it back! Little swine!'

With this his attack of fury subsided. The boy dropped his newspapers, slipped and fell down in a snowdrift. For a moment he pretended to burst into tears, and his eyes filled with a look of the most savage hatred that was no pretence.

'What's the matter with you? Who d'you think you are, mister? What've I done?' he snivelled, trying to cry and stumbling to his feet in the snow. A face stared at Turbin in astonishment, but was too afraid to say anything. Feeling stupid, confused and ashamed Turbin hunched his head into his shoulders and, turning sharply, ran past a lamp-post, past the circular white walls of the gigantic museum building, past some holes in the ground full of snow-covered bricks and towards the huge asphalt square in front of the Alexander I High School.

'*Voice of Liberty*! Paper! Paper!' came the cry from the street.

The huge four-storey building of Alexei Turbin's old school, with its hundred and eighty windows, was built around three sides of an asphalted square. He had spent eight years there. For eight years, in springtime during breaks between classes he had run around that playground, and in the winter semester when the air in the classrooms was stuffy and dust-laden and the playground was covered by the inevitable cold, solid layer of snow, he had gazed at it out of the window. For eight years that brick-and-mortar foster-mother had raised and educated Alexei Turbin and his two younger friends, Karas and Myshlaevsky.

And precisely eight years ago Turbin had said goodbye to the school playground for the last time. A spasm of something like fear snatched at his heart. He had a sudden feeling that a black cloud had blotted out the sky, that a kind of hurricane had blown up and carried away all of life as he knew it, just as a monster wave will sweep away a jetty. Ah, these eight years of school! There had been much in them that as a boy he had felt to be dreary, pointless

93

and unpleasant – but there had also been a lot of sheer fun. One monotonous classroom day had plodded after another – *ut* plus the subjunctive, Caius Julius Caesar, a zero for astronomy and an undying hatred of astronomy ever since; but then spring would come, eager spring and somehow the noise in the school grew louder and more excited, the high school girls would be out in their green pinafores on the avenue, May and chestnut blossom and above all the constant beacon ahead: the university, in other words – freedom. Do you realise what the university means? Boat trips on the Dnieper, freedom, money, fame, power.

And now he had been through it all. The teachers with their permanently enigmatic expressions; those terrible swimming baths in the math problems (which he still dreamed about) always draining themselves at so many gallons per minute but which never emptied; complicated arguments about the differences in character between Lensky and Onegin, about the disgraceful behaviour of Socrates; the date of the foundation of the Jesuit order; the dates of Pompey's campaigns and every other campaign for the past two thousand years.

But that was only a beginning. After eight years in high school, after the last swimming bath had emptied itself, came the corpses in the anatomy school, white hospital wards, the glassy silence of operating theatres; then three years in the saddle, wounded soldiers, squalor and degradation – the war, yet another ever-flowing, never-emptying pool. And now he had landed up here again, back in the same school grounds. He ran across the square feeling sick and depressed, clutching the revolver in his pocket, running God knew where or why: presumably to defend that life, that future on whose behalf he had racked his brains over emptying swimming-pools and over those damned men, one of whom was always walking from point 'A' and the other walking towards him from point 'B'.

The dark windows were grim and silent, a silence revealed at a glance as utterly lifeless. Strange, that here in the center of the City, amidst all the disintegration, uproar and bustle this great four-storey ship, which had once launched tens of thousands of young lives on to the open sea, should now be so dead. No one seemed to be in charge of it any longer; there was not a sound, not a movement to be found any longer in its windows or behind the yellow-washed walls dating from the reign of Nicholas I. A virginal layer of snow lay on its roofs, covered the tops of the chestnut trees like white caps, lay evenly like a sheet over the playground, and only a few random tracks showed that someone had recently tramped across it.

And most depressing of all, not only did nobody know, but nobody cared what had become of the school. Who was there now to come and study aboard that great ship? And if no one came to school – why not? Where was the janitor? What were those horrible, blunt-muzzled mortars doing there, drawn up under the row of chestnut trees by the railings around the main entrance? Why had the school been turned into an armory? Whose was it now? Who had done this? Why had they done it?

*

'Unlimber!' roared a voice. The mortars swung round and moved slowly forward. Two hundred men sprang into action, ran about, squatted down or heaved on the enormous cast-iron wheels. There was a confused blur of yellow sheepskin jerkins, gray coats and fur caps, khaki army caps and blue students' caps.

By the time Turbin had crossed the vast square four mortars had been drawn up in a row with their muzzles facing him. The brief period of instruction was over and the motley complement of a newly-formed mortar troop was standing to attention in two ranks.

'Troop all present and correct, sir!' sang out Myshlaevsky's voice.

Studzinsky marched up to the ranks, took a pace backwards and shouted:

'Left face! Quick-march!'

With a crunch of snow underfoot, wobbling and unsoldierly, the troop set off.

Among the rows of typical students' faces Turbin noticed several that were similar. Karas appeared at the head of the third troop. Still not knowing quite what he was supposed to do Turbin fell into step beside them. Karas stepped aside and marching backwards in front of them, began to shout the cadence:

'Left! Left! Hup, two, three, four!'

The troops wheeled toward the gaping black mouth of the school's basement entrance and the doorway began to swallow them rank by rank.

Inside, the school buildings were even gloomier and more funereal than outside. The silent walls and sinister half-light awoke instantly to the echoing crash of marching feet. Noises started up beneath the vaults as though a herd of demons had been awakened. The rustling and squeaking of frightened rats scuttling about in dark corners. The ranks marched on down the endless black underground corridors shored up by brick buttresses, until they reached a vast hall feebly lit by whatever light managed to filter through the narrow, cobwebbed, barred windows.

The silence was next shattered by an infernal outbreak of hammering as steel-banded wooden ammunition boxes were opened and their contents taken out – endless machine-gun belts and round, cake-like Lewis gun magazines. Out came spindle-legged machine-guns with the look of deadly insects. Nuts and bolts clattered, pincers wrenched, a saw whistled in a corner. Cadets sorted through piles of store-damaged fur caps, greatcoats in folds as rigid as iron, leather straps frozen stiff, cartridge pouches and cloth-covered waterbottles.

'Come on, look lively!' Studzinsky's voice rang out.

Six officers in faded gold shoulder-straps circled around like clumps of duckweed in a mill-race. Myshlaevsky's tenor, now fully restored, bawled out something above the noise.

'Doctor!' shouted Studzinsky from the darkness, 'please take command of the medical orderlies and give them some instruction.'

Two students materialised in front of Alexei Turbin. One of them, short and excitable, wore a red cross brassard on the sleeve of his student's uniform greatcoat. The other was in a gray army coat; his fur cap kept falling over his eyes, so he was constantly pushing it back with his fingers.

'There are the boxes of medical supplies,' said Tubirn, 'take out the orderlies' satchels, put them over your shoulder and pass me the surgeon's bag with the instruments ... Now go and issue every man with two individual field-dressing packets and give them brief instructions in how to open them in case of need.'

Myshlaevsky's head rose above the swarming gray mob. He climbed upon a box, waved a rifle, slammed the bolt open, noisily charged the magazine, then aimed out of a window, rattled the bolt and showered the surrounding cadets with ejected cartridges as he repeated the action several times. After this demonstration the cellar began to sound like a factory as the cadets rattling and slamming, filled their rifle-magazines with cartridges.

'Anyone who can't do it – take care. Cadets!' Myshlaevsky sang out, 'show the students how it's done.'

As straps fitted with cartridge pouches and water-bottles were pulled on over heads and shoulders, a miracle took place. The motley rabble became transformed into a compact, homogeneous mass crowned by a waving, disorderly, spiky steel-bristled brush made of bayonets.

'All officers report to me, please', came Studzinsky's voice.

In a dark passageway to the subdued clink of spurs, Studzinsky asked quietly:

'Well, gentlemen, what are your impressions?'

A rattle of spurs. Myshlaevsky, saluting with a practised and nonchalant touch of his cap, took a pace towards the staff-captain and said:

'It's not going to be easy. There are fifteen men in my troop who have never seen a rifle in their lives.'

Gazing upwards as though inspired towards a window where the last trickle of gray light was filtering through, Studzinsky went on:

'Morale?'

Myshlaevsky spoke again.

'Er, h'umm ... I think the students were somewhat put off by the sight of that funeral. It had a bad effect on them. They watched it through the railings.'

Studzinsky turned his eager, dark eyes on to him.

'Do your best to raise their morale.'

Spurs clinked again as the officers dispersed.

'Cadet Pavlovsky!' Back in the armory, Myshlaevsky roared out like Radames in *Aïda*.

'Pavlovsky . . . sky . . . sky!' answered the stony walls of the armory and a chorus of cadets' voices.

'Here, sir!'

'Were you at the Alexeyevsky Artillery School?'

'Yes, sir.'

'Right, let's smarten things up and have a song. So loud that it'll make Petlyura drop dead, God rot him . . .'

One voice, high and clear, struck up beneath the stone vaults:

'I was born a little gunner-boy . . .' Some tenors chimed in from among the forest of bayonets:

> 'Washed in a shell-case spent . . .'

The horde of students seemed to shudder, quickly picked up the tune by ear, and suddenly, in a mighty bass roar that echoed like gunfire, they rocked the whole armory:

> 'Christened with a charge of shrapnel,
> Swaddled in an army tent!
> Christened with . . .'

The sound rang in their ears, boomed among the ammunition boxes, rattled the grim windows and pounded in their heads until several long-forgotten dusty old glasses on the sloping window ledges began to rattle and shake . . .

> 'In my cradle made of trace-ropes
> The gun-crew would rock me to sleep.'

Out of the crowd of greatcoats, bayonets and machine-guns, Studzinsky selected two pink-faced ensigns and gave them a rapid, whispered order:

'Assembly hall . . . take down the drapes in front of the portrait
. . . look sharp . . .'

The ensigns hurried off.

*

The empty stone box of the school building roared and shook in
march time, while the rats lurked deep in their holes, cowering
with terror.

'Hup, two, three, four!' came Karas' piercing voice.

'Louder!' shouted Myshlaevsky in his high, clear tenor.

'What d'you think this is – a funeral!?'

*

Instead of a ragged gray mob, an orderly file bristling with
bayonets now marched off steadily along the corridor, the floor
groaning and bending under the crunch of feet. Along the endless
passages and up to the second floor marched the detachment
straight into the gigantic assembly hall bathed in light from its
glass dome, where the front ranks had already halted and were
beginning to fidget restlessly.

Mounted on his pure-bred Arab charger, saddle-cloth em-
blazoned with the imperial monogram, the Arab executing a
perfect caracole, with beaming smile and white-plumed tricorn hat
cocked at a rakish angle, the balding, radiant Tsar Alexander I
galloped ahead of the ranks of cadets and students. Flashing them
smile after smile redolent of insidious charm, Alexander waved his
baton at the cadets to show them the serried ranks of Borodino.
Clumps of cannon-balls were strewn about the fields and the
entire background of the fourteen foot canvas was covered with
black slabs of massed bayonets.

*

As the gorgeous Tsar Alexander galloped onwards and upwards to
heaven, the torn drapes which had shrouded him for a whole year
since October 1917 lay in a heap around the hooves of his charger.

'Can't you see the Emperor Alexander? Keep that cadence!

Left, left! Hup, two, three, four!' roared Myshlaevsky as the file mounted the staircase with the ponderous tread of Tsar Alexander's foot-soldiers, past the man who beat Napoleon, the battery wheeled to the right into the vast assembly hall. The singing broke off as they formed into an open square several ranks deep, bayonets clicking. A pale, whitish twilight reigned in the hall and the portraits of the last tsars, still draped, peered down faint and corpse-like through the cloth.

Studzinsky about-faced and looked at his wrist-watch. At that moment a cadet ran in and whispered something to him. The nearby ranks could hear the words '. . . regimental commander.'

Studzinsky signalled to the officers, who began dressing the ranks. Studzinsky went out into the corridor towards the commanding officer.

Turning and glancing at Tsar Alexander, his spurs ringing, Colonel Malyshev mounted the staircase towards the entrance to the assembly hall. His curved Caucasian sabre with its cherry-red sword-knot bumped against his left hip. He wore a black parade-dress service cap and a long greatcoat with a large slit up the back. He looked worried.

Studzinsky marched rapidly up to him, halted and saluted. Malyshev asked him:

'Have they all got uniforms?'

'Yes, sir. All orders carried out.'

'Well, what are they like?'

'They'll fight. But they're completely inexperienced. For a hundred and twenty cadets there are eighty students who have never handled a rifle.'

A shadow crossed Malyshev's face, but he said nothing.

'Thank God, though, we've managed to get some good officers,' Studzinsky went on, 'especially that new one, Myshlaevsky. We'll make out somehow.'

'I see. Thank you, captain. Now: as soon as I have inspected the battery I want you to send them home with orders to report back here in time to be on parade at seven o'clock tomorrow morning, except for the officers and a guard detachment of sixty of the best and most experienced cadets, who will mount guard over the guns, the armory and the buildings.'

Paralysed with amazement, Studzinsky glared at the colonel in the most insubordinate fashion. His mouth dropped open.

'But sir . . .' – in his excitement Studzinsky's Polish accent became more pronounced – '. . . if you'll allow me to say so, sir, that's impossible. The only way of keeping this battery in any state of military efficiency is to keep the men here overnight.'

Instantly the colonel demonstrated an unsuspected capacity for losing his temper on the grandest scale. His neck and cheeks turned a deep red and his eyes flashed.

'Captain', he said in a furious voice, 'if you talk to me like that again I will have an official notice published that you no longer rank as a staff-captain but as an instructor who regards it as his job to lecture senior officers. This will be most unfortunate, because I thought that in you I had an experienced executive officer and not a civilian professor. Kindly understand that I am in no need of lectures, and when I want your advice I shall ask for it. Otherwise it is your duty to listen, to take note – and then to carry out what I say!'

The two men stared at each other.

Studzinsky's face and neck turned the color of a hot samovar and his lips trembled. In a grating voice he forced himself to say:

'Very good, colonel.'

'Now do what you're told. Send them home. Tell them to get a good night's sleep; send them home unarmed, with orders to report back here by seven o'clock tomorrow morning. Send them home – and what's more, make sure they go in small parties, not whole troops at a time, and without their shoulder-straps, so that they don't attract any unwelcome attention from undesirable elements.'

A ray of comprehension passed across Studzinsky's expression and his resentment subsided.

'Very good, sir.'

The colonel's tone altered completely.

'My dear Studzinsky, you and I have known each other for

some time and I know perfectly well that you are a most experienced regimental officer. And I'm sure you know me well
enough not to be offended. In any case, taking offense is a luxury
we can hardly afford at the moment. I apologise for showing you
the rough side of my tongue – please forget it; I think you rather
forgot yourself, too. . . .'

Studzinsky blushed again.

'Quite right, sir. I'm sorry.'

'Well, that's in order. Let's not waste time, otherwise it will be
bad for their morale. Everything depends on what happens
tomorrow, because by then the situation will be somewhat clearer.
However, I may as well tell you now that there's not much
prospect of using the mortars: there are no horses to pull them and
no ammunition to fire. So as of tomorrow morning it's to be rifle
and shooting practice, shooting practice and more shooting
practice. By noon tomorrow I want this battery to be able to shoot
like a Guards regiment. And issue hand-grenades to all the more
experienced cadets. Understood?'

Studzinsky looked grim as he listened tensely.

'May I ask a question, sir?'

'I know what you're going to ask, and you needn't bother. I'll
tell you the answer straight away – it's sickening. It could be
worse – but not much. Get me?'

'Yes, sir!'

'Right then.' Malyshev raised his voice: 'So you see I don't
want them to spend the night in this great stone rat-trap, at an
uncertain time like this, when there's a good chance that by doing
so I would be signing the death warrant of two hundred boys,
eighty of whom can't even shoot.'

Studzinsky said nothing.

'So that's it. I'll tell you the rest later on this evening. We'll pull
through somehow. Let's go and have a look at 'em.'

They marched into the hall.

'Atten-*shun*!' shouted Studzinsky.

'Good day, gentlemen!'

Behind Malyshev's back Studzinsky waved his arm like an

anxious stage director and with a roar that shook the windowpanes the bristling gray wall sang out the Russian soldier's traditional response to their commanding officer's greeting.

Malyshev swept the ranks with a cheerful glance, snapped his hand down from the salute and said:

'Splendid! . . . Now gentlemen, I'm not going to waste words. You won't find me at political meetings, because I'm no speaker, so I shall be very brief. We're going to fight that son of a bitch Petlyura and you may rest assured that we shall beat him. There are cadets among you from the Vladimir, Constantine and Alexeyevsky military academies and no officer from any of these institutions has ever yet disgraced the colors. Many of you, too, were once at this famous school. Its old walls are watching you: I hope you won't make them redden with shame on your account. Gentlemen of the Mortar Regiment! We shall defend this great city in the hour of its assault by a bandit. As soon as we get Petlyura in range of our six-inchers, there won't be much left of him except a pair of very dirty underpants, God rot his stinking little soul!'

When the laugh from the ranks had died down the colonel finished:

'Gentlemen – do your best!'

Again, like a director off-stage, Studzinsky nervously raised his arm and once more the Mortar Regiment blew away several layers of dust all around the assembly hall as they gave three cheers for their commanding officer.

*

Ten minutes later the assembly hall, just like the battlefield of Borodino, was dotted with hundreds of rifles piled in threes, bayonet upwards. Two sentries stood at either end of the dusty parquet floor sprouting its dragon's teeth. From the distance came the sound of vanishing footsteps as the new recruits hastily dispersed according to instructions. From along the corridors came the crash of hobnailed boots and an officer's words of command – Studzinsky himself was posting the sentries. Then came the unexpected sound of a bugle-call. There was no menace in the ragged, jerky sound as it echoed around the school buildings, but merely an anxious splutter of sour notes. On the landing bounded by the railings of the double staircase leading from the first floor up to the assembly hall, a cadet was standing with distended cheeks. The faded ribbons of the Order of St George dangled from the tarnished brass of the bugle. His legs spread wide like a pair of compasses, Myshlaevsky was standing in front of the bugler and instructing him.

'Don't blow too hard . . . look – like this. Fill your cheeks with air and blow out. No, no, hopeless. Now try again – sound the "General Alarm".'

'Pa – pa – *pah* – pa – *pah*', shrieked the bugle, reducing the school's rat population to terror.

Twilight was swiftly advancing over the assembly hall, where Malyshev and Turbin stood beside the ranks of piled rifles. Colonel Malyshev frowned slightly in Turbin's direction, but at once arranged his face into an affable smile.

'Well, doctor, how are things? Is all well in the medical section?'

'Yes, colonel.'

'You can go home now, doctor. And tell your orderlies they can go too, but they must report back here at seven o'clock with the others. And you . . . (Malyshev reflected, frowned) . . . I should like you to report here tomorrow at two o'clock in the afternoon. Until then you're free. (Malyshev thought again) And there's one other thing: you'd better not wear your shoulder-straps. (Malyshev looked embarrassed) It is not part of our plans to draw attention to ourselves. So, in a word, just be back here at two o'clock tomorrow.'

'Very good, sir.'

Turbin shuffled his feet. Malyshev took out a cigarette case and offered him a cigarette, for which Turbin lit a match. Two little red stars glowed, emphasising how much darker it had grown. Malyshev glanced awkwardly upward at the dim white globes of the hall's arc-lamps, then turned and went out into the passage.

'Lieutenant Myshlaevsky, come here, please. I am putting you in full charge of the electric light in this building. Try and get the lights switched on as quickly as possible. Please have it organised so that at any moment you can not only put all the lights on, but also switch them off. Responsibility for the lighting is entirely yours.'

Myshlaevsky saluted and faced sharply about. The bugler gave a squeak and stopped. Spurs jingling – ca-link, ca-link, ca-link – Myshlaevsky ran down the main staircase so fast that he seemed to be skating down it. A minute later the sound of his hammering fists and barked commands could be heard from somewhere in the depths of the building. This was followed by a sudden blaze of light in the main downstairs lobby, which threw a faint reflected glow over the portrait of Alexander I. Malyshev was so delighted that his mouth even fell open slightly and he turned to Alexei Turbin:

'Well, I'm damned . . . Now there's an officer for you! Did you see that?'

A figure appeared at the bottom and began slowly climbing up the staircase. Malyshev and Turbin were able to make out who it was as he reached the first landing. The figure advanced on doddering, infirm legs, his white head shaking, and wore a broad double-breasted tunic with silver buttons and bright green lapels. An enormous key dangled in his shaking hand. Myshlaevsky was following him up the staircase with occasional shouts of encouragement.

'Come on, old boy, speed it up! You're crawling along like a flea on a tightrope.'

'Your . . . your', mumbled the old man as he shuffled along. Karas emerged out of the gloom on the landing, followed by another, tall officer, then by two cadets and finally the pointed snout of a machine-gun. The white-haired figure stumbled, bent down and bowed to the waist in the direction of the machine-gun.

'Your . . . your honor', muttered the figure.

The figure arrived at the top of the stairs, and with shaking hands, fumbling in the dark, opened a long oblong box on the wall from which shone a white spot of light. The old man thrust his hand in, there was a click and instantly the upper landing, the corridor and the entrance to the assembly hall were flooded with light.

The darkness rolled away to the ends of the corridor. Myshlaevsky immediately took possession of the key and thrust his hand inside the box where he began to try out the rows of black switches. Light, so blinding that it even seemed to be shot with pink, flared up and vanished again. The globes in the assembly hall were lit and then extinguished. Two globes at the far ends of the corridor suddenly blazed into life and the darkness somersaulted away altogether.

'How's that?' shouted Myshlaevsky.

'Out', several voices answered from downstairs.

'O.K.! On!' came a shout from the upper floor.

Satisfied, Myshlaevsky finally switched on the lights in the assembly hall, in the corridor and the spotlight over the Emperor Alexander, locked the switchbox and put the key in his pocket.

'All right, you can go back to bed now, old fellow,' he said reassuringly, 'all's well now.'

The old man's near-sighted eyes blinked anxiously:

'But what about the key, your . . . your honor . . . Are you going to keep it?'

'That's right. I'm going to keep the key.'

The old man stood trembling for a few moments longer then began slowly going downstairs.

'Cadet!'

A stout, red-faced cadet snapped to attention beside the switch box.

'You are to allow only three people to have access to the box: the regimental commander, the executive officer and myself. And nobody else. In case of necessity, on the orders of one of those three officers, you are to break open the box, but carefully so as not to damage the switchboard.'

'Very good, sir.'

Myshlaevsky walked over to Alexei Turbin and whispered:

'Did you see him – old Maxim?'

'God, yes, I did . . .' whispered Turbin.

The battery commander was standing in the entrance to the assembly hall, thousands of candle-power sparkling on the engraved silver of his scabbard. He beckoned to Myshlaevsky and said:

'Lieutenant, I am very glad you were able to join our regiment. Well done.'

'Glad to do my duty, sir.'

'One more thing: I just want you to fix the heating in this hall so that the cadets on sentry-duty will be kept warm. I'll take care of everything else. I'll see you get your rations and some vodka – not much, but enough to keep the cold out.'

Myshlaevsky gave the colonel a charming smile and cleared his throat in a way that conveyed tactful appreciation.

Alexei Turbin heard no more of their conversation. Leaning over the balustrade, he stared down at the little white-haired figure until it disappeared below. A feeling of hollow depression came over Turbin. Suddenly, leaning on the cold metal railings, a memory returned to him with extreme clarity.

. . . A crowd of high-school boys of all ages was rushing along that same corridor in a state of high excitement. Maxim, the thickset school beadle, made a grab at two small dark figures at the head of the mob. 'Well, well, well', he muttered. 'The school inspector will be pleased to see Mr Turbin and Mr Myshlaevsky, today of all days, when the school governor is visiting. He *will* be pleased!' Needless to say Maxim's remark was one of crushing sarcasm. Only someone of perverted taste could have gained any pleasure from the contemplation of Mr Turbin and Mr Myshlaevsky, especially on the day of the school governor's visit.

Mr Myshlaevsky, gripped in Maxim's left hand, had a split upper lip and his left sleeve was dangling by a thread. Mr Turbin, a prisoner of Maxim's right hand, had lost his belt and all his buttons – not only on his tunic but his fly-buttons as well, revealing a most indecent display of underwear.

'Please let us go, kind Maxim', begged Turbin and Mysh-laevsky gazing beseechingly at Maxim with bloodstained faces.

'Go on, Max, wallop him!' shouted the excited boys from behind. 'That'll teach him to beat up a junior!'

Oh God, the sunshine, noise and bustling of that day. And Maxim had been very different from this white-haired, hunched and famished old man. In those days Maxim's hair had been as thick and strong as a black boot-brush, scarcely touched with a few threads of grey, Maxim's hands had been as strong as a pair of steel pincers and round his neck he had worn a medallion the size of a wagon-wheel . . . Yes, the wheel, the wheel of fate had gone on rolling from village 'A', making 'x' number of turns on the way . . . and it had never reached village 'B' but had landed up in a stony void. God, it was cold. Now they had to defend . . . But defend what? A void? The sound of footsteps? . . . Can you save this doomed building, Tsar Alexander, with all the regiments of Borodino? Why don't you come alive and lead them down from the canvas? They'd smash Petlyura all right.

Turbin's legs took him downstairs of their own volition. He wanted to shout 'Maxim!', but he hesitated and then finally stopped. He imagined Maxim down below in the janitors' quarters in the basement, probably sitting huddled over his stove. Either he would have forgotten the old days, or he would burst into tears. And things were bad enough without that. To hell with the idea – sentimental rubbish. They had all ruined their lives by being too sentimental. So forget it.

*

Yet when Turbin had dismissed his medical orderlies he found himself wandering around one of the empty, twilit classrooms. The blackboards looked down blankly from the walls, the benches still stood in their ranks. He could not resist lifting the lid of one of the desks and sitting down at it. It felt difficult, awkward and uncomfortable. How near the blackboard seemed. He could have sworn that this was his old classroom, this or the next one, because there was that same familiar view of the City out of the window. Over there was the huge black, inert mass of the university buildings, there was the lamplit avenue running straight as an arrow, there were the same boxlike houses, the dark gaps in between them, walls, the vaulted sky. . . .

Outside it looked exactly like a stage set for *The Night Before Christmas*, snow and little flickering, twinkling lights . . . 'I wonder why there is gunfire out at Svyatoshino?' Harmless, far away, as though muffled in cotton wool, came the dull boo-oom, boom . . .

'Enough of this.'

Alexei Turbin lowered the desk-lid, walked out into the corridor and through the main lobby, past the sentries and out of doors. A machine-gun was posted at the main entrance. There were hardly any people out on the streets and it was snowing hard.

*

The colonel spent a busy night, making countless journeys back and forth between the school and Madame Anjou's shop nearby. By midnight the machinery of his command was working thoroughly and efficiently. Crackling faintly, the school arc-lights shone with their pinkish light. The assembly hall had grown noticeably warmer, thanks to the fires blazing all evening and all night in the old-fashioned stoves in the library bays of the hall.

Under Myshlaevsky's command several cadets had lit the white stoves with bound volumes of literary magazines of the 1860's, and then to a ceaseless clatter of axes had fed the flames by chopping up the old school benches. Having swallowed their ration of two glasses of vodka (the colonel had kept his promise and provided them with enough to keep the cold out – a gallon and a half), Studzinsky and Myshlaevsky took turns as officer of the guard. They slept for two hours, wrapped in their greatcoats, lying on the floor beside the stove with the cadets, the crimson flames and shadows playing on their faces. Then they got up, moving from sentry-post to sentry-post all through the night inspecting the guard. Relieved every hour, four cadets, muffled in sheepskin jerkins, stood guard over the broad-muzzled six-inch mortars.

The stove at Madame Anjou's glowed infernally, the draught roaring and crackling up the flue. A cadet stood on guard at the door keeping constant watch on the motor-cycle and sidecar parked outside, while four others slept like logs inside the shop, wrapped in their greatcoats. Towards midnight the colonel was finally able to settle down at Madame Anjou's. He was yawning, but was still too busy on the telephone to go to sleep. Then at two o'clock in the morning a motor-cycle drove hooting up to the shop. A military man in a gray coat dismounted.

'Let him pass. It's for me.'

The man handed the colonel a bulky package wrapped in cloth, tied criss-cross with wire. The colonel personally deposited it in the little safe at the back of the shop and locked it. The gray man drove off again on his motor-cycle. The colonel mounted to the balcony, where he spread out his greatcoat and put a bundle of rags under his head. Having ordered the duty cadet to waken him at precisely 6.30 a.m., he lay down and went to sleep.

Seven

THE coal-black gloom of the darkest night had descended on the terraces of the most beautiful spot on earth, St Vladimir's Hill, whose brick-paved paths and avenues were hidden beneath a thick layer of virgin snow.

Not a soul in the City ever set foot on that great terraced mound in wintertime. Still less was anyone likely to climb the hill at night, especially at times like these, which were grim enough to deter the bravest man. There was no good reason for going there and only one place that was lit: for a hundred years the black, cast-iron St Vladimir has been standing on his fearful heavy plinth and holding, upright, a twenty-foot-high cross. Every evening, as soon as twilight begins to enfold the snowdrifts, the slopes and the terraces, the cross is lighted and it burns all night. From far away it can be seen; from thirty miles away in the black distance stretching away towards Moscow. But here on the hilltop it lights up only very little: the pale electric light falls, brushing the greenish-black flanks of the plinth, picking out of the darkness the balustrade and a stretch of the railings that surround the central terrace. And that is all. Beyond this – utter darkness. Out there stand strange trees capped with snow, looking like chandeliers wrapped in muslin, and neck-deep snowdrifts all around. Terrifying.

Obviously no one, however courageous, is going to come here. Chiefly because there is nothing to come for. The City, though, is another matter. A night of alarm, of military decision. Street-lamps shining like strings of beads. The Germans asleep, but with half an eye open. A blue cone of light suddenly flashes into life in one of the City's darkest streets.

'Halt!'

Crunch ... crunch ... Helmeted soldiers, with black ear-muffs, walking down the middle of the street ... Crunch ... Rifles not slung, but at the ready. The Germans are not in a joking mood for the moment. Whatever else may be in doubt, the Germans are to be taken seriously. They look like dung-beetles.

'Papiere!'

'Halt!'

A cone from the flashlight ...

A big shiny black car with four headlamps. No ordinary car, because it is followed at a brisk canter by an escort of eight cavalrymen. The Germans are not impressed, and shout at the car:

'Halt!'

'Where to? Who? Why?'

'General Belorukov, commanding general.'

That is another matter. Proceed, general. Deep inside, behind the glass of the car's windows, a pale moustached face. Faint glimmer reflected from general's shoulder-straps. The German helmets saluted. Secretly they didn't care whether it was General Belorukov, or Petlyura, or a Zulu chief – it was a lousy country anyway. But when in Zululand, do as the Zulus do. So the helmets saluted. Courtesy is international, as the saying goes.

*

A night of martial deeds. Rays of light slanting out of Madame Anjou's windows, with their ladies' hats, corsets, underwear and crossed cannon. A cadet marched back and forth like a pendulum, freezing cold, tracing the tsarist cypher in the snow with the tip of his bayonet. Over in the Alexander I High School the arc-lights shone as though at a ball. Fortified by a sufficient quantity of vodka Myshlaevsky tramped around the corridors, glancing up at Tsar Alexander, keeping an eye on the switch-box. There at the school things might have been worse: the sentry-posts armed with eight machine-guns and manned by cadets – not mere students . . . and they would fight. Myshlaevsky's eyes were red as a rabbit's. He was unlikely to get much sleep that night, but there was plenty of vodka and just enough tension in the air for excitement. Provided it got no worse life in the City was tolerable in this state. If you had nothing on your conscience you could keep out of trouble. True, you might be stopped four times, but if you had your papers on you there was nothing to hold you up. It might look odd that you were out so late at night, but still – pass, friend . . .

Crazy as it might seem, there *were* people out on St Vladimir's Hill despite the icy wind whistling between the snowdrifts with a sound like the voice of the devil himself. If anyone were to climb up the Hill it could only be some complete outcast, a man who under no matter what government felt as much at home among his fellow men as a wolf in a pack of dogs – in a word, one of Victor Hugo's 'misérables'. The sort of man who had good reason not to show himself in the City, or if so then at his own risk. If he were in luck he might evade the patrols; if not, then it would be just too bad. If a man like that found his way up on to the Hill one could only feel sorry for him out of sheer human pity. The wind was so icy, one wouldn't send a dog out – after five minutes up there he would be back home and whining to be let in. But . . .

'Only five o'clock. Christ, we'll freeze to death . . .'

The trouble was that there was no way into the Upper City past the Belvedere and the water-tower because Prince Belorukov's headquarters was installed in the monastery building on Mikhailovsky Street, and cars with cavalry outriders or mounted machine-guns were passing by all the time . . .

'Damned officers, we'll never get through that way!'

And patrols everywhere.

It was no good trying to creep down the hillside terraces to the Lower City either, firstly because Alexandrovsky Street, which wound its way around the foot of the hill, was lit by rows of street-lamps, and secondly because it was heavily patrolled by the Germans, damn them. Maybe someone might be able to slip down that way toward dawn, but by then they would be frozen to death. As the icy wind whistled along the snowbound avenues there seemed to be another sound too – the mutter of voices somewhere near the snowbound railings.

'We can't stay here, Kirpaty, we'll freeze to death, I tell you.'

'Stick it out, Nemolyaka. The patrols will be out till morning, then they turn in and sleep. Once we can slip through to the Embankment we can hide at Sychukla's and warm ourselves up.'

There was a movement in the darkness along the railings as if three shadows blacker than the rest were huddling against the parapet and leaning over to look down at Alexandrovsky Street stretched out immediately below. It was silent and empty, but at any moment two bluish cones of light might appear and some German cars drive past or the dark blobs of steel-helmeted troops, casting their sharp, foreshortened shadows under the street-lamps . . . and so near, they might be within reach . . .

One shadow broke away from the group on the Hill and his wolfish voice grated:

'Come on, Nemolyaka, let's risk it. Maybe we can slip through . . .'

Something bad was afoot on the Hill.

*

Something equally bad was afoot in the Hetman's palace, where the activity seemed oddly out of place at that hour of night. An elderly footman in sideburns scuttled like a mouse across the shiny parquet floor of a chamber lined with ugly gilt chairs. From somewhere in the distance came the jerky ringing of an electric bell, the clink of spurs. In the state bedroom the mirrors in their gloomy crowned frames reflected a strange, unnatural scene. A thin, graying man with narrow, clipped moustaches on his foxy, clean-shaven, parchment-like face was pacing in front of the mirrors; he was dressed in a fancy Circassian coat with ornamental silver cartridge-cases. Around him hovered three German officers and two Russian. One of the latter wore a Circassian coat like the central figure, the other was in service tunic and breeches whose cut betrayed their tsarist Chevalier Guards origin despite the officer's wedge-shaped Hetmanite shoulder-straps. They were helping the foxy man to change his clothes. Off came the Circassian coat, the wide baggy trousers, the patent-leather boots. In their place the man was encased in the uniform of a German major and he became no different from hundreds of other majors. Then the door opened, the dusty palace drapes were pulled aside and admitted another man in the uniform of a German army medical officer carrying a large quantity of packages. These he opened and with the contents skilfully bandaged the head of the newly-created German major until all that remained visible were one foxy eye and a thin mouth open just wide enough to show some of its gold and platinum bridgework.

The improper nocturnal activity in the palace continued for some time. A German came out of the bedroom and announced in German to some officers loafing around in the chamber with the gilt chairs and in a nearby hall that Major von Schratt had accidentally wounded himself in the neck while unloading a revolver and must be taken urgently to the German military hospital. A telephone rang somewhere, followed by the shrill bird-like squeak of a field-telephone. Then a noiseless German ambulance with Red Cross markings drove through the wrought-iron gates of the palace to a side entrance and the mysterious Major von Schratt, swathed in bandages and wrapped in a greatcoat, was carried out on a stretcher and placed inside the ambulance. The ambulance drove away with a muffled roar as it turned out of the gates.

The bustle continued in the palace until the morning, lights burned on in gilded halls lined with portraits, the telephone rang frequently; a look something like insolence came over the expressions of the palace servants and their eyes glinted cheerfully ...

In a cramped little room on the first floor of the palace a man in the uniform of an artillery colonel picked up the telephone after carefully closing the door of the little whitewashed room. He asked the unsleeping girl on the exchange for number 212. When she had connected him he said 'merci', frowned hard and asked in a low, confidential voice:

'Is that the headquarters of the Mortar Regiment?'

*

Alas, Colonel Malyshev was not fated to be able to sleep until half past six, as he had assumed. At four o'clock in the morning the telephone bell in Madame Anjou's shop squealed with extreme insistence and the cadet on duty was obliged to waken the colonel. The colonel woke up with remarkable speed. He grasped the situation as quickly and perceptively as though he had never been to sleep at all, and did not reproach the cadet for having interrupted his rest. Soon afterwards he drove away in the motor-cycle and sidecar, and when the colonel returned to Madame Anjou at five o'clock his eyebrows were contracted in as deep a military frown as had crossed the forehead of the colonel at the palace who had called up the Mortar Regiment.

*

On the field of Borodino at seven o'clock that morning, lit by the great pink globes, hunched against the pre-dawn cold, buzzing with talk, stood the same extended string of young men which had marched up the staircase towards the portrait of Tsar Alexander. A little distance away, Staff Captain Studzinsky stood silent among a group of officers. Strangely enough his eyes had the same uneasy gleam of anxiety that Colonel Malyshev had shown since four o'clock that morning. But anyone who had seen both the staff captain and the colonel on that fateful night would have been able to say at once and with certainty where the difference lay: the anxiety in Studzinsky's eyes was one of foreboding, whereas Malyshev's was a certainty – the anxiety founded on a clear realisation that disaster was complete. A long list of the names of the regiment's complement was sticking out of the long turned-up cuff of the sleeve of Studzinsky's greatcoat. He had just finished calling the roll and had discovered that the unit was twenty men short. This was why the list was crumpled: it bore the traces of the staff captain's fingers.

Little bursts of smoke arose into the chilly air of the assembly hall as some of the officers smoked.

On the stroke of seven o'clock Colonel Malyshev appeared on parade to be greeted, as on the previous day, by a roar of greeting from the ranks in the hall. As on the previous day the colonel was wearing his sabre, but for some reason the chased silverwork of its scabbard no longer flashed with a thousand reflections. On the colonel's right hip his revolver lay in its holster, which with a carelessness quite untypical of Colonel Malyshev, was un-buttoned.

The colonel took up his position in front of the regiment, put his gloved left hand on the hilt of his sword and with his ungloved right hand resting gently on his holster he spoke the following words:

'I want all officers and men of the Mortar Regiment to listen carefully to what I have to say to them! Last night a number of sudden and violent changes took place which affect us, which affect the army as a whole – and which, I venture to say, affect the entire political situation of the Ukraine. I therefore have to inform you that this Regiment is disbanded! I propose that each one of you should remove all insignia and badges of rank, take anything from the armory you may want and which you can carry away and go home, stay there without showing yourselves and wait there until you are recalled to duty by me.'

The colonel stopped, and his abrupt silence was emphasised even more by the absolute stillness in the hall. Even the arc-lights had ceased to hiss. Every man in the room was staring at one point – the colonel's clipped moustache.

He went on:

'I shall issue orders for your recall as soon as there is the slightest change in the situation. But I must tell you that the hopes of any such change are slim . . . I can't predict how events will develop, but I think the best that every, . . . er . . . (the colonel suddenly yelled the next word) *loyal* man among you can hope for is to be sent to join General Denikin's forces on the Don. So my orders to the whole regiment – with the exception of the officers and those who were on sentry-duty last night – are to dismiss and return immediately to your homes!'

'What? What?! . . .' The incredulous murmur ran down the ranks and the bayonets dipped and swayed. Bewildered faces gazed around them, some were plainly relieved, some even delighted . . .

Staff Captain Studzinsky stepped forward from the group of officers. Bluish-white in the face, squinting, he took a few paces towards Colonel Malyshev, then glanced round at the officers. Myshlaevsky was not looking at Studzinsky but was still staring at Colonel Malyshev's moustache. From his expression he looked exactly as if he was about to indulge in his usual habit of breaking out in obscene abuse. Karas stupidly put his arms akimbo and blinked. In the separate group of young ensigns there suddenly came the rustling sound of the rash, dangerous word 'arrest' . . .

'What was that?' muttered a deep voice from the ranks of the cadets.

'Arrest!'

'Treachery!'

Studzinsky suddenly gave an inspired look upward at the

electric light globe above his head, then glanced down at the butt of his holster and barked:

'Number 1 Troop!'

The first rank broke up, several gray figures stepped forward. A strangely confused scene ensued.

'Colonel!' said Studzinsky in a thin, hoarse voice, 'you are under arrest!'

'Arrest him!' one of the ensigns suddenly shrieked hysterically and moved toward the colonel.

'Stop, gentlemen!' shouted Karas, who although his mind did not work fast had firmly grasped the import of the situation.

Myshlaevsky leaped swiftly forward, grabbed the impetuous ensign by the sleeve of his greatcoat and pulled him back.

'Let me go, lieutenant!' shouted the ensign, grimacing with fury.

'Quiet!' The colonel's voice rang out with complete self-assurance. Although his mouth was twitching as much as the ensign's and his face was mottled with red, there was more calm and confidence in his expression than any of the other officers could muster at that moment. All stood still.

'Quiet!' repeated the colonel. 'I order you all to stay where you are and listen to me!'

Silence reigned, and Myshlaevsky became sharply attentive. It was as if a sudden thought had occurred to him and he was now expecting some news from the colonel that was considerably more important than that which he just announced.

'I see,' said the colonel, his cheek twitching, 'that I would have made a fine fool of myself if I had tried going into battle with the motley crew which the good Lord saw fit to provide me with. Obviously it was just as well that I didn't. But what is excusable in a student volunteer or a young cadet, and possibly just excusable in an ensign is utterly inexcusable in you, Staff Captain Studzinsky!'

With this the colonel withered Studzinsky with a look of quite exceptional virulence, his eyes flashing with sparks of genuine exasperation. Again there was silence.

'Well, now', went on the colonel, 'I have never attended a meeting in my life, but it seems that I shall have to start now. Very well, let's hold a meeting! Now I agree that your attempt to arrest your commanding officer does credit to your patriotism, but it also shows that you are, er . . . how shall I put it, gentlemen? . . . inexperienced! Briefly – I have no time left and nor, I assure you,' the colonel said with baleful emphasis, 'have you. Let me ask you a question: whom are you proposing to defend?'

Silence.

'I'm asking you: whom do you mean to defend?' the colonel repeated threateningly.

His eyes burning with interest Myshlaevsky stepped forward, saluted and said:

'We are in duty bound to defend the Hetman, sir.'

'The Hetman?' the colonel questioned in return. 'Good. Regiment – atten-*shun*!' he suddenly roared in a voice that made the entire regiment jump to attention. 'Listen to me! This morning at approximately 4 a.m. the Hetman shamefully abandoned us all to our fate and ran away! Yes, he ran away, like the most miserable scoundrel and coward! This morning too, an hour after the Hetman, our commanding general, General Belorukov, ran away in the same way as the Hetman – in a German train. In no more than a few hours from now we shall be witnesses of a catastrophe in which the wretched people like yourselves who were tricked and involved into this absurd escapade will be slaughtered like dogs. Listen: on the outskirts of this city Petlyura has an army over a hundred thousand strong and tomorrow . . . what am I saying, tomorrow – today!' and the colonel pointed out of the window to where the sky was beginning to pale over the City, 'the isolated, disorganised units formed from officers and cadets, abandoned by those swine at headquarters and by those two unspeakable rogues Skoropadsky and Belorukov, who should both be hung, will be faced by Petlyura's troops who are well armed and who outnumber them by twenty to one . . . Listen, boys!' Colonel Malyshev suddenly exclaimed in a breaking voice, although his age made him more of an elder brother than a father to the rows of bayonet-toting youths in front of him – 'Listen! I am a regular officer. I went through the German war, as Staff Captain Studzinsky here will witness, and I know what I'm talking about! I assume full and absolute responsibility for what I'm doing! Understand? I'm warning you! And I'm sending you home! Do you understand why?' he shouted.

'Yes, yes', answered the crowd, bayonets swaying. Then loudly and convulsively a cadet in the second rank burst into tears.

To the utter surprise of the regiment and probably of himself, Staff Captain Studzinsky crammed his gloved fist into his eyes with a strange and most un-officer like gesture, at which the regiment's nominal roll fell to the floor, and burst into tears.

Infected by him several more cadets began weeping, the ranks disintegrated and the disorderly uproar was only stopped when Myshlaevsky, in his Radames voice, roared an order to the bugler:

'Cadet Pavlovsky! Sound the retreat!'

*

'Colonel, will you give me permission to set fire to the school building?' said Myshlaevsky, beaming at the colonel.

'No, I will not', Malyshev replied quietly and politely.

'But sir,' said Myshlaevsky earnestly, 'that means that Petlyura will get the armory, the weapons and worst of all –' Myshlaevsky pointed out into the hallway where the head of Tsar Alexander I could be seen over the landing.

'Yes, he'll get all that', the colonel politely agreed.

'You can't mean to let him, sir?'

Malyshev turned to face Myshlaevsky, stared hard at him and said:

'Lieutenant, in three hours' time hundreds of human lives will fall to Petlyura and my only regret is I am unable to prevent their destruction at the cost of my own life, or of yours. Please don't mention portraits, guns or rifles to me again.'

'Sir,' said Studzinsky, standing at attention in front of the colonel, 'I wish to apologise on my own behalf and on behalf of those officers whom I incited to an act of disgraceful behavior.'

'I accept your apology', replied the colonel politely.

*

By the time the morning mist over the town had begun to disperse, the blunt-muzzled mortars on the Alexander High School parade ground had lost their breech-blocks and the rifles and machine-guns, dismantled or broken up, had been hidden in the furthermost recesses of the attic. Heaps of ammunition had been thrown into snowdrifts, into pits and into secret crannies in the cellars, while the globes no longer radiated light over the assembly hall and corridors. The white insulated switchboard had been smashed by cadets' bayonets under Myshlaevsky's orders.

*

The reflection in the windows was blue sky. The two last men to leave the school building – Myshlaevsky and Karas – stood in the sunlight on the square.

'Did the colonel warn Alexei that the regiment was going to be disbanded?' Myshlaevsky asked Karas anxiously.

'Yes, I'm sure he did. After all, Alexei didn't turn up on parade this morning, so he must have been told', replied Karas.

'Shall we go and see the Turbins?'

'Better not by daylight, as things are. It won't be safe for officers to be seen congregating in groups . . . you never know. Let's go back to our apartment.'

Blue skies in the windows, white on the playground and the mist rose and drifted away.

Eight

MIST. Mist, and needle-sharp frost, claw-like frost flowers. Snow, dark and moonless, then faintly paling with the approach of dawn. In the distance beyond the City, blue onion-domes sprinkled with stars of gold leaf; and on its sheer eminence above the City the cross of St Vladimir, only extinguished when the dawn crept in across the Moscow bank of the Dnieper.

When morning came the lighted cross went out, as the stars went out. But the day did not warm up; instead it showed signs of being damp, with an impenetrable veil suspended low over the whole land of the Ukraine.

Ten miles from the City Colonel Kozyr-Leshko awoke exactly at daybreak as a thin, sour, vaporous light crept through the dim little window of a peasant shack in the village of Popelyukha. Kozyr's awakening coincided with the word: 'Advance.'

At first he thought that he was seeing the word in a very vivid dream and even tried to brush it away with his hand as something chill and threatening. But the word swelled up and crept into the shack along with a crumpled envelope and the repulsive red pimples on the face of an orderly. Kozyr pulled a map out of a gridded mica map-case and spread it out under the window. He found the village of Borkhuny, then Bely Hai, and from these used his fingernail to trace the route along the maze of roads, their edges dotted with woods like so many flies, leading to a huge black blob – the City. Added to the powerful smell of Kozyr's cheap tobacco, the shack reeked of homegrown shag from the owner of the red pimples, who assumed that the war would not be lost if he smoked in the colonel's presence.

Faced with the immediate prospect of going into battle, Kozyr was thoroughly cheerful. He gave a huge yawn and jingled his complicated harness as he slung the straps over his shoulders. He had slept last night in his greatcoat without even taking off his spurs. A peasant woman sidled in with an earthenware pot of milk. Kozyr had never drunk milk before and did not wish to start now. Some children crept up. One of them, the smallest, with a completely bare bottom, crawled along the bench and reached out for Kozyr's Mauser, but could not get his hands on it before Kozyr had put the pistol into his holster.

Before 1914 Kozyr had spent all his life as a village schoolmaster. Mobilised into a regiment of dragoons at the outbreak of war, in 1917 he had been commissioned. And now the dawn of

December 14th 1918, found Kozyr a colonel in Petlyura's army and no one on earth (least of all Kozyr himself) could have said how it had happened. It had come about because war was Kozyr's true vocation and his years of teaching school had been nothing more than a protracted and serious mistake.

This, of course, is something that happens more often than not in life. A man may be engaged in some occupation for twenty whole years, such as studying Roman law, and then in the twenty-first year it suddenly transpires that Roman law is a complete waste of time, that he not only doesn't understand it and dislikes it too, but that he is really a born gardener and has an unquench-able love of flowers. This is presumably the result of some im-perfection in our social system, which seems to ensure that people frequently only find their proper *métier* towards the end of their lives. Kozyr had found his at the age of forty-five. Until then he had been a bad teacher, boring and cruel to his pupils.

'Right, tell the boys to get out of those shacks and stand to their horses', said Kozyr in Ukrainian and tightened the creaking belt around his stomach.

Smoke was beginning to curl up from the chimneys of Popel-yukha as Colonel Kozyr's cavalry regiment, four hundred sabres strong, rode out of the village. An aroma of shag floated above the ranks, Kozyr's fifteen-hand bay stallion prancing nervously ahead of them, whilst strung out for a quarter of a mile behind the regiment creaked the waggons of the baggage train. As soon as they had trotted clear of Popelyukha a two-color standard was unfurled at the head of the column of horsemen – one yellow strip and one blue strip of bunting tacked to a lance-shaft.

Kozyr could not abide tea and preferred to breakfast on a swig of vodka. He loved 'Imperial' vodka, which had been unobtainable for four years, but which had reappeared all over the Ukraine under the Hetman's régime. Like a burst of flame the vodka poured out of Kozyr's gray army canteen and through his veins. In the ranks, too, a liquid breakfast was the order of the day, drunk from canteens looted from the stores at Belaya Tserkov; as soon as the vodka began to take effect an accordion struck up at the head of the column and a falsetto voice started a refrain which was at once taken up by a bass chorus.

The trooper carrying the colors whistled and flicked his whip, lances and shaggy black braided fur caps bobbing in time to the song. The snow crunched under a thousand iron-shod hoofs. A drum gaily tapped out the cadence.

'Fine! Cheerful does it, lads', said Kozyr approvingly. And the whip cracked and whistled its melody over the snowbound Ukrainian fields.

As they passed through Bely Hai the mist was clearing, the roads were black with troops and the snow crunching under the weight of marching feet. At the crossroads in Bely Hai the cavalry column halted to let pass a fifteen-hundred-strong body of infantry. The men in the leading ranks all wore identical blue long-skirted tunics of good quality German cloth; they were thin-faced, wiry, active little men who carried their weapons like trained troops: Galicians. In the rear ranks came men dressed in long heel-length hospital robes, belted in with yellow rawhide straps. On their heads, bouncing atop their fur caps, were battered German army helmets and their hob-nailed boots pounded the snow beneath them.

The white roads leading to the City were beginning to blacken with advancing troops.

'Hurrah!' – the passing infantry shouted in salute to the yellow and blue ensign.

'Hurrah!' echoed the woods and fields of Bely Hai.

The cry was taken up by the guns to the rear and on the left of the marching column. Under cover of night the commander of the support troops, Colonel Toropets, had already moved two batteries into the forest around the City. The guns were positioned in a half-circle amid the sea of snow and had started a bombardment at dawn. The six-inch guns shook the snow-capped pine trees with waves of thundering explosions. A couple of rounds fell short in the large village of Pushcha-Voditsa, shattering all the windows of four snowbound houses. Several pine trees were reduced to splinters and the explosions threw up enormous fountains of snow.

Then all sound died in the village. The forest reverted to its dreamy silence and only the frightened squirrels were left scuttling, with a rustle of paws, between the trunks of centuries-old trees. After that the two batteries were withdrawn from Pushcha and switched to the right flank. They crossed boundless acres of arable land, through the wood-girt village of Urochishche, wheeled on to a narrow country road, drove on to a fork in the road and there they deployed in sight of the City. From early in the morning a high-bursting shrapnel bombardment began to fall on Podgorodnaya, Savskaya and on Kurenyovka, a suburb of the City itself. In the overcast, snow-laden sky the shrapnel bursts made a rattling noise, as though someone were playing a game of dice. The inhabitants of these villages had taken cover in their cellars since daybreak, and by the early morning half-light thin lines of cadets, frozen to the bone, could be seen conducting a skirmishing withdrawal towards the heart of the City. Before long, however, the artillery stopped and gave way to the cheerful rattle of machine-gun fire somewhere on the northern outskirts of the City. Then it too died down.

*

The train carrying the headquarters of Colonel Toropets, commander of the support troops, stood deep in the vast forest at the junction about five miles from the village of Svyatoshino, lifeless, snowbound and deafened by the crash and thunder of gunfire. All night the electric light had burned in the train's six cars, all night the telephone had rung in the signal-box and the field-telephones squealed in Colonel Toropets' grimy compartment. As the glimmer of a snowy morning began to light up the surroundings, the guns were already thundering ahead up the line leading from Svyatoshino to Post-Volynsk, the bird-like calls of field-telephones in their yellow wooden boxes were growing more urgent and Colonel Toropets, a thin, nervous man, said to his executive officer Khudyakovsky:

'We've captured Svyatoshino. Find out please, whether we can move the train up to Svyatoshino.'

Toropets' train moved slowly forward between the timber walls of the wintry forest and halted near the intersection of the railroad and a great highroad which thrust its way like an arrow to the very heart of the City. Here, in the dining-car, Colonel Toropets started to put into operation the plan which he had worked out for two sleepless nights in that same bug-ridden dining-car No. 4173.

The City rose up in the mist, surrounded on all sides by a ring of advancing troops. From the forests and farmland in the north, from the captured village of Svyatoshino in the west, from the ill-fated Post-Volynsk in the south-west, through the woods, the cemeteries, the open fields and the disused shooting-ranges ringed by the railroad line, the black lines of cavalry trotted and jingled inexorably forward along paths and tracks or simply cut across country, whilst the lumbering artillery creaked along behind and the ragged infantry of Petlyura's army trudged through the snow to tighten the noose that they had been drawing around the City for the past month.

The field-telephones shrilled ceaselessly in the saloon car, its carpeted floor trodden and crumpled, until Franko and Garas, the two signalmen, began to go mad.

Toropets' plan was a cunning one, as cunning as the tense, black-browed, clean-shaven colonel himself. He had intentionally sited his two batteries behind the forest, intentionally blown up the streetcar lines in the shabby little village of Pushcha-Voditsa. He had then purposely moved his machine-guns away from the farmlands, deploying them towards the left flank. For Toropets wanted to fool the defenders of the City into thinking that he, Toropets, intended to assault the City from his left (the northern) flank, from the suburb of Kurenyovka, in order to draw the City's forces in that direction whilst the real attack on the City would be delivered frontally, straight along the Brest–Litovsk highway from Svyatoshino, timed to coincide with a simultaneous assault from the south, on his right flank, from the direction of the village of Demiyovka.

So, in accordance with Toropets' plan, Petlyura's regiments were moving across from the left to the right flank, and to the sound of cracking whips and accordion music, with a sergeant at the head of each troop marched the four squadrons of Kozyr-Leshko's regiment of horse.

'Hurrah!' echoed the woods around Bely Hai, 'Hurrah!'

Leaving Bely Hai, they crossed the railroad line by a wooden bridge and from there they caught their first glimpse of the City. It lay in the distance, still warm from sleep, wrapped in a vapor that was half mist, half smoke. Rising in his stirrups Kozyr stared through his Zeiss field-glasses at the innumerable roofs of many-storey houses and the domes of the ancient cathedral of Saint Sophia.

Fighting was already in progress on Kozyr's right. From a mile or so away came the boom of gunfire and the stutter of machine-guns; waves of Petlyura's infantry were advancing on Post-Volynsk as the noticeably thinner and more ragged lines of the motley White Guard infantry, shattered by the heavy enemy fire, were retreating from the village.

*

The City. A heavy, lowering sky. A street corner. A few suburban bungalows, a scattering of army greatcoats.

'I've just heard – people are saying they've made an agreement with Petlyura to allow all Russian-manned units to keep their arms and to go and join Denikin on the Don. . . .'

'Well? So what?'

A rumbling burst of gunfire. Then a machine-gun started to bark.

A cadet's voice, full of bewilderment and despair:

'But then that means we must cease resistance, doesn't it?'

Wearily, another cadet's voice:

'God alone knows . . .'

*

Colonel Shchetkin had been missing from his headquarters since early morning, for the simple reason that the headquarters no longer existed. Shchetkin's headquarters had already withdrawn to the vicinity of the railroad station on the night of the fourteenth and had spent the night in the Rose of Stamboul Hotel, right alongside the telegraph office. The field-telephone still squealed occasionally in Shchetkin's room, but towards dawn it grew silent. At daybreak two of Colonel Shchetkin's aides vanished without trace. An hour later, after searching furiously for something in his trunks and tearing certain papers into shreds, Shchetkin himself left the squalid little Rose of Stamboul, although no longer wearing his regulation greatcoat and shoulder straps. He was dressed in a civilian fur coat and trilby hat, which he had suddenly and mysteriously acquired.

Taking a cab a block away from the 'Rose', Shchetkin the civilian drove to Lipki, where he arrived at a small but cosy and well furnished apartment, rang the bell, kissed the buxom golden-haired woman who opened the door and retired with her to the secluded bedroom. The blonde woman's eyes widened with terror as he whispered to her face:

'It's all over! God, I'm exhausted . . .' With which Colonel Shchetkin sank down on to the bed and fell asleep after a cup of black coffee prepared by the loving hands of the lady with golden hair.

*

The cadets of the 1st Infantry Detachment knew nothing of this. This was a pity, for if they had known, it might have roused their imagination and instead of cowering under shrapnel fire at Post-Volynsk they might have set off for that comfortable apartment in Lipki, dragged out the sleepy Colonel Shchetkin and hanged him from the lamp-post right opposite the blonde creature's apartment.

They would have done well to do so, but they did not because they knew nothing and understood nothing. Indeed, no one in the City understood anything and it would probably be a long time before they did.

A few rather subdued steel-helmeted Germans could still be seen around the City, and for all anyone knew the foxy Hetman with his carefully trimmed moustaches (that morning only very few people yet knew of the wounding of the mysterious Major von Schratt) was still there, as were his excellency Prince Belorukov and General Kartuzov, busy forming detachments for the defense of the Mother of Russian Cities (nobody yet knew that they had run away that morning). In fact the City was ominously deserted. The name 'Petlyura' still aroused fury in the City and that day's issue of the *News* was full of jokes at Petlyura's expense, made by corrupt refugee journalists from St Petersburg; uniformed cadets were still walking around the City, yet out in the suburbs people could already hear the whistling sound of Petlyura's motley cavalry troops cracking their whips as his lancers crossed from the left to the right flank at an easy gallop. If the cavalry is only three miles out of town, people asked, what hope can there be for the Hetman? And it's his blood they're out for ... Perhaps the Germans will back him up? But in that case why were the tin-hatted Germans grinning and doing nothing as they stood on Fastov station and watched trainload after trainload of Petlyura's troops being brought up to the assault? Perhaps an agreement has been made with Petlyura to let his troops occupy the City peacefully? But if so, why the hell are the White officers' guns still shooting at Petlyura?

The fact was that no one in the City knew what was happening on that fourteenth of December.

The field-telephones still rang in the headquarters, but less and less often ...

Rrring ...

'What's happening? ...'

Rrring ...

'Send more ammunition to Colonel Stepanov ...'

'Colonel Ivanov ...'

'... Antonov ...'

'... Stratonov! ...'

'We should pull out and join Denikin on the Don ... things don't seem to be working out here ...'

'To hell with those swine at headquarters ...'

'. . . to the Don . . .'

By noon the telephones had almost stopped ringing altogether. There would be occasional bursts of firing in the City's outskirts, then they would die down. . . . But even at noon, despite the sound of gunfire, life in the City still kept up a semblance of normality. The shops were open and still doing business. Crowds of people were streaming along the sidewalks, doors slammed, and the streetcars still rumbled through the streets.

It was at midday that the sudden cheerful stutter of a machine-gun was heard coming from Pechorsk. The Pechorsk hills echoed to the staccato rattle and carried the sound to the center of the City. Hey, that was pretty near! . . . What's going on? Passers-by stopped and began to sniff the air, and suddenly the crowds on the sidewalks thinned out.

What was that? Who is it?

Drrrrrrrrrrrrrrat-tat-ta-ta. Drrrrrrrat-ta-ta. Ta. Ta.

'Who is it?'

'Who? Don't you know? It's Colonel Bolbotun.'

So much for the story that Bolbotun had turned his coat and deserted Petlyura.

*

Bored with trying to execute the complex manoeuvers devised by Colonel Toropets' general-staff mind, Bolbotun had decided that events needed a little speeding up. His mounted troops were freezing as they waited beyond the cemetery due south of the City, a stone's throw away from the majestic snowbound Dnieper. Bolbotun was frozen too. He suddenly raised his cane in the air and his regiment of horse began moving off in threes, swung on to the road and advanced towards the flat ground bordering the outskirts of the City. Here Bolbotun encountered no resistance. The noise of six of his machine-guns echoed around the garden suburb of Nizhnyaya Telichka. In a trice Bolbotun had cut across the line of the railroad and stopped a passenger train which had passed the switches across the railroad bridge, carrying a fresh load of Muscovites and Petersburgers with their elegant women and fluffy lap-dogs. The passengers were terrified, but Bolbotun had no time to waste on lap-dogs. The frightened crews of some empty freight trains were switched from the Freight Depot on to the Passenger Station, with much hooting of switching engines, while Bolbotun brought down an unexpected hail of bullets on the roofs of the houses in Svyatotroitzkaya Street. On and on went Bolbotun, on into the City, unhindered as far as the Military Academy, sending out mounted reconnaissance patrols down every side street as he went. He was only checked at the colonnaded building of the Nicholas I Military Academy, where he was met by a machine-gun and a ragged burst of rifle-fire from a handful of troops. A cossack, Butsenko, was killed in the leading troop of Bolbotun's forward squadron, five others were wounded and two horses were hit in the legs. Bolbotun's progress was checked. He had the impression that he was faced by forces of untold strength, whereas in reality the detachment which greeted the blue-capped colonel consisted of thirty cadets, four officers and one machine-gun.

The order was given and Bolbotun's troopers deployed at the gallop, dismounted, took cover and began an exchange of shots with the cadets. Pechorsk filled with the sound of gunfire which echoed from wall to wall and the district around Millionnaya Street seethed with action like a boiling tea-kettle.

Bolbotun's advance produced an immediate reaction in the center of the City, as steel shutters came crashing down on Elisavetinskaya, Vinogradnaya and Levashovskaya streets and all the gay shop-fronts turned sightless and blank. The sidewalks emptied at once and became eerily resonant. Janitors stealthily shut doors and gateways. The advance was also reflected in another way – the field-telephones in the defense headquarters fell silent one by one.

An outlying artillery troop calls up battery headquarters. What the hell's going on, they're not answering! An infantry detachment rings through to the garrison commander's headquarters and manages to get something done, but then the voice at headquarters mutters something nonsensical.

'Are your officers wearing badges of rank?'

'Well, so what?'

Rrrring . . .

'Send a detachment to Pechorsk immediately!'

'What's happening?'

And the sound of one name crept all over town: Bolbotun, Bolbotun, Bolbotun. . . .

How did people know that it was Bolbotun and not someone else? It was a mystery, but they knew. Perhaps they knew because from noon onward a number of men in overcoats with lambskin collars began mingling with the passers-by and the usual riff-raff of City idlers, and as they strolled about these men eavesdropped and watched. They stared after cadets, refugees and officers with long, insolent stares. And they whispered:

'Bolbotun's coming.'

And they whispered it without the least regret. On the contrary, their eyes showed that they were delighted, and the stuttering rattle of machine-gun fire round the hills of Pechorsk echoed their news.

Rumors flew like wildfire:

'Bolbotun is the Grand Duke Mikhail Alexandrovich.'

'No he isn't: Bolbotun is the Grand Duke Nikolai Nikolaevich.'

'Bolbotun is simply Bolbotun.'

'There'll be a pogrom against the Jews.'

'No there won't: The troops are wearing red ribbons in their caps.'

'Better go home.'

'Bolbotun's against Petlyura.'

'You're wrong – he's on the Bolsheviks' side.'

'Wrong again: he's for the Tsar, only without the officers.'

'Is it true the Hetman ran away?'

'Is it true . . . Is it true . . . Is it true . . . Is it true . . .?'

*

A reconnaissance troop of Bolbotun's force, led by Sergeant Galanba, was trotting down the deserted Millionnaya Street.

Then, if you can believe it, a front door opened and out of it, straight towards the troop of five lancers, ran none other than Yakov Grigorievich Feldman, the well-known army contractor. Had he gone mad, running out into the streets at a time like this? He certainly looked crazy. His sealskin fur hat had slipped down on to the back of his neck, his overcoat was undone and he was staring wildly around him.

Yakov Grigorievich Feldman had reason to look crazy. As soon as the firing had begun at the Military Academy, there came a groan from his wife's bedroom. Another groan, and then silence.

'Oi, weh', said Yakov Grigorievich as he heard the groan. He looked out of the window and decided that the situation looked very bad indeed. Nothing but empty streets and gunfire.

There came another groan, louder this time, which cut Yakov Grigorievich to the heart. His stooping old mother put her head round the bedroom door and shrieked:

'Yasha! D'you hear? She's started!'

All Yakov Grigorievich's thoughts turned in one direction – to the little house on the corner of Millionnaya Street with its familiar, rusting sign with gold lettering:

E. T. Shadurskaya
Registered Midwife

It was dangerous enough on Millionnaya Street, even though it was not a main thoroughfare, as they were firing along it from Pechorskaya Square towards the upper part of town.

If only he could just hop across . . . If only. . . . His hat on the back of his head, terror in his eyes, Yakov Grigorievich started to creep along close to the wall.

'Halt! Where d'you think you're going?'

Sergeant Galanba turned around in the saddle. Feldman's face turned purple, his eyes swivelling as he saw that the lancers wore the green cockades of Petlyura's Ukrainian cavalry.

'I'm a peaceful citizen, sir. My wife's just going to have a baby. I have to fetch the midwife.'

'The midwife, eh? Then why are you skulking along like that? Eh? You filthy little yid?'

'Sir. I. . . .'

Like a snake the sergeant's whip curled around his fur collar and his neck. Hellish pain. Feldman screamed. His colour changed from purple to white and he had a vision of his wife's face.

'Identity papers!'

Feldman pulled out his wallet, opened it, took out the first piece of paper that came to hand and then he shuddered as he suddenly remembered . . . Oh my God, what have I done? Why did he have to choose that piece of paper? But how could he be expected to remember, when he has just run out of doors, when his wife is in labor? Woe to Feldman! In a flash Sergeant Galanba snatched the document. Just a thin scrap of paper with a rubber stamp on it, but it spelled death for Feldman:

> The Bearer of this pass, Mr Y. G. Feldman, is hereby permitted freely to enter and leave the City on official business in connection with supplying the armored-car units of the City garrison. He is also permitted to move freely about the City after 12 o'clock midnight.
> Signed: Chief of Supply Services
> *Illarionov*, Major-General
> Executive Officer
> *Leshchinsky*, 1st Lieutenant.

Feldman had supplied General Kartuzov with tallow and vaseline for greasing the garrison's weapons.

Oh God, work a miracle!

'Sergeant, sir, that's the wrong document . . . May I . . .'

'No, it's the right one', said Sergeant Galanba, grinning diabolically. 'Don't worry, we're literate, we can read it for ourselves.'

Oh God, work a miracle. Eleven thousand roubles . . . Take it all. Only let me live! Let me! Shma-isroël!

There was no miracle. At least Feldman was lucky and died an easy death. Sergeant Galanba had no time to spare, so he simply swung his sabre and took off Feldman's head at one blow.

Nine

HAVING lost seven cossacks killed, nine wounded, and seven horses, Colonel Bolbotun had advanced a quarter of a mile from Pechorskaya Square, as far as Reznikovskaya Street, where he was halted again. It was here that the retreating detachment of cadets acquired some reinforcements, which included an armored car. Like a clumsy gray tortoise capped by a revolving turret it lumbered along Moskovskaya Street and with a noise like the rustling of dry leaves fired three rounds from its three-inch gun. Bolbotun immediately galloped up to take charge, the horses were led off down a side street, his regiment deployed on foot and took cover after pulling back a short way towards Pechorskaya Square and began a desultory exchange of fire. The armored tortoise blocked off Moskovskaya Street and fired an occasional shell, backed up by a thin rattle of rifle-fire from the intersection of Suvorovskaya Street. There in the snow lay the troops which had fallen back from Pechorsk under Bolbotun's fire, along with their reinforcements, which had been called up like this:

'Rrrring . . .'

'First Detachment headquarters?'

'Yes.'

'Send two companies of officers to Pechorsk.'

'Right away . . .'

The squad that reached Pechorsk consisted of fourteen officers, four cadets, one student and one actor from the Studio Theater.

*

One undermanned detachment, alas, was not enough. Even when reinforced by an armored car, of which there should have been no less than four. And it can be stated with certainty that if the other three armored cars had shown up, Colonel Bolbotun would have been forced to evacuate Pechorsk. But they did not appear.

This happened because no less a person than the celebrated Lieutenant Mikhail Shpolyansky, who had been personally decorated with the St George's Cross by Alexander Kerensky in May 1917, was appointed to command one of the four excellent vehicles which comprised the Hetman's armored car troop.

Mikhail Shpolyansky was dark and clean-shaven, except for a pair of velvet sideburns, and he looked exactly like Eugene Onegin. Shpolyansky made himself known throughout the City as soon as he arrived there from St Petersburg. He made a reputation as an excellent reader of his own verse at the poetry club known as The Ashes, also as an excellent organiser of his fellow-poets and as chairman of the school of poetry known as The Magnetic Triolet. Not only was Mikhail Shpolyansky an unrivalled orator and could drive any sort of vehicle, civilian or military, but he also kept a ballerina from the Opera Theater and another lady whose name Shpolyansky, like the perfect gentleman that he was, revealed to no one. He also had a great deal of money, which he disbursed in generous loans to the members of The Magnetic Triolet. He drank white wine, played chemin-de-fer, bought a picture called *Venetian Girl Bathing*; at night-time he lived on the Kreshchatik, in the mornings he lived in the Café Bilbocquet, in the afternoon in his comfortable room in the Hotel Continental, in the evening at The Ashes, whilst he devoted the small hours to a scholarly work on 'The Intuitive in Gogol'.

The Hetman's City perished three hours earlier than it should have done because on the evening of December 2nd 1918, in The Ashes club, Mikhail Shpolyansky announced the following to Stepanov, Sheiyer, Slonykh and Cheremshin (the leading lights of The Magnetic Triolet):

'They're all swine – the Hetman, and Petlyura too. But Petlyura's worse, because he's an anti-Semite as well. But that's not the real trouble. The fact is I'm bored, because it's so long since I threw any bombs.'

After dinner at The Ashes (paid for by Shpolyansky) all the members of The Magnetic Triolet plus a fifth man, slightly drunk and wearing a mohair overcoat, left with Shpolyansky, who was dressed in an expensive fur coat with a beaver collar, and a fur hat. Shpolyansky knew a little about his fifth companion – firstly, that he was syphilitic; secondly, that he wrote atheistic poetry which Shpolyansky with his better literary connections arranged to have published in one of the Moscow literary magazines; and thirdly that the man, whose name was Rusakov, was the son of a librarian.

The man with syphilis was weeping all over his mohair coat under the electric street lighting on the Kreshchatik and saying, as he buried his face in the beaver-fur lapels of Shpolyansky's coat:

'Shpolyansky, you are the strongest man in this whole city, which is rotting away just as I am. You're such a good fellow that one can even forgive you for looking so disgustingly like Eugene Onegin! Listen Shpolyansky . . . it's positively indecent to look like Onegin. Somehow you're *too* healthy . . . But you lack that spark of ambition which could make you the really outstanding personality of our day . . . Here am I rotting to death, and proud of it . . . You're too healthy, but you're strong, strong as a steel spike, so you ought to thrust your way upwards to the top! Look, like this . . .'

And Rusakov showed him how to do it. Clasping the lamp-post he started to wind his way up it, making himself as long and thin as a grass-snake. A bevy of prostitutes walked by dressed in green, red, black and white hats, pretty as dolls, and called out cheerfully:

'Hey, had a couple too many? How about it, darling?'

The sound of gunfire was very far away and Shpolyansky really did look like Onegin in the lamp-lit snow.

'Go to bed', he said to the syphilitic acrobat, turning his head away slightly so that the man should not cough over him. 'Go on.' He gave the mohair coat a push with the tips of his fingers. As his black fur gloves touched the coat, the other man's eyes were quite glassy. The two men parted. Shpolyansky called a cab, told the driver: 'Malo-Provalnaya', and drove away, as mohair staggered home to Podol.

*

That night in Podol, in his room in the librarian's apartment, the owner of the mohair coat stood naked to the waist in front of a mirror, holding a lighted candle in his hand. Diabolical fear flickered in his eyes, his hands were shaking, and as he talked his lips quivered like a child's.

'Oh my God, my God, my God . . . It's horrible . . . That evening! I'm so unhappy. Sheyer was there with me too, yet he's all right, he didn't catch this infection because he's a lucky man. Maybe I should go and kill that girl who gave it to me. But what's the point? Can anybody tell me – what would be the point? Oh Lord, Lord . . . I'm twenty-four and I might have . . . Another fifteen years' time, perhaps less, and the pupils of my eyes will have changed colour, my legs will have rotted, then the lapse into mad idiotic babbling and then – I shall be a rotten, sodden corpse.'

The thin naked torso was reflected in the dusty mirror, the candle guttered in his upraised hand and there was a faint blotchy rash on his chest. Tears poured uncontrollably down the sick man's cheeks, and his body shook and twitched.

'I ought to shoot myself. But I haven't the strength – why should I lie to you, oh my God? Why should I lie to my own reflection?'

From the drawer of a small, delicate, ladies' writing-desk he took out a thin book printed on horrible gray paper. On the cover was printed in red letters:

FANTOMISTS – FUTURISTS

Verses by:

M. SHPOLYANSKY

B. FRIEDMAN

V. SHARKEVICH

I. RUSAKOV

Moscow, 1918.

The wretched man opened the book at page thirteen and read the familiar lines:

Ivan Rusakov

DIVINE RAVINE
Heaven's above –
They say.
And there in heaven,
Deep in a vaporous
Ravine,
Like a shaggy old bear
Licking his paws,
Lurks the daddy of us all –
God.
Time to shoot the hairy old
Contrary old
Bear
In his lair:
Shoot God.
When the shooting starts
Use my words as bullets,
Crimson with hate.

'A-a-a-ah', moaned the syphilitic creature, grinding his teeth in pain. 'Oh, God', he muttered in unbearable agony.

Suddenly, his face contorting, he spat on the page of verse and threw the book to the floor, then knelt down, and crossing himself rapidly with trembling fingers, bowing until his cold forehead touched the dusty parquet floor, he began to pray, raising his eyes to the black, joyless window:

'Oh Lord, forgive me and have mercy on me for having written those foul words. But why art Thou so cruel? Why? I know Thou hast punished me – oh how terribly Thou hast punished me! Look at my skin. I swear to Thee by all that is holy, all that is dear to me in this world, by the memory of my dead mother – I have been punished enough. I believe in Thee! I believe with all my soul, my body, with every fibre of my brain. I believe and I seek refuge only in Thee, for there is no one in the whole world who can help me. I have no one to turn to save Thee. Forgive me, and grant that I be healed! Forgive me for denying Thee: if there were no God I should now be no more than a lousy dog, a creature without hope. But I am a man and my only strength is in Thee and I may turn to Thee in prayer in my hour of need. And I believe Thou wilt hear my prayer, Thou wilt pardon me and cure me. Cure me, oh Lord, forget about the filth I have written in a moment of insanity, when I was drunk on brandy and drugged with cocaine. Do not let me rot, and I swear I shall become a man again. Fortify me, save me from cocaine, save me from weakness of spirit and save me from Mikhail Shpolyansky!'

The candle flickered out as the room grew cold and dawn drew near. The rash spread over the sick man's skin, but his soul was much relieved.

*

Mikhail Shpolyansky spent the rest of the night on Malo-Provalnaya Street, in a large room with a low ceiling and an old portrait from which, slightly dulled by a patina of time, shone a pair of the epaulettes worn in the 1840's. Coatless, wearing nothing but a white lawn shirt and a handsome black vest with a deeply cut front, Shpolyansky was seated on a narrow little footstool and talking to a woman with a pale, matte complexion:

'Julia, I have finally made up my mind. I'm going to join the Hetman's armored-car troop.'

Her body still vibrating with Shpolyansky's passionate love-making, wrapping herself in a fluffy gray shawl, the woman replied:

'I'm sorry, but I don't understand what you're doing and I never have.'

Shpolyansky lifted a brandy glass from the little table in front of his stool, sniffed the aromatic cognac, gulped it down and said:

'Don't bother to try.'

*

Two days later Mikhail Shpolyansky was transformed. Instead of a top hat he now wore an officer's forage cap, instead of his civilian greatcoat a short combat jerkin with crumpled field-service shoulder straps, gauntlets on his hands and gaiters on his legs. He was covered from head to foot in engine oil (even his face) and, for some reason, in soot. On December 9th two of the armored cars went into action with remarkable success. They rumbled about fifteen miles out along the highway and no sooner had they loosed off a few of their three-inch shells and fired a few bursts from their machine-guns than Petlyura's advance troops broke and ran. The successful armored-car detachment commander, a pink-faced enthusiast called Ensign Strashkevich, swore to Shpolyansky that if all four cars were sent into action at once they could defend the whole City unaided. This conversation took place on the evening of the ninth, and at twilight on the eleventh Shpolyansky, who was officer of the day, gathered Shchur and Kopylov and their crews – two gunlayers, two drivers and a mechanic – around him and said:

'You must realise that the chief question is: are we doing right to stand by this Hetman? In his hands this armored-car troop is nothing but an expensive and dangerous toy, which he is using to impose a régime of the blackest reaction. Who knows, maybe this clash between Petlyura and the Hetman is historically inevitable and that out of it will emerge a third historic force which may be fated to win.'

His listeners greatly admired Shpolyansky for the same quality that his fellow-poets admired him at The Ashes – his exceptional eloquence.

'What is this third force?' asked Kopylov, puffing at a cheroot.

Shchur, a stocky, intelligent man with fair hair, gave a knowing wink and nodded towards the north-east. The men went on talking for a little longer and then dispersed. On the evening of December 12th Shpolyansky held another talk with the same tight little group behind the vehicle sheds. What was said then will never be known, but it is common knowledge that on the thirteenth, when Shchur, Kopylov and the snub-nosed Petrukhin were on duty, Mikhail Shpolyansky appeared at the sheds carrying a package wrapped in paper. Shchur, who was mounting guard, let him pass into the vehicle compound, lit by the feeble red glow from a lantern. With a somewhat insolent wink at the package, Kopylov asked:

'Sugar?'

'Uh-huh', replied Shpolyansky.

A small, flickering lantern was lit in the shed and Shpolyansky and a mechanic busied themselves with preparing the armored cars for tomorrow's action. The cause was a piece of paper in the possession of Captain Pleshko, the troop commander: '. . . dispatch all four vehicles on mission to Pechorsk district at o8oo hours, December 14th.'

The joint efforts of Shpolyansky and the mechanic to prepare the armored cars for action produced somewhat strange results. By the morning of the fourteenth, three vehicles which on the day before had been in perfect running order (the fourth was already in action, commanded by Strashkevich) were immobilised as completely as though stricken with paralysis. No one could understand what was wrong with them. Some kind of dirt was lodged in the carburettor jets, and however hard they tried to blow them through with tyre-pumps, nothing did any good. That morning they labored hopelessly by lantern-light to fix them. Looking pale, Captain Pleshko glanced around him like a hunted wolf and demanded the mechanic. It was then that the affair turned to disaster. The mechanic had disappeared. It transpired that against all rules and regulations troop headquarters had no record of his address. A rumor started that the mechanic had suddenly fallen sick with typhus. This was at eight a.m.; at eight thirty Captain Pleshko received a second blow. Ensign Shpolyansky, after finishing the maintenance work on the vehicles at four o'clock that morning, had set off for Pechorsk on a motor-cycle driven by Shchur and had not come back. Shchur had returned alone to tell a sad tale. They had driven as far as Telichka, where Shchur had tried in vain to dissuade Ensign Shpolyansky from doing anything rash. Shpolyansky, notorious throughout the troop for his exceptional bravery, had left Shchur, and taking a carbine and a hand-grenade had set off alone in the darkness to reconnoitre the area around the railroad tracks. Shchur heard shots, and was convinced that an enemy patrol, which had pushed forward as far as Telichka, had found Shpolyansky and had inevitably shot him in an unequal fight. Shchur had waited two hours for Shpolyansky, even though the ensign had ordered him to wait no longer than an hour before returning to troop headquarters, in order not to expose himself and his government-issue motor-cycle to excessive risk.

On hearing Shchur's story, Captain Pleshko turned even paler. The field-telephones from the headquarters of the Hetman and General Kartuzov were ringing ceaselessly with urgent demands for the armored cars to go into action. At nine o'clock the keen, pink-faced young Ensign Strashkevich reported back from duty and some of the color in his cheeks transferred itself to the face of the troop commander. Strashkevich drove his car off to Pechorsk where, as has been described, it successfully blocked Suvorovskaya Street against the advancing Bolbotun.

By ten o'clock Pleshko was looking paler than ever. Two of his gunlayers, two drivers and one machine-gunner had vanished without trace. Every effort to get the three armored cars moving proved fruitless. Shchur, who had been ordered out on a mission by Captain Pleshko, never returned. Needless to say his motor-cycle disappeared with him. The voices on the field-telephones grew threatening. The brighter grew the morning, the stranger the things that happened at the armored-car troop: two gunners, Duvan and Maltsev also vanished, together with a couple more machine-gunners. The vehicles themselves took on a forlorn, abandoned look as they stood there like three useless juggernauts, surrounded by a litter of spanners, jacks and buckets.

By noon the troop commander, Captain Pleshko himself, had disappeared too.

Ten

FOR three days a confused series of moves and counter-moves, some made in the heat of battle, others connected with the arrival of dispatch-riders and the squealing of field-telephones, had kept Colonel Nai-Turs' unit on the move among the snowdrifts and roadblocks around the City in a circuit that extended from Red Tavern to Serebryanka in the south and to Post-Volynsk in the south-west. By the evening of December 14th the unit was back in the City at a deserted barracks, half of whose window-panes were smashed in.

The unit commanded by Colonel Nai-Turs was a strange one. Everyone who saw it was surprised to find it so well equipped with the footgear – felt boots – so essential to winter campaigning. At its formation three days before the unit numbered a hundred and fifty cadets and three second lieutenants.

In early December an officer had reported to Major-General Blokhin, commander of the 1st Infantry Detachment. The officer was a cavalryman of medium height, dark, clean-shaven with a gloomy expression, wearing the shoulder-straps of a colonel of hussars, who had introduced himself as Colonel Nai-Turs, formerly squadron commander of No. 2 Squadron of the former Regiment of Belgrade Hussars. Nai-Turs' sad eyes had a look in them which had the effect of making anyone who met this limping colonel, with his grubby St George's Cross ribbon sewn to a worn enlisted-man's greatcoat, pay absolute attention to whatever the colonel had to say. After only a short conversation with Nai-Turs, Major-General Blokhin entrusted him with the formation of the Detachment's second infantry company, with orders that the task was to be completed by December 13th. Astoundingly, the job of mustering and organising the company was finished by December 10th, and on that date Colonel Nai-Turs, by nature a man of few words, reported briefly to Major-General Blokhin, distracted on all sides by the insistent buzz of telephones from headquarters, that he, Nai-Turs, and his cadets were now ready for combat, but only on the essential condition that his entire squad were issued with fur caps and felt boots for a hundred and fifty men, without which he, Nai-Turs, considered military action as totally unfeasible. When the laconic colonel had made his report, General Blokhin gladly signed him a requisition order to the supply section but warned Nai-Turs that with this piece of paper he was unlikely to obtain the equipment he wanted in less than a week's time, because both headquarters and the supply section were hotbeds of inefficiency, red tape and disorganisation.

Colonel Nai-Turs took the piece of paper and, with his habitual twitch of the left half of his clipped moustache, marched out of General Blokhin's office without turning his head to left or right (he could not turn it, because as the result of a wound his neck was rigid and whenever he needed to look sideways he was obliged to turn his whole body). At the Detachment's quarters on Lvov Street Nai-Turs collected ten cadets (armed, for some reason) and a couple of two-wheeled carts, and set off with them to the supply section.

At the supply section, housed in a most elegant villa on Kudryavskaya Boulevard, in a comfortable office adorned with a map of Russia and a portrait of the ex-Empress Alexandra left over from the days of the wartime Red Cross, Colonel Nai-Turs was received by Lieutenant-General Makushin, a short unnaturally flushed little man dressed in a gray tunic, a clean shirt peeping over its high collar, which gave him an extraordinary resemblance to Milyutin, Alexander II's war minister.

Flinging down a telephone receiver, the general enquired in a childish voice that sounded like a toy whistle:

'Well, colonel, what can I do for you?'

'Unit about to go into action', replied Nai-Turs laconically. 'Please issue felt boots and fur hats for two hundred men immediately.'

'H'mm', said the general, pursing his lips and crumpling Nai's requisition order in his hand. 'Can't issue them today I'm afraid, colonel. Today we're taking an inventory of stores issued to all units. Come back again in about three days time. And in any case I can't issue a quantity like two hundred.'

He placed the requisition order at the top of a pile under a paperweight in the shape of a naked woman.

'I said felt boots', Nai-Turs rejoined in a monotone, squinting down at the toes of his boots.

'What?' the general asked in perplexity, staring at the colonel with amazement.

'Give me those felt boots at once.'

'What are you talking about?' The general's eyes nearly popped out of their sockets.

Nai-Turs turned to the door, opened it a little and shouted out into the passage:

'Hey there, platoon!'

The general turned a grayish white, his glance swivelling from Nai-Turs' face to the telephone receiver, from there to the ikon of the Virgin hanging in the corner, then back to the colonel's face.

There was a clinking and shuffling in the passage, then several red-banded cadets' forage caps of the Alexeyevsky Military Academy and some black bayonets appeared in the doorway. The general started to rise from his padded armchair.

'I have never heard anything like it . . . this is mutiny . . .'

'Please countersign the requisition order, sir', said Nai. 'We haven't much time, we move off in an hour. The enemy is right outside the city.'

'What on earth do you mean by . . .'

'Come on, hurry up', said Nai-Turs in a funereal voice.

Hunching his head between his shoulders, his eyes starting from his head, the general pulled the piece of paper from under the naked woman and with a shaking hand, spattering ink, scrawled in the corner: 'Issue the above stores.'

Nai-Turs took the paper, tucked it into the cuff of his sleeve, turned to his cadets and gave the order:

'Load up the felt boots. Look sharp.'

Clumping and rattling, the cadets began to file out. As Nai waited for them to leave, the general, purple in the face, said to him:

'I shall immediately ring the commander-in-chief's headquarters and raise the matter of having you court-martialled. This is unheard-of . . .'

'Go ahead and try', replied Nai-Turs, swallowing his saliva. 'Just try. Just out of interest, go ahead and try.' He put his hand on the revolver-butt peeping out of his unbuttoned holster. The general's face turned blotchy and he was silent.

'If you pick up that telephone, you silly old man,' Nai suddenly said in a gentle voice, 'I'll give you a hole in your head from this Colt and that will be the end of you.'

The general sat back in his chair. The folds of his neck were still purple, but his face was gray. Nai-Turs turned around and went out.

For a few more minutes the general sat motionless in his arm-chair, then crossed himself towards the ikon, picked up the tele-phone receiver, raised it to his ear, heard the operator's muffled yet intimate voice . . . suddenly he had a vision of the grim eyes of that laconic colonel of hussars, replaced the receiver and looked out of the window. He watched the cadets in the yard busily carrying gray bundles of felt boots out of the black doorway of the stores, where the quartermaster-sergeant could be seen holding a piece of paper and staring at it in utter amazement. Nai-Turs was standing with his legs astraddle beside a two-wheeled cart and gazing at it. Weakly the general picked up the morning paper from the table, unfolded it and read on the front page:

On the river Irpen clashes occurred with enemy patrols which were attempting to penetrate towards Svyatoshino . . .

He threw down the newspaper and said aloud:

'Cursed be the day and the hour when I took on this . . .'

The door opened and the assistant chief of the supply section entered, a captain who looked like a tailless skunk. He stared meaningly at the folds of purpling flesh above the general's collar and said:

'Permission to report, sir.'

'See here, Vladimir Fyodorich', the general interrupted him, sighing and gazing about him in obvious distress, 'I haven't been feeling too good . . . a slight attack of . . . er . . . and I'm going home now. Will you please take over?'

'Yes, sir,' replied the skunk, staring curiously at the general. 'But what am I to do? The Fourth Detachment and the engineers are asking for felt boots. Did you just give an order to issue two hundred pairs?'

'Yes. Yes, I did,' replied the general in his piercing voice. 'Yes, I gave the order. I personally allowed it. Theirs is an exceptional case! They are just going into combat. Yes, I gave the order!'

A look of curiosity flashed in the skunk's eyes.

'Our total stock is only four hundred pairs . . .'

'What can I do?' squeaked the general. 'Do you think I can produce them like rabbits out of a hat? Eh? Issue them to anybody who asks for them!'

Five minutes later General Makushin was taken home in a cab.

＊

During the night of December 13th to the 14th the moribund barracks on Brest-Litovsk Street came to life. In the vast, dirty barrack-rooms the lights came on again, after some cadets had spent most of the day stringing wires from the barracks and connecting them up to the streetlamps. A hundred and fifty rifles stood neatly piled in threes, whilst the cadets slept sprawled fully dressed on dirty cots. At a rickety wooden table, strewn with crusts of bread, mess-tins with the remains of congealed stew, cartridge pouches and ammunition clips, sat Nai-Turs unfolding a large colored plan of the City. A small kitchen oil lamp threw a blob of light on to the maze-like map, on which the Dnieper was shown like a huge, branching, blue tree.

By about two o'clock in the morning sleep began to overtake Nai-Turs. His nose twitched, and occasionally his head nodded towards the map as though he wanted to study some detail more closely. Finally he called out in a low voice:

'Cadet!'

'Yes, sir', came the reply from the doorway, and with a rustle of felt boots a cadet approached the table.

'I'm going to turn in now', said Nai. 'If a signal comes through by telephone, waken Lieutenant Zharov and depending on its contents he will decide whether to waken me or not.'

There were no telephone messages and headquarters did not disturb Nai-Turs' detachment that night. At dawn a squad armed with three machine-guns and three two-wheeled carts set out along the road leading out of the City, past rows of dead, shuttered suburban houses . . .

Nai-Turs deployed his unit around the Polytechnic School, where he waited until later in the morning when a cadet arrived on a two-wheeler and handed him a pencilled signal from headquarters: 'Guard the Southern Highway at Polytechnic and engage the enemy on sight.'

Nai-Turs had his first view of the enemy at three o'clock in the afternoon when far away to the left a large force of cavalry appeared, advancing across an abandoned, snow-covered army training-ground. This was Colonel Kozyr-Leshko, who in accordance with Colonel Toropets' plan was attempting to penetrate to the center of the City along the Southern Highway. In reality Kozyr-Leshko, who had met no resistance of any kind until reaching the approaches to the Polytechnic, was not so much attacking as making a victorious entry into the City, knowing full well that his regiment was being followed by another squadron of Colonel Gosnenko's cossacks, by two regiments of the Blue Division, a regiment of South Ukrainian riflemen and six batteries of guns. As the leading horsemen began trotting across the training-ground, shrapnel shells, like a flock of cranes, began bursting in the heavy, snow-laden sky. The scattered riders closed up into a single ribbon-like file and then, as the main body came in sight, the regiment spread itself across the whole width of the highway and bore down on Nai-Turs' position. A rattle of rifle-bolts ran along the lines of

149

cadets, Nai pulled out a whistle, blew a piercing blast and shouted:

'At cavalry ahead! Rapid . . . fire!'

Sparks flickered along the gray ranks as the cadets loosed off their first volley at Kozyr. Three times after that the enemy batteries sent a salvo of shrapnel raining down against the walls of the Polytechnic and three times more, with an answering rattle of musketry Nai-Turs' detachment fired back. The distant black lines of horsemen broke up, melted away and vanished from the highway.

It was then that something odd seemed to happen to Nai-Turs. No one in the detachment had ever seen him frightened, but at that moment the cadets had the impression that Nai either saw, heard or sensed something in the distance . . . in short, Nai gave the order to withdraw toward the City. One platoon remained behind to give covering fire to the other platoons as they pulled out, then withdrew in turn when the main body was safely ensconced in a new position. Like this they leap-frogged back for two miles, throwing themselves down and making the broad highway echo with rifle-fire at regular intervals until they reached the intersection where Brest-Litovsk Street crossed the highway, the place where they had spent the previous night. The crossroads were quite dead, not a soul was to be seen on the streets.

Here Nai-Turs selected three cadets and gave them their orders:

'Run back to Polevaya Street and find out where our units are and what's become of them. If you come across any carts, two-wheelers or other means of transportation retreating in a dis-organised fashion, seize them. In case of resistance threaten the use of firearms, and if that doesn't work, use them . . .'

As the cadets ran off and disappeared, the detachment suddenly came under fire from ahead. At first it was wild and sporadic, mostly hitting the roofs and walls of houses, but then it grew heavier and one cadet collapsed face down into the snow and colored it red with blood. Then with a groan another cadet fell away from the machine-gun he was manning. Nai's ranks scattered and began a steady rapid fire at the dark bunches of enemy troops which now seemed to be rising out of the ground in front of them as if by magic. The wounded cadets were lifted up, white bandages unwound. Nai's cheekbones stood out like two swellings. He kept turning his body more and more often in order to keep a watch out on his flanks, and by now his expression betrayed his anxiety and impatience for the return of his three messengers. Finally they arrived, panting like foxhounds. Nai looked up sharply and his face darkened. The first cadet ran up to him, stood to attention and reported, gasping:

'Sir, there are none of our units to be found at Shulyavka – or anywhere else, either.' He paused for breath. 'We could hear machine-gun fire to our rear and just now enemy cavalry was sighted, apparently about to march into the City . . .'

The rest of what the cadet had to say was drowned by a deafening shriek from Nai's whistle.

The three two-wheeled carts galloped noisily off down Brest-Litovsk Street, then turned down Fonarnaya Street, bouncing along over the rutted snow and carrying with them the two wounded cadets, fifteen cadets unscathed and armed, and all three of the detachment's machine-guns. This was as big a load as they could carry. Then Nai-Turs faced his ranks and in a clipped, hoarse voice issued them with orders they had never expected to hear . . .

In the shabby but warmly heated building of the former barracks on Lvov Street the third company of the 1st Infantry Detachment, consisting of twenty-eight cadets, was growing restless. The interesting fact about this uneasy party was that the person in charge of it was none other than Nikolka Turbin. The company commander, Staff Captain Bezrukov and two ensigns, his platoon commanders, had left for headquarters that morning and had not come back. Nikolka, who as a corporal was now the senior ranker in the company, wandered around the barrack rooms, now and again walking up to the telephone and looking at it.

So it went on until three in the afternoon, by which time the cadets were growing demoralised from a mixture of nerves and boredom. At three o'clock the field-telephone squealed:

'Is that Number 3 Company?'

'Yes.'

'Put the company commander on the line.'

'Who's speaking?'

'Headquarters.'

'The company commander isn't back yet.'

'Who's that speaking?'

'Corporal Turbin.'

'Are you the senior rank?'

'Yes, sir.'

'Get your squad out on to the street and into action right away.'

So Nikolka mustered his twenty-eight men and led them out along the street.

*

Until two o'clock that afternoon Alexei Turbin slept the sleep of the dead. He woke up as though someone had thrown water over him, glanced at the little clock on his bedside chair, saw that it was ten minutes to two, got up and began stumbling about the room. Alexei pulled on his felt boots, fumbled in his pockets, in his haste forgetting first one thing and then another – matches, cigarette case, handkerchief, automatic pistol and two magazines, – buttoned his greatcoat, then remembered something else, but hesitated – it seemed shameful and cowardly, but he did it nonetheless: out of his desk drawer he took his civilian doctor's identity card. He turned it around in his hands, decided to take it with him, but just at that moment Elena called him and he forgot it, leaving it lying on the desk.

'Listen, Elena', said Alexei, nervously tightening and buckling his belt. An uncomfortable premonition had taken hold of him and he was tormented by the thought that apart from Anyuta, Elena would be alone in their big, empty apartment. 'There's nothing for it – I must go. Let's hope nothing happens to me. The mortar regiment is unlikely to operate outside the City limits and I will probably be in some safe place. Pray God to protect Nikolka. I heard this morning that the situation was a little more serious, but I'm sure we will beat off Petlyura. Goodbye, my dear . . .'

Alone in the empty sitting-room Elena walked from the piano, where the open music of *Faust* had still not been tidied away, towards the doorway of Alexei's study. The parquet floor creaked beneath her feet and she felt very unhappy.

*

At the corner of his own street and Vladimirskaya Street Alexei Turbin hailed a cab. The driver agreed to take him, but puffing gloomily, named a monstrous price and it was obvious that he would settle for no less. Grinding his teeth, Alexei Turbin climbed into the sled and set off towards the museum. There was frost in the air.

Alexei was extremely worried. As he drove, he caught the sound of machine-gun fire that seemed to be coming from the direction of the Polytechnic Institute and moving in the direction of the railroad station. Alexei wondered what it might mean (he had slept through Bolbotun's afternoon incursion into the City) and he turned his head from side to side to stare at the passing sidewalks. There were plenty of people about, although there was an air of unease and confusion.

'St . . . Stop . . .' said a drunken voice.

'What does this mean?' asked Alexei Turbin angrily.

The driver pulled so hard on the reins that Alexei almost fell forward on to his knees. A man with a very red face stood swaying beside the cab's shafts, holding the reins and making his way towards the passenger seats. A crumpled pair of lieutenant's shoulder-straps glittered on a short, fur-collared greatcoat. From two feet away Alexei was nauseated by a powerful reek of moonshine vodka and onion. With his free hand the lieutenant was waving a rifle.

'Turn . . . turn around', said the red-faced drunk. 'Ta . . . take on a passenger.' For some reason the word 'passenger' struck the man as funny and he began to giggle.

'What does this mean?' Alexei repeated angrily. 'Can't you see who I am? I'm reporting for duty. Kindly let go of this cab! Drive on!'

'No, don't drive on . . .' said red-face in a threatening voice.

153

Only then, blinking and peering, did he recognise the Medical Corps badges on Alexei's shoulder straps. 'Ah, doctor, we can travel together . . . let me get in . . .'

'We're not going the same way . . . Drive on!'

'Now see here . . .'

'Drive on!'

The cabman, head hunched between his shoulders, was about to crack his whip and move off, but thought better of it. Turning round, he glared at the drunk with a mixture of anger and fear. However, red-face let go the reins of his own accord. He had just noticed an empty cab, which was about to drive away but did not have time to do so before the drunken officer raised his rifle in both hands and threatened the driver. The terrified cabman froze to the spot and red-face staggered over to him, swaying and hiccuping.

'I knew I shouldn't have taken you on, even for five hundred', Alexei's driver muttered angrily, lashing the rump of his ancient nag. 'What's in it for me if all I get's a bullet in my back?'

Turbin sat glumly silent.

'The swine . . . it's louts like him who give the whole White cause a bad name', he thought furiously.

The crossroads by the opera house was alive with activity. Right in the middle of the streetcar tracks stood a machine-gun, manned by two small, frozen cadets, one in a black civilian over-coat with ear-muffs, the other in a gray army greatcoat. Passers-by, clustered in heaps along the sidewalk like flies, stared curiously at the machine-gun. By the corner druggist, just in sight of the museum, Alexei paid off his cab.

'Make it a bit more, your honor', said the cab-driver, grimly insistent. 'If I'd known what it was going to be like! Look what's going on here.'

'Shut up. That's all you're getting.'

'They've even dragged kids into it now . . .' said a woman's voice.

Only then did Alexei notice the crowd of armed men around the museum, swaying and growing thicker. Machine-guns could be vaguely seen on the sidewalk among the long-skirted greatcoats.

Just then came the furious drumming of a machine-gun from the Pcchorsk direction.

'What the hell's going on?' Alexei wondered confusedly as he quickened his pace to cross the intersection toward the museum.

'Surely I'm not too late? . . . What a disgrace. . . . They might think I've run away . . .'

Officers, cadets, and a few soldiers were crowding and running excitedly around the gigantic portico of the museum and the broken gates at the side of the building which led on to the parade-ground in front of the Alexander I High School. The enormous glass panes of the main doors shuddered constantly and the doors groaned under the pressure of the milling horde of armed men. Exct ed, unkempt cadets were crowding into the side door of the circular white museum building, whose pediment was embellished with the words:

'For the Edification of the Russian People'.

'Oh God!' exclaimed Alexei involuntarily. 'The regiment has already left.'

The mortars grinned silently at Alexei, standing idle and abandoned in the same place as they had been the day before.

'I don't understand . . . what does this mean?'

Without knowing why, Alexei ran across the parade-ground to the mortars. They grew larger as he moved towards the line of grim, gaping muzzles. As he reached the first mortar at the end of the row, Alexei stopped and froze: its breech mechanism was missing. At a fast trot he cut back across the parade ground and jumped over the railings into the street. Here the mob was even thicker, many voices were shouting at once, bayonets were bobbing up and down above the heads of the crowd.

'We must wait for orders from General Kartuzov!' shouted a piercing, excited voice. A lieutenant crossed in front of Alexei, who noticed that he was carrying a saddle with dangling stirrups.

'I'm supposed to hand this over to the Polish Legion.'

'Where is the Polish Legion?'

'God only knows!'

'Everybody into the museum! Into the museum!'

'To the Don!'

The lieutenant suddenly stopped and threw his saddle down on to the sidewalk.

'To hell with it! Who cares now, anyway – it's all over', he screamed furiously. 'Christ, those bastards at headquarters.'

He turned aside, threatening someone with a raised fist.

'Disaster . . . I see now . . . But how awful – our mortar regiment must have gone into action as infantry. Yes, of course. Presumably Petlyura attacked unexpectedly. There were no horses, so they were deployed as riflemen, without the mortars . . . Oh my God. . . . I must get back to Madame Anjou . . . Maybe I'll be able to find out there. . . . Surely someone will have stayed behind. . . .'

Alexei forced his way out of the milling crowd and ran, oblivious to everything else, back to the opera house. A dry gust of wind was blowing across the asphalted path around the opera house and flapping the edge of a half-torn poster on the theatre wall beside a dim, unlit side entrance. Carmen. Carmen . . .

At last, Madame Anjou. The artillery badges were gone from the window, the only light was the dull, flickering reflection of something burning. Was the shop on fire? The door rattled as Alexei pushed, but did not open. He knocked urgently. Knocked again. A gray figure emerged indistinctly on the far side of the glass doorway, opened it and Alexei tumbled into the shop and glanced hurriedly at the unknown figure. The person was wearing a black student's greatcoat, on his head was a moth-eaten civilian cap with ear-flaps, pulled down low over his forehead. The face was oddly familiar, but somehow altered and disfigured. The stove was roaring angrily, consuming sheets of some kind of paper. The entire floor was strewn with paper. Having let Alexei in, the figure left him without a word of explanation, walked away and squatted down on his haunches by the stove, which sent a livid red glow flickering over his face.

'Malyshev? Yes, it's Colonel Malyshev.' Alexei at last recognised the man.

The colonel no longer had a moustache. Instead, there was a bluish, clean-shaven strip across his upper lip.

Spreading his arms wide, Malyshev gathered up sheets of paper from the floor and rammed them into the stove.

'What's happened? Is it all over?' Alexei asked dully.

'Yes', was the colonel's laconic reply. He jumped up, ran over to a desk, carefully looked it over, pulled out the drawers one by one and banged them shut, bent down again, picked up the last heap of documents from the floor and shoved them into the stove. Only then did he turn to Alexei Turbin and added in an ironically calm voice: 'We've done our bit – and now that's that!' He reached into an inside pocket, hurriedly pulled out a wallet, checked the documents in it, tore up a few of them criss-cross and threw them on the fire. As he did so Alexei stared at him. He no longer bore any resemblance to Colonel Malyshev. The man facing Alexei was simply a rather fat student, an amateur actor with slightly puffy red lips.

'Doctor – you're not still wearing your shoulder-straps?' Malyshev pointed at Alexei's shoulders. 'Take them off at once. What are you doing here? Where have you come from? Don't you know what's happened?'

'I'm late, sir, I'm afraid . . .' Alexei began.

Malyshev gave a cheerful smile. Then the smile suddenly vanished from his face, he shook his head anxiously and apologetically and said:

'Oh God, of course – it's my fault . . . I told you to report at this time. . . . Obviously you stayed at home all day and haven't heard . . . Well, no time to go into all that. There's only one thing for you to do now – remove your shoulder-straps, get out of here and hide.'

'What's happened? For God's sake tell me what's happened?'

'What's happened?' Malyshev echoed his question with ironical jocularity. 'What's happened is that Petlyura's in the City. He's reached Pechorsk and may even be on the Kreshchatik now for all I know. The City's taken.' Suddenly Malyshev ground his teeth, squinted furiously and began unexpectedly to talk like the old Malyshev, not at all like an amateur actor. 'Headquarters betrayed us. We should have given up and run this morning. Fortunately I had some reliable friends at headquarters and I found out the true state of affairs last night, so was able to disband the mortar regiment in time. This is no time for reflection, doctor – take off your badges!'

'. . . but over there, at the museum, they don't know all this and they still think. . . .'

Malyshev's face darkened.

'None of my business', he retorted bitterly. 'Not my affair. Nothing concerns me any longer. I was there a short while ago and I shouted myself hoarse warning them and begging them to disperse. I can't do any more. I've saved all my own men, and prevented them from being slaughtered. I saved them from a shameful end!' Malyshev suddenly began shouting hysterically. Obviously his control over some powerful and heavily-suppressed emotion had snapped and he could no longer restrain himself. 'Generals – huh!' He clenched his fists and made threatening gestures. His face had turned purple.

Just then a machine-gun began to chatter at the end of the street and the bullets seemed to be hitting the large house next door.

Malyshev stopped short, and was silent.

'This is it, doctor. Goodbye. Run for your life! Only not out on to the street. Go out there, by the back door, and then through the back yards. That way's still safe. And hurry.'

Malyshev shook the appalled Alexei Turbin by the hand, turned sharply about and ran off through the dark opening behind a partition. The machine-gun outside stopped firing and the shop was silent except for the crackling of paper in the stove. Although he suddenly felt very lonely, and despite Malyshev's urgent warnings, Alexei found himself walking slowly and with a curious languor towards the door. He rattled the handle, let fall the latch and returned to the stove. He acted slowly, his limbs oddly unwilling, his mind numb and muddled. The fire was dying down, the flames in the mouth of the stove sinking to a dull red glow and the shop suddenly grew much darker. In the graying, flickering shadows the shelves on the walls seemed to be gently moving up and down. As he stared around them Alexei noticed dully that

Madame Anjou's establishment still smelled of perfume. Faintly and softly, but it could still be smelled.

The thoughts in Alexei's mind fused into a formless jumble and for some time he gazed completely senselessly towards the place where the newly-shaven colonel had disappeared. Then, helped by the silence, his tangled thinking began slowly to unravel. The most important strand emerged clearly: Petlyura was here. 'Peturrá, Peturrá', Alexei repeated softly to himself and smiled, not knowing why. He walked over to a mirror on the wall, dimmed by a film of dust like a sheet of fine taffeta.

The paper had all burned out and the last little red tongue of flame danced to and fro for a while, then expired at the bottom of the stove. It was now almost quite dark.

'Petlyura, it's crazy. . . . Fact is, this country's completely ruined now', muttered Alexei in the twilit shop. Then, coming to his senses: 'Why am I standing around like this and dreaming? Suppose they start breaking into this place?'

He jumped into action, as Malyshev had done before leaving and began tearing off his shoulder-straps. The threads gave a little crackling sound as they ripped away and he was left holding two silver-braided rectangles from his tunic and two green ones from his greatcoat. Alexei looked at them, turned them over in his hands, was about to stuff them into his pocket as souvenirs but thought better of it as being too dangerous, and decided to burn them. There was no lack of combustible material, even though Malyshev had burned all the documents. Alexei scooped up a whole sheaf of silk clippings from the floor, pushed them into the stove and lit them. Once more weird shapes began flickering around the walls and the floor, and for a while longer Madame Anjou's premises brightened fitfully. In the flames the silver rectangles curled, broke out in bubbles, scorched and then turned to ash . . .

The next most urgent problem now arose in Alexei's mind – what should he do about the door? Should he leave the latch down, or should he open it? Suppose one of the volunteers, like Alexei himself, ran here and then found it shut and there was nowhere to shelter? He unfastened the latch. Then came another searing thought: his doctor's identity card. He searched one pocket, then another – no trace of it. Hell, of course. He had left it at home. What a disgrace. Suppose he were stopped and caught. He was wearing a gray army greatcoat. If they questioned him and he said he was a doctor, how could he prove it? Damn his own carelessness.

'Hurry' whispered a voice inside him.

Without stopping to reflect any longer Alexei rushed to the back of the shop by the way Malyshev had gone, through a narrow door into a dim passage, and from there out by the back door into a yard.

Eleven

OBEDIENT to the voice on the telephone, Corporal Nikolka Turbin led his twenty-eight cadets across the City by the route laid down in his order, which ended at a completely deserted crossroads. Although it was lifeless, it was extremely noisy. All around – in the sky, echoing from roofs and walls – came the chatter of machine-gun fire.

Obviously the enemy was supposed to be here because it was the final point on their route indicated by the voice on the telephone. But so far there was no enemy to be seen and Nikolka was slightly put out – what should he do next? His cadets, a little pale but as brave as their commander, lay down in a firing line on the snowy street and Ivashin the machine-gunner squatted down behind his machine-gun at the kerb of the sidewalk. Raising their heads, the cadets peered dutifully ahead, wondering what exactly was supposed to happen.

Their leader was thinking so hard that his face grew pinched and turned slightly pale. He was worried, firstly, by the complete absence at the crossroads of what the voice on the telephone had led him to expect. Nikolka was supposed to have found here a company of the 3rd Detachment, which he was to 'reinforce'. Of the company there was not a trace. Secondly, Nikolka was worried by the fact that now and again the rattle of machine-gun fire could be heard not only ahead of him but also to his left and even, he noticed uneasily, slightly to his rear. Thirdly, he was afraid of showing fear and he constantly asked himself: 'Am I afraid?' 'No I'm not', replied a brave voice in his head, and Nikolka felt so proud that he was turning out to be quite brave that he went even paler. His pride led him on to the thought that if he were killed he would be buried to the strains of a military band. It would be a simple but moving funeral: the open white silk-lined coffin would move slowly through the streets and in the coffin would lie Corporal Turbin, with a noble expression on his wax-like features. It was a pity that they didn't give medals any longer, because then he would have worn the ribbon and cross of the St George's Cross around his neck. Old women would be standing at the cemetery gates. 'Who are they burying, my dear?' 'Young Corporal Turbin.' 'Ah, the poor, handsome lad . . .' And the music. It is good to die in battle, they say. He hoped he would feel no pain. Thoughts of military funerals, bands and medal ribbons proved a slight distraction from the uncomfortable business of waiting for an enemy who obviously had no intention of obeying the voice on the telephone and had no intention of appearing.

'We shall wait here', Nikolka said to his cadets, trying to make his voice sound more confident, although without much success because the whole situation was somehow vaguely wrong, and stupidly so. Where was the other company? Where was the enemy? Wasn't it odd that sounds of firing should be coming from behind them?

*

So Nikolka and his little force waited. Suddenly, from the street that crossed theirs at the intersection, which led from Brest-Litovsk Street, came a burst of fire, and a detachment of gray-clad figures poured down the street at a furious pace. They were heading straight for Nikolka's cadets and were carrying rifles.

'Surrounded?' flashed through Nikolka's mind, as he tried wildly to think what order he was supposed to give; but a moment later he caught sight of the gold-braided shoulder-straps on several of the running men and realised that they were friendly.

Tall, well-built, sweating with exertion, the group of cadets from the Constantine Military Academy halted, turned around, dropped on one knee and fired two volleys down the street from whence they had come. Then they jumped up and ran across the intersection past Nikolka's detachment, throwing away their rifles as they went. On the way they tore off their shoulder-straps, cartridge pouches and belts and threw them down on the wheel-rutted snow. As he drew level with Nikolka, one gray-coated, heavily-built cadet turned his head towards Nikolka's detachment and shouted, gasping for breath:

'Come on, run for it! Every man for himself!'

Uncertain and confused, Nikolka's cadets began to stand up. Nikolka was completely stupefied, but a moment later he pulled himself together, thinking in a flash: 'This is the moment to be a hero.' He shouted in his piercing voice:

'Don't dare to stand up! Obey my orders!' At the same time he was wondering numbly: 'What are they doing?'

Once over the intersection and rid of their weapons, the fleeing cadets – twenty of them – scattered down Fonarny Street, some of them taking hasty refuge behind the first big gateway. The great iron gates shut with a hideous crash and the sound of their boots could be heard ringing under the arch leading into the courtyard. A second bunch disappeared through the next gateway. The remaining five, quickening their pace, ran off down Fonarny Street and vanished into the distance.

Finally the last runaway appeared at the crossroads, wearing faded gold shoulder-straps. Nikolka's keen eyes recognised him at a glance as the commanding officer of the second squad of the 1st Detachment, Colonel Nai-Turs.

'Colonel!' Nikolka called out to him, puzzled and at the same time relieved. 'Your cadets are running away in a panic.'

Then the most amazing thing happened. Nai-Turs ran across the trampled snow of the intersection. The skirts of his greatcoat were looped back on both sides, like the uniform of the French infantry;

his battered cap had fallen back on the nape of his neck and was only held on by the chinstrap. In his right hand was a revolver, whose open holster flapped against his hip. Unshaven for several days, his bristly face looked grim and his eyes were set in a squint. He was now close enough for Nikolka to make out the zig-zag braid of a hussar regiment on his shoulder-straps. Nai-Turs ran right up to Nikolka and with a sweeping movement of his free left hand he tore off from Nikolka's shoulders first the left and then the right shoulder-strap. Most of the threads tore free, although the right strap pulled a lump of the greatcoat material with it. Nikolka felt such a pull that he was instantly aware of the remarkable strength of Nai-Turs' hands. The force of the movement made Nikolka lose his balance and he sat down on something that gave way beneath him with a shriek: it was Ivashin the machine-gunner. Confusion broke out and all that Nikolka could see were the astonished faces of the cadets milling around above him. Nikolka was only saved from going out of his mind at that moment by the violence and urgency of Nai-Turs' behaviour. Turning to face the disorganised squad he roared an order in a strange, cracked voice. Nikolka had an irrational feeling that a voice like that must be audible for miles, if not over the whole City.

'Cadets! Listen and do as I tell you: rip off your shoulder-straps, your cap-badges and cartridge pouches and throw your rifles away! Go through the backyards from Fonarny Street towards Razezhaya Street and make your way to Podol! To Podol, you hear? Tear up your identity papers as you go, hide, disperse and tell anyone you meet on the way to do the same!'

Then, brandishing his revolver, Nai-Turs added in a voice like a cavalry trumpet:

'Down Fonarny Street – don't go any other way! Get away home and lie low! The fight's over! On the double!'

For a few seconds the squad could not take it in, then the cadets' faces turned absolutely white. In front of Nikolka, Ivashin ripped off his shoulder-straps, his cartridge pouches flew over the snow and his rifle crashed down against the kerbstone. Half a minute later the crossroads was littered with belts, cartridge pouches and someone's torn cap, and the cadets were disappearing into the gateways that would lead through backyards into Razyezhaya Street.

With a flourish Nai-Turs thrust his revolver back into its holster, strode over to the machine-gun, squatted down behind it, swung its muzzle round in the direction from which he had come and adjusted the belt with his left hand. From his squatting position he turned, looked up at Nikolka and roared in fury:

'Are you deaf? Run!'

Nikolka felt a strange wave of drunken ecstasy surge up from his stomach and for a moment his mouth went dry.

'I don't want to, colonel', he replied in a blurred voice, squatted down, picked up the ammunition belt and began to feed it into the machine-gun.

Far away, from where the remnants of Nai-Turs' squad had come running, several mounted men pranced into view. Their horses seemed to be dancing beneath them as though playing some game, and the gray blades of their sabres could just be seen. Nai-Turs cocked the bolt, the machine-gun spat out a few rounds, stopped, spat again and then gave a long burst. Instantly bullets whined and ricocheted off the roofs of houses to right and left down the street. A few more mounted figures joined the first ones, but suddenly one of them was thrown sideways towards the window of a house, another's horse reared on its hind legs to an astonishing height, almost to the level of the second-floor windows, and several more riders disappeared altogether. Then all the others vanished as though they had been swallowed up by the earth.

Nai-Turs dismantled the breech-block, and as he shook his fist at the sky his eyes blazed and he shouted:

'Those swine at headquarters – run away and leave children to fight . . . !'

He turned to Nikolka and cried in a voice that struck Nikolka like the sound of a muted cavalry trumpet:

'Run for it, you stupid boy! Run for it, I say!'

He looked behind him to make sure that all the cadets had

already disappeared, then peered down the road from the inter-section to the distant street running parallel to Brest-Litovsk Street and shouted in pain and anger:

'Ah, hell!'

Nikolka followed his glance and saw that far away on Kadetskaya Street, among the bare snow-covered trees of the avenue, lines of gray-clad men had begun to materialise and were dropping to the ground. Then a sign above Nai-Turs and Nikolka's heads on the corner house of Fonarny Street, reading:

Berta Yakovlevna Printz
Dental Surgeon

swung with a clang and a window-pane shattered somewhere in the courtyard of the same house. Nikolka noticed some lumps of plaster bouncing and jumping on the sidewalk. Nikolka looked questioningly at Colonel Nai-Turs for an explanation of these lines of gray men and the fragments of plaster. Colonel Nai-Turs' response was very strange. He hopped up on one leg, waved the other as though executing a waltz step, and an inappropriate grimace, like a dancer's fixed smile, twisted his features. The next moment Colonel Nai-Turs was lying at Nikolka's feet. A black fog settled on Nikolka's brain. He squatted down and with a dry, tearless sob tried to lift the colonel by the shoulders. In doing so he noticed that blood was seeping through the colonel's left sleeve and his eyes were staring up into the sky.

'Colonel, sir. . . .'

'Corporal', said Nai-Turs. As he spoke blood trickled from his mouth on to his chin and his voice came in droplets, thinning and weakening at each word. 'Stop playing the hero, I'm dying. . . . Make for Malo-Provalnaya Street. . . .'

Having said all that he wanted to say, his lower jaw began to shake. It twitched convulsively three times as though Nai-Turs was being strangled, then stopped, and the colonel suddenly became as heavy as a sack of flour.

'Is this how people die?' thought Nikolka. 'It can't be. He was alive only a moment ago. Dying in battle isn't so terrible. I wonder why they haven't hit me. . . .'

Dent . . .

Surg . . .

rattled and swung above his head a second time and somewhere another pane of glass broke. 'Perhaps he's just fainted?' thought Nikolka stupidly and started to drag the colonel away. But he could not lift him. 'Am I frightened?' Nikolka asked himself, and knew that he was terrified. 'Why? Why?' Nikolka wondered and realised at once that he was frightened because he was alone and helpless and that if Colonel Nai-Turs had been on his feet at that moment there would have been nothing to fear . . . But Colonel Nai-Turs was completely motionless, was no longer issuing orders, was oblivious to the fact that a large red puddle was spreading alongside his sleeve, that broken and pulverised stucco was lying scattered in a crazy pattern along the nearby wall. Nikolka was frightened because he was utterly alone. . . . And loneliness drove Nikolka from the crossroads. He crawled away on his stomach, pulling himself along first with his hands, then with his right elbow as his left hand was grasping Nai-Turs' revolver. Real fear overcame him when he was a mere two paces away from the street corner. If they hit me in the leg now, he thought, I won't be able to crawl any further, Petlyura's men will come riding up and hack me to bits with their sabres. How terrible to be lying helpless as they slash at you . . . I'll fire at them, provided there's any ammunition left in this revolver . . . Just another step away . . . pull myself, pull . . . again . . . and Nikolka was around the corner and in Fonarny Street.

'How amazing, absolutely amazing, that I wasn't hit. A sheer miracle. God must have worked a miracle', thought Nikolka as he stood up. 'Now I've actually seen a miracle. Notre Dame de Paris. Victor Hugo. I wonder what's happened to Elena? And Alexei? Obviously the order to tear off our shoulder-straps means disaster.'

Nikolka jumped up, smothered from head to foot in snow, thrust the revolver into his greatcoat pocket and ran off down the street. Finding the first pair of gates on his right hand still open, Nikolka ran through the echoing gateway and found himself in a dim, squalid courtyard with sheds of red brick along its right-hand side and a pile of firewood on the left. Assuming that the back door leading to the adjoining courtyard was in the middle, he ran towards it across the slippery snow and bumped heavily into a man in a sheepskin jerkin. The man had a red beard and little eyes that were quite plainly dripping with hatred. Snub-nosed, with a sheepskin hat on his head, he was a caricature of the Emperor Nero. As though playfully the man clasped Nikolka in a hug with his left arm and with his right seized Nikolka's left arm and started to twist it behind his back. For a few seconds Nikolka was completely dazed. 'God, he's caught me and he hates me . . . He's one of Petlyura's men . . .'

'Ah, you swine!' croaked the red-bearded man, breathing hard. 'Where d'you think you're going, eh?' Then he suddenly howled: 'Got you, cadet! Think we wouldn't recognise you just because you've torn off your shoulder-straps? Now I've got you!'

Nikolka was seized with fury. He sat down backwards so hard that the half-belt at the back of his greatcoat snapped, rolled over and freed himself from red-beard's grasp with a superhuman effort. For a second he lost sight of him as they were back to back, then he swung around and saw him. The man with the red beard was not only unarmed, he was not even a soldier, merely a janitor. A pall of rage like a red blanket floated across Nikolka's eyes and immediately gave way to a sensation of complete self-confidence. Cold frosty air was sucked into Nikolka's mouth as he bared his teeth like a wolf-cub. Determined to kill the beast if only the chamber were loaded, he wrenched the revolver out of his pocket. His voice, when he spoke, was so strange and terrible that he did not recognise it.

'I'll kill you, you bastard!' Nikolka hissed as he fumbled with the Colt, realising as he did so that he had forgotten how to fire it. Seeing that Nikolka was armed the janitor fell to his knees in terror and despair and whined, changing miraculously from a Nero into a snake:

'Ah, your honor! Oh sir . . .'

Nikolka would still have fired, but the revolver refused to work. 'Hell! It's unloaded!' flashed through Nikolka's mind. Shaking and covering his face with his hand the janitor fell back from his knees on to his haunches and let out a sickening howl that infuriated Nikolka. At a loss how to close that gaping maw framed in its copper-red beard, and desperate because the revolver would not fire, Nikolka leaped upon the janitor like a fighting cock and smashed the butt into the man's teeth, running the risk of shooting himself as he did so. Nikolka's fury instantly drained away. The janitor leaped to his feet and ran away out of the gateway through which Nikolka had come. Crazed with fear, the janitor could no longer howl, and just ran, stumbling and slipping on the icy ground. Once he looked round and Nikolka saw that half his beard was stained dark red. Then he vanished. Nikolka turned and ran past the sheds to the end of the yard where the back gate should have opened onto Razezhaya Street, but as he reached it he was overcome with despair. 'Done for. I'm too late. Caught. God, even my revolver's useless.' In vain he shook the enormous pad-locked bolt. There was nothing to be done. As soon as Nai-Turs' cadets had escaped through the courtyard the red-bearded janitor had obviously locked the gate giving on to Razezhaya Street and now Nikolka was faced by a completely insurmountable obstacle – an iron wall, smooth and solid from bottom to top. Nikolka turned around, glanced up at the lowering, overcast sky, and noticed a black fire-escape leading all the way up to the roof of the four-storey house. 'Maybe I could climb up there?' he wondered, and at that moment he had a sudden foolish recollection of a colored illustration in a book: Nat Pinkerton in a yellow jacket and a red mask climbing up just the same sort of fire-escape. 'Maybe Nat Pinkerton can do that in America . . . but suppose I climb up – what then? I'll sit up there on the roof and by that time the janitor will have called Petlyura's troops. He's bound to give me away. He won't forgive me for knocking his teeth in.'

And so it was. Through the open gateway into Fonarny Street Nikolka could hear the janitor's desperate shouts for help: 'In here! In here!' – and the sound of horses' hoofs. Nikolka realised that Petlyura's cavalry must have penetrated the City by a surprise move from the flank, and by now they were as far as Fonarny Street. That's why Nai-Turs had shouted his warning . . . There was no going back along Fonarny Street now.

All this flashed through his mind before he found himself, he knew not how, on top of the pile of firewood alongside a lean-to built against the wall of the neighbouring house. The ice-covered logs wobbled under his tread as Nikolka scrambled, fell down, tore his breeches, finally reached the top of the wall, looked over it and saw exactly the same kind of courtyard as the one he was in. It was so alike that he even expected to see another red-bearded janitor leap out at him in a sheepskin jerkin. But none did. Feeling a terrible wrench in the region of his stomach and kidneys, Nikolka dropped to the ground and at that very moment his revolver jerked in his hand and fired a deafening shot. After a moment's amazement Nikolka said to himself: 'Of course, the safety catch was on and the shock of my fall released it. I'm in luck.'

Hell. The gate on to Razezhaya Street was shut here too, and locked. That meant climbing over the wall again, but alas there was no convenient pile of firewood in this courtyard. He climbed on to a heap of broken bricks and, like a fly on a wall, started clambering up by sticking the toes of his boots into cracks so small that under normal circumstances a kopeck piece would not have fitted into them. With torn nails and bleeding fingers he clawed his way up the wall. As he lay atop it on his stomach he heard the janitor's voice and the deafening crack of a rifle-shot from the first courtyard. In this, the third courtyard, he caught a glimpse of a woman's face distorted with fear, which for a moment stared at him from a second-floor window and then immediately disappeared. Dropping down from the wall he chose a better spot to fall, landing in a snowdrift, but even so the shock jolted his spine and a searing pain shot through his skull. With his head buzzing and spots dancing before his eyes Nikolka picked himself up and made for the gate.

Oh joy! Although the gate was locked it presented no problem, being made of wrought iron open-work. Like a fireman Nikolka climbed up to the top, slid over, dropped down and found himself on Razezhaya Street. It was utterly deserted. 'Fifteen seconds' rest to get my breath back, no more, otherwise my heart will crack up', thought Nikolka, gulping down air into his burning lungs. 'Oh yes . . . my papers . . .' From his tunic pocket Nikolka pulled out a handful of grubby certificates and identity documents and tore them up, scattering the shreds like snowflakes. Behind him, from the direction of the crossroads where he had left Nai-Turs, he heard a burst of machine-gun fire, echoed by more machine-guns and rifle volleys from ahead, from the heart of the City. This is it. Fighting in the City centre. The City's captured. Disaster. Still panting, Nikolka brushed the snow from his clothes with both hands. Should he throw away the revolver? Nai-Turs' revolver? No, never. He might well succeed in slipping through. After all, Petlyura's men couldn't be everywhere at once.

Taking a deep breath, and aware that his legs were noticeably weaker and less able to obey him, Nikolka ran along the deserted Razezhaya Street and safely reached the next intersection, from which two streets branched off – Lubochitskaya Street leading to Podol and Lvovskaya Street which forked away to the right and to the centre of the City. Here he noticed a pool of blood alongside the kerbstone, an overturned cart, two abandoned rifles and a blue student's peaked cap. Nikolka threw away his own army-issue fur hat and put on the student's cap. It turned out to be too small and gave him the look of an untidy, raffish civilian – a high-school expellee with a limp. Nikolka peered cautiously around the corner and up Lvovskaya Street. At the far end of it he could just make out a scattering of mounted troops with blue badges on their fur hats. Petlyura. Some sort of a scuffle was in progress there, and stray shots were whistling through the air, so he turned and made off down Lubochitskaya Street. Here he saw his first sign of normal human life. A woman was running along the opposite sidewalk, her black feathered hat fallen to one side, holding a gray bag from which protruded an anguished rooster loudly squawking 'cock-adoodle-doo', or as it seemed to Nikolka 'pet-a-luu-ra'! Some carrots were falling out of a hole in the basket on the woman's left arm. She was weeping and moaning as she staggered along, hugging the wall. A well-dressed man rushed out of a doorway, crossed himself feverishly and shouted:

'Jesus Christ! Volodya, Volodya! Petlyura's coming!'

At the end of Lubochitskaya Street there were signs of more life as people scurried to and fro and disappeared indoors. Crazed with fear, a man in a black overcoat hammered at a gateway, thrust his stick between the bars and broke it with a violent crack.

Meanwhile time was flying by and twilight had already come. As Nikolka turned off Lubochitskaya Street and down Volsky Hill the electric street lamp on the corner was turned on and began to burn with a very faint hiss. The shutters clanged down on a shopfront, instantly hiding piles of gaily-colored cartons of soap powder. Turning the corner, a cabman overturned his sleigh into a snowdrift and lashed furiously at his miserable horse. Nikolka dashed past a four-storey apartment block with three walk-up entrances, in all three of which the doors were being constantly slammed as residents hustled inside. One of them, in a sealskin fur collar, ran out in front of Nikolka and yelled at the janitor:

'Ivan! Have you gone crazy? Shut the doors! Shut the front doors, man!'

One of the huge doors slammed shut and a piercing woman's voice could be heard on the darkened staircase shrieking:

'Petlyura! Petlyura's coming!'

The farther Nikolka ran towards the haven of Podol, as Nai-Turs had told him to, the greater became the bustle and confusion on the street, although there was less of a sense of fear and not everyone was going the same way as Nikolka. Some were even heading in the opposite direction.

At the very top of the hill leading down to Podol, there stepped out of the doorway of a gray stone building a solemn-looking young cadet wearing an army greatcoat and white shoulder-straps embroidered with a gold badge. The cadet had a snub nose the size of a button. Glancing boldly around him, he gripped the sling of a huge rifle slung across his back. Passers-by scurried by glancing up in terror at this armed cadet, and hurried on. As he stepped down on to the sidewalk the cadet stopped, cocked an ear to listen to the firing with the knowing look as of a trained military man, stuck his nose in the air and was about to stride off. Nikolka swerved aside sharply, planted himself across the sidewalk, pressed close to the cadet and said in a whisper:

'Get rid of that rifle and hide at once.'

The little cadet shuddered with fright and took a step back, but then took a more threatening grip on his rifle. With the ease born of experience Nikolka gently but firmly edged the boy backward, pushed him into a doorway and went on urgently:

'Hide, I tell you. I'm a cadet-officer. It's all up. Petlyura's taken the City.'

'What d'you mean – how can he have taken the City?' asked the cadet. His mouth hung open, showing a gap where a tooth was missing on the left side of his lower jaw.

'That's how', Nikolka answered, with a sweep of his arm in the direction of the Upper City, adding: 'D'you hear? Petlyura's cavalry are in the streets up there. I only just got away. Run home, hide that rifle and warn everybody.'

Dumbstruck, the cadet froze to the spot. There Nikolka left him, having no time to waste on people who were so dense.

In Podol there was less alarm, but considerable bustle and activity. Passers-by quickened their pace, often turning their heads to listen, whilst cooks and servant girls were frequently to be seen running indoors, hastily wrapping themselves in shawls. An unbroken drumming of machine-gun fire could now be heard coming from the Upper City, but on that twilit December 14th there was no more artillery fire to be heard from near or far.

Nikolka had a long way to go. As he crossed through Podol the twilight deepened and enveloped the frostbound streets. Swirling in the pools of light from the street-lamps, a heavy fall of snow began to muffle the sound of anxious, hurrying footsteps. Occasional lights twinkled through the fine network of snowflakes, a few shops and stores were still gaily lit, though many were closed and shuttered. The snowfall grew thicker. As Nikolka reached the bottom of his own street, the steep St Alexei's Hill, and started to climb up it, he noticed an incongruous scene outside the the doorway of No. 7: two little boys in gray knitted sweaters and woolen caps had just ridden down the hill on a sled. One of them, short and round as a rubber ball, covered with snow, was sitting on the sled and laughing. The other, who was older, thinner and serious-looking, was unravelling a knot in the rope. A youth was standing in the doorway and picking his nose. The noise of rifle fire grew more audible, breaking out from several directions at once.

'Vaska, did you see how I fell off and hit my bottom on the kerb!' shouted the youngest.

'Look at them, playing so peacefully', Nikolka thought with amazement. He turned to the youth and asked the youth in an amiable voice:

'Tell me, please, what's all the shooting going on up there?'

The young man removed his finger from his nose, thought for a moment and said in a nasal whine:

'It's our people, beating the hell out of the White officers.'

Nikolka scowled at him and instinctively fingered the revolver in his pocket. The older of the two boys chimed in angrily:

'They're getting even with the White officers. Serve 'em right. There's only eight hundred of them, the fools. Petlyura's got a million men.'

He turned and started to pull the sled away.

*

At the sound of Nikolka opening the front gate the cream-colored blind flew up in the dining-room window. The old clock ticked away, tonk-tank, tonk-tank . . .

'Has Alexei come back?' Nikolka asked Elena.

'No', she replied, and burst into tears.

The whole apartment was in darkness, except for a lamp in the kitchen where Anyuta, leaning her elbows on the table, sat and wept for Alexei Turbin. In Elena's bedroom logs flamed in the stove, light from the flames leaping behind the grate and dancing on the floor. Her eyes red from crying about Alexei, Elena sat on a stool, resting her cheek on her bunched fist, with Nikolka sprawling at her feet across the fiery red pattern cast on the floor.

Who was this Colonel Bolbotun? Earlier that day at the Shcheglovs some had been saying that he was none other than the Grand Duke Mikhail Alexandrovich. In the half darkness and the glow from the fire the mood was one of despair. What was the use of crying over Alexei? Crying did no good. He had obviously been killed – that was clear. The enemy took no prisoners. Since he had not come back it meant that he had been caught, along with his regiment, and he had been killed. The horror of it was that Petlyura, so it was said, commanded a force of eight hundred thousand picked men. We were fooled, sent to face certain death . . .

Where had that terrible army sprung from? Conjured up out of the freezing mist, the bitter air and the twilight . . . it was so sinister, mysterious . . .

Elena stood up and stretched out her arm.

'Curse the Germans. Curse them. If God does not punish them, then he is not a God of justice. They must surely be made to answer for this – they *must*. They are going to suffer as we have suffered. They will suffer, they will . . .'

She repeated the word 'will' like an imprecation. Her face and neck were flushed, her unseeing eyes were suffused with black hatred. Her shrieks reduced Nikolka to misery and despair.

'Mightn't he still be alive?' he asked gently. 'After all he is a doctor . . . Even if he had been caught they may not have killed him but only taken him prisoner.'

'They will eat cats, they will kill each other just as we have done,' said Elena in a loud voice, wagging a threatening finger at the stove.

'Rumors, rumors . . . They said Bolbotun's a grand duke – ridiculous. So's the story of Petlyura having a million men. Even eight hundred thousand is an exaggeration. Lies, confusion. The hard times are really starting now. Looks like Talberg was doing the right thing after all by getting out in time . . . Flames dancing on the floor. Once everything was so peaceful and the world was full of wonderful places. There never was such a hideous monster as that red-bearded janitor. They all hate us, of course, but he's like a mad dog. Tried to twist my arm behind my back.'

*

Outside, gunfire began again. Nikolka jumped up and ran to the window.

'Did you hear that? Did you? And that? It could be the Germans. Or maybe the Allies come to help us at last? Who is it? Petlyura wouldn't be shelling the City if he's already taken it.'

Elena folded her arms across her chest and said:

'It's no good, Nik, I'm not letting you go. I beg you not to go out. Don't be crazy.'

'I only wanted to go as far as the little square in front of St Andrew's church. I could look and listen from there. It overlooks the whole of Podol.'

'All right, go. If you feel like leaving me alone at a moment like this, then go.'

Nikolka looked embarrassed.

'Well, then I'll just go out into the yard and listen.'

'And I'll go with you.'

'But Lena, suppose Alexei comes back while we're both in the yard? We won't hear the front door bell out there.'

'No, we won't. And it'll be your fault.'

'Very well, Lena, I give you my word of honor I won't move a step outside the yard.'

'Word of honor?'

'Word of honor.'

'You won't go past the gate? You won't climb up the hill? You promise to stay in the yard?'

'I promise.'

'All right, go then.'

*

The City was swathed in the deep, deep snow of December 1918. Why were those unidentified guns firing at nine o'clock at night – and only for a quarter of an hour? The snow was melting on

Nikolka's collar, and he fought the temptation to climb up the snow-covered hillside. From the top he would be able to see not only Podol but part of the Upper City, the seminary, hundreds of rows of lights in big apartment houses, the hills of the city dotted with countless flickering lights. But no one should break his word of honor, or life becomes impossible. So Nikolka believed. At every distant menacing rumble he prayed: 'Please, God . . .'

Then the gunfire stopped.

'Those were our guns', Nikolka thought miserably. As he walked back from the gate he glanced in at the Shcheglovs' window. The white blind was rolled up and through the little window in their wing of the house he could see Maria Petrovna Shcheglov giving her little boy Peter his bath. Peter was sitting up naked in the tub and soundlessly crying because the soap was trickling into his eyes. Maria Petrovna squeezed out a sponge over Peter. There was some washing hanging on a line and Maria Petrovna's bulky shadow passed back and forth behind, occasionally bending down. Nikolka suddenly felt how warm and secure the Shcheglovs were and how cold he was in his unbuttoned greatcoat.

*

Deep in the snow, some five miles beyond the outskirts of the City to the north, in an abandoned watchman's hut completely buried in white snow sat a staff-captain. On the little table was a crust of bread, the case of a portable field-telephone and a small hurricane-lamp with a bulbous, sooty glass. The last embers were fading in the stove. The captain was a short man with a long sharp nose, and wearing a greatcoat with a large collar. With his left hand he squeezed and crumbled the crust of bread, whilst pressing the knob of the telephone with his right. But the telephone seemed to have died and gave no response.

For three miles around the captain there was nothing but darkness, blizzard and snowdrifts.

By the time another hour had passed the captain had abandoned the telephone. At about 9 p.m. he snorted and for some reason said aloud:

'I'm going mad. Really the right thing would be to shoot myself.' And as though in answer to him the telephone rang.

'Is that Number 6 Battery?' asked a distant voice.

'Yes, yes', the captain replied, wild with excitement.

The agitated, faraway voice, though muffled, sounded delighted:

'Open fire at once on the target area . . .' quacked the blurred voice down the line, '. . . with maximum fire-power . . .' the voice broke off. '. . . I have the impression . . .' At this the voice was again cut off.

'Yes, I'm listening', the captain screamed into the receiver, grinding his teeth in despair. There was a long pause.

'I can't open fire', the captain said into the mouthpiece, compelled to speak although well aware that he was talking into nothingness. 'All the gun crews and my three lieutenants have deserted. I'm the only man left in the battery. Pass the message on to Post-Volynsk.'

The captain sat for another hour, then went out. The snowstorm was blowing with great violence. The four grim, terrible field-guns were already half buried in snow and icicles had already begun to festoon their muzzles and breech-mechanisms. In the cold of the screaming, whirling snowstorm the captain fumbled like a blind man. Working entirely by feel, it was a long time before he was able to remove the first breech-block. He was about to throw it into the well behind the watchman's hut, but changed his mind and went into the hut. He went out three more times, until he had removed the four breech-blocks from all the guns and hidden them under a trap-door in the floor, where potatoes were stored. Then, having first put out the lamp, he went out into the darkness. He walked for about two hours, unseen and unseeing through the darkness until he reached the highway leading into the City, lit by a few faint sparse street lamps. Under the first of these lamps he was sabred to death by a party of pigtailed horsemen, who removed his boots and his watch.

The same voice came to life in the receiver of a telephone in a dug-out four miles to the west of the watchman's hut.

'Open fire at once on the target area. I have the impression that the enemy has passed between your position and ours and is making for the City.'

'Can you hear me? Can you hear me?' came the reply from the dugout. 'Ask headquarters . . .' He was cut off. Without listening, the voice quacked in reply:

'Harassing fire on cavalry in the target area . . .' The message stopped abruptly and finally.

Three officers and three cadets clambered out of the dugout with lanterns. The fourth officer and two cadets were already in the gun position, standing around a lantern which the storm was doing its best to put out. Five minutes later the guns began to jump and fire into the darkness. They filled the countryside for ten miles around with their terrible roar, which was heard at No. 13 St Alexei's Hill . . . Please God . . .

Prancing through the snow, a troop of cavalry leaped out of the dark beyond the lamplight and killed all the cadets and four of the officers. The battery commander, who had stayed by the telephone in the dugout, shot himself in the mouth.

The battery commander's last words were: 'Those swine at headquarters. It's enough to make one turn Bolshevik.'

*

That night Nikolka lit the lamp hanging from the ceiling in his room in the corner of the apartment; then with a penknife he carved on the door a large cross and an irregular inscription:

'Col. Turs. Dec. 14th. 1918. 2 p.m.'

He left out the 'Nai' from the colonel's name for security, in case Petlyura's men searched the apartment.

He did not want to sleep, in case he missed hearing the doorbell He knocked on the wall of Elena's room and said:

'Go to sleep – I'll stay awake.'

After which he at once fell asleep as though dead, lying fully dressed on his bed. Elena did not sleep until dawn and stayed listening in case the bell should ring. But the bell did not ring and there was no sign of their elder brother Alexei.

*

A tired, exhausted man needs sleep, and by eleven o'clock next morning Nikolka was still asleep despite the discomforts of sleeping in tight boots, a belt that dug into his lower ribs, a throttling collar and a nightmare that crouched over him with its claws dug into his chest.

Nikolka had fallen asleep flat on his back with his head on one side. His face had turned purple and a whistling snore came from his throat . . . There was a whistling snowstorm and a kind of damned web that seemed to envelop him from all sides. The main thing was to break through this web but the accursed thing grew and grew until it had reached up to his very face. For all he knew it could envelop him so completely that he might never get out, and he would be stifled. Beyond the web were great white plains of the purest snow. He had to struggle through to that snow, and quickly, because someone's voice had apparently just called out 'Nikolka!' Amazingly, some very lively kind of bird seemed to be caught in the net too, and was pecking and chirping to get out . . . Tik, tik, tikki, Tweet, Too-weet! 'Hell.' He couldn't see it, but it was twittering somewhere nearby. Someone else was bewailing their fate, and again came the other voice: 'Nicky! Nikolka!'

'Ugh!' Nikolka grunted as he tore the web apart and sat up in one movement, dishevelled, shaken, his belt-buckle twisted round to one side. His fair hair stood on end as though someone had been tousling it for a long time.

'Who? Who? Who is it?' asked Nikolka in horror, utterly confused.

'Who. Who, who, who, who's it? Who's it? Tweet, tweet!' the web replied and the mournful voice, quivering with suppressed tears, said:

'Yes, with her lover!'

Horrified, Nikolka backed against the wall and stared at the apparition. The apparition was wearing a brown tunic, riding-breeches of the same color and yellow-topped jockey's boots. Its dull, sad eyes stared from the deepest of sockets set in an improbably large head with close-cropped hair. Undoubtedly the apparition was young, but the skin on its face was the grayish skin of an old man, and its teeth were crooked and yellow. The apparition was holding a large birdcage covered with a black cloth and an unsealed blue letter . . .

'I must be still asleep', Nikolka thought, with a gesture trying to brush the apparition aside like a spider's web and knocking his fingers painfully against the wires of the cage. Immediately the bird in the cage screeched in fury, whistled and clattered.

'Nikolka!' cried Elena's voice anxiously somewhere far, far away.

'Jesus Christ', thought Nikolka. 'No, I'm awake all right, but I've gone mad, and I know why – combat fatigue. My God! And I'm seeing things too . . . and what's happening to my fingers? Lord! Alexei's not back yet . . . yes, now I remember . . . he's not back . . . he's been killed . . . Oh, God . . .'

'With her lover on the same divan,' said the apparition in a tragic voice, 'where I once read poetry to her.'

The apparition turned towards the door, obviously to someone who was listening, then turned round again and bore down on Nikolka:

'Yes, on the very same divan . . . They're sitting there now and kissing each other . . . after I signed those IOU's for seventy-five thousand roubles without thinking twice about it, like a gentleman. Because I am and always shall be a gentleman. Let them kiss!'

'Oh, Lord!' thought Nikolka. His eyes stared and a shiver ran down his back.

'I'm sorry', said the apparition, gradually emerging from the shimmering fog of sleep and turning into a real live body. 'Perhaps you may not quite understand. Look, this letter will explain it all. Like a gentleman, I won't hide my shame from anyone.'

And with these words the stranger handed Nikolka the blue letter. Feeling he had gone quite insane, Nikolka took it and moving his lips, began to read the large sprawling, agitated handwriting. Undated, the letter on the thin sky-blue paper read thus:

'Lena darling, I know how good-hearted you are and I am sending him to you because you're one of the family. I did send a telegram, but he'll tell you all about it himself, poor boy. Lariosik has had a most terrible blow and for a long time I was afraid he wouldn't get over it. You know he married Milochka Rubtsova a year ago. Well, she has turned out to be a snake in the grass! Take him in I beg you, and look after him as only you can. I will send you a regular allowance for his keep. He has come to hate Zhitomir and I can quite understand why. I won't write any more – I'm too upset. The hospital train is just leaving and he'll tell you all about it himself. A big, big kiss for you and Seryozha.'

This was followed by an indecipherable signature.

'I brought the bird with me', said the stranger, sighing. 'A bird is man's best friend. I know many people think they're a nuisance to keep, but all I can say is that at least a bird never does anyone any harm.'

Nikolka very much liked that last sentence. Making no effort to understand it, he shyly scratched his forehead with the incomprehensible letter and slowly swung his legs down from the bed, thinking: 'I can't ask him his name . . . it would sound so rude . . . What an extraordinary thing to happen . . .'

'Is it a canary?' he asked.

'It certainly is', replied the stranger enthusiastically. 'Actually it's not a hen-canary as most of them are, but a real cock-canary. I have fifteen of them at home in Zhitomir. I took them to mother, so that she can look after them. I'm sure that *beast* would wring their necks. He hates birds. May I put him down on your desk for a moment?'

'Please do', Nikolka replied. 'Are you from Zhitomir?'

'Yes, I am', answered the stranger. 'And wasn't it a coincidence – I arrived here at the same time as your brother.'

'What brother?'

'What d'you mean – what brother? Your brother arrived here as I did', the stranger replied with astonishment.

'But what brother?' Nikolka exclaimed miserably. 'What brother? From Zhitomir!'

'Your elder brother . . .'

Elena's voice came piercingly from the drawing-room: 'Nikolka! Nikolka! Illarion – please! Wake him up!'

'Tweet, tweet, tweee-ee, tik, tik, tikki', screeched the bird.

Nikolka dropped the blue letter and shot like a bullet through the library and dining-room into the drawing-room, where he stopped in horror, his arms spread wide.

Wearing another man's black overcoat with a torn lining and a pair of strange black trousers Alexei Turbin lay motionless on the divan below the clock. His face was pale, with a bluish pallor, and his teeth were clenched. Elena was fussing around him, her dressing-gown untied and showing her black stockings and lace-trimmed underwear. She was tugging at her brother's arms and at the buttons on his chest and shouting: 'Nik! Nik!'

Within three minutes, a student's cap crammed on to the back of his head and his grey overcoat flapping open, Nikolka was running up St Alexei's Hill, panting hard and muttering: 'What if he's not at home? And this extraordinary creature in the jockey's boots has to turn up at a moment like this! It's out of the question to call on Dr Kuritsky after Alexei laughed at him for speaking Ukrainian . . .'

An hour later a bowl was standing on the dining-room floor, full of red-stained water, scraps of red bandage lay scattered among fragments of broken crockery which the stranger in the yellow-topped boots had knocked down from the sideboard while fetching a glass. Everybody walked back and forth on the broken pieces, crunching them underfoot. Still pale but no longer looking blue, Alexei still lay on his back, his head on a cushion. He had recovered consciousness and was trying to say something, but the doctor, a man with a pointed beard with rolled-up sleeves and a pince-nez said as he wiped his bloodstained hands:

'Be quiet, doctor . . .'

Anyuta, the color of chalk and wide-eyed, and Elena, her red hair dishevelled, were lifting Alexei to take off his wet, blood-stained shirt with a torn sleeve.

'Cut it off him, it's ruined anyway', said the bearded doctor.

They cut up Alexei's shirt with scissors and took it off in shreds, baring his thin yellowish body and his left arm freshly bandaged up to the shoulder. The ends of splints protruded above and below the bandaging. Nikolka knelt down carefully undoing Alexei's buttons, and removed his trousers.

'Undress him completely and straight into bed', said the pointed beard in his bass voice. Anyuta poured water from a jug on to his hands and blobs of lather fell into the bowl as he washed. The stranger stood aside from the confusion and bustle, at one moment gazing unhappily at the broken plates, at the next blushing as he looked at the dishevelled Elena who had ceased to care that her dressing-gown was completely undone. The stranger's eyes were wet with tears.

They all helped to carry Alexei from the dining-room into his bedroom, and in this the stranger took part: he linked his hands under Alexei's knees and carried his legs.

In the drawing-room Elena offered the doctor money. He pushed it aside. 'No really, for heaven's sake,' he said, 'not from a colleague. But there's a much more serious problem. The fact is, he ought to go into hospital . . .'

'No,' came Alexei's weak voice, 'impossible. Not into hosp . . .'

'Be quiet, doctor. We shall manage quite well without you. Yes, of course, I understand the situation perfectly well . . . God knows what's going on in the City at the moment . . .' He nodded towards the window. 'He's probably right, I suppose, hospital's out of the question at the moment . . . All right then, he'll have to be treated at home. I'll come again this evening.'

'Is he in danger, doctor?' asked Elena anxiously.

The doctor stared at the parquet floor as though a diagnosis were imprisoned in the bright yellow wood, grunted and replied, twisting his beard:

'The bone is not fractured . . . H'm . . . major blood-vessels intact . . . the nerve too . . . But it's bound to fester . . . strands of wool from the overcoat have entered the wound . . . Temperature . . .' Having delivered himself of these cryptic scraps of thought, the doctor raised his voice and said confidently: 'Complete rest, . . . Morphia if he's in pain. I will give him an injection this evening. Food – liquids, bouillon and so on . . . He mustn't talk too much . . .'

'Doctor, doctor, please – one thing: he begs you not to talk to anyone about this . . .'

The doctor glowered sidelong at Elena and muttered:

'Yes, I understand . . . How did it happen?'

Elena only gave a restrained sigh and spread her hands.

'All right', growled the doctor and sidled, bear-like, out into the lobby.

Twelve

IN Alexei's small bedroom dark-colored blinds had been pulled down on the two windows that gave on to the glazed verandah. Twilight filled the room. Elena's golden-red hair seemed a source of light, echoed by another white blur on the pillow – Alexei's face and neck. The wire from the plug snaked its way to a chair, where the pink-shaded lamp shone and turned day into night. Alexei signed to Elena to shut the door.

'Warn Anyuta not to talk about me . . .'

'I know, I know . . . Try not to talk too much, Alyosha.'

'Yes . . . I'm only whispering . . . God, if I lose my arm!'

'Now, Alyosha, lie still and be quiet . . . Shall we keep that woman's overcoat here for a while?'

'Yes, Nikolka mustn't try and take it back to her. Otherwise something might happen to him . . . in the street. D'you hear? Whatever happens, for God's sake don't let him go out anywhere.'

'God bless her', Elena said with sincere tenderness. 'And they say there are no more good people in this world . . .'

A faint color rose in the wounded man's cheeks. He stared up at the low white ceiling then turned his gaze on Elena and said with a frown:

'Oh yes – and who, may I ask, is that block-head who has just appeared?'

Elena leaned forwards into the beam of pink light and shrugged.

'Well, this creature appeared at the front door no more than a

184

couple of minutes before you arrived. He's Sergei's nephew from Zhitomir. You've heard about him – Illarion Surzhansky . . . Well, this is the famous Lariosik, as he's known in the family.'

'Well?'

'Well, he came to us with a letter. There's been some drama. He'd only just started to tell me about it when she brought you here.'

'He seems to have some sort of bird, for God's sake.'

Laughing, but with a look of horror in her eyes, Elena leaned towards the bed:

'The bird's nothing! He's asking to live here. I really don't know what to do.'

'*Live* here?'

'Well, yes . . . Just be quiet and lie still, please Alyosha. His mother has written begging us to have him. She simply worships him. I've never seen such a clumsy idiot as this Lariosik in my life. The first thing he did when he got here was to smash all our china. The blue dinner service. Now there are only two plates of it left.'

'I see. I don't know what to suggest . . .'

For a long time they whispered in the pink-shadowed room. The distant voices of Nikolka and the unexpected visitor could be heard through closed doors. Elena wrung her hands, begging Alexei to talk less. From the dining-room came a tinkling sound as Anyuta angrily swept up the remains of the blue dinner service. Finally they came to a whispered decision. In view of the uncertainty of life in the City from now on and the likelihood of rooms being requisitioned, and because they had no money and Lariosik's mother would be paying for him, they would let him stay, but on condition that he observed the rules of behaviour of the Turbin household. The bird would be put on probation. If it proved unbearable having the bird in the house, they would demand its removal and its owner could stay. As for the smashed dinner service, since Elena could naturally not bring herself to complain about it, and to complain would in any case be insufferably vulgar and rude, they agreed to consign it to tacit oblivion. Lariosik could sleep in the library, where they would put in a bed with a sprung mattress and a table.

Elena went into the dining-room. Lariosik was standing in a mournful pose, hanging his head and staring at the place on the sideboard where a pile of twelve plates had once stood. His cloudy blue eyes expressed utter remorse. Nikolka, with his mouth open and a look of intense curiosity, stood facing Lariosik and listening to him.

'There is no leather in Zhitomir', Lariosik was saying perplexedly. 'Simply none to be had at all, you see. At least of the kind of leather I'm used to wearing. I sent round to all the shoemakers, offering them as much money as they liked, but it was no good. So I had to . . .'

As he caught sight of Elena Lariosik turned pale, shifted from foot to foot and for some reason staring down at the emerald-green fringe of her dressing-gown, he said:

'Elena Vasilievna, I'm going straight out to the shops to hunt around, and you shall have a new dinner service today. I don't know what to say. How can I apologise to you? I should be shot for ruining your china. I'm so terribly clumsy', he added to Nikolka. 'I shall go out to the shops at once', he went on, turning back to Elena.

'Please don't try and go to any shops. You couldn't anyway, because they're all shut. Don't you know what's happening here in the City?'

'Of course I know!' exclaimed Lariosik. 'After all, I came here on a hospital train, as you know from the telegram.'

'What telegram?' asked Elena. 'We've had no telegram.'

'What?' Lariosik opened his wide mouth. 'You never *got* it? Aha! Now I realise', he turned to Nikolka, 'why you were so amazed to see me . . . But how . . . Mama sent a telegram of sixty-three words.'

'Phew, sixty-three words!' Nikolka said in astonishment. 'What a pity. Telegrams are very slow in getting through these days. Or to be more accurate, they're not getting through at all.'

'What's to happen then?' Lariosik said in a pained voice. 'Will you let me stay with you?' He looked around helplessly, and it was at once obvious from his expression that he liked it very much at the Turbins' and did not want to go away.

'It's all arranged', replied Elena and nodded graciously. 'We have agreed. Stay here and make yourself as comfortable as you can. But you can see what a misfortune . . .'

Lariosik looked more upset than ever. His eyes became clouded with tears.

'Elena Vasilievna!' he said with emotion, 'I'll do everything I can to help. I can go without sleep for three or four days on end if necessary.'

'Thank you.'

'And now,' Lariosik said to Nikolka, 'could you please lend me a pair of scissors?'

Nikolka, so amazed and fascinated that he was still as dishevelled as when he had woken up, ran out and came back with the scissors. Lariosik started to unbutton his tunic, then blinked and said to Nikolka:

'Excuse me, I think I'd better go into your room for a minute, if you don't mind . . .'

In Nikolka's room Lariosik took off his tunic, revealing an extremely dirty shirt. Then armed with the scissors he ripped open the glossy black lining of the tunic and pulled out of it a thick greenish-yellow wad of money. This he bore solemnly into the dining-room and laid on the table in front of Elena, saying:

'There, Elena Vasilievna, allow me to present you with the money for my keep.'

'But why are you in such a hurry?' Elena asked, blushing. 'You could have paid later . . .'

Lariosik protested hotly:

'No, no, Elena Vasilievna, please take it now. At difficult times like this money is always extremely necessary, I understand that very well!' He unwrapped the package, from which a woman's picture fell out as he did so. Lariosik swiftly picked it up and with a sigh thrust it into his pocket. 'In any case it will be safer with you. What do I want it for? I shall only need to buy a few cigarettes and some canary seed for the bird . . .'

For a moment Elena forgot about Alexei's wound and she was so favourably impressed by Lariosik's sensible and timely action that a gleam of cheerfulness came into her eyes.

'Maybe he's not such a booby as I thought he was at first', she thought. 'He's polite and conscientious, even if he is a bit eccentric. It's an awful shame about the dinner service, though.'

'What a type', thought Nikolka. Lariosik's miraculous appearance had driven the gloomy thoughts from his mind.

'There's eight thousand roubles here', said Lariosik, pushing the packet across the table, which from the color of the money looked like scrambled eggs with chopped chives. 'If there's not enough we'll count it again and I'll write home for some more.'

'No, no, that doesn't matter, later will do', replied Elena. 'I'm going to tell Anyuta right away to heat the water so you can have a bath. But tell me – how did you come here? I don't understand how you managed to get through.' Elena began to roll the money into a bundle and stuff it into the huge pocket of her dressing-gown.

Lariosik's eyes filled with horror at the memory.

'It was a nightmare!' he exclaimed, clasping his hands like a Catholic at prayer. 'It took me nine days . . . no, sorry, was it ten? Just a moment . . . Sunday, yes, Monday . . . No, it took me eleven days travelling here from Zhitomir!'

'Eleven days!' cried Nikolka. 'You see?' he said reproachfully, for some reason, to Elena.

'Yes, eleven days. When I left the train belonged to the Hetman's government, but on the way it was taken over by Petlyura's men. One day we stopped at a station – what's it called now? Oh dear, I've forgotten . . . anyway, it doesn't matter . . . and there if you please, they wanted to shoot me. These troops of Petlyura's appeared, wearing pigtails . . .'

'Blue ones?' Nikolka asked with curiosity.

'No, red . . . yes, red ones . . . and they shouted: "Get out! We're going to shoot you on the spot!" They had decided I was an officer, hiding in a hospital train. And the only reason I had been able to get on that train was because Mama knew Doctor Kuritsky.'

'Kuritsky?' Nikolka exclaimed meaningfully. 'I see . . . our Ukrainian nationalist friend. We know him.'

'Yes, that's him . . . it was he who brought the train to us at Zhitomir . . . God! I started to pray, believe me. I thought this was the end. And d'you know what? The bird saved me. I wasn't an officer, I said, I was an ornithologist, and I showed him the bird. I'm a bird-breeder, I said . . . Well, one of them punched me on the back of the neck and said "All right, bird-man, you can go to hell for all I care!" The insolence! As a gentleman I ought to have killed him, but I could hardly . . . you understand . . .'

'Elena', came a weak voice from Alexei's bedroom. Elena swung round and ran out without waiting to hear the rest of the story.

*

On December 15th, according to the calendar, the sun sets at half past three in the afternoon, so by three o'clock twilight began to settle on the apartment. But at that hour the hands on Elena's face were showing the most depressed and hopeless time on the human clock-face – half past five. The hands of the clock were formed by two sad folds at the corners of her mouth which were drawn down towards her chin, whilst in her eyes, depression and resolution had begun their struggle against disaster.

Nikolka's face showed a jagged, wavering twenty to one, because Nikolka's head was full of chaos and confusion evoked by the significant enigmatic words: Malo-Provalnaya . . .', words spoken by the dying man in the fighting at the crossroads yesterday, words which somehow had to be deciphered no later than the next few days. The chaos and difficulties had also been evoked by the puzzling and interesting figure of Lariosik falling from the sky into the Turbins' life and by the fact that a monstrous, grand event had befallen them: Petlyura had captured the city. Petlyura, of all people – and the City, of all places. And what would happen in it now was incomprehensible and inconceivable even to the most intelligent of human minds. One thing was quite clear – yesterday saw the most appalling catastrophe: all our forces were thoroughly beaten, caught with their pants down. Their blood shrieks to heaven – that is one thing. Those criminals, the generals, and the swine at headquarters deserve to be killed – that is another. But as well as sickening horror, a burning interest grew in Nikolka's mind – what, after all, is going to happen? How are seven hundred thousand people going to live in a City in the power of an enigmatic personality with such a terrible, ugly name – Petlyura? Who is he? Why is he here? Hell, though, all that takes second place for the moment in comparison with the most important thing, Alexei's bloody wound . . . horrible, horrible business. Nothing is known for sure of course, but in all probability Myshlaevsky and Karas can be counted as dead too.

On the slippery, greasy kitchen table Nikolka was crushing ice with a broad-bladed hatchet. The lumps of ice either split with a crunch or slithered out from under the hatchet and jumped all over the kitchen, whilst Nikolka's fingers grew numb. Nearby was an ice-bag with a silvery cap.

'Malo . . . Provalnaya . . .' Nikolka mouthed silently, and across his mind's eye passed the images of Nai-Turs, of the red-haired janitor, and of Myshlaevsky. And just as the image of Myshlaevsky, in his slashed greatcoat, had entered Nikolka's thoughts, the clock on the face of Anyuta, busy at the stove with her sad, confused dreams, pointed ever more clearly to twenty to five – the hour of sorrow and depression. Were his different-colored eyes still alive and safe? Would she hear his broad stride again, the clinking sound of his spurs?

'Bring the ice', said Elena, opening the door into the kitchen.

'Right away', said Nikolka hurriedly, screwing up the cap, and running out.

'Anyuta, my dear', said Elena. 'Make sure you don't say a word to anyone about Alexei Vasilievich being wounded. If they find out, God forbid, that he was fighting against them, there'll be trouble.'

'I understand, Elena Vasilievna. Of course I won't tell anyone!' Anyuta looked at Elena with wide, anxious eyes. 'Mother of God, the things that are happening in town. I was walking down the street today and there were two dead men without boots . . . and blood, blood everywhere! People were standing around and looking . . . Someone said the two dead men were officers. They were just lying there, no hats on their heads or anything . . . I felt my legs go all weak and I just ran away, nearly dropped my basket . . .'

Anyuta hunched her shoulders as though from cold as she remembered something else, and immediately a frying-pan slid sideways out of her hands on to the floor . . .

'Quiet, please, for God's sake', said Elena, wringing her hands.

At three o'clock that afternoon the hands on Lariosik's face were pointing to the zenith of strength and high spirits – twelve o'clock. Both hands overlapped at noon, sticking together and pointing upwards like two sharp sword-blades. This had come about because after the catastrophe which had shattered Lariosik's tender soul in Zhitomir, after his terrible eleven-day journey in a hospital train and after so many violent sensations, Lariosik liked it very much indeed at the Turbins'. He could not yet have told them why he liked it, because he had not so far properly explained it to himself.

The beautiful Elena seemed a person deserving of unusual respect and attention. And he liked Nikolka very much too. As a way of showing this, Lariosik chose the moment when Nikolka had stopped dashing in and out of Alexei's room, and began to help him set up the folding steel bed in the library.

'You have the sort of frank expression which makes people trust you', Lariosik said politely and stared so hard at that frank expression that he did not notice that he had caused the complicated, creaking bed to snap shut and crush Nikolka's arm between the two halves of the frame. The pain was so violent that Nikolka gave a yell which, although muffled, was so powerful that it brought Elena rushing into the room. Although Nikolka exerted all his strength to stop himself from howling, great tears burst spontaneously from his eyes. Elena and Lariosik both gripped the patent folding bed and tugged long and hard at it from opposite sides until they released Nikolka's wrist, which had turned blue.

Lariosik almost burst into tears himself when the crushed arm came out limp and mottled.

'Oh my God!' he said, his already miserable face grimacing even harder, 'What's the matter with me? Everything I touch goes wrong! Does it hurt terribly? Please forgive me, for God's sake . . .'

Without a word Nikolka rushed into the kitchen, where at his instructions Anyuta ran a stream of cold water from the tap over his wrist.

By the time the diabolical patent bed had been prised apart and straightened out and it was clear that Nikolka had suffered no great damage to his arm, Lariosik was once more overcome by a delightful sense of quiet joy at being surrounded by so many books. Besides his passion and love for birds, he also had a passion for books. Here, on open shelves that lined the room from floor to ceiling, was a treasure-house. In green and red gold-tooled bindings, in yellow dust-covers and black slip-cases, books stared out at Lariosik from all four walls. The bed had been long made up; beside it was a chair with a towel draped over its back, whilst on the seat, among the usual male accessories – soap-dish, cigarettes, matches and watch – there was propped up a mysterious photograph of a woman. All the while Lariosik stayed in the library, voyaging around the book-lined walls, squatting down on his haunches by the bottom rows, staring greedily at the bindings, undecided as to which to take out first, *The Pickwick Papers* or the bound volumes of the *Russian Herald* for 1871. The clock-hands on his face pointed to twelve o'clock.

But as twilight approached the mood in the Turbins' apartment grew sadder and sadder, and as a result the clock did not strike twelve, the hands stood still and silent, like a glittering sword wrapped in a flag of mourning that stood at half-mast.

The cause of the air of mourning, the cause of the discord on the clock-faces of all the people in the dusty, slightly old-fashioned comfort of the Turbins' apartment was a thin column of mercury. At three o'clock in Alexei's bedroom it showed 39.6° Centigrade. Turning pale, Elena was just about to shake it but Alexei turned his head, looked up at her and said weakly but insistently: 'Show it to me.' Silently and reluctantly Elena showed him the thermo-meter. Alexei looked at it and sighed deeply.

By five o'clock he was lying with a cold gray bag on his head, little lumps of ice melting and floating in the bag. His face had turned pink, his eyes glittered and looked very handsome.

'Thirty-nine point six . . . good . . .' he said, occasionally licking his dry, cracked lips. 'Ye-es . . . May be all right . . . Though I won't be able to practice . . . for a long time. If only I don't lose my arm . . . without an arm I'm useless . . .'

'Please don't talk, Alyosha', begged Elena, straightening the blanket around his shoulders . . . Alexei was silent, closing his eyes. From his wound in his left armpit, a dry prickly heat spread out over his whole body. Occasionally he filled his chest with a deep breath, which gave his head a misty feeling, but his legs were turning unpleasantly cold. Towards evening, when the lamps were lit everywhere and the other three – Elena, Nikolka and Lariosik – slowly ate their supper in silence and anxiety, the column of mercury, expanding and bursting magically out of its silver globule crawled up to the 40.2 mark. Then Alexei's alarm and depression began to melt away and dissipate. The depression, which had come to him like a gray lump that spread itself over the blanket, was now transformed into yellow strands which trailed out like seaweed in water. He forgot about his practice, forgot his anxiety about the future because everything was smothered by those yellow strands. The tearing pain in the left side of his chest grew numb and still. Fever gave way to cold. Now and again the burning flame in his chest was turned into an ice-cold knife twisting somewhere within his lung. When this happened, Alexei shook his head, threw off the ice-bag and crawled deeper under the blankets. The pain in his wound altered from a dull ache to a spasm of such intensity that the wounded man began involuntarily to complain, in a weak, dry voice. When the knife went away and was replaced by the flame, the fever flooded back again through his body and through the whole of the little cavity under the bedclothes and the patient asked for a drink. The faces of Nikolka, then of Elena and then of Lariosik appeared through the mist, bent over him and listened. The eyes of all three looked terribly alike, frowning and angry. The hands on Nikolka's face dropped at once and stayed – like Elena's – at half past six. Every minute Nikolka went out into the dining-room – somehow that evening the lights all seemed to be flickering and dim – and looked at the clock. Tonkhh . . . tonkhh . . . the clock creaked on with an angry, warning sound as its hands pointed at nine, then at a quarter past, then half past nine . . .

'Oh lord', sighed Nikolka, wandering like a sleepy fly from the dining-room, through the lobby into the drawing-room, where he pushed aside the net curtain and stared through the french window into the street . . . 'Let's hope the doctor hasn't lost his nerve and isn't afraid to come . . .' he thought. The street, steep and crooked, was emptier than it had ever been recently, but it also looked somehow less menacing. The occasional cabman's sleigh creaked past. But they were very few and far between . . . Nikolka realised that he would probably have to go out and fetch the doctor, and wondered how to persuade Elena to let him go.

'If he doesn't come by half past ten,' said Elena, 'I will go myself with Larion Larionovich and you stay and keep an eye on Alyosha . . . No, don't argue . . . Don't you see, you look too like an officer cadet . . . We'll give Lariosik Alyosha's civilian clothes, and they won't touch him if he's with a woman . . .'

Lariosik assured them that he was prepared to take the risk and go alone, and went off to change into civilian clothes.

The knife had gone altogether, but the fever had returned, made worse by the onset of typhus, and in his fever Alexei kept seeing the vague, mysterious figure of a man in gray.

'I suppose you know he's turned a somersault? Is he gray?' Alexei suddenly announced sternly and clearly, staring hard at Elena. 'Nasty . . . All birds, of course, are the same. You should put him in the larder, make them sit down in the warm and they'll soon recover.'

'What are you talking about, Alyosha?' asked Elena in fright noticing as she bent over him how she could feel the heat from Alexei's face on her own face. 'Bird? What bird?'

In the black civilian suit Larosik looked hunched and broader than usual. He was frightened, his eyes swivelling in misery. Swaying, on tiptoe, he crept out of the bedroom across the lobby into the dining-room, through the library into Nikolka's room. There, his arms swinging purposefully, he strode up to the bird-cage on the desk and threw a black cloth over it. But it was un-necessary – the bird had long since fallen asleep in one corner, curled up into a feathery ball and was silent, oblivious to all the alarms and anxiety round about. Lariosik firmly shut the door into the library, then the door from the library into the dining-room.

'Nasty business . . . very nasty', said Alexei uneasily, as he stared at the corner of the room. 'I shouldn't have shot him . . . Listen . . .' He began to pull his unwounded arm from under the bedclothes. 'The best thing to do is to invite him here and explain, ask him why he was fooling about like that. I'll take all the blame, of course . . . It's no good though . . . all over now, all so stupid . . .'

'Yes, yes', said Nikolka unhappily, and Elena hung her head. Alexei started to get excited, tried to sit up, but a sharp pain pulled him down and he groaned, then said irritably:

'Get him out of here!'

'Shall I put the bird in the kitchen? I've covered it with a cloth, and it's not making any noise', Lariosik whispered anxiously to Elena.

Elena waved him away: 'No, that's not it, don't worry . . .' Nikolka strode purposefully out into the dining-room. His hair dishevelled, he glanced at the clock face: the hands were pointing to around ten o'clock. Worried, Anyuta came into the dining-room.

'How is Alexei Vasilievich?' she asked.

'He's delirious', Nikolka replied with a deep sigh.

'Oh my God', whispered Anyuta. 'Why doesn't the doctor come?'

Nikolka looked at her and went back into the bedroom. He leaned close to Elena's ear and began to whisper urgently:

'I don't care what you say, I'm going out for a doctor. It's ten o'clock. The street is completely quiet.'

'Let's wait until half past ten', whispered Elena in reply, nodding and twisting a handkerchief in her hands. 'It wouldn't be right to call in another doctor. I know our doctor will come.'

Soon after ten o'clock a great, clumsy heavy mortar moved into the crowded little bedroom. Alexei was in despair: how were they all to survive? And now there stood this mortar, filling the room from wall to wall, with one wheel pressing against the bed. Life would be impossible, because one would have to crawl between those thick spokes, then arch one's back and squeeze through the other wheel, carrying all one's luggage which seemed to be hanging from one's left arm. It was pulling one's arm down to the ground, cutting into one's armpit with a rope. No one could move the mortar. The whole apartment was full of them, according to instructions, and Colonel Malyshev and Elena could only stare helplessly through the wheels, unable to do anything to remove the gun or at least to move a sick man into a more tolerable room that wasn't crowded out with mortars. Thanks to that damned heavy, cold piece of ordnance the whole apartment had turned into a cheap hotel. The doorbell was ringing frequently . . . rrring . . . and people were coming to call. Colonel Malyshev flitted past, looking awkward, in a hat that was too big for him, wearing gold epaulettes, and carrying a heap of papers. Alexei shouted at him and Malyshev disappeared into the muzzle of the mortar and was replaced by Nikolka, bustling about and behaving with stupid obstinacy. Nikolka gave Alexei something to drink, but it was not a cold spiralling stream of water from a fountain but some disgusting lukewarm liquid that smelled of washing-up water.

'Ugh . . . horrible . . . take it away', mumbled Alexei.

Startled, Nikolka raised his eyebrows, but persisted obstinately and clumsily. Frequently Elena changed into the black, unfamiliar figure of Lariosik, Sergei's nephew, and then as it turned back into Elena he felt her fingers somewhere near his forehead, which gave him little or no relief. Elena's hands, usually warm and deft now felt as rough and as clumsy as rakes and did everything to make a peaceful man's life miserable in this damned armorer's yard he was lying in. Surely Elena was not responsible for this pole on which Alexei's wounded body had been laid? Yet now she was sitting on it . . . what's the matter with her? . . . sitting on the end of the pole and her weight was making it start to spin sickeningly round . . . How can a man live if a round pole is cutting into his body? No, no, they're behaving intolerably! As loudly as he could, though it came out as a mere whisper, Alexei called out:

'Julia!'

Julia, however, did not emerge from her old-fashioned room with its portrait of a man in gold epaulettes and the uniform of the 1840's, and she did not hear the sick man's cry. And that poor sick man would have been driven mad by the gray figures which began pacing about the room alongside his brother and sister, had there not also come a stout man in gold-rimmed spectacles, a man of skill and firm confidence. In honor of his appearance an extra light was brought into the bedroom – the light of a flickering wax candle in a heavy, old black candlestick. At one moment the light glimmered on the table, at the next it was moving around Alexei, above it the ugly, distorted shadow of Lariosik, looking like a bat with its wings cut off. The candle bent forward, dripping white wax. The little bedroom reeked with the heavy smells of iodine, surgical spirit and ether. On the table arose a chaos of glittering boxes, spirit lamps reflected in shining nickel-plate, and heaps of cotton wool, like snow at Christmas. With his warm hands the stout man gave Alexei a miraculous injection in his good arm, and in a few minutes the gray figures ceased to trouble him. The mortar was pushed out on to the verandah, after which its black muzzle, poking through the draped windows, no longer seemed menacing. He began to breathe more easily, because the huge wheel had been removed and he was no longer obliged to crawl through its spokes. The candle was put out and the angular coal-black shadow of Larion Surzhansky from Zhitomir disappeared from the wall, whilst Nikolka's face became clearer to see and not so infuriatingly obstinate, perhaps because the hands on his clock, thanks to the hope inspired by the skill of the stout man in gold-rimmed spectacles, had moved apart and did not point so implacably and despairingly towards the point of his sharp chin. The time on

Nikolka's face had moved backwards from half past six to twenty to five, whilst the clock in the dining-room, although it did not tell the same time, although it insistently pushed its hands ever forward, was now doing so without any senile croaking and grumbling, but in the good old manner, marking the seconds with a clear, healthy baritone: tonk! And the chimes, coming from the tower of the beautiful toylike Louis Quatorze château, struck: bom! bom! Midnight, listen . . . midnight, listen . . . the chimes gave their warning note, then a sentry's halberd began to strike the silvery hour. The sentries marched back and forth, guarding their tower, for without knowing it, man had made towers, alarm-bells and weapons for one purpose only – to guard the peace of his hearth and home. For this he goes to war, which if the truth be known, is the only cause for which anyone ought to fight.

Only when Alexei had reached a state of calm and peace did Julia, that selfish, sinful but seductive woman, agree to appear. And she appeared – her black-stockinged leg, the top of a black fur-trimmed boot flashed by on the narrow brick staircase, and the hasty sound of her footsteps and the rustle of her dress were accompanied by the gavotte played on tinkling little bells from where Louis Quatorze basked in a sky-blue garden on the banks of a lake, intoxicated by his glory and by the presence of charming, brightly-colored ladies.

*

At midnight Nikolka undertook a most important and very timely piece of work. First he took a dirty wet rag from the kitchen, and rubbed off the belly of the tiled Dutch stove the words:

Long live Russia!

God Save the Tsar!

Down with Petlyura!

Then, with the enthusiastic participation of Lariosik, a more important task was put in hand. Alyosha's Browning automatic was neatly and soundlessly removed from the desk, together with two spare magazines and a box of ammunition for it. Nikolka checked the weapon and found that his elder brother had fired six of the seven rounds in the magazine.

'Good for him . . ' Nikolka murmured to himself.

There was not, of course, the slightest likelihood of Lariosik being a traitor. It was inconceivable that an educated man should be on Petlyura's side at all, and in particular a gentleman who signed promissory notes for seventy-five thousand roubles and who sent sixty-three-word telegrams. The Colt automatic that had belonged to Nai-Turs and Alyosha's Browning were thoroughly greased with engine oil and paraffin. Imitating Nikolka, Lariosik rolled up his shirtsleeves and helped to grease and pack the weapons into a long, deep cake tin. They worked in a hurry, for as every decent man who has taken part in a revolution knows very well – no matter who is in power – searches take place from 2.30 a.m. to 6.15 a.m. in winter and from midnight to 4 a.m. in summer. Even so the work was held up, thanks to Lariosik, who in examining the mechanism of the ten-round Colt-system automatic pushed the magazine into the butt the wrong way round, and the job of getting it out again took a great deal of effort and a considerable quantity of oil. Apart from that, there was a further unexpected hindrance: the tin, containing the revolvers, Nikolka's and Alexei's shoulder-straps, Nikolka's chevrons and Alexei's picture of the murdered Tsarevich, wrapped tightly inside with waterproof oilcloth and outside with long, sticky strips of electrical insulating tape – the tin was too big to go through the little upper pane, the only part of the window left unsealed in winter.

The box had to be really well hidden. Not everybody was as idiotic as Vasilisa. Nikolka had already worked out that morning how to hide the box. The wall of their house, No. 13, almost but not quite touched the wall of No. 11 next door, leaving a gap of only about two feet. Only three of the windows of No. 13 were in that wall – one on the corner, from Nikolka's room, two from the library next to it which were quite useless (it was permanently dark) and lower down there was a dim little window covered by a grating which belonged to Vasilisa's cellar, whilst the wall of the neighbouring No. 11 was completely blind and windowless. Imagine a perfect artificial canyon two feet wide, dark, and invisible from the street and even inaccessible from the back yard except to the occasional small boy. It was as a boy that Nikolka, once when playing cops and robbers, had squeezed into the gap between the houses, stumbling over piles of bricks, and he remembered exactly how there had been a double line of metal spikes in the wall of No. 13 stretching from ground level right up to the roof. Earlier, before No. 11 had been built, there had probably been a fire escape bolted to these spikes, which had later been removed, the spikes being left in place. That evening, as he thrust his hand out through the little upper window-pane, it did not take Nikolka two minutes of fumbling to find one of the spikes. The solution was plain, but the tin, tied up with a triple thickness of stout cord, with a loop at one end, was too large to go through the window.

'Obviously we must open up the rest of the window', said Nikolka, as he jumped down from the window-ledge.

Having paid suitable tribute to Nikolka's intelligence and ingenuity, Lariosik set about unsealing the main casement. This back-breaking work took at least half an hour, as the swollen frames refused to open. Finally they managed to open first one side and then the other, in the course of which the glass on Lariosik's side shattered in a long, web-like crack.

'Put the light out!' Nikolka ordered.

The light went out, and a freezing blast of air lashed into the room. Nikolka eased himself half way out into the icy black space and hooked the loop round one of the spikes, from which the tin hung at the end of a two foot length of cord. Nothing was visible from the street, since the fireproof wall of No. 13 was built at an angle to the street. The very narrow gap between the two houses was covered by the large signboard belonging to a dressmaker's workshop in No. 11. The tin could only be seen by someone actually climbing into the gap, which no one was likely to do before spring thanks to the huge piles of snow which had been shovelled out of the yard, forming an ideal fence in front of the house. The chief advantage of the hiding place, however, was that it could be checked without opening the main casement of the window: one only had to open the little pane at the top, push one's hand through and feel for the cord, taut as a 'cello string. Perfect.

The light was switched on again, and kneading the putty which Anyuta had left over from the fall, Nikolka sealed up the casement again. Even if by some miracle the tin were found, they would always be ready with the answer: 'What? Whose box? What revolvers, Tsarevich . . . ? Impossible! No idea. God only knows who put it out there! Somebody must have climbed up on the roof and hung it from there. Not many other people around here? Well, so what? We're peaceful, law abiding folk, why should we want a picture of the Tsarevich . . .'

'A perfect job, brilliantly done, I swear it', said Lariosik. It could not have been better – easy to reach, yet outside the apartment.

*

It was three o'clock in the morning. Evidently no one would be coming tonight. Her eyelids heavy with exhaustion Elena tiptoed out into the dining-room. It was Nikolka's turn to take over from her by Alexei's bedside. He would keep watch from three till six, then Lariosik from six till nine.

They spoke in whispers.

'So if anyone asks, he's got typhus', Elena whispered. 'We must stick to that story, because Wanda has already been up from downstairs trying to find out what's the matter with Alexei. I said it was suspected typhus. She probably didn't believe me, because she gave me a very funny look . . . and she kept on asking questions – how were we, where had we all been, wasn't one of us wounded. Not a word about his being wounded.'

'No, of course not', Nikolka gestured forcibly. 'Vasilisa is the biggest coward in the world! If anything happened he'd babble to anybody that Alexei had been wounded if it meant saving his own skin.'

'The swine!' said Lariosik. 'What a filthy thing to do.'

Alexei lay in a coma. After the injection his expression had become quite calm, his features looked sharper and finer. The soothing poison coursed through his bloodstream and kept vigil. The gray figures had ceased to act as though they belonged to his room, they departed about their affairs, the mortar had finally been removed altogether. Whenever strangers did appear they now behaved decently, fitting in with the people and things which belonged legitimately in the Turbins' apartment. Once Colonel Malyshev appeared and sat down in an armchair, but he smiled as much as to say that all would be for the best. He no longer growled menacingly, no longer filled the room with heaps of paper. It was true he did burn some documents, but he refrained from touching Alexei's framed diplomas and the picture of his mother, and he did his burning in the pleasant blue flame of a spirit lamp, which was reassuring because the lighting of the spirit lamp was usually followed by an injection. Madame Anjou's telephone bell rang constantly.

'Rrring . . .' said Alexei, trying to pass on the sound of the telephone bell to the person sitting in the armchair, who was by turns Nikolka, then a stranger with mongoloid eyes (the drug kept Alexei from protesting at this intrusion), then the wretched Maxim, the school janitor, gray and trembling.

'Rrring', murmured the wounded man softly, as he tried to make a moving picture out of the writhing shadows, a difficult and agonising picture but one with an unusual, delightful but painful ending.

On marched the hours, round went the hands on the dining-room clock, and when the short one on the white clock-face pointed to five, he fell into a half-sleep. Alexei stirred occasionally, opening his narrowed eyes and mumbling indistinctly:

'I'll never make it . . . never get to the top of the stairs, I'm getting weaker, I'm going to fall . . . And she's running so fast . . . boots, on the snow . . . You'll leave a trail . . . wolves . . . Rrring, rrring . . .'

Thirteen

THE last time that Alexei had heard the sound of a bell ringing was when he had been running out of the back door of Madame Anjou's sensually perfumed boutique. The door bell rang. Someone had just come to the door of the shop, possibly someone like Alexei himself, a straggler from the Mortar Regiment, but equally possibly an enemy in pursuit. In any case, there was no question of going back into the shop, which would have been a totally superfluous piece of heroics.

A slippery flight of steps took Alexei down into the yard. There he could quite plainly hear the sound of rifle-fire very close by, somewhere on the broad street which sloped down to the Kreshchatik, possibly even as close as the museum. It was now obvious that he had wasted too much time musing sadly in the twilit shop and that Malyshev had been quite right in advising him to hurry. His heart-beat quickened with anxiety.

Looking round, Alexei saw that the long and endlessly tall yellow box-like building which housed Madame Anjou's boutique extended backwards into an enormous courtyard and that this courtyard stretched as far as a low wall dividing it from the adjoining property, the head office of the railroad. Glancing around through narrowed eyes Alexei set off across the open space straight towards the wall. There was a gate in it, which to his great surprise was unlocked, and he passed through it into the grim courtyard of the empty railroad building, whose blind, ugly little windows heightened the sense of desolation. Passing through the building under an echoing archway, Alexei emerged from the asphalted passageway on to the street. It was exactly four o'clock in the afternoon by the old clock on the tower of the house opposite, and just starting to get dark. The street was completely deserted. Nagged by an uncomfortable presentiment Alexei again looked grimly around and turned, not uphill but down towards the Golden Gates which loomed up, covered in snow, in the middle of the wet, slushy square. A solitary pedestrian ran towards Alexei with a frightened look and vanished.

An empty street always looks depressing, but here the feeling was augmented by an uncomfortable sense of foreboding somewhere in the pit of Alexei's stomach. Scowling in order to overcome his indecision – he had to go in *some* direction, he couldn't fly home through the air – he turned up his coat collar and set off.

He soon realised part of the reason for his unease – the gunfire had suddenly stopped. It had been booming away almost without cease for the past two weeks, and now there was silence in the surrounding sky. Yet in town, in fact right ahead of him down on the Kreshchatik, he could plainly hear bursts of rifle-fire. Alexei should have turned sharp left at the Golden Gates along a side-street, and then by keeping close to the back of St Sophia's Cathedral, he could have slipped home through a network of alleyways. If Alexei had done this, life would have turned out quite differently, but he did not do it. There is a kind of power which sometimes makes us turn and look over a mountain precipice, which draws us to experience the chill of fear and to the edge of the abyss. It was the same instinct which now made Alexei head towards the museum. He simply had to see, even if from a distance, just what was going on there; and instead of turning away Alexei took ten unnecessary steps and walked into Vladimirskaya Street. At this point an inner voice of alarm prompted him and he distinctly heard Malyshev's voice whispering 'Run!' Alexei looked to his right, towards the distant museum. He managed to catch a glimpse of part of the museum's white wall, the towering dome and a few small black figures scuttling into the distance . . . and that was all.

Coming straight toward him up the slope of Proreznaya Street from the Kreshchatik, veiled in a distant frosty haze, a herd of little gray men in soldiers' greatcoats was advancing, strung out across the whole width of the street. They were not far away –

thirty paces at the most. It was instantly obvious that they had been on the move for a long time and were showing signs of exhaustion. Not his eyes, but some irrational movement of his heart told Alexei that these were Petlyura's troops.

'Caught', Malyshev's voice said clearly from the pit of his stomach.

The next few seconds were effaced from Alexei's life and he never knew what happened in them. He only became conscious of himself again when he was round the corner in Vladimirskaya Street, his head hunched between his shoulders, and running on legs which were carrying him as fast as they could go, away from the fatal corner of Proreznaya Street, by the French pâtisserie, La Marquise.

'Come on, come on, come on, keep going . . . keep going . . .' The blood in his temples beat time to his pace.

For a little while there was still no sound from behind. If only he could turn into a razor blade and slip into a crack in the wall. But inevitably the silence was broken:

'Stop!' A hoarse voice shouted at Alexei's retreating back.

'This is it', from the pit of his stomach.

'Stop!' the voice repeated urgently.

Alexei Turbin looked around and even stopped for a second, because of a crazy, momentary thought that he might pretend to be a peaceful citizen. I'm just going about my business . . . leave me alone . . . His pursuer was about fifteen paces away and hurriedly unslinging his rifle. The moment the doctor turned around, amazement showed in the eyes of the pursuer and the doctor thought they were squinting, mongoloid eyes. A second figure dashed round the corner, tugging at his rifle-bolt. The astonishment on the first man's face changed to an incomprehensible, savage joy.

'Hey!' he shouted, 'Look, Petro – an officer!' At that moment he looked exactly like a hunter who had spotted a hare on the path right in front of him.

'What the hell? How do they know?' The thought struck Alexei like a hammer-blow.

The second man's rifle was suddenly reduced to a tiny black hole no bigger than a ten-kopeck piece. Alexei then felt himself turn and fly like an arrow up Vladimirskaya Street, desperate because his felt boots were slowing him down. Above and behind him came a whip-crack through the air – crack-thump . . .

'Stop! Get him!' Another crack. 'Get that officer!' The whole of Vladimirskaya Street echoed to the baying of the pack. Twice more the air was split by a high-pitched report.

A man only has to be chased with firearms for him to turn into a cunning wolf: in place of his weak, and in really desperate situations useless intellect, the wisdom of animal instinct will suddenly take over. Turning the corner of Malo-Provalnaya Street like a hunted wolf, Alexei caught a glimpse of the black rifle-muzzle behind him suddenly blotted out by a pale ring of fire. Putting on a spurt he swerved into Malo-Provalnaya Street, making a life-and-death choice for the second time in the course of the last five minutes.

Instinct told him that the men were chasing him hard and obstinately, that they wouldn't stop and that once they had caught up with him they would inevitably kill him. They would kill him because he had turned and run, there was not a single identification paper in his pocket, there was a revolver, and he was wearing a gray coat. They would kill him because men in pursuit might miss once, might miss twice, but the third time they would hit him. Third time lucky. It was a law as old as mankind. That meant that with these heavy felt boots on his feet he had about another half minute, and then it would be over. Once he realised that it was irrevocable, a wave of fear passed right through his body, out of his feet and into the ground. But it was at once replaced, like icy water creeping up his legs, by a savage fury which he exhaled with his panting breath. Already he was glancing wolfishly about him as he ran. Two of the gray men, followed by a third, rushed around the corner of Vladimirskaya Street and all three rifles flashed in turn. Slowing down, gritting his teeth, Alexei fired three shots at them without aiming. He quickened his pace again, dimly noticing ahead of him a slight black shadow pressed up against the wall alongside a drainpipe, then he felt as though someone with wooden pincers was tugging at his side under his left armpit, which made him run jerkily in an odd, crooked, sideways fashion. Turning round again he carefully fired three shots, deliberately stopping himself when he had fired his sixth round:

'Keep the last one for myself. Think of Elena and Nikolka. Done for. They'll torture me, carve epaulettes on my shoulders with their knives. Keep the seventh one for myself.'

Limping sideways, he had an odd sensation: although he could feel the weight of the revolver in his right hand, it was his left arm which was somehow growing heavier. He had to stop. He was out of breath and he would never get away. Nevertheless Alexei somehow reached the turn of that most beautiful street in the world, disappeared round the corner and gained a brief respite. The prospect looked hopeless: that wrought-iron doorway was firmly shut, those huge double doors over there were bolted . . . He remembered a stupid old proverb: 'Don't give up, brother, till you hit bottom.'

Then, in one miraculous moment, he saw her beside a black, moss-grown wall that almost hid a row of trees in the garden behind it. Half collapsing against the wall, she was stretching out her arms and like the heroine in a melodrama her huge, terror-stricken eyes shone as she screamed:

'You – officer! Here! Here . . .'

His felt boots slipping, breathing in ragged, hot gulps, Alexei stumbled towards the rescuing arms and threw himself after them through the narrow gateway in the black wooden wall. Instantly everything changed. The woman pushed the gate to close the gap in the wall, the lock clicked shut. Alexei found her eyes close to his. In them he was vaguely conscious of determination, energy and blackness.

'Follow me', the woman whispered as she turned and ran along the narrow brick-paved path. Alexei ran very slowly after her. The walls of courtyards flashed past to his left, then the woman turned. To his right was what looked like a beautiful white terraced garden. Stopping at a low fence the woman passed through another gate, and Alexei followed her, panting. She slammed the gate shut. A shapely black-stockinged leg flashed before his eyes, there was a swish of her coat and she was climbing nimbly up a brick stairway. Alexei's sharpened hearing could hear the sounds of his pursuers in the street which they had left behind. There . . . they had just turned the corner and were looking for him. 'She might have saved me . . . might have . . .' thought Alexei, 'but I don't think I shall make it . . . my heart.' Suddenly he collapsed on to his left knee and his left hand at the very top of the steps. Everything started to revolve. The woman bent down and gripped Alexei under his right arm.

'Just a little . . . a little bit further!' she screamed. Fumbling wildly with her left hand she opened a third little wicket gate, pulled along the stumbling Alexei by his arm and began running again along a tiny narrow alleyway. 'What a labyrinth . . . thank God for it, though', Alexei thought hazily as he found himself in the white garden, but now at a much higher level and mercifully far away from Malo-Provalnaya Street. He felt the woman pulling him, felt that his left side and arm were very hot while the rest of his body was cold and his icy heart scarcely beating. 'She might have saved me, but this is the end now . . . legs getting weaker . . .' He dimly saw what looked like some lilac bushes under the snow, a door, a lantern hanging outside an old-fashioned porch covered in snow. There was the sound of a key. The woman was still there at his right side and was straining with the last of her strength to drag Alexei toward the lantern. Then after the sound of a second key, into the gloom of a place with an old, lived-in smell. Overhead a dim little light flared, the floor skidded sideways to the left under his feet . . . Some unfamiliar poison-green blobs with fiery edges flashed past his eyes, and in the darkness that followed he felt a great relief . . .

*

A row of tarnished brass knobs in the dim, flickering light. Something cold was running down his open shirt-front, enabling him to breathe more easily, but his left sleeve was full of a damp, ominous, lifeless warmth. 'That's it. I'm wounded.' Alexei realised that he was lying on the floor, his head leaning painfully against something hard and uncomfortable. The brass knobs in front of him belonged to a trunk. The cold, so great that it took his breath away, was her throwing water over him.

'For God's sake,' said a faint, husky voice over his head, 'drink this. Are you breathing? What am I to do now?'

A glass clattered against his teeth and Alexei noisily gulped down some icy cold water. Now, very close, he could see her fair curls and her dark, dark eyes. Squatting on her haunches the woman put down the glass on the floor and gently putting her arm behind his neck she began to lift Alexei up.

'How's my heart?' he wondered. 'Seem to be coming round . . . maybe I haven't lost too much blood . . . must fight.' His heart was beating, but fast, unevenly and in sudden jerks and Alexei said weakly:

'Cut my clothes off if necessary, but whatever you do put on a tourniquet at once . . .'

Her eyes widened as she strained to hear him, then as she understood she jumped up and ran to a closet, and pulled out heaps of material.

Biting his lip, Alexei thought: 'At least there's no bloodstain on the floor, with luck I may not have been bleeding too hard.' With the woman's help he wriggled out of his coat and sat up, trying to ignore the dizziness. She began to take off his tunic.

'Scissors', said Alexei.

He was short of breath and it was hard to talk. The woman disappeared, sweeping the floor with the silk hem of her dress, and wrenched off her hat and fur coat in the lobby. Then she came back and squatted down again. With the scissors she sliced clumsily and painfully into the sleeve, already wet and sticky with blood, ripped it open and freed Alexei's arm. The shirt was quickly dealt with. The whole left sleeve and side was dark red and soaking. Blood started to drip on to the floor.

'Don't worry, cut away . . .'

The shirt fell away in tatters and Alexei, white-faced, naked and yellow to the waist, blood-stained, determined to live and not to faint a second time, clenched his teeth and prodded his left shoulder with his right hand.

'Thank God . . . bone's not broken. Tear off a square or a long strip.'

'I have a bandage', she said weakly, but happily. She disappeared, returned, tearing open the wrapping of a bandage and saying: 'There's no one else here . . . I'm alone . . .'

Again she sat down beside him. Alexei saw the wound. It was a small hole in the upper arm, near the inner surface at the point where the arm lies closest to the body. A thin stream of blood was seeping out of it.

'Wound on the other side?' he asked jerkily and laconically, instinctively conserving the breath of life.

'Yes, there is', she said with horror.

'Tie the tourniquet above it . . . yes, there . . . right.'

There came a new, violent pain, green rings danced before his eyes. Alexei bit his lower lip.

She pulled from one side, he helped from the other end with his teeth and his right hand, until the burningly painful knot encircled his arm above the wound. At once the bleeding stopped.

*

The woman moved him thus: he got to his knees and put his right arm round her shoulder while she helped him to stand up on his weak, trembling legs, and led him into the next room, supporting him with her whole body. Around him in the twilight he saw deep, dark shadows in a very low, old-fashioned room. When she had sat him down on something soft and dusty, she turned aside and turned up the light in a cerise-shaded lamp. He made out a velvet fringe, part of a double-breasted frock-coat and a yellowish-gold epaulette in a frame on the wall. Stretching out her arms to Alexei and breathing heavily from excitement and exertion, she said:

'I have some brandy . . . Perhaps you should have some? . . . Brandy?'

He replied:

'Yes, right away . . .'

And collapsed on to his right elbow.

The brandy seemed to help, at least Alexei began to feel he might not die and might survive the pain which was gnawing and cutting into his shoulder. Kneeling, the woman bandaged his wounded arm, then sidled down to his feet and pulled off his felt boots. This done she brought him a pillow and a long Japanese robe that smelled faintly of a sweet, long-faded perfume and was embroidered with exotic sprays of flowers.

'Lie down', she said.

Obediently he lay down, she spread the robe over him and then a blanket, and stood beside the narrow ottoman looking in to his face.

He said:

'You . . . you're a remarkable woman.' After a silence: 'I'll lie down for a bit until I get my strength back, then I'll get up and go home . . . Just put up with me for a little longer.'

Fear and despair came over him. 'What's happened to Elena? Oh God, and Nikolka. Why did Nikolka have to die? He's dead, for sure . . .'

She pointed silently at a little window, covered by a ruched blind with pompoms. Far away he clearly heard the crack of rifle-fire.

'They'll kill you at once if you try and go now', she said.

'I wouldn't like to drag you into it . . . They may come suddenly, they'll see a revolver, blood . . . there in my greatcoat pocket . . .' He licked his dry lips. He was feeling slightly light-headed from the loss of blood and the brandy. The woman's face looked frightened, then thoughtful.

'No,' she said resolutely, 'no, if they had been going to find you they would already be here by now. This place is such a labyrinth that no one could find our tracks. We crossed through three gardens. But all the same I must clear up at once . . .'

He heard the splash of water, rustle of material, the sound of things being rearranged in closets. She returned holding his

Browning automatic by the butt with two fingers as though it were red hot and asked:

'Is it loaded?'

Pulling out his sound arm from under the blanket, Alexei tested the safety catch and said:

'It won't harm you, but only hold it by the butt.'

She came back again and said in embarrassment:

'Just in case they do come . . . I shall have to take off your breeches . . . Then you can lie there and I'll say you're my husband and you're sick . . .'

Frowning and grimacing Alexei began to unbutton his breeches. She walked firmly up to the ottoman and knelt down, then put her hands under the blanket and having pulled off his breeches by the footstraps, folded them up and took them away. In the short time that she was away he noticed that the apartment was divided into two rooms by an arch. The ceilings were so low that if a grown man had stood on tiptoe he could have touched the ceiling with his hand. In the far room beyond the arch it was dark, but the varnished side of an old piano gleamed, there was something else shining and what looked like a flowering cactus. Nearby the wall was dominated by the portrait of the man in gold epaulettes.

God, the place was so full of antiques, it was like a museum! The epaulettes in the portrait fascinated him. A tallow candle in a candlestick gave a gentle light. There had once been peace and now peace was dead. Those years could not be brought back. Behind him were two small, low windows and another at his side. What was this funny little house? She lived alone. Who was she? She had saved him . . . no peace . . . shooting out on the streets . . .

*

She came in, laden with a pile of firewood and dropped it noisily in the corner by the stove.

'What are you doing? Why bother?' he asked irritably.

'I had to light the stove anyway', she answered with a hint of a smile in her eyes. 'I can manage . . .'

'Come here', Alexei asked her quietly. 'Look, I haven't thanked

you for everything you've . . . done . . . And I don't know how to
. . .' He stretched out his hand and took her fingers. As she
obediently drew nearer he kissed her thin wrist twice. Her face
softened as though a shadow of anxiety had been lifted from it and
in that moment her eyes looked extraordinarily beautiful.

'If it hadn't been for you,' Alexei went on, 'I would certainly
have been killed.'

'Of course,' she replied, 'of course you would . . . After all you
did kill one of them.'

'I killed one of them?' he asked, feeling a new weakness as his
head began to spin.

'M'hm.' She nodded approvingly and looked at Alexei with a
mixture of fear and curiosity. 'Oh, it was terrible . . . they almost
shot me too.' She shuddered.

'How did I kill him?'

'Well, they leaped round the corner, you began shooting and
the man in front fell down . . . Perhaps you just wounded him.
Anyway you were brave . . . I thought I was going to faint. You
were running, turned round and shot at them, then ran on again
. . . What are you – a captain?'

'What made you think I was an officer? Why did you shout
"officer" at me?'

Her eyes shone.

'I decided you must be an officer when I saw your badge in your
fur cap. Why did you have to take such a risk by wearing your
badge?'

'Badge? Oh my God, of course . . . I see now . . .' He remembered
the shop bell ringing . . . the dusty mirror . . . 'I ripped off everything else – but had to go and forget my badge! I'm not an
officer,' he said, 'I'm just an army doctor. My name is Alexei
Vasilievich Turbin . . . Please tell me – what is your name?'

'I am Julia Alexandrovna Reiss.'

'Why are you alone?'

Her answer was somehow strained and she looked away as she
said:

'My husband's not here at the moment. He went away. And his mother too. I'm alone . . .' After a pause she added:

'It's cold in here. Brrr . . . I'll light the stove.'

*

As the logs burned up in the stove his head ached with growing violence. His wound had stopped hurting him, all the pain was concentrated in his head. It began in his left temple, then spread to the crown of his head and the back of his neck. Some little vein under his left eyebrow tautened and radiated waves of desperate pain in all directions. Julia Reiss knelt down at the stove and raked the fire with a poker. Alternately opening and closing his eyes in pain, Alexei watched her as she turned her head aside from the heat, screening it with her pale wrist. Her hair seemed to be an indefinite color which at one moment looked ash-blond shot with flame, at the next almost gold; but her eyebrows were as coal-black as her eyes. He could not decide whether that irregular profile with its aquiline nose was beautiful or not. The look in her eyes was a riddle. There was fear, anxiety and perhaps – sensuality . . . Yes, sensuality.

As she sat there lapped in a wave of heat she was miraculously attractive. She had saved his life.

*

For hours that night, when the heat of the stove had long since died down and burned instead in his head and arm, someone was twisting a red-hot nail into the top of his head and destroying his brain. 'I've got a fever', Alexei repeated drily and soundlessly, and tried to instil into his mind that he must get up in the morning and somehow make his way home. As the nail bored into his brain it finally drove out his thoughts of Elena, of Nikolka, of home and of Petlyura. Nothing mattered. Peturra . . . Peturra . . . He could only long for one thing – for the pain to stop.

Deep in the night Julia Reiss came in wearing soft fur-trimmed slippers, and sat beside him and again, his arm weakly hooked around her neck, he passed through the two small rooms. Before this she had gathered her strength and said to him:

214

'Get up, if only you can. Don't pay any attention to me. I'll help you. Then lie right down . . . Well, if you can't . . .'

He replied:

'No, I'll go . . . only help me . . .'

She led him to the little door of that mysterious house and then helped him back. As he lay down, his teeth chattering from the cold, he felt some lessening and respite from his headache and said:

'I swear I won't forget what you've done. Go to bed . . .'

'Be quiet, I'll soothe your head', she replied.

Then the dull, angry pain flowed out of his head, flowed away from his temples into her soft hands, through them and through her body into the floor, covered with a dusty, fluffy carpet, and there it expired. Instead of the pain a delicious even heat spread all over his body. His arm had gone numb and felt as heavy as cast-iron, so he did not move it but merely closed his eyes and gave himself up to the fever. How long he lay there he could not have said: perhaps five minutes, perhaps hours. But he felt that he could have lain like that, bathed in heat, for ever. Whenever he opened his eyes, gently so as not to alarm the woman sitting beside him, he saw the same picture: the little lamp burning weakly but steadily under its red shade giving out a peaceful light, and the woman's unsleeping profile beside him. Her lips pouting like an unhappy child, she sat staring out of the window. Basking in the heat of fever, Alexei stirred and edged towards her . . .

'Bend over me', he said. His voice had become dry, weak and high-pitched. She turned to him, her eyes took on a frightened guarded look and the shadows around them deepened. Alexei put his right arm around her neck, pulled her to him and kissed her on the lips. It seemed to him that he was touching something sweet-tasting and cold. The woman was not surprised by what Alexei did, but only gazed more searchingly into his face. Then she said:

'God, how hot you are. What are we going to do? We ought to call a doctor, but how are we going to do it?'

'No need', Alexei replied gently. 'I don't need a doctor. To-morrow I'll get up and go home.'

'I'm so afraid,' she whispered, 'that you'll get worse. Then how can I help you? It's not bleeding any more, is it?' She touched his bandaged arm so lightly that he did not feel it.

'Don't worry, nothing's going to happen to me. Lie down and sleep.'

'I'm not going to leave you', she answered, caressing his hand. 'You have such a fever.'

He could not stop himself from embracing her again and drawing her to him. She did not resist. He drew her until she was leaning right over him. Then, as she lay down beside him he sensed through his own sickly heat the clear live warmth of her body.

'Lie down and don't move,' she whispered, 'and I'll soothe your head.'

She stretched out alongside him and he felt the touch of her knees. She began to smooth back his hair from his temples. He felt such pleasure that he could only think of how to prevent himself from falling asleep.

But he did fall asleep, and slept long, peacefully and well. When he awoke he felt that he was floating in a boat on a river of warmth, that all his pain had gone, and that outside the night was turning gradually paler and paler. Not only the little house but the City and the whole world were full of silence. A glassy, limpid blue light was pouring through the gaps in the blinds. The woman, warm from his body, but with her face set in a look of unhappiness, was asleep beside him. And he went to sleep again.

*

In the morning, around nine o'clock, one of the rare cab-drivers took on two passengers on the deserted Malo-Provalnaya Street – a man in a black civilian overcoat, looking very pale, and a woman. Carefully supporting the man by the arm, the woman drove him to St Alexei's Hill. There was no traffic on the hill, except for a cab outside No. 13 which had just brought a strange visitor with a trunk, a bundle and a cage.

Fourteen

THAT evening all the habitués of No. 13 began to converge on the house of their own accord. None of them had been cut off or driven away.

'It's him', echoed the cry in Anyuta's breast, and her heart fluttered like Lariosik's bird. There had come a cautious tap at the little snow-covered window of the Turbins' kitchen. Anyuta pressed her face to the window to make out the face. It was him, but without his moustache . . . Him . . . With both hands Anyuta smoothed down her black hair, opened the door into the porch, then from the porch into the snow-covered yard and Myshlaevsky was standing unbelievably close to her. A student's overcoat with a beaver collar and a student's peaked cap . . . his moustache was gone . . . but there was no mistaking his eyes, even in the half-darkness of the porch. The right one flecked with green sparks, like a Urals gemstone, and the left one dark and languorous . . . And he seemed to be shorter.

With a trembling hand Anyuta unfastened the latch, then the courtyard vanished and the patch of light from the open kitchen door vanished too, because Myshlaevsky's coat had enveloped Anyuta and a very familiar voice whispered:

'Hallo, Anyutochka . . . You'll catch cold . . . Is there anyone in the kitchen, Anyuta?''

'No one', answered Anyuta, not knowing what she was saying, and also whispering for some reason. 'How sweet his lips have become . . .' she thought blissfully and whispered: 'Viktor Viktororich . . . let me go . . . Elena . . .'

'What's Elena to do with it', whispered the voice reproachfully, a voice smelling of eau-de-cologne and tobacco. 'What's the matter with you, Anyutochka . . .'

'Let me go, I'll scream, honestly I will', said Anyuta passionately as she embraced Myshlaevsky round the neck. 'Something terrible's happened – Alexei Vasilievich's wounded . . .'

The boa-constrictor instantly released her.

'What – wounded? And Nikolka?'

'Nikolka's safe and well, but Alexei Vasilievich has been wounded.'

The strip of light from the kitchen, then through more doors . . .

In the dining-room Elena burst into tears when she saw Myshlaevsky and said:

'Vitka, you're alive . . . Thank God . . . But we're not so lucky . . .' She sobbed and pointed to the door of Alexei's room. 'His temperature's forty . . . badly wounded . . .'

'Holy Mother', said Myshlaevsky, pushing his cap to the back of his head. 'How did he get caught?'

He turned to the figure at the table bending over a bottle and some shining metal boxes.

'Are you a doctor, may I ask?'

'No, unfortunately', answered a sad, muffled voice. 'Allow me to introduce myself: Larion Surzhansky.'

＊

The drawing-room. The door into the lobby was shut and the portière drawn to prevent the noise and the sound of voices from reaching Alexei. Three men had just left his bedroom and driven away – one with a pointed beard and gold pince-nez, another clean shaven, young, and finally one who was gray and old and wise, wearing a heavy fur coat and a tall fur hat, a professor, Alexei's old teacher. Elena had seen them out, her face stony. She had pretended that Alexei had typhus, and now he had it.

'Apart from the wound – typhus . . .'

The column of mercury showed forty and . . . 'Julia' . . . A feverish flush, silence, and in the silence mutterings about a staircase and a telephone bell ringing . . .

＊

'Good day, sir', Myshlaevsky whispered maliciously in Ukrainian, straddling his legs wide. Red-faced, Shervinsky avoided his look.

His black suit fitted immaculately; an impeccable shirt and a bow tie; patent-leather boots on his feet. 'Artiste of Kramsky's Opera Studio.' There was a new identity-card in his pocket to prove it. 'Why aren't you wearing epaulettes, *sir*?' Myshlaevsky went on. ' "The imperial Russian flag is waving on Vladimirskaya Street ... Two divisions of Senegalese in the port of Odessa and Serbian billeting officers ... Go to the Ukraine, gentlemen, and raise your regiments" ... Remember all that, Shervinsky? Why, you mother-...'

'What's the matter with you?' asked Shervinsky. 'It's not my fault is it? What did I have to do with it? I was nearly shot myself. I was the last to leave headquarters, exactly at noon, when the enemy's troops appeared in Pechorsk.'

'You're a hero', said Myshlaevsky, 'but I hope that his excellency, the commander-in-chief managed to get away sooner. Just like his highness, the Hetman of the Ukraine ... the son of a bitch ... I trust that he is in safety. The country needs men like him. Yes – perhaps *you* can tell me exactly where they are?'

'Why do you want to know?'

'I'll tell you why.' Myshlaevsky clenched his right fist and smashed it into the palm of his left hand. 'If those *excellencies* and those *highnesses* fell into my hands I'd take one of them by the left leg and the other by the right, turn them upside down and bang their heads on the ground until I got sick of it. And the rest of your bunch of punks at headquarters ought to be drowned in the lavatory ...'

Shervinsky turned purple.

'See here – you be more careful what you're saying, if you please', he began. 'Don't forget that the Hetman abandoned his headquarters staff too. He took no more than two personal aides with him, all the rest of us were just left to our fate.'

'Do you realise that at this moment a thousand of our men are cooped up as prisoners in the museum, hungry, guarded by machine-guns ... And whenever they feel inclined, Petlyura's men will simply squash them like so many bed-bugs. Did you know that Colonel Nai-Turs was killed? He was the only one who ...'

'Keep your distance!' shouted Shervinsky, now genuinely angry. 'What do you mean by that tone of voice? I'm as much a Russian officer as you are!'

'Now, gentlemen, stop!' Karas wedged himself between Myshlaevsky and Shervinsky. 'This is a completely pointless conversation. He's right, Viktor – you're being too personal. Stop it, this is getting us nowhere . . .'

'Quiet, quiet,' Nikolka whispered miserably, 'he'll hear you . . .' Embarrassed, Myshlaevsky changed his tune.

'Don't get upset, Mr Opera-singer. I get carried away . . . you know me.'

'Funny way you have . . .'

'Gentlemen, please be quiet . . .' Nikolka gave a warning look and tapped his foot on the floor. They all stopped and listened. Voices were coming from Vasilisa's apartment below. They could just make out the sound of Vasilisa laughing cheerfully, though a shade hysterically. As if in reply, Wanda said something in a confident, ringing voice. Then they quietened down a little, the voices burbling on for a while.

'How extraordinary', said Nikolka thoughtfully. 'Vasilisa has visitors. People to see him. And at a time like this. A real party too, by the sound of it.'

'He's weird all right, is your Vasilisa', grunted Myshlaevsky.

*

It was around midnight that Alexei fell asleep after his injection, and Elena settled down in the armchair by his bedside. Meanwhile, a council of war was taking place in the drawing-room.

It was decided that they should all stay for the night. Firstly, it was pointless to try and go anywhere at night, even with papers that were in order. Secondly, it would be better for Elena if they stayed – they could help in case it was needed. And above all, at a time like this it was better *not* to be at home, but to be out visiting. An even more pressing reason was that there was no alternative; here at least they could play whist.

'Do you play?' Myshlaevsky asked Lariosik.

Lariosik blushed, looked embarrassed, and said hastily that he did play, but very, very badly . . . that he hoped they wouldn't swear at him in the way his partner, the tax inspector, used to swear at him in Zhitomir . . . that he had been through a terrible crisis, but that here in Elena Vasilievna's house he was regaining his spirits, that Elena Vasilievna was a quite exceptional person and that it was so warm and cosy here, especially the cream-colored blinds on all the windows, which made you feel insulated from the outside world . . . And as for that outside world – you had to agree it was filthy, bloody and senseless.

'Do you write poetry, may I ask?' Myshlaevsky asked, staring intently at Lariosik.

'Yes, I do', Lariosik said modestly, blushing.

'I see, . . . Sorry I interrupted you . . . Senseless, you were saying. Please go on.'

'Yes, senseless, and our wounded souls look for peace some-where like here, behind cream-colored blinds . . .'

'Well, as for peace, I don't know what things are like in Zhito-mir, but I don't think you'll find it here, in the City . . . Better give your throat a good wetting with vodka before we start, or you'll feel very dry. May we have some candles? Excellent. In that case someone will have to stand down. Playing five-handed, with one dummy, is no good . . .'

'Nikolka plays like a dummy, anyway', put in Karas.

'What? What a libel! Who lost hands down last time? You revoked.'

'The right place to live is behind cream-colored blinds. I don't know why, but everyone seems to laugh at poets . . .'

'God forbid . . . Why did you take my question amiss? I've nothing against poets. I admit I don't read poetry but . . .'

'And you've never read any other books either except for the artillery manual and the first fifteen pages of Roman law . . . the war broke out on page sixteen and he gave it up . . .'

'Nonsense, don't listen to him . . . What is your name and patronymic – Larion Ivanovich?'

Lariosik explained that he was called Larion Larionovich, but he found the company so congenial, which wasn't so much company as a friendly family and he would like it very much if they simply called him 'Larion' without his patronymic . . . Provided, of course, no one had any objections.

'Seems a decent fellow . . .' the usually reserved Karas whispered to Shervinsky.

'Good . . . let's get down to the game, then . . . He's lying, of course. If you really want to know, I've read *War and Peace*. Now there's a book for you. Read it right through – and enjoyed it. Why? Because it wasn't written by any old scribbler but by an artillery officer. Have you drawn a ten? Right, you're my partner . . . Karas partners Shervinsky . . . Out you go, Nikolka.'

'Only don't swear at me please', begged Lariosik in a nervous voice.

'What's the matter with you? We're not cannibals, you know – we won't eat you! I can see the tax inspectors in Zhitomir must be a terrible breed. They seem to have frightened the life out of you . . . We play a very strict game here.'

'So you've no need to worry', said Shervinsky as he sat down. 'Two spades . . . Ye . es . . . now there was a writer for you, Lieutenant Count Lev Nikolaevich Tolstoy of the artillery . . . Pity he left the army . . . pass . . . he'd have made general . . . Instead of retiring to his estate, where anyone might turn to novel-writing out of boredom . . . nothing to do in those long winter evenings. Easy enough in the country. No ace . . .'

'Three diamonds', said Lariosik shyly.

'Pass', answered Karas.

'What's all this about being a bad player? You play very well. You deserve to be congratulated, not sworn at. Well then, if you call three diamonds, I'll say four spades. I wouldn't mind going to my estate myself at the moment . . .'

'Four diamonds', Nikolka prompted Lariosik, glancing at his cards.

'Four? Pass.'

'Pass.'

In the flickering light of the candle, amid the cigarette smoke,

Lariosik nervously bought more cards. Like spent cartridges flicking out of a rifle Myshlaevsky dealt the players a card apiece.

'A low spade', he announced, adding encouragingly to Lariosik: 'Well done!'

The cards flew out of Myshlaevsky's hands as noiselessly as maple leaves. Shervinsky threw down neatly, Karas harder and more clumsily. Sighing, Lariosik put down his cards as gently as if each one was an identity card.

'Aha,' said Karas, 'so that's your game – king-on-queen.'

Myshlaevsky suddenly turned purple, flung his cards on the table and swivelling round to stare furiously at Lariosik, he roared:

'Why the hell did you have to trump my queen? Eh, Larion?!'

'Good, Ha, ha, ha!' Karas gloated. 'Our trick I believe!'

A terrible noise broke out over the green table and the candle-flames stuttered. Waving his arms, Nikolka tried to calm the others down and rushed to shut the door and close the portière.

'I thought Fyodor Nikolaevich had a king', Lariosik murmured faintly.

'How could you think that . . .' Myshlaevsky tried not to shout, which gave his voice a hoarse rasp that made it sound even more terrifying: '. . . when you bought it yourself and handed it to me? Eh? That's a hell of a way to play' – Myshlaevsky looked round at them all – 'isn't it? He said he came here for peace and quiet, didn't he? Well, trumping your partner's trick is a funny way to look for a peaceful life, I must say! This is a game of skill, dammit! You have to use your head, you know, this isn't like writing poetry!'

'Wait. Perhaps Karas . . .'

'Perhaps what? Perhaps nothing. I'm sorry if that's the way they play in Zhitomir, but to me it's sheer murder! Don't get me wrong . . . Pushkin and Lomonosov wrote poetry, they wouldn't have pulled a trick like that . . .'

'Oh, shut up Viktor. Why lose your temper with him? It happens to everybody.'

'I knew it,' mumbled Lariosik, 'I knew I'd be unlucky . . .'

'Ssh. Stop . . .'

There was instant, total silence. Far away, through many closed doors, a bell trembled in the kitchen. Pause. Then came the click of footsteps, doors were opened, and Anyuta came into the room. Elena passed quickly through the lobby. Myshlaevsky drummed on the green baize cloth and said:

'A bit early, isn't it?'

'Yes, it is', said Nikolka, who regarded himself as the expert on house-searches.

'Shall I open the door?' Anyuta asked uneasily.

'No, Anna Timofeyevna,' replied Myshlaevsky, 'wait a moment.' He rose groaning from his chair. 'Let me go to the door, don't you bother . . .'

'We'll both go', said Karas.

'Right', said Myshlaevsky, suddenly looking exactly as if he were standing in front of a platoon of troops. 'I assume everything is all right in the bedroom . . . Doctor Turbin has typhus. Elena, you're his sister . . . Karas – you pretend to be a doctor . . . no, a medical student. Go into the bedroom, make it look convincing. Fiddle about with a hypodermic or something . . . There are quite a lot of us . . . we should be all right . . .'

The bell rang again impatiently, Anyuta gave a start; they all looked anxious.

'No hurry', said Myshlaevsky as he took a small toy-like black revolver from his hip-pocket.

'That's too risky', said Shervinsky, frowning. 'I'm surprised at you. You of all people ought to be more careful. D'you mean to say you walked through the streets carrying it?'

'Don't worry,' Myshlaevsky replied calmly and politely, 'we'll take care of it. Take it, Nikolka, and if necessary throw it out of a window or out of the back door. If it's Petlyura's men at the door, I'll cough. Then throw it out – only throw it so that we can find it again afterwards. I'm fond of this little thing, it went with me all the way to Warsaw . . . Everyone ready?'

'Ready', said Nikolka grimly and proudly as he took the revolver.

'Right.' Myshlaevsky poked Shervinsky in the chest with his

finger, and said: 'You're a singer, invited to give a recital.' To Karas: 'You're a doctor, come to see Alexei.' To Nikolka: 'You're the brother.' To Lariosik: 'You're a student and you're a lodger here. Got an identity card?'

'I have a tsarist passport,' said Lariosik turning pale, 'and a student identity card from Kharkov University.'

'Hide the tsarist one and show your student card.'

Lariosik clutched at the portière, pushed it aside and went out.

'The women don't matter', Myshlaevsky went on. 'Right – has everybody got identity cards? Nothing suspicious in your pockets? Hey, Larion! Somebody ask him if he's carrying a weapon.'

'Larion!' Nikolka called out from the dining-room. 'Do you have a gun?'

'No, God forbid', answered Larion from somewhere in the depths of the apartment.

Again there came a long, desperate, impatient ring at the door-bell.

'Well, here goes', said Myshlaevsky and made for the door. Karas disappeared into Alexei's bedroom.

'I'll make it look as if someone's playing patience', said Shervinsky and blew out the candles.

There were three doors to pass through to get into the Turbins' apartment. The first was from the lobby on to the staircase, the second was a glass door which marked off the limit of the Turbins' property. Beyond the glass door and downstairs was a cold, dark hallway, on one side of which was the Lisovichs' front door; at the end of the hallway was the third door giving on to the street.

Doors slammed, and Myshlaevsky could be heard downstairs shouting:

'Who's there?'

Behind him at the top of the stairs he sensed the shadowy figures of his friends, listening. Outside a muffled voice said imploringly:

'How many more times do I have to ring? Does Mrs Talberg-Turbin live here? Telegram for her. Open up.'

'This is an old trick', Myshlaevsky thought to himself, and he began coughing hard. One of the figures on the staircase disappeared indoors. Cautiously Myshlaevsky opened the bolt, turned the key and opened the door, leaving the chain in position.

'Give me the telegram', he said, standing sideways to the door so that he was invisible to the person outside. A hand in a gray sleeve pushed itself through and handed him a little envelope. To his astonishment Myshlaevsky realised that it really was a telegram.

'Sign please', said the voice behind the door angrily.

With a quick glance Myshlaevsky saw that there was only one person standing outside.

'Anyuta, Anyuta', he shouted cheerfully, his bronchitis miraculously cured. 'Give me a pencil.'

Instead of Anyuta, Karas ran down and handed him a pencil. On a scrap of paper torn from the flap of the envelope Myshlaevsky scribbled 'Tur', whispering to Karas:

'Give me twenty-five . . .'

The door was slammed shut and locked.

In utter amazement Myshlaevsky and Karas climbed up the staircase. All the others had gathered in the lobby. Elena tore open the envelope and began mechanically reading aloud:

'Lariosik suffered terrible misfortune stop. Operetta singer called Lipsky . . .'

'My God!' shouted Lariosik, scarlet in the face. 'It's the telegram from my mother!'

'Sixty-three words', groaned Nikolka. 'Look, they've had to write all round the sides and on the back!'

'Oh lord!' Elena exclaimed. 'What have I done? Lariosik, please forgive me for starting to read it out aloud. I'd completely forgotten about it . . .'

'What's it all about?' asked Myshlaevsky.

'His wife's left him', Nikolka whispered in his ear. 'Terrible scandal . . .'

The apartment was suddenly invaded by a deafening noise of hammering on the glass door as if it had been hit by a landslide. Anyuta screamed. Elena turned pale, and started to collapse against the wall. The noise was so monstrous, so horrifying and absurd that even Myshlaevsky's expression changed. Shervinsky, pale himself, caught Elena . . . A groan came from Alexei's bedroom.

'The door', shrieked Elena.

Completely forgetting their strategic plan Myshlaevsky ran down the staircase, followed by Karas, Shervinsky and the mortally frightened Lariosik.

'Sounds bad', muttered Myshlaevsky.

A single black silhouette could be seen beyond the frosted-glass door. The noise stopped.

'Who's there?' roared Myshlaevsky in his parade-ground voice.

'For God's sake, open up. It's me, Lisovich . . . Lisovich!' screamed the black silhouette. 'It's me – Lisovich . . .'

Vasilisa was a terrible sight. His hair, with pink bald patches showing through, was wildly dishevelled. His necktie was pulled sideways and the tails of his jacket flapped like the doors of a broken closet. His eyes had the blurred, unfocused look of someone who has been poisoned. He reached the first step, then suddenly swayed and collapsed into Myshlaevsky's arms. Myshlaevsky caught him, but he was off-balance. He sat back heavily on to the stairs and shouted hoarsely:

'Karas! Water . . .'

Fifteen

IT was evening, almost eleven o'clock. Because of events the street, never very busy, was empty and deserted rather earlier than usual.

There was a thin fall of snow, the flakes floating evenly and steadily past the window, and the branches of the acacia tree, which in summer gave shade to the Turbins' window, bent lower and lower under their coating of snow.

The snowfall had begun at lunchtime and from then on the day had turned into a dull, lowering evening full of ill-omen. The electric current was reduced to half strength, and Wanda served brains for supper. Brains are a horrible form of food anyway, and when cooked by Wanda they were disgusting. Before the brains there was soup, which Wanda had cooked with vegetable oil, and Vasilisa had risen from table in a bad temper with the unpleasant feeling of having eaten nothing at all. That evening he had innumerable things to do, all of them difficult and unpleasant. The dining-room table had been turned upside down and a bundle of Lebid-Yurchik's money was lying on the floor.

'You're a fool', Vasilisa said to his wife.

Wanda turned on him and she answered:

'I've always known you were a despicable beast, but lately you've been outdoing yourself.'

Vasilisa felt an agonising desire to fetch her a swinging blow across the face that would knock her over and make her hit her head on the edge of the sideboard. And then again and again until that damned, bony creature shut up and admitted she was beaten. He, Vasilisa, was worn out, he worked like a slave, and he felt he had a right to demand that she obey him at home. Vasilisa gritted his teeth and restrained himself. Attacking Wanda was a rather more dangerous undertaking than one might think.

'Just do as I say', said Vasilisa through clenched teeth. 'Don't you see – they may move the sideboard and what then? But they'd never think of looking under the table. Everybody in town does it.'

Wanda gave in to him and they set to work together, pinning banknotes to the underside of the table with thumb-tacks. Soon the whole underside of the table was covered with a multi-colored pattern like a well-designed silk carpet.

Grunting, his face covered in sweat, Vasilisa stood up and glanced over the expanse of paper money.

'It's going to be so inconvenient', said Wanda. 'Every time I want some money I shall have to turn the dining-room table over.'

'So what, it won't kill you', replied Vasilisa hoarsely. 'Better to have to turn the table over than lose everything. Have you heard what's going on in the City? They're worse than the Bolsheviks.

They're searching houses indiscriminately, looking for officers who fought against them.'

At eleven o'clock Wanda carried the samovar from the kitchen into the dining-room and put out the lights everywhere else in the apartment. She produced a bag of stale bread and a lump of green cheese from the sideboard. The single lamp hanging over the table from one socket of a triple chandelier shed a dim reddish light from its semi-incandescent filament.

Vasilisa chewed a piece of bread roll and green cheese, which was so unpleasant that it made his eyes water as if he had a raging toothache. At every bite fine crumbs of the sickening stuff spattered his jacket and his tie. Uneasy, though not knowing quite why, Vasilisa glared at Wanda as she chewed.

'I'm amazed how easily they get away with it', said Wanda, glancing upwards towards the Turbins. 'I was certain that one of them had been killed. But no, they're all back, and now the apartment is full of officers again . . .'

At any other time Wanda's remarks would not have made the slightest impression on Vasilisa, but now, when he was tortured by fear and unease, he found them intolerably spiteful.

'I'm surprised at you', he replied, glancing away to avoid the irritation of looking at her, 'you know perfectly well that really they were doing the right thing. Somebody had to defend the City against those (Vasilisa lowered his voice) swine . . . Besides you're wrong if you think they got off lightly . . . I think he's been . . .'

Wanda looked thoughtful and nodded.

'Yes, I thought so too when I went up there . . . You're right, he's been wounded . . .'

'Well, then, it's nothing to be pleased about – got away with it, indeed . . .'

Wanda licked her lips.

'I'm not pleased, I only say they seem to have "got away with it" because what I want to know is, when Petlyura's men come to you – which God forbid – and ask you, as chairman of the house committee, who are the people upstairs – what are you going to say? Were they in the Hetman's army, or what?'

Vasilisa scowled.

'I can say with absolute truth that he's a doctor. After all, there's no reason why I should know anything else about him. How could I?'

'That's the point. In your position you're *supposed* to know.'

At that moment the door-bell rang. Vasilisa turned pale, and Wanda turned her scrawny neck.

His nose twitching, Vasilisa stood up and said:

'D'you know what? Maybe I'd better run straight up to the Turbins and call them.'

Before Wanda had time to reply the bell rang again.

'Oh my God', said Vasilisa anxiously. 'Nothing for it – I shall have to go.'

Terrified, Wanda followed him. They opened their front door into the communal hallway, which smelled of the cold. Wanda's angular face, eyes wide with fear, peeped out. Above her head the electric bell gave another importunate ring.

For a moment the idea crossed Vasilisa's mind of knocking on the Turbins' glass door – someone would be bound to come down and things might not be so terrible. But he was afraid to do it. Suppose the intruders were to ask him: 'Why did you knock? Afraid of something? Guilty conscience?' Then came the hopeful thought, though a faint one, that it might not be a search-party but perhaps someone else . . .

'Who's there?' Vasilisa asked weakly at the door.

Immediately a hoarse voice barked through the keyhole at the level of Vasilisa's stomach and the bell over Wanda's head rang again.

'Open up', rasped the keyhole in Ukrainian. 'We're from headquarters. And don't try running away, or we'll shoot through the door.'

'Oh, God . . .' sighed Wanda.

With lifeless hands Vasilisa slid open the bolt and then lifted the heavy latch, after fumbling with the chain for what seemed like hours.

'Hurry up . . .' said the keyhole harshly.

Vasilisa looked outside to see a patch of gray sky, an acacia branch, snowflakes. Three men entered, although to Vasilisa they seemed to be many more.

'Kindly tell me why . . .'

'Search', said the first man in a wolfish voice, marching straight up to Vasilisa. The corridor revolved and Wanda's face in the lighted doorway seemed to have been powdered with chalk.

'In that case, if you don't mind', Vasilisa's voice sounded pale and colorless, 'please show me your warrant. I'm a peaceful citizen – I don't know why you want to search my house. There's nothing here', said Vasilisa, painfully aware that his Ukrainian had suddenly deserted him.

'Well, we've come to have a look', said the first man.

Edging backwards as the men pushed their way in, Vasilisa felt he was seeing them in a dream. Everything about the first man struck Vasilisa as wolf-like. Narrow face, small deep-set eyes, gray skin, long straggling whiskers, unshaven cheeks furrowed by deep grooves, he had a curious shifty look and even here, in a confined space, he managed to convey the impression of walking with the inhuman, loping gait of a creature at home in snow and grassland. He spoke a horrible mixture of Russian and Ukrainian, a language familiar to those inhabitants of the City who know the riverside district of Podol, where in summertime the quayside is alive with groaning, rattling winches and where ragged men unload watermelons from barges . . . On the wolf's head was a fur hat, a scrap of blue material with tinsel piping dangling loosely from one side.

The second man, a giant, almost touched the ceiling of Vasilisa's lobby. His complexion was as ruddy as a jolly, rosy-cheeked peasant woman's, and so young that there was no hair on his face. He wore a coarse sheepskin cap with moth-eaten earflaps, a gray overcoat, and his unnaturally small feet were clad in filthy, tattered rags.

The third man had a broken nose, one side of which was covered in a suppurating scab, and his upper lip was disfigured by a crudely stitched scar. On his head was an officer's old peaked cap with a red band and a pale mark where the badge had once been. He wore an old-fashioned double-breasted army tunic with brass buttons covered in verdigris, a pair of black trousers, and bast foot-cloths round his instep over a pair of thick gray army-issue socks. His face in the lamplight was compounded of two colors – a waxy yellow and a dull violet, whilst his eyes stared with a look of malice and self-pity.

'We've come to have a look,' the wolf repeated, 'and here's our warrant.'

With this he dived into his trouser pocket, pulled out a crumpled piece of paper and thrust it at Vasilisa. While one of his eyes kept Vasilisa in a state of palsied fear, his other eye, the left, made a cursory inspection of the furniture in the lobby.

The crumpled sheet was folded into four, and was embossed: 'Headquarters 1st Cossack Corps.' Beneath that, written with indelible pencil in large sloping characters, was an order in Ukrainian:

> You are instructed to carry out a search of the premises of citizen Vasily Lisovich, No. 13 St Alexei's Hill. Resistance to this order is punishable by summary execution.
>
> > signed: *Protsenko*, Chief of Staff
> > *Miklun*   Adjutant

In the lower left-hand corner was the indecipherable impression of a blue rubber stamp.

The sprays of flowers on the lobby wallpaper swam slightly in front of Vasilisa's eyes and he said as the wolf regained possession of the piece of paper:

'Come in, please, but there's nothing here . . .'

The wolf pulled a black, oil-smeared automatic out of his pocket and pointed it at Vasilisa. Wanda gave a muffled scream. A long, businesslike revolver, also gleaming with oil, appeared in the hand of the man with the disfigured face. Vasilisa's knees weakened and he seemed to grow shorter. Suddenly the electric light flashed brightly on to full power.

'Who's here?' asked the wolf in a hoarse voice.

'No one', Vasilisa replied through white lips. 'Just me and my wife.'

'Come on, lads – let's have a look. And quick', grunted the wolf to his companions. 'No time to waste.'

The giant picked up a heavy wooden chest and shook it like a box of matches, whilst the disfigured man darted towards the stove. Pocketing his revolver, he hammered with his fists on the wall, noisily flung open the stove door sending out a wave of tepid heat.

'Any weapons?' asked the wolf.

'No, on my word of honor . . . why should I have a weapon . . .'

'No', echoed Wanda's shadow breathlessly.

'Better say if you have. Ever seen a man shot?' asked the wolf meaningfully.

'Why should I have a gun?'

The green-shaded lamp was burning brightly in the study where Alexander II, indignant to the depth of his cast-iron soul, stared at the three intruders. In the green light of the study Vasilisa discovered for the first time in his life the dizzy feeling that comes before a fainting-fit. All three men began immediately to examine the wallpaper. In great heaps, as if they were toys, the giant flung down row upon row of books from the bookshelf, whilst six hands tapped their way all over the wallpaper. Tap, tap, tap . . . the wall echoed dully. Suddenly the box in the secret cache rang out: tonk. The wolf's eyes shone with glee.

'What did I say?' he whispered noiselessly. The giant stamped a hole with his feet through the leather of the armchair and rose almost to the ceiling. There was a cracking sound as the giant's fingers broke into the cache. He pulled out the tin box and threw the string-tied paper package down to the wolf. Vasilisa staggered and leaned against the wall. The wolf began to shake his head and shook it for a long time as he stared at the half-dead Vasilisa.

'Well, well, well', he said bitterly. 'What's all this? Nothing here, you said, but seems you've sealed up your money in the wall. You ought to be shot!'

'Oh, no!' cried Wanda.

Something odd happened to Vasilisa, and he suddenly burst into convulsive laughter. It was a terrible laugh because Vasilisa's eyes were alive with fear and only his lips, nose and cheeks were laughing.

'But I haven't broken the law. There's nothing there except some papers from the bank and a few little things . . . There's not much money . . . I've earned it all . . . Anyway, all tsarist money is cancelled now . . .'

As Vasilisa spoke he stared at the wolf as though the sight of him gave him a morbid, unnatural pleasure.

'You should be arrested', said the wolf reprovingly as he shook the packet and dropped it into the bottomless pocket of his tattered greatcoat. 'Come on, lads, see to the desk.'

From the desk drawers, opened by Vasilisa himself, there poured forth heaps of paper, seals, signets, postcards, pens, cigarette cases. The green carpet and the red cloth of the table-top were strewn with paper, sheets of paper fell rustling to the floor. The disfigured man overturned the wastepaper basket. In the drawing-room they tapped the walls superficially, almost reluctantly. The giant pulled back the carpet and stamped on the floor, purposely leaving a row of marks like burns in the wood. Now that the current had been increased for night-time, the electricity sputtered cheerfully on full power and the phonograph horn glittered brightly. Vasilisa followed the three men, stumbling and dragging his feet. A certain stunned calm came over Vasilisa and his thoughts seemed to flow more coherently. Then into the bedroom – instant chaos as clothes, sheets poured out of the mirror-fronted wardrobe and the mattress was turned upside down. The giant suddenly stopped, a shy grin broke out over his face and he looked down. From beneath the ravaged bed peeped Vasilisa's new kid boots with lacquered toes. The giant laughed, glanced timidly at Vasilisa.

'There's a smart pair of boots', he said in a high-pitched voice. 'I wonder if they fit me?'

Vasilisa had no time to think of a reply before the giant bent down and tenderly picked up the boots. Vasilisa shuddered.

'They're kid', he said vaguely.

As the wolf turned on him, bitter anger flashed in his squinting eyes:

'Quiet, you bastard', he said grimly. 'Shut up!' he said again, suddenly losing his temper. 'You ought to thank us for not shooting you as a thief and a bandit for hoarding that fortune of yours. So you be quiet.' His eyes glistened with menace as he advanced on the deathly pale Vasilisa. 'You've been sitting here, making your pile, feeding your ugly mug till you're as pink as a pig – and now you can see what people like us have to wear on their feet. See? His feet are frost-bitten and wrapped in rags, he rotted in the trenches for you while you were sitting at home and playing the phonograph. Ah, you mother-f . . .' In his eyes flashed an urge to punch Vasilisa in the ear, and he swung his arm. Wanda screamed: 'No . . .' The wolf did not quite dare to punch the respectable Vasilisa and only poked him in the chest with his fist. Chalk-white, Vasilisa staggered, feeling a stab of pain and anguish in his chest at the blow from that bony fist.

'That's revolution for you', he thought in his pink, neat head. 'Fine state of affairs. We should have strung them all up, and now it's too late . . .'

'Put those boots on, Vasilko', the wolf said in a kindly voice to the giant, who sat down on the springy mattress and pulled off his foot-cloths. The boots would not fit over his thick gray socks.

'Give the cossack a pair of thin socks', the wolf said sternly, turning to Wanda, who at once squatted down to pull out the bottom drawer of the chest-of-drawers and took out a pair of socks. The giant threw away his thick gray socks showing feet with red toes and black corns, and pulled on the new pair. The boots went on with difficulty and the laces on the left boot broke with a snap. Delighted, grinning like a child, the giant tied the frayed ends and stood up. And immediately it was as if something snapped in the tense relationship between those five ill-assorted people. They began to act more naturally. With a glance at the giant's boots the disfigured man suddenly reached out and deftly snatched Vasilisa's trousers that were hanging on a hook alongside the washstand. The wolf simply gave Vasilisa another suspicious glance – would he say anything? – but Vasilisa and Wanda said nothing; their faces were both the same shade of unrelieved white, their eyes wide and round. The bedroom began to look like a corner of a ready-made clothing store. The man with the disfigured face stood there in nothing but his torn, striped underpants and examined the trousers in the light.

'Nice bit of serge, this . . .' he said in a nasal whine, sat down in a blue armchair and began to pull them on. The wolf exchanged his dirty tunic for Vasilisa's grey jacket, and said as he handed some papers back to Vasilisa: 'Here take these, mister, you may need them.' He picked up a globe-shaped glass clock from the table, its face adorned with broad Roman figures, and as the wolf pulled on his greatcoat the clock could be heard ticking underneath it.

'Useful thing, a clock. Being without a clock's like being without hands', the wolf said to broken-nose, his attitude to Vasilisa noticeably relenting. 'I like to be able to see what time it is at night.'

Then all three moved off, back through the drawing-room to the study. Together Vasilisa and Wanda followed after them. In the study the wolf, squinting hard, looked thoughtful and said to Vasilisa:

'Better give us a receipt, Mister . . .' (His forehead creased like an accordion as he wrestled with some obviously disturbing thought.)

'What?' whispered Vasilisa.

'Receipt, saying you gave us these things', the wolf explained, staring at the floor.

Vasilisa's expression changed, his cheeks turned pink.

'But how can I . . . What . . .' (He wanted to shout 'What! you mean to say I have to give you a receipt as well!' but quite different words came out.) 'Why do you need a receipt?'

'Ah, you ought to be shot like a dog, you . . . you blood sucker. I know what you're thinking, I know. If your people were in power you'd squash us like insects. I can see there's no good to be

236

had out of you. Boys, put him up against the wall. I'll give you such a thrashing . . .'

Working himself up until he was shaking with fury, he pushed Vasilisa against the wall and clutched him by the throat, at which Vasilisa instantly turned red.

'Oh!' shrieked Wanda in horror, tugging at the wolf's arm. 'Stop it! Mercy, for God's sake! Vasya, do as he says and write it!'

The wolf released the engineer's throat, and with a crack one half of his collar burst away from the stud as though on a spring. Vasilisa did not remember how he came to be sitting in his chair. With shaking hands he tore a sheet from a note-pad, dipped his pen into the ink. In the silence the crystal globe could be heard ticking in the wolf's pocket.

'What shall I write?' Vasilisa asked in a weak, cracked voice.

The wolf began to think, his eyes blinking.

'Write . . . "By order of headquarters of the cossack division . . . I surrendered . . . articles . . . articles . . . to the sergeant as follows" . . .'

'As follows . . .' croaked Vasilisa, and was silent.

'Then say what they are . . . "In the course of search. I have no claims." Then sign . . .'

Here Vasilisa gathered the last remnants of the breath in his body and turning his glance away from the wolf, he asked:

'Who shall I say I gave them to?'

The wolf looked suspiciously at Vasilisa, but he restrained his displeasure and only sighed.

'Write: Sergeant Nemolyak . . .' He thought for a moment, glancing at his companions. '. . . Sergeant Kirpaty and Hetman Uragan.'

Staring muzzily at the paper, Vasilisa wrote to the wolf's dictation. Having written it, instead of his proper signature he wrote 'Vasilis' and handed the paper to the wolf, who took it and stared at it.

Just then the glass door at the top of the staircase slammed, footsteps were heard and Myshlaevsky's voice rang out.

The wolf scowled, his companions shuffled uneasily. The wolf turned red in the face and hissed: 'Quiet!' He pulled the automatic out of his pocket and pointed it at Vasilisa, who gave a martyred smile. From the corridor came more footsteps, muffled talk. Then there was the sound of the bolt being drawn, the latch, the chain – and the door was locked again. Footsteps again, men laughing. After that the glass door slammed, the sound of steps receding upstairs and all was quiet. The disfigured man went out into the lobby, leaned his head against the door and listened. When he returned he exchanged meaning glances with the wolf and all three jostled their way out into the lobby. There the giant wriggled his fingers inside his boots, which were rather tight.

'They'll be cold.'

And he put on Vasilisa's rubber overshoes.

The wolf turned to Vasilisa and said shiftily in a low voice:

'See here, mister . . . Don't you tell anyone we've been here. If you inform on us, our boys will beat you up. Don't go out of the house till tomorrow, or you'll be in trouble . . .'

'Sorry', whined the man with the shattered nose.

The rosy-cheeked giant said nothing, but only looked shyly at Vasilisa, then delightedly at his gleaming overshoes. As they walked quickly out of Vasilisa's door and along the passage to the front door, for some reason they tiptoed, jostling each other as they went. The door was noisily unlocked, there was a glimpse of dark sky and with cold hands Vasilisa closed the bolts. His head swam, and for a moment he thought he was dreaming. His heart almost stopped, then started beating faster and faster. In the lobby Wanda was sobbing. She collapsed on to a chest, knocking her head against the wall, and big tears poured down her face.

'God, what's happened to us? God, oh God, Vasya . . . in broad daylight. What are we to do?'

Shaking like a leaf, Vasilisa stood in front of her, his face contorted.

'Vasya,' screamed Wanda, 'do you know – they weren't soldiers, they weren't from any headquarters! They were just hoodlums!'

'I know, I realised that', Vasilisa mumbled, spreading his hands in despair.

'Lord!' Wanda exclaimed. 'You must go this minute, report them at once and try and catch them! Mother of God! All our things! Everything! If only there was somebody who . . .' She shuddered and slid from the chest to the floor, covering her face with her hands. Her hair was dishevelled, her blouse unbuttoned at the back.

'But where do we report them?' asked Vasilisa.

'To headquarters, for God's sake, to the police! Make a formal complaint. Quickly. What's the matter?'

Vasilisa, who had been shuffling his feet, suddenly rushed for the door. He ran to the Turbins' glass door and hammered on it noisily.

*

Everybody except Shervinsky and Elena crowded into Vasilisa's apartment. Lariosik, looking pale, stayed in the doorway. Legs planted wide, Myshlaevsky inspected the foot-cloths and other rags abandoned by the unknown visitors and said to Vasilisa:

'Well, you won't see your things again, I'm afraid. They weren't soldiers, just burglars. You can thank God you're still alive. To tell you the truth I'm amazed they let you off so lightly.'

'God – the things they did to us!' said Wanda.

'They threatened to kill me.'

'Thank the Lord they didn't carry out their threat. First time I've ever seen anything like it.'

'Neat piece of work', Karas added quietly.

'What do we do now?' asked Vasilisa miserably. 'Go and complain? But where to? For God's sake advise me, Viktor Viktorovich.'

Myshlaevsky grunted thoughtfully.

'I advise you not to complain to anyone', he said. 'Firstly, they'll never catch them.' He crooked his middle finger. 'Secondly . . .'

'Don't you remember, Vasya, they said you'd be killed if you made a complaint.'

'That's nonsense', Myshlaevsky frowned. 'No one's going to kill you, but as I say, they'll never be caught, no one will even try and catch them, and secondly . . .' He crooked his second finger, 'you'll have to describe what they stole, and that means admitting that you were hoarding tsarist money . . . No, if you make a complaint to their headquarters or to anywhere else they will almost certainly have you searched again.'

'Yes, very likely', said Nikolka the specialist.

Shattered, soaking with the water thrown over him when he fainted, Vasilisa hung his head. Wanda quietly burst into tears and leaned against the wall. They all felt sorry for them. Lariosik sighed deeply in the doorway and turned up his lacklustre eyes.

'We each have our grief to bear', he murmured.

'What weapons did they have?' asked Nikolka.

'My God, two of them had revolvers. Did the third man have anything, Vasya?'

'Two of them had revolvers', Vasilisa confirmed weakly.

'Did you notice what type they were?' Nikolka pressed him in a business-like voice.

'I don't really know,' Vasilisa replied with a sigh, 'I don't know the various types. One was big and black, the other one was smaller, with a lanyard fixed to a ring on the butt.'

'Yes, that's right,' said Wanda, 'one of them had a lanyard on it.'

Nikolka frowned and cocked his head to one side like a bird as he looked at Vasilisa. He shuffled awkwardly for a moment, then with an uneasy movement he slipped unobtrusively out of the door, followed by Lariosik. Upstairs, Lariosik had not even reached the dining-room when the sound of breaking glass and a howl came from Nikolka's room. Lariosik hastened after him. The light shone brightly in Nikolka's room, a stream of cold air was coming through the open upper pane and there was a gaping hole in the lower casement which Nikolka had made with his knees as he had jumped down from the window-ledge in despair. There was a wild look in his eyes.

'It can't be!' cried Lariosik, clasping his hands together. 'Pure witchcraft!'

Nikolka rushed out of the room, through the library, through the kitchen and past the horrified Anyuta, who shouted: 'Nikol, Nikol, where are you going without a hat? Oh Lord, don't say something else has happened?' Then he was out of the porch and into the yard. Crossing herself, Anyuta shut the door in the porch, then ran back into the kitchen and pressed her face to the window, but Nikolka was already out of sight.

He turned sharp left, ran to the corner of the house and stopped in front of the snowdrift blocking the way into the gap between the houses. The snowdrift was completely untouched. 'I don't understand', Nikolka muttered in despair, and bravely plunged into the drift. He felt he was suffocating. For a long time he waded, almost swam in snow, snorting, until he had finally broken through the barrier and cleared the snow away from the space between the two walls. He looked up and saw, far above, where the light fell from the fateful window of his room, that there was the row of black spikes and their broad, sharp-pointed shadows, but no sign of the tin box.

In a last hope that maybe the cord had broken Nikolka fell on his knees and fumbled around among the rubble of broken bricks. No box.

At this point Nikolka suddenly had an idea. 'Aha!' he shouted, and crawled forward to the fence which closed off the gap to the street. Reaching the fence, he prodded it, several planks fell away and he found himself looking through a large hole on to the dark street. It was obvious what had happened. The men had ripped away the planks leading into the gap, had climbed in and – of course! – they had tried to get into Vasilisa's apartment by way of his cellar, but the window was barred.

White and silent Nikolka went back into the kitchen.

'Lord, you're filthy – let me clean you up', cried Anyuta.

'Leave me alone, for God's sake', replied Nikolka and passed on into the apartment wiping his frozen hands on his trousers. 'Larion, you may punch me on the jaw', he said to Lariosik, who blinked, then stared and said:

'Why, Nikolashka? There's no need for despair.' He began

timidly to brush the snow from Nikolka's back with his hands.

'Apart from the fact that if Alyosha recovers – which pray God he does – he will never forgive me,' Nikolka went on, 'it means I've lost the Colt that belonged to Colonel Nai-Turs! I'd rather have been killed myself! It's God's punishment on me for sneering at Vasilisa. I feel bad enough about Vasilisa as it is, but it's far worse for me now because *those* were the guns they used to rob him. Although anyone could rob him without a gun at all, he's so feeble . . . What a man. God, it's a terrible business. Come on, Larion, get some paper and we'll mend the window.'

*

That night Nikolka, Myshlaevsky and Lariosik crawled into the gap with axe, hammer and nails to mend the fence. Nikolka himself frenziedly drove in the long, thick nails so far that their points stuck out on the far side. Later still they went out with candles on to the verandah, from where they climbed through the cold storeroom into the attic. There, above the apartment, they clambered everywhere, squeezing between the hot water pipes and trunks full of clothes, until they had cut a listening-hole in the ceiling.

When he heard about the expedition to the attic, Vasilisa showed the liveliest interest and joined them in crawling around among the beams, thoroughly approving of everything that Myshlaevsky was doing.

'What a pity you didn't warn us somehow. You should have sent Wanda Mikhailovna up to us by the back door', said Nikolka, wax dripping from his candle.

'That wouldn't have done much good', Myshlaevsky objected. 'By the time they were in the apartment the game was up. You don't believe they wouldn't have put up a fight, do you? Of course they would – and how. You'd have had a bullet in your belly before there was time to reach us. And that would have been that. No – your best bet was never to have let them in by the front door at all.'

'But they threatened to shoot through the door, Viktor Viktorovich', said Vasilisa pathetically.

'They would never have done that', Myshlaevsky replied as he banged away with the hammer. 'Not a chance of it. That would have brought the whole street down on their heads.'

Later still that night Karas found himself luxuriating like Louis XIV in the Lisovichs' apartment. This was preceded by the following conversation:

'Oh no, they won't come back again tonight', said Myshlaevsky.

'No, no, no', Wanda and Vasilisa replied in chorus on the staircase, 'please – we beg you or Fyodor Nikolaevich to come down and spend the rest of the night with us – please! It won't be any trouble to you. Wanda Mikhailovna will make tea for you, and we'll make you up a comfortable bed. Please come tonight – and tomorrow too. We must have another man in the apartment.'

'Otherwise I won't sleep a wink', added Wanda, wrapping herself in an angora shawl.

'And there's a drop or two of brandy in the house to keep the cold out', said Vasilisa in an unexpectedly devil-may-care voice.

'Go on, Karas', said Myshlaevsky.

So Karas went and settled in comfortably. Brains and thin soup with vegetable oil were, as might be expected, no more than a symptom of the loathsome disease of meanness with which Vasilisa had infected his wife. In reality there were considerable treasures concealed in the depths of their apartment, treasures known only to Wanda. There appeared on the dining-room table a jar of pickled mushrooms, veal, cherry jam and a bottle of real, good Shustov's brandy with a bell on the label. Karas called for a glass for Wanda Mikhailovna and poured some out for her.

'Not a full glass!' cried Wanda.

With a despairing gesture Vasilisa obeyed Karas and drank a glassful.

'Don't forget, Vasya – it's not good for you', said Wanda tenderly.

After Karas had explained authoritatively that brandy never harmed anyone and that mixed with milk it was even given to people suffering from anaemia, Vasilisa drank a second glass. His cheeks turned pink and his forehead broke out in sweat. Karas drank five glasses and was soon in excellent spirits. 'Feed her up a bit and she wouldn't be at all bad', he thought as he looked at Wanda.

Then Karas praised the layout of the Lisovichs' apartment and discussed the arrangements for signalling to the Turbins: one bell was installed in the kitchen, another in the lobby. At the slightest sign they were to ring upstairs. And if anyone had to go and open the front door it would be Myshlaevsky, who knew what to do in case of trouble.

Karas was loud in praise of the apartment: it was comfortable and well furnished. There was only one thing wrong – it was cold.

That night Vasilisa himself fetched logs and with his own hands lit the stove in the drawing-room. Having undressed, Karas lay down on a couch between two luxurious sheets and felt extremely well and comfortable. Vasilisa, in shirtsleeves and suspenders, came in, sat down in an armchair and said:

'I can't sleep, so do you mind if we sit and talk for a while?'

The stove was burning low. Calm at last, settled in his armchair, Vasilisa sighed and said:

'That's how it goes, Fyodor Nikolaevich. Everything I've earned in a lifetime of hard work has disappeared in one evening into the pockets of those scoundrels . . . by violence. Don't think I rejected the revolution – oh no, I fully understand the historical reasons which caused it all.'

A crimson glow played over Vasilisa's face and on the clasps of his suspenders. Feeling pleasantly languorous from the brandy, Karas was beginning to doze, whilst trying to keep his face in a look of polite attention.

'But you must agree that here in Russia, this most backward country, the revolution has already degenerated into savagery and chaos . . . Look what has happened: in less than two years we have been deprived of any protection by the law, of the very minimal protection of our rights as human beings and citizens. The English have an expression . . .'

'M'mm, yes, the English . . . They, of course . . .' Karas mumbled, feeling that a soft wall was beginning to divide him from Vasilisa.

'. . . but here – how can one say "my home is my castle" when even in your own apartment, behind seven locks, there's no guarantee that a gang like that one which got in here today won't come and take away not only your property but, who knows, your life as well!'

'We'll prevent it with our signalling system', Karas replied rather vaguely in a sleepy voice.

'But Fyodor Nikolaevich! There's more to the problem than just a signalling system! No signalling system is going to stop the ruin and decay which have eaten into people's souls. Our signalling system is a particular case, but let's suppose it goes wrong?'

'Then we'll fix it', answered Karas happily.

'But you can't build a whole way of life on a warning system and a few revolvers. That's not the point. I'm talking in broader terms, generalising from a single instance, if you like. The fact is that the most important thing of all has disappeared – I mean respect for property. And once that happens, it's the end. We're finished. I'm a convinced democrat by nature and I come from a poor background. My father was just a foreman on the railroad. Everything you can see here and everything those rogues stole from me today – all that was earned by my own efforts. And believe me I never defended the old régime, on the contrary, I can admit to you in secret I belonged to the Constitutional Democrat party, but now that I've seen with my own eyes what this revolution's turning into, then I swear to you I am horribly convinced that there's only one thing that can save us . . .' From some point in the fuzzy cocoon in which Karas was wrapped came the whispered word: '. . . Autocracy. Yes, sir . . . the most ruthless dictatorship imaginable . . . it's our only hope . . . Autocracy . . .'

'God, how he goes on', Karas thought beatifically. 'M'yes . . . autocracy – good idea. Aha . . . h'm . . .' he mumbled through the surrounding cotton wool.

'Yes, mumble, mumble, mumble . . . habeas corpus, mumble

245

mumble . . . Yes, mumble, mumble . . .' The voice droned on through the wadding, 'mumble, mumble they're making a mistake if they think this state of affairs can last for long, mumble, mumble and they shout hurrah and sing "Long Live." No sir! It will *not* be long lived, and it would be ridiculous to think . . .'

'Long live Fort Ivangorod.' Vasilisa's voice was unexpectedly interrupted by the dead commandant of the fort in which Karas had served during the war.

'And long live Ardagan and Kars!' echoed Karas from the mists.

From far away came the thin sound of Vasilisa's polite laughter.

'Long may he live!' sang joyous voices in Karas' head.

Sixteen

'LONG may he live. Long may he live. Lo-o-ong li-i-ive . . .' sang the nine basses of Tolmashevsky's famous choir.

'Long may he li-i-i-ive . . .' rang out the crystalline descant.

'Long may . . . long may . . . long may . . .' the soprano soared up to the very dome of the cathedral.

'Look! Look! It's Petlyura . . .'

'Look, Ivan . . .'

'No, you fool, Petlyura's out in the square by now . . .'

Hundreds of heads in the choir-loft crowded one on another, jostling forward, hanging down over the balustrade between the ancient pillars adorned with smoke-blackened frescoes. Craning, excited, leaning forward, pushing, they surged towards the balustrade trying to look down into the well of the cathedral, but could see nothing for the hundreds of heads already there, like rows of yellow apples. Down in the abyss swayed a reeking, thousand-headed crowd, over which hovered an almost incandescent wave of sweat, steam, incense smoke, the lamp-black from hundreds of candles, and soot from heavy chain-hung ikon-lamps.

The ponderous gray-blue drape creaked along on its rings and covered the doors of the altar screen, floridly wrought in centuries-old metal as dark and grim as the whole gloomy cathedral of St Sophia. Crackling faintly and swaying, the flaming tongues of candles in the chandeliers drifted upwards in threads of smoke. There was not enough air for them. Around the altar there was incredible confusion. From the doors of side-chapels, down the worn granite steps, poured streams of gold copes and fluttering stoles. Priestly headdresses, like short violet stovepipes, slid out of their cardboard boxes, religious banners were taken down, flapping, from the walls. Somewhere in the thick of the crowd boomed out the awesome bass of Archdeacon Seryebryakov. A headless, armless cope swayed above the crowd and was swallowed up again; then there rose up one sleeve of a quilted cassock, followed by the other as its wearer was enrobed in the cope. Check handkerchiefs fluttered and were twisted into plaits.

'Tie up your checks tighter, Father Arkady, the frost outside is wicked. Please let me help you.'

Like the flags of a conquered army the sacred banners were dipped as they passed under the doorway, brown faces and mysterious gold words swaying, fringes scraping along the ground.

'Make way, there . . .'

'Where are they going?'

'Manya! Look out! You'll be crushed . . .'

'What are they celebrating? (whisper:) Is it the Ukrainian people's republic?'

'God knows' (whisper).

'That's not a priest, that's a bishop . . .'

'Look out, careful . . .'

'Long may he live . . .!'

sang the choir, filling the whole cathedral. The fat, red-faced precentor Tolmashevsky extinguished a greasy wax candle and thrust his tuning-fork into his pocket. The choir, in brown heel-length surplices with gold braid, the swaying choirboys whose cropped fair hair made their little heads look almost bald, the bobbing of Adam's apples and horse-like heads of the basses streamed out of the dark, eerie choir-loft. Thicker and thicker, jostling through all the doors, like a swelling avalanche, like water gushing from drainpipes flowed the murmuring crowd.

From the doors of the sacristy floated a stream of vestments, their wearers' heads wrapped up as if they all had toothache, eyes anxious and uneasy beneath their toylike, mauve stovepipe hats. Father Arkady, dean of the cathedral, a puny little man, wearing a sparkling jewelled mitre above the gray check scarf wrapped around his head, glided along with little mincing steps. There was a desperate look in his eyes and his wispy beard trembled.

'There's going to be a procession round the cathedral. Out of the way, Mitya.'

'Hey, you – not so fast! Come back! Give the priests room to walk.'

'There's plenty of room for them to pass.'

'For God's sake – this child is suffocating . . .'

'What is happening?'

'If you don't know what's happening you'd better go home, where there's nothing for you to steal . . .'

'Somebody's cut the strap of my handbag!'

'But Petlyura's supposed to be a socialist, isn't he? So why are all the priests praying for him?'

'Look out!'

'Give the fathers twenty-five roubles, and they'll say a mass for the devil himself.'

'We ought to go straight off to the bazaar now and smash in some of the Yids' shop windows. I once did . . .'

'Don't speak Russian.'

'This woman's suffocating! Clear a space!'

'Kha-a-a-a . . .'

Shoulder to shoulder, unable to turn, from the side chapels, from the choir-lofts, down step after step the crowd slowly moved out of the cathedral in one heaving mass. On the wall frescoes the brown painted figures of fat-legged buffoons, of unknown antiquity, danced and played the bagpipes. Half suffocated, half intoxicated by carbon dioxide, smoke and incense the crowd flowed noisily out of the doors, the general hum occasionally pierced by the strangled cries of women in pain. Pickpockets, hat brims pulled low, worked hard and with steady concentration, their skilled hands slipping expertly between sticky clumps of compressed human flesh. The crowd rustled and buzzed above the scraping of a thousand feet.

'Oh Lord God . . .'

'Jesus Christ . . . Holy Mary, queen of heaven . . .'

'I wish I hadn't come. What is supposed to be happening?'

'I don't care if you are being crushed . . .'

'My watch! My silver watch! It's gone! I only bought it yesterday . . .'

'This may be the last service in this cathedral . . .'

'What language were they holding the service in, I didn't understand?'

'In God's language, dear.'

'It's been strictly forbidden to use Russian in church any more.'

'What's that? Aren't we allowed to use our own Orthodox language any more?'

'They pulled her ear-rings off and tore half her ears away at the same time . . .'

'Hey, cossacks, stop that man! He's a spy! A Bolshevik spy!'

'This isn't Russia any longer, mister. This is the Ukraine now.'

'Oh my God, look at those soldiers – wearing pigtails . . .'

'Oh, I'm going . . . to faint . . .'

'This woman's feeling bad.'

'We're all feeling bad, dear. Everybody's feeling terrible. Look out, you'll poke my eye out – stop pushing! What's the matter with you? Gone crazy?'

'Down with Russia! Up the Ukraine!'

'There ought to be a police cordon here, Ivan Ivanovich. Do you remember the celebrations in 1912? Ah, those were the days . . .'

'So you want Bloody Nicholas back again, do you? Ah, we know your sort . . . we know what you're thinking.'

'Keep away from me, for Christ's sake. I'm not in your way, so keep your hands to yourself . . .'

'God, let's hope we get out of here soon . . . get a breath of fresh air.'

'I won't make it. I shall die of suffocation in a moment.'

Like soda-water from a bottle the crowd burst swirling out of the main doors. Hats fell off, people groaned with relief, crossed themselves. Through the side door, where two panes of glass were broken in the crush, came the religious procession, silver and gold, the priests breathless and confused, followed by the choir. Flashes of gold among the black vestments, mitres bobbed, sacred banners were held low to pass under the doorway, then straightened and floated on upright.

There was a heavy frost, a day when smoke rose slowly and heavily above the City. The cathedral courtyard rang to the ceaseless stamp of thousands of feet. Frosty clouds of breath swayed in the freezing air and rose up towards the belfry. The great bell of St Sophia boomed out from the tallest bell-tower, trying to drown the awful, shrieking confusion. The smaller bells tinkled away at random, dissonant and tuneless, as though Satan had climbed into the belfry and the devil in a cassock was amusing himself by raising bedlam. Through the black slats of the multi-storied belfry, which had once warned of the coming of the slant-eyed Tartars, the smaller bells could be seen swinging and yelping like mad dogs on a chain. The frost crunched and steamed. Shocked by noise and cold, the black mob poured across the cathedral courtyard.

In spite of the cruel frost, mendicant friars with bared heads, some bald as ripe pumpkins, some fringed with sparse orange-colored hair, were already sitting cross-legged in a row along the stone-flagged pathway leading to the main entrance of the old belfry of St Sophia and were chanting in a nasal whine.

Blind ballad-singers droned their eerie song about the Last Judgment, their tattered peaked caps lying upwards to catch the sparse harvest of greasy rouble bills and battered coppers.

Oh, that day, that dreadful day,
When the end of the world will come.
The judgment day . . .

The terrible heart-rending sounds floated up from the crunching, frosty ground, wrenched whining from these yellow-toothed old instruments with their palsied, crooked limbs.

'Oh my brethren, oh my sisters, have mercy on my poverty, for the love of Christ, and give alms.'

'Run on to the square and keep a place, Fedosei Petrovich, or we'll be late.'

'There's going to be an open-air service.'

'Procession . . .'

'They're going to pray for victory for the revolutionary people's army of the Ukraine.'

'What victory? They've already won.'

'And they'll win again!'

'There's going to be a campaign.'

'Where to?'

'To Moscow.'

'Which Moscow?'

'The usual.'

'They'll never make it.'

'What did you say? Say that again! Hey, lads, listen to what this Russian's saying!'

'I didn't say anything!'

'Arrest him! Stop, thief!'

'Run through that gateway, Marusya, otherwise we'll never get through this crowd. They say Petlyura's in the square. Let's go and see him.'

'You fool, Petlyura's in the cathedral.'

'Fool yourself. They say he's riding on a white horse.'

'Hurrah for Petlyura! Hurrah for the Ukrainian People's Republic!'

Bong . . . bong . . . bong . . . tinkle – clang-clang . . . Bong-clang-bong . . . raged the bells.

'Have pity on an orphan, Christian people, good people . . . A blind man . . . A poor man . . .'

Dressed in black, his hindquarters encased in leather like a broken beetle, a legless man wriggled between the legs of the crowd, clutching at the trampled snow with his sleeves to pull himself along. Crippled beggars displayed the sores on their bruised shins, shook their heads as though from *tic douloureux* or paralysis, rolled the whites of their eyes pretending to be blind. Tearing at the heart-strings of the crowd, reminding them of poverty, deceit, despair, hopelessness and sheer animal misery, creaking and groaning, they howled the refrain of the damned.

Shivering dishevelled old women with crutches thrust out their desiccated, parchment-like hands as they moaned:

'God give you good health, handsome gentleman!'

'Have pity on a poor old woman . . .'

'Give to the poor, my dear, and God will be good to you . . .'

Capes, coats, bonnets with ear-flaps, peasants in sheepskin caps, red-cheeked girls, retired civil servants with a pale mark on their cap where the badge had been removed, elderly women with protruding bellies, nimble-footed children, cossacks in greatcoats and shaggy fur hats with tops of different colors – blue, red, green, magenta with gold and silver piping, with tassels from the fringes of coffin-palls: they poured out on to the cathedral courtyard like a black sea, yet the cathedral doors still gave forth wave upon wave.

Heartened by the fresh air, the procession gathered its forces, rearranged itself, straightened up and glided off in an orderly and proper sequence of heads wearing check scarves, mitres, stovepipe hats, bareheaded deacons with their long flowing hair, skullcapped monks, painted crosses on gilded poles, banners of Christ the Saviour and the Virgin and Child and a host of ikons in curved and wrought covers, gold, magenta, covered in Slavonic script.

Now like a gray snake winding its way through the City, now like brown turbulent rivers flowing along the old streets, the innumerable forces of Petlyura made their way to the parade on St Sophia's Square. First, shattering the frost with the roaring of trumpets and the clash of glittering cymbals, cutting through the black river of the crowd, marched the tight ranks of the Blue Division.

In blue greatcoats and blue-topped astrakhan caps set at a jaunty angle the Galicians marched past. Slanting forward between bared sabres two blue and yellow standards glided along behind a large brass band and after the standards, rhythmically stamping the crystalline snow, rank on rank of men marched jauntily along dressed in good, sound German cloth. After the first battalion ambled a body of men in long black cloaks belted at the waist with ropes, with German steel helmets on their heads, and the brown thicket of bayonets crept on parade like a bristling swarm.

In uncountable force marched the ragged gray regiments of Cossack riflemen and battalion on battalion of *haidamak* infantrymen; prancing high in the gaps between them rode the dashing regimental, battalion and company commanders. Bold, brassy, confident marches blared out like nuggets of gold in a bright, flashing stream.

After the infantry detachments came the cavalry regiments riding at a collected trot. The excited crowd was dazzled by rank on rank of crumpled, battered fur caps with blue, green and red tops and gold tassels. Looped on to the riders' right hands, their lances bobbed rhythmically like rows of needles. Jingling gaily, the bell-hung hetmen's standards jogged along among the ranks of horsemen and the horses of officers and trumpeters strained forward to the sound of martial music. Fat and jolly as a rubber ball, Colonel Bolbotun pranced ahead of his regiment, his low, sweating forehead and his jubilant, puffed-out cheeks thrusting forward into the frosty air. His chestnut mare, rolling her bloodshot eyes, champing at the bit and scattering flecks of foam, reared now and again on her hind legs, shaking even the 200-pound weight of Bolbotun and making his curved sabre rattle in its scabbard as the colonel lightly touched her nervous flanks with his spurs.

For our headmen are with us,
Shoulder to shoulder
Alongside as brothers . . .

chorused the bold *haidamaks* as they trotted along, pigtails jogging.

With their bullet-torn yellow-and-blue standard fluttering and accordions playing, rode the regiment of the dark, moustached Colonel Kozyr-Leshko mounted on a huge charger. The colonel looked grim, scowling and slashing at the rump of his stallion with a whip. The colonel had cause to be angry – in the misty early hours of that morning the rifle-fire from Nai-Turs' detachment on the Brest-Litovsk highway had hit Kozyr's best troops hard and as the regiment trotted into the square its ranks had been closed up to conceal the gaps in them.

Behind Kozyr came the brave, hitherto unbeaten 'Hetman Mazeppa' regiment of cavalry. The name of the glorious hetman, who had almost destroyed Peter the Great at the battle of Poltava, glittered in gold letters on a sky-blue silk standard.

Streams of people flowed around the gray and yellow walls, people pushed forward and climbed on to advertisement-hoardings, little boys clambered up the lamp-posts and sat on the crossbars, stood on rooftops, whistled and shouted hurrah . . .

'Hurrah! Hurrah!' they shouted from the sidewalks.

Faces crowded behind glassed-in balconies and window-panes.

Cab-drivers climbed unsteadily on to the boxes of the sleighs, waving their whips.

'They said Petlyura's troops were just a rabble . . . Some rabble. Hurrah!'

'Hurrah! Hurrah for Petlyura! Hurrah for our Leader!'

'Hurrah!'

'Look, Manya, look! There's Petlyura himself, look, on the gray horse. Isn't he handsome . . .'

'That's not Petlyura, ma'am, that's a colonel.'

'Oh, really? Then where is Petlyura?'

'Petlyura's at the palace receiving the French emissaries from Odessa.'

'What's the matter with you, mister, gone crazy? What emissaries?'

'Pyotr Vasilievich, they say Petlyura (whisper) is in Paris, did you know?'

'Some rabble . . . there's a million men in this army.'

'Where's Petlyura? If they'd only give us one look at him.'

'Petlyura, madam, is on the square at this moment taking the salute as the parade marches past.'

'Nothing of the sort. Petlyura's in Berlin at the moment meeting the president to sign a treaty.'

'What president? Are you trying to spread rumors, mister?'

'The president of Germany. Didn't you know? Germany's been declared a republic.'

'Did you see him? Did you see him? He looked splendid . . . He's just driven down Rylsky Street in a coach and six horses.'

'But will they recognise the Orthodox Church?'

'I don't know. Work it out for yourself . . .'

'The fact is that the priests are praying for him, anyway . . .'

'He'll be stronger if he keeps the priests on his side . . .'

'Petlyura. Petlyura. Petlyura. Petlyura . . .'

There was a fearsome rumbling of heavy wheels and rattling limbers and after the ten regiments of cavalry rolled an endless stream of artillery. Blunt-muzzled, fat mortars, small-caliber howitzers; the crews sat on the limbers, cheerful, well-fed, victorious, the drivers riding calmly and sedately. Straining and creaking, the six-inch guns rumbled past, hauled by teams of powerful, well-fed, big-rumped horses and smaller hard-working peasant ponies that looked like pregnant fleas. The light mountain artillery clattered briskly along, the little guns bouncing up and down between their jaunty crews.

'Who said Petlyura only had fifteen thousand men? It was all a lie. Just a rabble, they said, no more than fifteen thousand and demoralised . . . God, there are so many I've lost count already. Another battery . . . and another . . .'

His sharp nose thrust into the upturned collar of his student's greatcoat, Nikolka was shoved and jostled by the crowd until he

255

finally succeeded in climbing up into a niche in a wall and installed himself. A jolly little peasant woman in felt boots was already in the niche and said cheerfully to Nikolka:

'You hold on to me, mister, and I'll hang on to this brick and we'll be all right.'

'Thanks,' Nikolka sniffled dejectedly inside his frozen collar, 'I'll hold on to this hook.'

'Where's Petlyura?' the talkative woman babbled on. 'Oh, I do want to see Petlyura. They say he's the handsomest man you've ever seen.'

'Yes,' Nikolka mumbled vaguely into the beaver fur, 'so they say . . .' ('Another battery . . . God, now I understand . . .')

'Look, there he goes, driving in that open car . . . Didn't you see?'

'He's at Vinnitsa', Nikolka replied in a dry, dull voice, wriggled his freezing toes inside his boots. 'Why the hell didn't I put felt boots on? Hellish cold.'

'Look, look, there's Petlyura.'

'That's not Petlyura, that's the commander of the bodyguard.'

'Petlyura has a palace in Belaya Tserkov. Belaya Tserkov will be the capital now.'

'Won't he come to the City, then?'

'He'll come in his own good time.'

'I see, I see . . .'

Clang, clank, clank. The muffled boom of kettledrums rolled across St Sophia's Square; then down the street, machine-guns thrust menacingly from their gun-ports, swaying slightly from the weight of their turrets, rolled the four terrible armored cars. But the enthusiastic, pink-cheeked Lieutenant Strashkevich was no longer inside the leading car. A dishevelled and far from pink-cheeked Strashkevich, waxy-gray and motionless, was lying in the Mariinsky Park at Pechyorsk, immediately inside the park gates. There was a small hole in Strashkevich's forehead and another, plugged with clotted blood, behind his ear. The lieutenant's naked feet stuck out of the snow and his glassy eyes stared straight up into the sky through the bare branches of a maple tree. It was very quiet round about, there was not a living soul in the park and scarcely anyone was to be seen even on the street; the sound of music from St Sophia's Square did not reach as far as here, so there was nothing to upset the complete calm on the lieutenant's face.

Hooting and scattering the crowd, the armored cars rolled onward to where Bogdan Khmelnitzky sat and pointed north-eastwards with a mace, black against the pale sky. The great bell was still sending thick, oily waves of sound over the snowbound hills and roofs of the City; in the thick of the parade the drums thumped untiringly and little boys, maddened with excitement, swarmed around the hooves of the black Bogdan. Next in the parade was a line of trucks, snow-chains clanking on their wheels, carrying choirs and dancing groups in Ukrainian costume — brightly colored embroidered skirts under sheepskin tunics, plaited straw wreaths on the girls' heads and the boys in baggy blue trousers tucked into their boot-tops . . .

At that moment a volley of rifle-fire came from Rylsky Street. Just before it there had been a sudden whirlwind of peasant women screaming in the crowd. There was a shriek and someone started running, then a staccato, breathless, rather hoarse voice shouted:

'I know those men! Kill them! They're officers! I've seen them in uniform!'

A troop of the 10th Cavalry Regiment, waiting their turn to march into the square, forced their way into the crowd and seized a man. Women screamed. The man who had been seized, Captain Pleshko, cried out weakly and jerkily:

'I'm not an officer. Nothing of the sort. What are you doing? I'm a bank clerk.'

Beside him another man was arrested, white-faced and silent, who wriggled in the soldiers' grip.

Then the crowd scattered down the street, jostling each other like animals let out of a sack, running away in terror, leaving an empty space on the street that was completely white except for one black blob – someone's lost hat. A flash and a bang, and Captain

Pleshko, who had thrice denied himself, paid for his curiosity to see the parade. He lay face upward by the fence of the presbytery of St Sophia's cathedral, spreadeagled, whilst the other, silent man fell across his legs with his face to the ground. Just then came a roll of drums from the corner of the square, the crowd surged back again and the band struck up with a boom and a crash. A confident voice roared: 'Walk – march!' Rank upon rank, gold-tasselled caps glittering, the 10th Cavalry Regiment moved off.

*

Quite suddenly a gray patch between the domes of the cathedral broke open and the sun burst through the dull, overcast sky. The sun was bigger than anyone had ever seen it in the Ukraine and quite red, like pure blood. Streaks of clotted blood and plasma flowed steadily from that distant globe as it struggled to shine through the screen of clouds. The sun reddened the dome of St Sophia with blood, casting a strange shadow from it on to the square, so that in that shadow Bogdan turned violet, and made the seething crowd of people look even blacker, even denser, even more confused. And gray men in long coats belted with rope and waving bayonets could be seen climbing up the steps leading up the side of the rock and trying to smash the inscription that stared down from the black granite plinth. But the bayonets broke or slithered uselessly away from the granite, and Bogdan wrenched his horse away from the rock at a gallop as he tried to fly away from the people who were clinging on to the hooves of his horse and weighing them down. His face, turned directly towards the red globe, was furious and he continued steadfastly to point his mace into the distance.

At that moment a man was raised on to the slippery frozen basin of the fountain, above the rumbling, shifting crowd facing the statue of Bogdan. He was wearing a dark overcoat with a fur collar and despite the frost he took off his fur hat and held it in his hands. The square still hummed and seethed like an ant-heap, but the belfry of St Sophia had stopped ringing and the bands had marched off in various directions down the snowbound streets. An enormous crowd had collected around the base of the fountain:

'Petka, who's that up on the fountain?'

'Looks like Petlyura.'

'Petlyura's making a speech.'

'Rubbish . . . that's just an ordinary speaker . . .'

'Look, Marusya, the man's going to make a speech. Look, look . . .'

'He's going to read a proclamation . . .'

'No, he's going to read the Universal.'

'Long live the free Ukraine!'

With an inspired glance above the thousands of heads towards the point in the sky where the sun's disc was emerging even more clearly and gilding the crosses with thick red gold, the man waved his arm and shouted in a weak voice:

'Hurrah for the Ukrainian people!'

'Petlyura . . . Petlyura . . .'

'That's not Petlyura. What are you talking about?'

'Why should Petlyura have to climb up on a fountain?'

'Petlyura's in Kharkov.'

'Petlyura's just gone to the palace for a banquet . . .'

'Nonsense, there aren't going to be any banquets.'

'Hurrah for the Ukrainian people!' the man repeated, at which a lock of fair hair flicked up and dangled over his forehead.

'Quiet!'

The man's voice grew louder and began to make itself heard clearly above the murmur of the crowd and the crunch of feet on snow, above the retreating clatter of the parade, above the distant beat of drums.

'Have you seen Petlyura?'

'Of course I have – just now.'

'Ah, you're lucky. What's he like?'

'Black moustaches pointing upward like Kaiser Wilhelm, and wearing a helmet. Look, there he is, look, look Maria Fyodorovna, look – riding on a horse . . .'

'What d'you mean by spreading rumors like that? That's the chief of the City fire brigade.'

'Petlyura's in Belgium, madame.'

'Why should he go to Belgium?'

'To sign a treaty with the Allies . . .'

'No, no. He's gone to the Duma with a mounted escort.'

'What for?'

'To take the oath . . .'

'Will he take an oath?'

'Why should he take an oath? *They* are going to swear an oath to *him*.'

'Well, I'd rather die, (whisper) I won't swear . . .'

'No need for you. They won't touch women.'

'They'll touch the Jews all right, that's for sure . . .'

'And the officers. They'll rip their guts out.'

'And the landlords! Down with 'em!'

'Quiet!'

With a strange look of agony and determination in his eyes the fair-haired orator pointed at the sun.

'Citizens, brothers, comrades!' he began. 'You heard the cossacks singing "Our leaders are with us, with us like brothers". Yes, they are with us!' The speaker thumped his chest with his hat, which was adorned with a huge red ribbon. 'They are with us. Because our leaders are men of the people, they were born among the people and will die with them. They stood beside us freezing in the snow when we were besieging the City and now they've captured it – and the red flag is already flying over our towns and villages here in the Ukraine . . .'

'Hurrah!'

'What red flag? What's he saying? He means yellow and blue.'

'The Bolsheviks' flag is red.'

'Quiet!'

'Hurrah!'

'He speaks bad Ukrainian, that fellow.'

'Comrades! You are now faced by a new task – to raise and strengthen the independent Ukrainian republic for the good of the toiling masses, the workers and peasants, because only those who have watered our native soil with their fresh blood and sweat have the right to rule it!'

'Hear, hear! Hurrah!'

'Did you hear that? He called us "comrades". That's funny . . .'

'Qui-et.'

'Therefore, citizens, let us swear an oath now in the joyous hour of the people's victory.' The speaker's eyes began to flash, he stretched his arms towards the sky in mounting excitement and the Ukrainian words in his speech grew fewer and fewer – 'and let us take an oath that we will not lay down our arms until the red flag – the symbol of liberty – is waving over a world in which the workers have been victorious.'

'Hurrah! Hurrah! . . . The "Internationale" . . .'

'Shut up, Vasya. Have you gone crazy?'

'Quiet, you!'

'No, I can't help it, Mikhail Semymovich, I'm going to sing it: "Arise, ye starvelings from your slumbers . . ." '

The black sideburns disappeared into their owner's thick beaver collar and all that could be seen were his eyes glancing nervously towards his excited companion in the crowd, eyes which were strangely similar to those of the late Lieutenant Shpolyansky who had died on the night of December 14th. His hand in a yellow glove reached out and pulled Shchur's arm down . . .

'All right, all right, I won't', muttered Shchur, staring intently at the fair-haired man. The speaker, who was now well into his stride and had gripped the attention of the mass of people nearest to him, was shouting:

'Long live the Soviets of workers', peasants' and cossacks' deputies. Long live . . .'

Suddenly the sun went in and a shadow fell on the domes of St Sophia; Bogdan's face and the speaker's face were more sharply outlined. His blond lock of hair could be seen bouncing on his forehead.

'Aaah . . . aaah . . .' murmured the crowd.

'. . . the Soviets of workers', peasants' and Red Army soldiers' deputies. Workers of the world, unite!'

'What's that? What? Hurrah!'

A few men's voices and one high, resonant voice at the back of the crowd began singing 'The Red Flag'.

Suddenly, in another part of the crowd a whirlpool of noise and movement burst into life.

'Kill him! Kill him!' shouted an angry, quavering, tearful man's voice in Ukrainian 'Kill him! It's a put-up job! He's a Bolshevik! From Moscow! Kill him! You heard what he said . . .'

A pair of arms shot up into the air. The orator leaned sideways, then his legs, torso and finally his head, still wearing its hat, disappeared.

'Kill him!' shouted a thin tenor voice in response to the other. 'He's a traitor! Get him, lads!'

'Stop! Who's that? Who's that you've got there? Not him – he's the wrong one!'

The owner of the thin tenor voice lunged toward the fountain, waving his arms as though trying to catch a large, slippery fish. But Shchur, wearing a tanned sheepskin jerkin and fur hat, was swaying around in front of him shouting 'Kill him!' Then he suddenly screamed:

'Hey, stop him! He's taken my watch!'

At the same moment a woman was kicked, letting out a terrible shriek.

'Whose watch? Where? Stop thief!'

Someone standing behind the man with the thin voice grabbed him by the belt and held him whilst a large cold palm, weighing a good pound and a half, fetched him a ringing smack across his nose and mouth.

'Ow!' screamed the thin voice, turning as pale as death and realising that his fur hat had been knocked off. In that second he felt the violent sting of a second blow on the face and someone shouting:

'That's him, the dirty little thief, the son of a bitch! Beat him up!'

'Hey!' whined the thin voice. 'What are you hitting me for? I'm not the one! You should stop *him* – that Bolshevik! – Ow!' he howled.

'Oh my God, Marusya, let's get out of here, what's going on?'

There was a furious, whirling scuffle in the crowd by the fountain, fists flew, someone screamed, people scattered. And the orator had vanished. He had vanished as mysteriously and magically as though the ground had swallowed him up. A man was dragged from the centre of the mêlée but it turned out to be the wrong one: the traitorous Bolshevik orator had been wearing a black fur hat, and this man's hat was gray. Within three minutes the scuffle had died down of its own accord as though it had never begun, because a new speaker had been lifted up on to the fountain and people were drifting back from all directions to hear him until, layer by layer around the central core, the crowd had built up again to almost two thousand people.

*

By the fence in the white, snow-covered side-street, now deserted as the gaping crowd streamed after the departing troops, Shchur could no longer hold in his laughter and collapsed helplessly and noisily on to the sidewalk where he stood.

'Oh, I can't help it!' he roared, clutching his sides. Laughter cascaded out of him, his white teeth glittering. 'I'll die laughing! God, when I think how they turned on him – the wrong man! – and beat him up!'

'Don't sit around here for too long, Shchur, we can't take too many risks', said his companion, the unknown man in the beaver collar who looked the very image of the late, distinguished Lieutenant Shpolyansky, chairman of The Magnetic Triolet.

'Coming, coming', groaned Shchur as he rose to his feet.

'Give me a cigarette, Mikhail Semymovich', said Shchur's other companion, a tall man in a black overcoat. He pushed his gray fur hat on to the back of his head and a lock of fair hair fell down over his forehead. He was breathing hard and looked hot, despite the frosty weather.

'What? Had enough?' the other man asked kindly as he thrust back the skirt of his overcoat, pulled out a small gold cigarette-case and offered a short, stubby German cigarette. Cupping his hands around the flame, the fair-haired man lit one, and only when he had exhaled the smoke did he say:

'Whew!'

Then all three set off rapidly, swung round the corner and vanished.

Two figures in student uniforms turned into the side-street from the square. One short, stocky and neat in gleaming rubber overshoes. The other tall, broad-shouldered, with legs as long as a pair of dividers and a stride of nearly seven feet. Both of them wore their collars turned right up to their peaked caps, and the tall man's clean-shaven mouth and chin were swathed in a woollen muffler – a wise precaution in the frosty weather. As if at a word of command both figures turned their heads together and looked at the corpse of Captain Pleshko and the other man lying face downward across him, his knees crumpled awkwardly to one side. Without a sound they passed on.

Then, when the two students had turned from Rylsky Street into Zhitomirskaya Street, the tall one turned to the shorter one and said in a husky tenor:

'Did you see that? Did you see that, I say?'

The shorter man did not reply but shrugged and groaned as though one of his teeth had suddenly started aching.

'I'll never forget it as long as I live,' went on the tall man, striding along, 'I shall remember that.'

The shorter man followed him in silence.

'Well, at least they've taught us a lesson. Now if I ever meet that swine . . . the Hetman . . . again . . .' – A hissing sound came from behind the muffler – 'I'll . . .' The tall man let out a long, complicated and obscene expletive. As they turned into Bolshaya Zhitomirskaya Street their way was barred by a kind of procession making its way towards the main police station in the Old City precinct. To pass into the square the procession only had to go straight ahead, but Vladimirskaya Street, where it crossed

Bolshaya Zhitomirskaya, was still blocked by cavalry marching away after the parade, so the procession, like everyone else, was obliged to stop.

It was headed by a horde of little boys, running, leapfrogging and letting out piercing whistles. Next along the trampled snow of the roadway came a man with despairing terror-stricken eyes, no hat, and a torn, unbuttoned fur coat. His face was streaked with blood and tears were streaming from his eyes. From his wide, gaping mouth came a thin, hoarse voice, shouting in an absurd mixture of Russian and Ukrainian:

'You have no right to do this to me! I'm a famous Ukrainian poet! My name's Gorbolaz. I've published an anthology of Ukrainian poetry. I shall complain to the chairman of the Rada and to the minister. This is an outrage!'

'Beat him up – the pickpocket!' came shouts from the sidewalk.

Turning desperately to all sides, the bloodstained man shouted: 'But I was trying to arrest a Bolshevik agitator . . .'

'What? What's that?'

'Who's he?'

'Tried to shoot Petlyura.'

'What?'

'Took a shot at Petlyura, the son of a bitch.'

'But he's a Ukrainian.'

'He's no Ukrainian, the swine', rumbled a bass voice. 'He's a pickpocket.'

'Phee-eew!' whistled the little boys contemptuously.

'What are you doing? What right have you to do this to me?'

'We've caught a Bolshevik agitator. He ought to be shot on the spot.'

Behind the bloodstained man came an excited crowd, amongst them an army fur hat with a gold-braided tassel and the tips of two bayonets. A man with a tightly-belted coat was striding alongside the bloodstained man and occasionally, whenever the victim screamed particularly loudly, mechanically punched him on the neck. Then the wretched prisoner, at the end of his tether, stopped shouting and instead began to sob violently but soundlessly.

The two students stepped back to let the procession go by. When it had passed, the tall one seized the short one by the arm and whispered with malicious pleasure:

'Serve him right. A sight for sore eyes. Well, I can tell you one thing, Karas – you have to hand it to those Bolsheviks. They really know their stuff. What a brilliant piece of work! Did you notice how cleverly they fixed things so that their speaker got clean away? They're tough and by God, they're clever. That's why I admire them – for their brazen impudence, God damn them.'

The shorter man said in a low voice:

'If I don't get a drink in a moment I shall pass out.'

'That's a thought. Brilliant idea', the tall man agreed cheerfully. 'How much do you have on you?'

'Two hundred.'

'I have a hundred and fifty. Let's go to Tamara's bar and get a couple of bottles . . .'

'It's shut.'

'They'll open up for us.'

The two men turned on to Vladimirskaya Street and walked on until they came to a two-storey house with a sign that read:

'Grocery'

Alongside it was another: 'Tamara's Castle – Wine Cellars.' Sidling down the steps to the basement the two men began to tap cautiously on the glass of the double door.

Seventeen

THROUGHOUT the last few days, since events had rained down on his family like stones, Nikolka had been preoccupied with a solemn obligation, an act bound up with the last words of his commanding officer, who had died stretched out on the snow. Nikolka succeeded in discharging that obligation, but to do so he had had to spend the whole of the day before the parade running around the city and calling on no less than nine addresses. Several times during this hectic chase Nikolka had lost his presence of mind, had given up in despair, then started again, until eventually he succeeded.

In a little house on Litovskaya Street at the very edge of town he found another cadet who had served in the second company of their detachment and from him he learned the first name, patronymic and address of Colonel Nai-Turs.

As he tried to cross St Sophia's Square, Nikolka struggled against swirling waves of people. It was impossible to get across the square. Frozen, Nikolka then lost a good half-hour as he tried to struggle free of the grip of the crowd and return to his starting point – St Michael's Monastery. From there Nikolka tried, by making a wide detour along Kostelnaya Street, to work his way round to the lower end of the Kreshchatik, and from there to get through to Malo-Provalnaya Street by devious backstreets. This too proved impossible. Like everywhere else, Kostelnaya Street was blocked by troops moving uphill towards the parade. Then Nikolka made an even bigger and more curving sweep away from the center until he found himself completely alone on St Vladimir's Hill. There, along the terraces and avenues of the park, Nikolka trudged on between walls of white snow. His way took him past the open space around St Vladimir's statue, where there was much less snow, and from where he could see, in the sea of snow on the hills opposite, the Imperial Gardens. Further away to the left, stretching towards Chernigov, lay the endless plains in their deep winter sleep divided from him by the river Dnieper – white and majestic between its frozen banks.

It was peaceful and utterly calm, but Nikolka had no time for calm. Fighting his way through the snow he made his way down from terrace after terrace, surprised by the occasional tracks in the snow which meant that someone beside himself had been wandering about the park in the depths of winter.

Finally, at the end of an avenue, Nikolka sighed with relief as he saw that there were no troops at this end of the Kreshchatik, and he made straight for the long-sought goal: No. 21 Malo-Provalnaya Street. This was the address that Nikolka had taken so much trouble to find and although he had not written it down, that address was deeply etched into his brain.

Nikolka felt both excited and shy. 'Who should I ask for? I don't know anything about them . . .' He rang the bell of a side door at the far end of a terraced garden. For a long time there was no answer, but at last came the slap of footsteps and the door opened a little to the extent of a short chain. A woman's face with a pince-nez peered out and asked brusquely from the darkness of the lobby:

'What d'you want?'

'Could you tell me, please – does the Nai-Turs family live here?'

The woman's face became even grimmer and more unwelcoming, and the lenses of her pince-nez glittered.

'There's no one here called Turs', said the woman in a low voice.

Blushing, Nikolka felt miserable and embarrassed.

'This is Apartment 5, isn't it?'

'Well, yes, it is', the woman replied suspiciously and reluctantly. 'Tell me what you want.'

'I was told that the Nai-Turs family lived here . . .'

The face thrust itself out a little further and glanced rapidly around the garden in an attempt to see whether there was anyone else standing behind Nikolka . . . Nikolka found himself staring at a fat female double chin.

'So what d'you want? Tell me . . .'

With a sigh Nikolka glanced around and said:

'I've come about Felix Felixovich . . . I have news.'

The expression on the face changed abruptly. The woman blinked and said:

'Who are you?'

'A student.'

'Wait there.' The door slammed and footsteps died away.

Half a minute later came the click of heels from behind the door, which opened to let Nikolka in. A light from the drawing-room fell into the lobby and Nikolka was able to make out the edge of a soft upholstered armchair and then the woman in the pince-nez. Nikolka took off his cap, at which another woman appeared, short, thin, with traces of a faded beauty in her face. From several slight, indefinable features about her – her forehead, the color of her hair – Nikolka realised that this was Nai-Turs' mother, and he was suddenly appalled – how could he tell her . . . The women stared at him with a steady, bright gaze which embarrassed Nikolka even more. Another woman appeared, young and with the same family resemblance.

'Well, say what you have to say', said the mother firmly.

Nikolka crumpled his cap in his hands, turned to look at the older woman and stammered:

'I . . . I . . .'

The mother gave Nikolka a look that was black and, so it seemed to him, full of hatred, and suddenly she cried out in a voice so piercing that it resounded from the glass doorway behind Nikolka:

'Felix has been killed!'

She clenched her fists, shook them in front of Nikolka's face and shouted:

'He's been killed . . . Do you hear, Irina? Felix has been killed!'

Nikolka's eyes clouded with fear and he thought despairingly: 'My God . . . and I haven't even said a word!' Instantly the fat woman slammed the door behind Nikolka. Then she rushed to the thin, older woman, took her by the shoulders and whispered hurriedly:

'Maria Frantsevna my dear, calm yourself . . .' She leaned towards Nikolka and asked: 'Perhaps he isn't dead after all? Oh, lord . . . You tell us – is he . . . ?'

Nikolka could say nothing but look helplessly ahead of him towards the edge of the armchair.

'Hush, Maria Frantsevna, hush my dear . . . For heaven's sake – They'll hear next door . . . it's the will of God . . .' stammered the fat woman.

Nai-Turs' mother collapsed backwards, screaming: 'Four years! Four years I've been waiting for him . . . waiting . . .' The younger woman rushed past Nikolka towards her mother and caught her. Nikolka should have helped them, but quite unexpectedly he burst into violent, uncontrollable sobbing and could not stop.

The blinds were drawn on all the windows, the drawing-room was in semi-darkness and complete silence; there was a nauseating smell of medicine.

Finally the young woman broke the silence: she was Nai-Turs' sister. She turned away from the window and walked over to Nikolka, who rose from his chair still clutching the cap which he could not bring himself to relinquish in this appalling situation. The sister mechanically patted her black curls, grimaced and asked:

'How did he die?'

'He died,' Nikolka replied in his very best voice, 'he died, you know, like a hero . . . A real hero . . . He saw to it that all the cadets were in safety and then, at the very last moment, he himself,' – Nikolka wept as he told the story – 'he himself gave them covering fire. I was nearly killed with him. We were caught by machine-gun fire' – Nikolka wept and talked at the same time – 'we . . . there were only us two left, and he tried to make me run for it and swore at me and fired the machine-gun . . . There was cavalry coming at us from every direction, because we had been caught in a trap. Literally from every direction.'

'And then he was wounded?'

'No,' Nikolka answered firmly and began wiping his eyes, nose and mouth with a dirty handkerchief, 'no, he was killed. I felt him myself. He was hit in the head and in the chest.'

It had grown still darker. There was not a sound from the next room; Maria Frantsevna was silent. In the drawing-room three people stood whispering in a tight group: Nai's sister Irina; the fat woman with the pince-nez, Lydia Pavlovna, who Nikolka discovered was the owner of the apartment; and Nikolka himself.

'I haven't any money on me', whispered Nikolka. 'If necessary I can run and get some right away, then we can go.'

'I'll give you the money now,' said Lydia Pavlovna, 'the money's not important. The important thing is that you succeed. Irina, don't say a word to her about where and how . . . I really don't know quite what to do . . .'

'I'll go with him,' Irina whispered, 'and we'll manage it some-how. You said he was in the barracks and that we have to get permission to see his body.'

'Well, that can be arranged . . .'

The fat woman then tiptoed into the next-door room, and her voice could be heard whispering persuasively:

'Now lie still, Maria Frantsevna, for God's sake . . . They're going now and they'll find out everything. The cadet says that he's lying in the barracks.'

'On planks?' asked the penetrating and, to Nikolka, hate-filled voice.

'No, of course not my dear, in the chapel, in the chapel . . .'

'He may still be lying at that crossroads, with the dogs gnawing at him.'

'What nonsense, Maria Frantsevna . . . you lie down quietly my dear, I beg of you . . .'

'Mama simply hasn't been normal these last three days . . .' whispered Nai's sister, pushing back the same unruly curl and staring past Nikolka. 'But then, nothing is normal any longer . . .'

'I'm going with them', rang out the voice from the next room. The sister turned round with a start and ran.

'Mama, mama, you're not coming. You're not coming. The cadet will refuse to help us if you come. He may be arrested. Lie there, I beg you, mama . . .'

'Ah Irina, Irina, Irina,' came the voice, 'he's dead, they've killed him and what can you do now? What's to become of you, Irina? And what am I to do now that Felix is dead? Dead . . . lying in the snow . . . Do you think . . .' There was the sound of sobbing, the bed creaked and Lydia Pavlovna's voice said:

'Calm yourself and be brave, Maria Frantsevna . . .'

'Oh God, oh God', said the young woman as she ran through the drawing-room. In horror and despair Nikolka thought dimly: 'Whatever will happen if we can't find him?'

*

By that terrible doorway, where despite the frost they could already smell the dreadful, suffocating stench, Nikolka stopped and said:

'Perhaps you'd better sit down here. There's such a smell in there that it may make you sick.'

Irina looked at the green door, then at Nikolka and said:

'No, I'm coming with you.'

Nikolka pulled at the handle of the heavy door and they went in. At first it was dark. Then they began to make out endless rows of empty coat-hooks. A dim lamp hung overhead.

Nikolka turned round anxiously to his companion, but she was walking beside him apparently unperturbed; only her face was pale and her brows were drawn together in a frown. She frowned in a way that reminded Nikolka of Nai-Turs, although the resemblance was fleeting – Nai-Turs had iron features, a plain and manly face, whilst his sister was a beautiful girl, with a beauty that was not so much Russian as somehow foreign. An astounding, remarkable girl.

The smell, which Nikolka feared so much, was everywhere. The floors, the wall, the wooden coat-hooks all smelled of it. The stench was so awful that it was almost visible. It seemed as if the walls were greasy and sticky, and the coat-hooks sticky, the floors greasy and the air thick and saturated, reeking of decaying flesh. He very soon got used to the smell itself, but he felt it safer not to look too hard at the surroundings and not to think too much. The chief thing was to stop oneself from thinking, or nausea would quickly follow. A student in an overcoat hurried past and disappeared. Over to the left, behind the row of coat-hooks, a door creaked open and a man came out, wearing boots. Nikolka looked at him and quickly looked away again to avoid seeing the man's jacket. Like the coat-hooks his jacket glistened, and the man's hands were glistening too.

'What do you want?' asked the man sternly.

'We have come,' said Nikolka, 'to see the man in charge . . . We have to find the body of a man who has been killed. Would he be here?'

'What man?' the man asked, staring suspiciously.

272

'He was killed here in the City, three days ago.'

'Aha, I suppose he was a cadet or an officer . . . and the *haidamaks* caught him. Who is he?'

Nikolka was afraid to admit that Nai-Turs had been an officer, so he said:

'Well yes, he was killed too . . .'

'He was an officer serving under the Hetman', said Irina as she approached the man. 'His name is Nai-Turs.'

The man, who obviously could not have cared who Nai-Turs was, glanced side-ways at Irina, coughed, spat on the floor and replied:

'I don't really know what to do. It's past working hours now, and there's nobody here. All the other janitors have gone. It will be difficult to find him, very difficult. All the bodies have been transferred down to the cellars. It's difficult, very difficult . . .'

Irina Nai-Turs unfastened her handbag, took out some money and handed it to the janitor. Nikolka turned away, afraid that the man might be honest and protest against this. But the janitor did not protest.

'Thanks, miss', he said, and at once grew livelier and more businesslike. 'We might be able to find him. Only we shall need permission. We can do it if the professor allows it.'

'Where's the professor?' asked Nikolka.

'He's here, only he's busy. I don't know whether I ought to announce you or not . . .'

'Please, please inform the professor at once,' begged Nikolka, 'I shall be able to recognise the body at once . . .'

'All right', said the janitor and led them away. They went up some stairs to a corridor, where the smell was even more overpowering. Then they went down the corridor and turned left; the smell grew fainter and the corridor lighter as it passed under a glass roof. Here the doors to right and left were painted white. At one of them the janitor stopped, knocked, then took off his cap and entered. It was quiet in the corridor, and a diffused light came through the glass ceiling. Twilight was gradually beginning to set in. At last the janitor came out again and said:

'Come in.'

Nikolka went in, followed by Irina Nai-Turs. Nikolka took off his cap, noticing the gleaming black blinds drawn down over the windows and a beam of painfully bright light falling on to a desk, behind which was a black beard, a crumpled, exhausted face, and a hooked nose. Then he glanced nervously around the walls at the line of shiny, glass-fronted cabinets containing rows of monstrous things in bottles, brown and yellow, like hideous Chinese faces. Further away stood a tall man, priest-like in a leather apron and black rubber gloves, who was bending over a long table. There like guns, glittering with polished brass and reflecting mirrors in the light of a low green-shaded lamp, stood a row of microscopes.

'What do you want?' asked the professor.

From his weary face and beard Nikolka realised that this was the professor, and the priest-like figure presumably his assistant.

He stared at the patch of bright light that streamed from the shiny, strangely contorted lamp, and at the other things: at the nicotine-stained fingers and at the repulsive object lying in front of the professor – a human neck and lower jaw stripped down to the veins and tendons, stuck with dozens of gleaming surgical needles and forceps.

'Are you relatives?' asked the professor. He had a dull, husky voice which went with his exhausted face and his beard. He looked up and frowned at Irina Nai-Turs, at her fur coat and boots.

'I am his sister', she said, trying not to look at the thing lying on the professor's desk.

'There, you see how difficult it is, Sergei Nikolaevich. And this isn't the first case . . . Yes, the body may still be here. Have they all been transferred to the general mortuary?'

'It's possible', said the tall man, throwing aside an instrument.

'Fyodor!' shouted the professor.

*

'No, wait here. You mustn't go in there . . . I'll go . . .' said Nikolka timidly.

'I shouldn't go, miss, if I were you', the janitor agreed. 'Look,' he said, 'you can wait here.'

Nikolka took the man aside, gave him some more money and asked him to find a clean stool for the lady to sit on. Reeking of cheap home-grown tobacco, the janitor produced a stool from a corner where there stood a green-shaded standard lamp and several skeletons.

'Not a medical man, are you, sir? Medical gentlemen soon get used to it.' He opened the big door and clicked the light switch. A globe-shaped lamp shone brightly under the glass ceiling. The room exuded a heavy stench. White zinc tables stood in rows. They were empty and somewhere water was dripping noisily into a basin. The stone floor gave a hollow echo under their feet. Suffering horribly from the smell, which must have been hanging there for at least a hundred years, Nikolka walked along trying not to think. The janitor led him through the door at the far end and into a dark corridor, where the janitor lit a small lamp and walked on a little further. The janitor slid back a heavy bolt, opened an iron door and unlocked another door. Nikolka broke out in a cold sweat. In the corner of the vast black room stood several huge metal drums filled to overflowing with lumps and scraps of human flesh, strips of skin, fingers and pieces of broken bone. Nikolka turned away, gulping down his saliva, and the janitor said to him:

'Take a sniff, sir.'

Nikolka closed his eyes and greedily inhaled a lungful of unbearably strong sal ammoniac from a bottle. Almost as though he were dreaming, screwing up his eyes, Nikolka heard Fyodor strike a match and smelled the delicious odour of a pipeful of home-grown shag. Fyodor fumbled for a long time with the lock of the elevator door, opened it and then he and Nikolka were standing on the platform. Fyodor pressed the button and the elevator creaked slowly downward. From below came an icy cold draft of air. The elevator stopped. They passed into the huge storeroom. Muzzily, Nikolka saw a sight that he had never seen before. Piled one upon another like logs of wood lay naked, emaciated human bodies. Despite the sal ammoniac, the stench of decay was intolerable. Rows of legs, some rigid, some slack, protruded in layers. Women's heads lay with tangled and matted hair, their breasts slack, battered and bruised.

'Right, now I'll turn them over and you look', said the janitor bending down. He grasped the corpse of a woman by the leg and the greasy body slithered to the floor with a thump. To Nikolka she seemed sticky and repulsive, yet at the same time horribly beautiful, like a witch. Her eyes were open and stared straight at Fyodor. With difficulty Nikolka tore his fascinated gaze from the scar which encircled her waist like a red ribbon, and looked away. His eyes clouded and his head began to spin at the thought that they might have to turn over every layer of that pile of sticky bodies.

'That's enough. Stop', he said weakly to Fyodor and thrust the bottle of smelling salts into his pocket. 'There he is. I've found him. On top. There, there.'

Moving carefully in order not to slip on the floor, Fyodor grasped Nai-Turs by the head and pulled hard. A flat-chested, broad-hipped woman was lying face down across Nai's stomach. There was a cheap little comb in the hair at the back of her neck, glittering dully, like a fragment of glass. Without stopping what he was doing Fyodor deftly pulled it out, dropped it into the pocket of his apron and gripped Nai-Turs under the armpits. As it was pulled out of the pile his head lolled back, his sharp, unshaven chin pointed upwards and one arm slipped from the janitor's grasp.

Fyodor did not toss Nai aside as he had tossed the woman, but carefully holding him under the armpits and bending the dangling body, turned him so that Nai's legs swung round on the floor until the body directly faced Nikolka. He said:

'Take a good look and see if it's him or not. We don't want any mistakes . . .'

Nikolka looked straight into Nai's glassy, wide-open eyes which stared back at him senselessly. His left cheek was already tinged green with barely detectable decay and several large, dark patches of what was probably blood were congealed on his chest and stomach.

'That's him', said Nikolka.

Still gripping him under the armpits Fyodor dragged Nai to the elevator and dropped him at Nikolka's feet. The dead man's arm was flung out wide and once again his chin pointed upwards. Fyodor entered the elevator, pushed the button and the cage moved upward.

*

That night in the chapel everything was done as Nikolka had wanted it, and his conscience was quite calm, though sad and austere. The light shone in the bare, gloomy anatomical theater attached to the chapel. The lid was placed on another coffin standing in the corner, containing an unknown man, so that this ugly unpleasant stranger should not disturb Nai's rest. Lying in his coffin, Nai himself had taken on a distinctly more cheerful look.

Nai, washed by two well bribed and talkative janitors; Nai, clean, in a tunic without badges; Nai, with a wreath on his forehead and three candles at the head of the bier; and, best of all, Nai wearing the bright ribbon of the St George's Cross which Nikolka himself had arranged under the shirt on the cold, clammy chest and looped through one buttonhole. Her head shaking, Nai's old mother turned aside from the three candles to Nikolka and said to him:

'My son. Thank you, my dear.'

At this Nikolka burst into tears and went out of the chapel into the snow. All around, above the courtyard of the anatomical theater, was the night, the snow, criss-crossed stars and the white Milky Way.

Eighteen

ALEXEI TURBIN began dying on the morning of December 22nd. The day was a dull white and overcast, and full of the advent of Christmas. This was particularly noticeable in the shine on the parquet floor in the drawing-room, polished by the joint efforts of Anyuta, Nikolka and Lariosik, who had spent the whole of the day before silently rubbing back and forth. There was an equally Christmassy look about the silver holders of the ikon lamps, polished by Anyuta's hands. And finally there was a smell of pine-needles and a bright display of greenery in the corner by the piano, where the music of *Faust* was propped up, as though forgotten for ever, above the open keys.

At about mid-day Elena came out of Alexei's room with slightly unsteady steps and passed silently through the dining-room where Karas, Myshlaevsky and Lariosik were sitting in complete silence. Not one of them moved as she passed by, afraid to look into her face. Elena closed the door of her room behind her and the heavy portière fell back motionless into place.

Myshlaevsky shifted in his seat.

'Well,' he said in a hoarse whisper, 'the mortar regiment commander did his best, but he didn't manage to arrange for Alyosha to get away . . .'

Karas and Lariosik had nothing to add to this. Lariosik blinked, mauve shadows spreading across his cheeks.

'Ah, hell', said Myshlaevsky. He stood up and tiptoed, swaying, to the door, then stopped irresolutely, turned round and winked toward Elena's door. 'Look, fellows, keep an eye on her . . . or she may . . .'

After a moment's hesitation he went out into the library, where his footsteps died away. A little later there came the sound of his voice and strange grieving noises from Nikolka's room.

'Poor Nikolka is crying', Lariosik whispered in a despairing voice, then sighed, tiptoed to the door of Elena's room and bent over to the keyhole, but he could not see anything. He looked round helplessly at Karas and began making silent, questioning gestures. Karas walked over to the door, looked embarrassed, then plucked up courage and tapped on the door several times with his fingernail and said softly:

'Elena Vasilievna, Elena . . .'

'Don't worry about me', came Elena's muffled voice through the door. 'Don't come in.'

The tense expression on the two men's faces relaxed, and they both went back to their places, in chairs beside the Dutch stove, and sat down in silence.

In Alexei Turbin's room there was nothing more for his friends and kin to do. The three men in the room made it crowded enough. One was the bear-like man with gold-rimmed spectacles; the other was young, clean-shaven and with a bearing more like a guards officer than a doctor, whilst the third was the gray-haired professor. His skill had revealed to him and to the Turbin family the joyless news when he had first called on December 16th. He had realised that Alexei had typhus and had said so at the time. Immediately the bullet wound near the left armpit seemed to become of secondary importance. An hour ago he had come out to Elena in the drawing-room and there, in answer to her urgent question, a question spoken not only with her tongue but with her dry eyes, her quivering lip and her disarranged hair, he had said that there was little hope, and had added, looking Elena straight in the eyes, with the gaze of a man of very great experience and therefore of very great compassion – 'very little'. Everybody, including Elena, knew that this meant that there was no hope at all and, therefore, that Alexei was dying. After Elena had gone into her brother's room and had stood for a long time looking at his face, and from this she too understood perfectly that there really was no hope. Even without the skill and experience of that good, gray-haired old man it was obvious that Doctor Alexei Turbin was dying.

He lay there, still giving off a feverish heat, but a fever that was already wavering and unstable, and which was on the point of declining. His face had already begun to take on an odd waxy tinge, his nose had changed and grown thinner, and in particular there was a suggestion of hopelessness about the bridge of his nose, which now seemed unnaturally prominent. Elena's legs turned cold and she felt overcome with a moment of dull despair in the reeking, camphor-laden air of the bedroom, but the feeling quickly passed.

Something had settled in Alexei's chest like a stone and he whistled as he breathed, drawing in through bared teeth a sticky, thin stream of air that barely penetrated to his lungs. He had long ago lost consciousness and neither saw nor understood what was going on around him. Elena stood and looked. The professor took her by the arm and whispered:

'Go now, Elena Vasilievna, we'll do all there is to do.'

Elena obeyed and went out. But the professor did not do anything more.

He took off his white coat, wiped his hands with some damp balls of cotton wool and looked again into Alexei's face. The bluish shadow around the folds of his mouth and nose was growing deeper.

'Hopeless', the professor said very quietly into the ear of the clean-shaven man. 'Stay with him, please, Doctor Brodovich.'

'Camphor?' asked Doctor Brodovich in a whisper.

'Yes, yes.'

'A full syringe?'

'No.' The professor looked out of the window and thought a moment. 'No, just three grams at a time. And often.' He thought again, then added: 'Telephone me in case of a termination' – the professor whispered very cautiously so that even through the haze of delirium Alexei should not hear him, – 'I'll be at the hospital. Otherwise I'll come back here straight after my lecture.'

*

Year after year, for as long as the Turbins could remember, the ikon lamps had been lit at dusk on December 24th, and in the evening they had lit the warm, twinkling candles on the Christmas tree in the drawing-room. But now that insidious bullet-wound and the rattle of typhus had put everything out of joint, had hastened the lighting of the ikon lamp. As she closed her bedroom door behind her, Elena went over to her bedside table, took from it a box of matches, climbed up on a chair and lit the wick in the lamp hanging on chains in front of the old ikon in its heavy metal covering. When the flame burned up brightly the halo above the dark face of the Virgin changed to gold and her eyes shone with a look of welcome. The face, inclined to one side, looked at Elena. In the two square panes of the window was a silent, white December day, and the flickering tongue of flame helped to create a sense of the approaching festival. Elena got down from the chair, took the shawl from her shoulders and dropped onto her knees. She rolled back a corner of the carpet to reveal an open space of gleaming parquet and she silently bowed down until her forehead touched the floor.

Myshlaevsky returned to the dining-room, followed by Nikolka, whose eyelids were puffy and red. They had just come from Alexei's room. As Nikolka returned to the dining-room he said to his companions:

'He's dying . . .' and took a deep breath.

'Look,' said Myshlaevsky, 'hadn't we better call a priest? Don't you agree, Nikol? Otherwise he may die without confession . . .'

'I shall have to tell Lena', Nikolka replied anxiously. 'I can't do it without her. And something seems to be the matter with her now . . .'

'What does the doctor say?' asked Karas.

'What is there to say? There's no more to say', said Myshlaevsky hoarsely.

For a long time they spoke in uneasy whispers, punctuated by the sighs of the pale, worried Lariosik. Again they consulted Doctor Brodovich, who came out into the lobby, lit a cigarette and whispered that the patient was in the terminal stage and that of course they could call a priest if they wanted to, he had no objection since the patient was in any case unconscious and it could do him no harm.

'Silent confession . . .'

They whispered and whispered but could not decide whether it was yet time to send for the priest. They knocked on Elena's door, and in a dull voice she replied:

'Don't come in yet . . . I'll come out later . . .'

And they went away.

From her knees Elena looked up at the fretted halo above the dark face with its clear eyes and she stretched out her arms and said in a whisper:

'Holy Mother of God, intercede for us. You have sent us too much sorrow. In one year you have destroyed this family. Why? You have taken our mother away from us, my husband has gone and will not come back, I know, I see that clearly now. And now you are taking away our eldest. Why? How will Nikolka and I survive, the two of us alone? Look and see what is happening all around . . . Mother of God, intercede for us and have mercy on us . . . Perhaps we are sinful people, but why should we be punished like this?'

She bowed down once more, fervently touching the floor with her forehead, crossed herself and stretching out her arms, prayed again:

'You are our only hope, Immaculate Virgin, you alone. Pray to your Son, pray to the Lord God to perform a miracle . . .'

Elena's whispering grew more passionate, she stumbled over the words, but her prayer flowed on like an unbroken stream. More and more often she bowed her forehead to the ground, shaking her head to throw back the lock of hair that escaped from its comb and fell over her eyes. Outside the square window-panes the daylight disappeared, the white falcon disappeared, the tinkling gavotte which the clock played as it struck three went unheard, as unheard as the coming of the One to whom Elena prayed through the intercession of the dark Virgin. He appeared beside the open grave, arisen, merciful and barefoot. Elena's breast seemed to have grown broader, feverish patches had spread over her cheeks, her eyes were filled with light, brimming with unshed tears. She pressed her forehead and cheek to the floor, then, yearning with all her soul she stretched toward the ikon lamp, oblivious to the hard floor under her knees. The lamp flared up, the dark face within the fretted halo grew more and more alive and the eyes inspired Elena to ceaseless prayer. Outside there was complete silence, darkness was setting in with terrible speed and another momentary vision filled the room – the hard, glassy light of the sky, unfamiliar yellowish-red sandstone rocks, olive trees, the cold and the dark silence of centuries within the sanctuary of the temple.

'Holy Mother, intercede for us', Elena muttered fervently. 'Pray to Him. He is there beside you. What would it cost you? Have mercy on us. Have mercy. Your day, the festival of the birth of your Son is approaching. If Alexei lives he will do good for others, and I will not cease to pray for forgiveness of our sins. Let Sergei not come back – take him away, if that is your will. But don't punish Alexei with death . . . We are all guilty of this blood-shed, but do not punish us. Do not punish us. There He is, your Son . . .'

The lamp began to flicker and one ray from it stretched out like a beam towards Elena. At that moment her wild, imploring eyes discerned that the lips on the image surrounded by its golden coif had parted and that the eyes had a look so unearthly that terror and intoxicated joy wrenched at her heart, she sank to the ground and did not rise again.

*

Alarm and disquiet wafted through the apartment like a ,dry, parching wind. Someone was tiptoeing through the dining-room. Another person was tapping on the door, whispering: 'Elena . . . Elena . . . Elena . . .' Wiping the cold sweat from her forehead with the back of her hand, tossing back her stray lock of hair, she stood up, looking up ahead of her blindly, like a savage. Without looking back to the lamp-lit corner, she walked to the door with a heart of steel. Without waiting for her permission the door burst open of its own accord and Nikolka was standing in the frame made by the portière. Nikolka's eyes bored into Elena with terror, and he seemed out of breath.

'Elena . . . don't worry . . . don't be afraid . . . come here . . . it seems as though . . .'

*

Waxen, like a candle that has been crushed and kneaded in sweaty hands, his bony hands with their unclipped finger nails thrust above the blanket, lay Doctor Alexei Turbin, his sharp chin pointing upwards. His body was bathed in sticky sweat, and his wet, emaciated chest was poking through the gaps in his shirt. He lowered his head, dug his chin into his chest, unclenched his yellowing teeth and half opened his eyes. In a thin, hoarse and very weak voice he said:

'The crisis, Brodovich. Well . . . am I going to live? . . . A-ha.'

Karas was holding the lamp in shaking hands, and it lit up the gray shadows and folds of the crumpled bedclothes.

With a slightly unsteady hand the clean-shaven doctor squeezed up a lump of flesh as he inserted the needle of a small hypodermic syringe into Alexei's arm. The doctor's forehead was beaded with small drops of sweat. He was excited and almost unnerved.

Nineteen

PETLYURA. His days in the City numbered forty-seven. Frozen, icy and dusted with snow, January 1919 flew over the heads of the Turbins, and February came, wrapped in a blizzard.

On February 2nd a black figure with a shorn head covered by a black skull cap began to walk about the Turbins' apartment. It was Alexei, risen again. He was greatly changed. On his face two deep furrows had etched themselves, apparently for ever, into the corners of his mouth, there was a wax-like colour to his skin, his eyes were sunk in shadow and were permanently unsmiling and grim.

In the Turbins' drawing-room, just as he had done forty-seven days ago, he leaned against the window-pane and listened, and, as before, when all that could be seen were twinkling lights and snow, like an opera-set, there came the distant boom of gunfire. Frowning hard, Alexei leaned with all his weight on a stick and looked out at the street. He noticed that the days had grown magically longer, and there was more light, despite the fact that there was a blizzard outside, swirling with millions of snowflakes.

Harsh, clear and cheerless, his thoughts flowed on beneath the silk skullcap. His head felt light and empty, like some strange, unfamiliar box sitting on his shoulders, and the thoughts seemed to enter his mind from outside and in a sequence chosen by them. Alexei was glad to be alone by the window and stared out:

'Petlyura . . . Tonight, at the latest, he will be thrown out and there will be no more Petlyura. Did he ever even exist, though? Or did I dream it all? No way of telling. Lariosik is really very nice. He fits into the family very well – in fact we need him. I must thank him for the way he helped to nurse me . . . What about Shervinsky? Oh, God knows . . . That's the trouble with women. Elena's bound to get tied up with him, it's inevitable . . . What is it about him that makes him so attractive to women? Is it his voice? He has a splendid voice, but after all one can listen to someone's voice without marrying him, can't one? But that's not really important. What is important, though? Ah yes, it was Shervinsky himself who was saying that they had red stars in their caps . . . I suppose that means trouble again in the City? Bound to be . . . Well, tonight it must be. Their wagon-trains are already moving through the streets . . . Nevertheless, I'll go, I'll go in daytime . . . And take it to her . . . I'm a murderer. No, I fired in battle, in self-defense. Or I wounded the man. Who does she live with? Where is her husband? And Malyshev. Where is he now? Swallowed up by the ground. And Maxim, the old school janitor . . . and what's become of the Alexander I High School?'

As his thoughts flowed on they were interrupted by the doorbell. There was no one in the apartment besides Anyuta, they had all gone into town in the attempt to finish all they had to do while it was still light.

'If it's a patient, show him in, Anyuta.'

'Very well, Alexei Vasilievich.'

A man followed Anyuta up the staircase, took off his mohair overcoat and went into the drawing-room.

'Please come in here', said Alexei.

A thin, yellowish young man in a gray tunic rose from his chair. His eyes were clouded and staring. In his white coat, Alexei stood aside and ushered the man into the consulting-room.

'Sit down, please. What can I do for you?'

'I have syphilis', said the visitor in a husky voice, staring steadily and gloomily at Alexei.

'Have you already had treatment?'

'Yes, but the treatment was bad and ineffective. It didn't help much.'

'Who sent you to me?'

'The vicar of St Nicholas' Church, Father Alexander.'

'What?'

'Father Alexander.'

'You mean you know him?'

'I have been saying confession to him, and what the saintly old man has had to say to me has brought me great relief', explained the visitor, staring out at the sky. 'I didn't need treatment. Or so I thought. I should have patiently borne this trial visited upon me by God for my terrible sin, but the father persuaded me that my reasoning was false. And I have obeyed him.'

Alexei gazed intently into the patient's pupils and began by testing his reflexes. But the pupils of the owner of the mohair coat seemed to be normal, except that they were filled with a profound, black sadness.

'Well, now', said Alexei as he put down his little hammer. 'You are obviously a religious man.'

'Yes, I think about God night and day. He is my only refuge and comforter.'

'That is very good, of course,' said Alexei, without taking his gaze from the patient's eyes, 'and I respect your views, but this is my advice to you: while you are undergoing treatment, give up thinking so hard about God. The fact is that in your case it is beginning to develop into an *idée fixe*. And in your condition that's harmful. You need fresh air, exercise and sleep.'

'I pray at night.'

'No, you must change that. You must reduce the time you spend praying. It will fatigue you, and you need rest.'

The patient lowered his eyes in obedience.

He stood naked in front of Alexei and submitted himself to examination.

'Have you been taking cocaine?'

'That too was one of the degrading sins in which I indulged. But I don't do it any longer.'

'God knows . . . he may turn out to be a fraud and a thief . . . malingering. I'll have to make sure there are no fur coats missing from the lobby when he leaves.'

Alexei drew a question mark on the patient's chest with the handle of his hammer. The white mark turned red.

'Stop this obsession with religion. In fact, give up thinking about things that are painful or disturbing. Get dressed. From tomorrow I shall start you on a course of mercury injections, then after a week I shall give you the first transfusion.'

'Very well, doctor.'

'No cocaine. No alcohol. And no women, either . . .'

'I have given up women and intoxicants. And I shun the company of evil men', said the patient as he buttoned up his shirt. 'The evil genius of my life, the forerunner of the Antichrist, has departed for the city of the devil.'

'My dear fellow, stop it,' Alexei groaned, 'or you'll end up in a psychiatric clinic. Who is this Antichrist you're talking about?'

'I'm talking about his precursor, Mikhail Semyonovich Shpolyansky, a man with the eyes of a snake and black sideburns. He has gone away to Moscow, to the kingdom of the Antichrist, to give the signal for a horde of fallen angels to descend on this City

287

in punishment for the sins of its inhabitants. Just as once Sodom and Gomorrah . . .'

'By fallen angels I suppose you mean Bolsheviks? Agreed. But I still insist you clear your mind of these thoughts . . . You'd better take bromide. A teaspoonful three times a day.'

'He's young. But he is as full of corruption as a thousand-year-old devil. He leads women into debauchery, young men to sin, and already the war-trumpets of the legions of evil are sounding and behind them is seen the countenance of Satan himself.'

'Trotsky?'

'Yes, that is the name the Evil One has taken. But his real name in Hebrew is Abaddonna, in Greek Apollyon, which means "the destroyer".'

'I'm telling you seriously that unless you stop this you, well . . . it's developing into a mania with you . . .'

'No, doctor, I'm quite normal. What is the fee, doctor, for your sacred work?'

'Look, why do you keep using the word "sacred"? I see nothing particularly sacred in my work. I charge the same for a course of treatment as every other doctor. If you want me to treat you, leave a deposit.'

'Very well.'

He unbuttoned his tunic.

'Perhaps you're short of money', muttered Alexei, glancing at the threadbare knees of his patient's trousers. 'No, he's no swindler . . . or burglar . . . but he may go out of his mind.'

'No, doctor, I'll raise the money. In your own way you ease the lot of mankind.'

'And sometimes very successfully. Now please be sure and take exactly the prescribed amount of bromide.'

'With respect, doctor, it is only *above* that we can obtain complete relief.' With an inspired gesture the patient pointed up to the white ceiling. 'Now we can all look forward to a time of trial such as we have never seen . . . And it will come very soon.'

'Thanks for the warning. I have already experienced quite enough of a trial.'

'There will be no escaping it, doctor. No escape', muttered the patient, as he struggled into his mohair overcoat in the lobby. 'For it is written: the third angel poured out his vial upon the rivers and fountains of waters; and they became blood.'

. . . Where have I heard that before? Ah yes, of course, when I was talking politics with the priest. So he's found a kindred spirit – remarkable . . . 'Take my advice and don't spend so much time reading the Book of Revelations. I repeat, it's doing you harm. Goodbye. Tomorrow at six, please. Anyuta, show the patient out, please . . .'

*

'Don't refuse it . . . I wanted the person who saved my life to have something to remember me by . . . this bracelet belonged to my late mother . . .'

'No, you mustn't . . . What for? . . . I don't want you to . . .' replied Julia Reiss, warding off Alexei with a gesture. But he insisted and fastened the dark, heavy metal bracelet around her pale wrist. It made her look altogether more beautiful . . . even in the half-light he could see her blushing.

Unable to help himself, Alexei put his right arm around Julia's neck, drew her to him and kissed her several times on the cheek. As he did so his walking-stick dropped from his weakened hand and it fell noisily against the legs of a chair.

'Go . . .' whispered Julia, 'you must go now. Before it's too late. Petlyura's wagons are driving through the streets. Take care they don't catch you.'

'You are very dear to me', whispered Alexei. 'Please let me come and see you again.'

'Yes, do come . . .'

'Tell me, why are you alone and whose picture is that on the table? The dark man with sideburns.'

'That's my cousin', replied Julia, lowering her eyes.

'What is his name?'

'Why do you want to know?'

'You saved me . . . I want to know.'

'Just because I saved you, does that give you the right to know? His name is Shpolyansky.'

'Is he here?'

'No, he's left. Gone to Moscow. How inquisitive you are.'

Something stirred within Alexei and he stared for a long time at the black sideburns and black eyes. A gnawing, uncomfortable thought refused to leave him as he stared at the mouth and forehead of the chairman of the Magnetic Triolet club. But the thought was confused and indistinct . . . The forerunner. That wretched man in the mohair coat . . . What was it that was worrying him, nagging him? Still, who cares. To hell with him . . . As long as Alexei could come again to this strange, silent little house with its portrait of a man wearing epaulettes . . .

'It's time you were going.'

*

'Nikolka? Is that you?'

The brothers met face to face on the lowest terrace of the mysterious garden behind Malo-Provalnaya Street. Nikolka seemed embarrassed, as though he had somehow been caught red-handed.

'Alyosha! Yes, I've been to see the Nai-Turs family', he explained, with a look as though he had been found climbing the fence after stealing apples.

'Very right and proper. His mother is still alive, I hear.'

'Yes. And his sister. You see, Alyosha . . . well, that's how it is.'

Alexei gave Nikolka a sideways glance and did not ask any more questions.

The brothers walked half of way home without saying a word. Then Alexei broke the silence:

'Obviously fate, in the person of Petlyura, has brought both of us to Malo-Provalnaya Street. Well, I expect we'll both be going back there again. And who knows what may come of it. Eh?'

Nikolka listened to this enigmatic remark with great interest and asked in his turn:

'Have you been taking some news to somebody on Malo-Provalnaya too, Alyosha?'

'M'hm', answered Alexei. Turning up his coat collar, he buried his face in it and said no more until they reached home.

*

They were all at the Turbins' for lunch on that historic day – Myshlaevsky, Karas and Shervinsky. It was their first meal together since Alexei had been lying in bed wounded. And everything was as before, except for one thing – there were no more brooding, full-blown roses on the table, because the florist's shop no longer existed, its owner having vanished, probably to the same resting-place as Madame Anjou. There were no officers' epaulettes on the shoulders of any of the men sitting at table, because their epaulettes too had faded away and melted in the snowstorm outside.

With mouths wide open, they were all listening to Shervinsky, even Anyuta, who had come from the kitchen and was leaning against the door.

'What sort of stars?' asked Myshlaevsky grimly.

'Little five-pointed stars, like badges, in their caps', said Shervinsky. 'There were hordes of them, they say. In short, they'll be here by midnight . . .'

'How do you know that it will be exactly at midnight?'

But Shervinsky had no time to reply, as the door-bell rang and Vasilisa came into the apartment.

Bowing to right and left, with handshakes for all and a specially warm one for Karas, Vasilisa made straight for the piano, his boots squeaking. Smiling radiantly, Elena offered him her hand and with a jerky little bow Vasilisa kissed it. 'God knows why, but Vasilisa is somehow much nicer since he had his money stolen,' thought Nikolka, reflecting philosophically: 'Perhaps money stops people from being nice. Nobody here has any money, for example, and they're all nice.'

Vasilisa declined the offer of tea. No, thank you very much. Most kind. (Giggle) How cosy it is here, despite the terrible times.

(Giggle) No, really, thank you very much. Wanda Mikhailovna's sister had arrived from the country, and he had to go right back home. He had only come to deliver a letter to Elena Vasilievna. He had just opened the letter-box at the front door and there it was. 'Thought I should bring it up right away. Goodbye.' With another little jerk, Vasilisa took his leave.

Elena took the letter into the bedroom.

'A letter from abroad? Can it really be? Obviously there are such letters – you only have to touch the envelope to feel the difference. But how did it get here? No mail is being delivered. Even from Zhitomir to the City letters have to be sent by hand. How stupid and crazy everything is in this country. After all, people still travel by train – why not letters? Yet this one got here. Bad news can always be sure of getting through. Where's it from? War . . . Warsaw. But the handwriting's not Talberg's. I don't like the look of it.'

Although the bedroom lamp was shaded, Elena had an unpleasant impression as if someone had ripped off the colored silk shade and the unshaded light had struck her eyes. The expression on Elena's face changed until it looked like the ancient face of the Virgin in the fretted silver ikon-cover. Her lips trembled, then her mouth twitched and set into folds of contempt. The sheet of gray deckle-edged paper and its torn envelope lay in the pool of light.

> . . . I have only just heard that you have divorced your husband. The Ostroumovs saw Sergei at the embassy – he was leaving for Paris with the Hertz family; they say he's going to marry Lydia Hertz. What strange things happen in all this muddle and chaos. I'm sorry you didn't leave Russia, sorry for all of you left behind in the clutches of the muzhiks. The newspapers here are saying that Petlyura is advancing on the City. We all hope the Germans won't let him . . .

A march tune which Nikolka was strumming next door thumped mechanically in Elena's head, as it came through the walls and the door muffled with its tapestry portière that showed a smiling

Louis XIV, one arm thrust out and holding a long beribboned stick.

The door-handle clicked, there was a knock and Alexei entered. He glanced down at his sister's face, his mouth twitched in the same way as hers had done and he asked:

'From Talberg?'

Elena was too ashamed and embarrassed to reply at first, but after a moment she pulled herself together and pushed the sheet of paper towards Alexei:

'From Olga . . . in Warsaw . . .'

Alexei stared at the letter, running his eyes along the lines until he had read it all, then read the opening words again:

My dear Lena, I don't know whether this will reach you, but . . .

Various colors played over his face: against a background of ashen-yellow his cheek bones were tinged with pink and his eyes changed from blue to black.

'How I would like,' he ground out through clenched teeth, 'to punch him in the teeth . . .'

'Who?' asked Elena, twitching her nose to keep back the gathering tears.

'Myself', Alexei replied, deeply ashamed. 'Myself, for having kissed him when he left.'

Elena burst into tears.

'Do me a favor,' Alexei went on, 'and get rid of that thing.' He jabbed his finger at the portrait on the table. Sobbing, Elena handed the portrait to her brother. Alexei immediately ripped the photograph of Sergei Talberg out of the frame and tore it into shreds. Elena moaned like a peasant woman, her shoulders heaving, and leaned her head against Alexei's starched shirt-front. With superstitious terror she glanced up at the brown image in the ikon, before which the lamp was still burning in its golden filigree holder.

'Yes, I agreed . . . when I prayed to you . . . on this condition . . .

don't be angry with me, Mother of God, don't be angry . . .
thought the superstitious Elena. Alarmed, Alexei said:

'Hush, my dear, hush . . . it wouldn't do for the others to hear
you.'

But no one in the drawing-room had heard her. Nikolka was
thumping out a march tune, 'The Double-Headed Eagle', and the
others were laughing.

Twenty

GREAT was the year and terrible the year of Our Lord 1918, but
the year 1919 was even more terrible.

On the night of February 2nd to the 3rd, at the snow-covered
approach to the Chain Bridge across the Dnieper two men were
dragging a man in a torn black overcoat, his face bruised and
bloodstained. A cossack sergeant was running alongside them and
hitting the man over the head with a ramrod. His head jerked at
each blow, but the bloodstained man was past crying out and only
groaned. The ramrod cut hard and viciously into the tattered coat
and each time the man responded with a hoarse cry.

'Ah, you dirty Yid!' the sergeant roared in fury. 'We're going to
see you shot! I'll teach you to skulk in the dark corners. I'll show
you! What were you doing behind those piles of timber? Spy! . . .'

But the bloodstained man did not reply to the cossack sergeant.
Then the sergeant ran ahead, and the two men jumped aside to
escape the flailing rod with its heavy, glittering brass tip. Without
calculating the force of his blow the sergeant brought down the
ramrod like a thunderbolt on to the man's head. Something cracked
inside it and the man in black did not even groan. Thrusting up his
arm, head lolling, he slumped from his knees to one side and with
a wide sweep of his other arm he flung it out as though he wanted
to scoop up more of the trampled and dung-stained snow. His
fingers curled hook-wise and clawed at the dirty snow. Then the

figure lying in the dark puddle twitched convulsively a few times and lay still.

An electric lamp hissed above the prone body, the anxious shadows of the two pig-tailed *haidamaks* fluttered around him, and above the lamp was a black sky and blinking stars.

As the man slumped to the ground, the star that was the planet Mars suddenly exploded in the frozen firmament above the City, scattered fire and gave a deafening burst.

After the star the distant spaces across the Dnieper, the distance leading to Moscow, echoed to a long, low boom. And immediately a second star plopped in the sky, though lower, just above the snow-covered roofs.

At that moment the Blue Division of the *haidamaks* marched over the bridge, into the City, through the City and out of it for ever.

Behind the Blue Division, the frost-bitten horses of Kozyr-Leshko's cavalry regiment crossed the bridge at a wolfish lope followed by a rumbling, bouncing field-kitchen . . . then it all disappeared as if it had never been. All that remained was the stiffening corpse of a Jew on the approach to the bridge, some trampled hay and horse-dung.

And the corpse was the only evidence that Petlyura was not a myth but had really existed . . . But why had he existed? Nobody can say. Will anybody redeem the blood that he shed?

No. No one.

The snow would just melt, the green Ukrainian grass would grow again and weave its carpet over the earth . . . The gorgeous sunrises would come again . . . The air would shimmer with heat above the fields and no more traces of blood would remain. Blood is cheap on those red fields and no one would redeem it.

No one.

*

That evening they had stoked up the Dutch stove until it glowed, and it was still giving out heat late into the night. The scribbled inscriptions had been cleaned from the tiles depicting Peter the Great as 'The Shipwright of Saardam', and only one had been left:

'Lena . . . I've bought tickets for Aïd . . .'

The house on St Alexei's Hill, covered with snow like a White general's fur hat, slept on in a long, warm sleep that dozed away behind the blinds, stirred in the shadows.

Outside, there flourished the freezing, all-conquering night, as it glided soundlessly over the earth. The stars glittered, contracting and broadening again, and especially high in the sky was Mars – red, five-pointed.

Many were the dreams dreamed in the warm rooms of the house.

Alexei slept in his bedroom, and a dream hovered over him like a blurred picture. The hallway of the school swayed in front of him and the Emperor Alexander I had come down from his picture to burn the list of names of the Mortar Regiment in the stove . . . Julia Reiss passed in front of him and laughed, other shadows leaped out at him shouting 'Kill him!'

Soundlessly they fired their rifles at him and Alexei tried to run away from them, but his feet stuck to the sidewalk of Malo-Provalnaya Street and Alexei died in his dream. He awoke with a groan, heard Myshlaevsky snoring from the drawing-room, the quiet whistle of breathing from Karas and Lariosik in the library. He wiped the sweat from his forehead, remembered where he was, then smiled weakly and stretched out for his watch.

It was three o'clock.

'They must have gone by now . . . Petlyura . . . Won't see him again.'

And he went to sleep again.

*

The night flowed on. Morning was already not far away and the house slept, buried under its shaggy cap of snow. The tormented Vasilisa lay asleep between cold sheets, warming them with his skinny body, and he dreamed a stupid, topsy-turvy dream. He dreamed that there had been no revolution, the whole thing was pure nonsense. In his dream a dubious, insecure kind of happiness

296

hovered over Vasilisa. It was summer and Vasilisa had just bought a garden. Instantly, fruit and vegetables sprang out of the ground. The beds were covered with gay little tendrils and bulbous green cucumbers were peeping through them. Vasilisa stood there in a pair of canvas trousers looking at the cheerful face of the rising sun, and scratching his stomach . . .

Then Vasilisa dreamed of the stolen globe-shaped clock. He wanted to feel regret at the loss of the clock, but the sun shone so sweetly that he could summon up no regret.

It was at this happy moment that a crowd of chubby pink piglets invaded the garden and began to root up the beds with their little round snouts. The earth flew up in fountains. Vasilisa picked up a stick and started to chase the piglets away, but there turned out to be something frightening about these pigs – they had sharp fangs. They began to jump and snap at Vasilisa, leaping three feet into the air as they did so because they had springs inside them. Vasilisa moaned in his sleep. A large black fence-post fell on the pigs, they vanished into the earth and Vasilisa woke up to see his damp, dark bedroom floating in front of him.

*

The night flowed on. The dream passed on over the City, flapping like a vague, white night-bird, flew past the cross held aloft by St Vladimir, crossed the Dnieper, into the thickest black of the night. It sped along the iron track to Darnitsa station and stopped above it. There, on track No. 3, stood an armored train. Its sides were fully armored right down to the wheels with gray steel plates. The locomotive rose up like a black, multi-faceted mass of metal, red-hot cinders dropping out of its belly on to the rails, so that from the side it looked as if the womb of the locomotive was stuffed with glowing coals. As it hissed gently and malevolently, something was oozing through a chink in its side armor, while its blunt snout glowered silently toward the forest that lay between it and the Dnieper. On the last flat-car the bluish-black muzzle of a heavy caliber gun, gagged with a muzzle-cover, pointed straight towards the City eight miles away.

The station was gripped in cold and darkness, pierced only by the light from dim, flickering yellow lamps. Although it was almost dawn there was constant movement and activity on its platforms. Three windows shone brightly in the low, single-storey yellow hut that housed the telegraph, and the ceaseless chatter of three morse-keys could be heard through the panes. Regardless of the burning frost men ran up and down the platform, figures in knee-length sheepskin jerkins, army greatcoats and black reefer jackets. On the next track alongside the armored train and stretching out far behind it, stood the heated cars of a troop-train, a constant un-sleeping bustle as men called out, doors opened and slammed shut again.

Beside the armored train, level with the locomotive and the steel sides of the first armored car, there marched up and down like a pendulum a man in a long greatcoat, torn felt boots and a sharp-pointed hood. He cradled his rifle in his arms as tenderly as an exhausted mother holding her baby, and beside him, under the meager light of a station lamp, there marched over the snow the silent foreshortened black shadow of the man and his bayonet. The man was very tired and suffering from the savage, inhuman cold. In vain he thrust the wooden fingers of his cold, blue hands into his ragged sleeves to seek refuge and warmth. From the ragged, frozen black mouth of his cowl, fringed with white hoar frost, his eyes stared out from under frost-laden eyelashes. The eyes were blue, heavy with sleeplessness and pain.

The man strode methodically up and down, swinging his bayonet, with only one thought in his mind: when would his hour of freezing torture be up? Then he could escape from the hideous cold into the heavenly warmth of the heated cars with their glowing stoves, where he could crawl into a crowded kennel-like compartment, collapse on to a narrow cot, cover himself up and stretch out. The man and his shadow marched from the fiery glow of the armored belly as far as the dark wall of the first armored car, to the point where stood the black inscription:

'The Proletarian'

Now growing, now hunching itself to the shape of a monster,

but never losing its sharp point, the shadow dug into the snow with its black bayonet. The bluish rays of the lamp shone feebly down behind the man. Like two blue moons, giving out no heat and trying to the eyes, two lamps burned, one at each end of the platform. The man looked around for any source of heat, but there was none; having lost all hope of warming his toes, he could do nothing but wriggle them. He stared fixedly up at the stars. The easiest star to see was Mars, shining in the sky ahead of them, above the City. As he looked at it, the gaze from his eyes travelled millions of miles and stared unblinkingly at the livid, reddish light from the star. It contracted and expanded, clearly alive, and it was five-pointed. Occasionally, as he grew more and more tired, the man dropped his rifle-butt on to the snow, stopped, dozed off for a moment, but the black wall of the armored train did not depart from that sleep, nor did the sounds coming from the station But he began to hear new sounds. A vast sky opened out above him in his sleep, red, glittering, and spangled with countless red-pointed stars. The man's soul was at once filled with happiness. A strange unknown man in chain-mail appeared on horseback and floated up to the man. The black armored train was just about to dissolve in the man's dream, and in its place rose up a village deep in snow – the village of Maliye Chugry. He, the man, was standing on the outskirts of Chugry, and a neighbor of his was coming toward him.

'Zhilin?' said the man's brain, silently his lips motionless. At once a grim voice struck him in the chest with the words:

'Sentry . . . your post . . . keep moving . . . freeze to death.'

With a superhuman effort the man gripped his rifle again, placed it on his arm, and began marching again with tottering steps.

Up and down. Up and down. The sky that he had seen in his sleep disappeared, the whole frozen world was again clothed in the silky, dark-blue night sky, pierced by the sinister black shape of a gun-barrel. The reddish star in the sky shone, twinkling, and in response to the rays of the blue, moon-like station lamp a star on the man's chest occasionally flashed. The star was small and also five-pointed.

*

The urgent spirit of the night flew on and on above the Dnieper. It flew over the deserted riverside wharves and descended on Podol, the Lower City. There, all the lights had long been put out. Everyone was asleep. Only in a three-storey stone building on Volynskaya Street, in a room in the house of a librarian, like a room in a cheap hotel, the blue-eyed Rusakov sat beside a lamp with a green glass shade. In front of him lay a heavy book bound in yellow leather. His gaze travelled slowly and solemnly along the lines.

> And I saw the dead small and great stand before God; and the books were opened: and another book was opened, which is the book of life: and the dead were judged out of those things which were written in the books, according to their works.
>
> And the sea gave up the dead which were in it; and death and hell delivered up the dead which were in them: and they were judged every man according to their works.
>
> . . . And whosoever was not found written in the book of life was cast into the lake of fire.
>
> And I saw a new heaven and a new earth: for the first heaven and the first earth were passed away; and there was no more sea.

As he read the shattering book his mind became like a shining sword, piercing the darkness.

Illness and suffering now seemed to him unimportant, unreal. The sickness had fallen away, like a scab from a withered, fallen branch in a wood. He saw the fathomless blue mist of the centuries, the endless procession of millenia. He felt no fear, only the wisdom of obedience and reverence. Peace had entered his soul and in that state of peace he read on to the words:

> And God shall wipe away all tears from their eyes; and there

shall be no more death, neither sorrow, nor crying, neither shall there be any more pain: for the former things are passed away.

*

The dim mist parted and revealed Lieutenant Shervinsky to Elena. His slightly protuberant eyes smiled cheerfully.

'I am a demon,' he said, clicking his heels, 'and Talberg is never coming back. I shall sing to you . . .'

He took from his pocket a huge tinsel star and pinned it on to the left side of his chest. The mists of sleep swirled around him, and his face looked bright and doll-like among the clouds of vapor. In a piercing voice, quite unlike his waking voice, he sang:

'We shall live, we shall live!'

'Then will come death, and we shall die', Nikolka chimed in as he joined them.

He was holding a guitar, but his neck was covered in blood and on his forehead was the wreath worn by the dead. Elena at once thought he had died, burst into bitter sobs and woke up in the night screaming:

'Nikolka! Nikolka!'

For a long time, sobbing, she listened to the muttering of the night.

And the night flew on.

*

Later Petka Shcheglov, the little boy next door, dreamed a dream too.

Petka was very young, so he was not interested in the Bolsheviks, in Petlyura, or in any sort of demon. His dream was as simple and joyful as the sun.

Petka dreamed he was walking through a large green meadow, and in it lay a glittering, diamond ball, bigger than Petka himself. When grown-ups dream and have to run, their feet stick to the ground, they moan and groan as they try to pull their feet free of the quagmire. But children's feet are free as air. Petka ran to the diamond ball, and nearly choking with happy laughter, he clasped it in his arms. The ball sprinkled Petka with glittering droplets. And that was all there was of Petka's dream. He laughed aloud with pleasure in his sleep. And the cricket behind the stove chirped gaily back at him. Petka began dreaming more sweet, happy dreams, while the cricket sang its song somewhere in a crack, in the white corner behind the bucket, enlivening the night for the Shcheglov family.

The night flowed on. During its second half the whole arc of the sky, the curtain that God had drawn across the world, was covered with stars. It was as if a midnight mass was being celebrated in the measureless height beyond that blue altar-screen. The candles were lit on the altar and they threw patterns of crosses, squares and clusters on to the screen. Above the bank of the Dnieper the midnight cross of St Vladimir thrust itself above the sinful, bloodstained, snowbound earth toward the grim, black sky. From far away it looked as if the cross-piece had vanished, had merged with the upright, turning the cross into a sharp and menacing sword.

But the sword is not fearful. Everything passes away – suffering, pain, blood, hunger and pestilence. The sword will pass away too, but the stars will still remain when the shadows of our presence and our deeds have vanished from the earth. There is no man who does not know that. Why, then, will we not turn our eyes toward the stars? Why?

Moscow,
1923–1924.